"A taut, near-future police procedural with a plot as sinewy as that cyborg snake in *Blade Runner*. Hayden Trenholm works the mean streets and millionaires' mansions of mid-21st century Calgary and comes up with a winner."
—Matthew Hughes, Author of the *Tales of Henghis Hapthorn*.

THE STEELE CHRONICLES

STEEL
WHISPERS

THE STEELE CHRONICLES

A NOVEL BY

HAYDEN TRENHOLM

For Doug & Helen
Ss hhhh!
Hayd
Trenhol

§Bundoran Press
Publishing House

Cover Illustration: Dan O'Driscoll

Trenholm, Hayden, 1955-
Steel whispers / by Hayden Trenholm;
Cover illustration, Dan O'Driscoll

(The Steele chronicles ; v.2)
ISBN 978-0-9782052-3-2

I. Title II. Series: Trenholm, Hayden, 1955- .
Steele Chronicles ; v.2

PS8589.R483S72 2009   C813'.54   C2009-904092-1

Published in Canada by
Bundoran Press
4378 1st Ave
Prince George, BC Canada
V2M 1C9
www.bundoranpress.com
Printed in Canada

This book is dedicated to my great friends, Michael Whittington and Robert J. Sawyer, who have both taught me more than I can say.

I would like to acknowledge the help of Tony King, Al Onia, Derek Künsken, Matt Moore, Herb Kauderer, Elizabeth Westbrook, Peter Halasz and Scott Trenholm who read and commented on the first draft of this novel. My thanks as well to my publishers and editors, Virginia O'Dine and Dominic Maguire, for their support and assistance.

Chapter 1

I deal in death every day. That's my job. I've learned not to let it touch me. You can't function as a cop if you do. Even twenty years behind a desk, where you're twice removed from death itself, can't change that.

The call came, as these calls always do, at 3 a.m. 3:14 a.m. to be exact. Wednesday, March 16th, 2044.

I answered the phone on the second ring.

"Superintendent Steele?" The voice on the other end of the line sounded young. These days they all sounded young.

"You got him," I said.

"I hope I didn't wake you," said the cop.

"Naw, I had to get up to answer the phone anyway." An old joke but it still got a laugh. Truth was I'd been up for over an hour. I checked the caller I.D. "What can I do for you, Constable Phalen?"

"You left orders to be called if we had another Borg murder. Same M.O. as the last four."

"Where are you?" Phalen gave me an address in the industrial Southeast. "I'm on my way."

Superintendents aren't supposed to get involved in crime scene investigations. We're supposed to sit in our offices and read reports and send younger, brighter minds to do the dirty work. But as other senior officers around the Calgary Police Force will tell you, Frank Steele is a special case. A headcase according to most.

I sat back in my chair and drank the last of my hot milk, thankful I'd resisted the call of my old friend, Jack Daniels, from where he rested in the cupboard above the kitchen sink. I'd been rereading *Illegal Alien* by Robert J. Sawyer and I slipped a bookmark into place and put it back on the shelf. I don't read a lot of science fiction—mysteries are more my forte—but this one was a great courtroom drama. Maybe I was hoping his exploration of alien motivations would help me figure out what was happening with the Borg. These days I needed all the inspiration I could get.

I'd asked Phalen to call for a cruiser and by the time I'd gotten on a tie and a suit jacket and rounded up my badge and gun, they were buzzing for me from downstairs.

At this time of night, traffic on the Deerfoot freeway was almost manageable and we made it from my northwest apartment to the crime scene in under twenty minutes. I had a pretty good idea of what to expect.

The Borg, as they were known in the popular press, had been a growing subculture in most of the Western world for the last ten years, ever since the cost of mechanical and cybernetic upgrades had fallen from astronomical to merely exorbitant. What they call themselves, I couldn't tell you; you need a high-end vocoder to make the sound. Some of the Borg didn't look much different than regular humans with all of the modifications and augmentation hidden under their skin. Most liked to flaunt their changes: artificial eyes and ears, new limbs ending in claws or tentacles or both, metal skull caps of gleaming chrome.

People overestimate the number of Borg—in part because people tend to do that with minorities, but also because Borg culture had spawned a whole crowd of wannabes—kids with nonfunctional copies of Borg modifications pasted on their skin or fitted over their real arms or legs.

But the four dead bodies that had turned up in Calgary dumpsters over the last few weeks had been the real thing, though what they were after all their modifications had been carved out of their flesh was difficult to say. We'd been able to identify three of the victims through DNA records in the national identity bank but the fourth was still listed as a Jane Doe and seemed likely to remain so unless we caught the perps. Based on the microscopic residue found in the wounds, she'd had her face largely rebuilt out of metal and ceramic and both arms replaced, probably turned into multi-use tools, so what was left after her killers were done was pretty difficult to I.D.

The dumpster where the fifth victim was housed was under a spotlight and I had the cruiser pull right up to the scene. The ambulance was waiting to make its delivery to the crime lab but the body was still in situ. Detective Lily Chin was talking to our new forensics guru, Dr.

Vanessa Pham. I walked past them before they noticed me and climbed up on the stepstool that had been placed beside the metal bin.

This Borg had barely started the modification process so his body was mostly intact. His right hand had been severed and the vocoder had been cut out of his throat. An artificial ear had been torn away along with the top of his skull but the face was intact, staring up at me with wide-open eyes. All expression had leached out in the hours since death but I had no real problem recognizing him.

I deal in death every day. But it's different when it's your own son.

I was still standing there, feeling stupid like I was half-asleep, trying to wake up from a bad dream, when Lily Chin came up to me and put her hand on my arm.

"Sorry, Frank, I didn't see you until it was too late. The identification came in after Phalen called you. I would have warned you but…"

"But my cell was turned off," I said, surprised at how calm my voice was. My cell was sitting on the bedside table, I thought, as if that somehow mattered. As if anything mattered right now other than the fact I was standing in front of a dumpster looking into the face of my dead son and wondering how the hell he could afford modifications and when did he get them anyway.

Josh and I had never been close and the distance between us had grown into a gulf since his mother and I divorced seven years ago. He'd been seventeen then, just starting his fine arts degree at the Southern Alberta Institute of Technology, and now he was lying in a dumpster like a stranger.

I reached out to touch his face.

"Frank," Chin's voice came from far away. "Superintendent Steele!"

The hard edge in her voice brought me back to the here and now.

"Forensics hasn't cleared the scene yet, sir. You can't touch the body."

"It's not a body, it's my goddamn son!" But I jerked my hand back. "I'm sorry, Lily, I'm sorry. Getting old, I guess."

I took a couple of steps away from the dumpster and fumbled for a cigarette, forgetting for a moment that I'd quit on the day my divorce from Dorothy, Josh's mother, had become final.

"Maybe you should head home, Frank, I can wrap up here," Chin said, her voice surprisingly gentle. I didn't think she had that in her but I guess you never stop learning about people. I looked over at the dumpster. Yeah, right.

"No," I said. "I'll head downtown and get an early start on the day. I should call…the victim's mother."

It's the first thing they teach you in detective school. Don't let it get personal. Keep your distance from death or it will swallow you whole. I wondered what chapter of the manual told you how to tell your ex-wife her baby boy was dead.

| | |

I sat at my desk, staring at the phone, trying to remember the last time I had seen Josh. Was it two years ago, or three? I thought of calling Amber, the daughter I'd had during my brief, tumultuous first marriage. But I hadn't seen her since her mother's funeral five years ago. I didn't expect she'd want to hear from me now.

At 5:30, I dialed Dorothy's number. It was an hour later in Chicago where she'd been living for the last year. She had always been an early riser. I didn't suppose the habits of twenty years had changed simply because she no longer had to escape my morning breath.

I debated about whether to turn the video pick-up on but figured Dorothy deserved that much at least. The news would be hard enough without getting it from a blank screen. I could have had the local cops go by her house. That's what the book probably suggested in these cases.

She answered on the third ring, a little out of breath and slightly flushed. I'd interrupted her morning aerobics routine. Her endorphins would be elevated which might help with the trauma of the next few minutes. Dorothy hadn't changed much over the years, still tall, willowy and blonde, with the kind of face designed to carry the years well, even without the benefits of modern medical science. She looked a lot more than five years younger than me.

I didn't say anything, not even hello, sat there staring at her and past her at the usual clutter of her trendy apartment. In the background a wall screen was showing coverage of the American Mars mission launch from the Endeavour space platform. It had been moved ahead two weeks to keep pace with the Chinese and European programs. I stared stupidly at the video image of the video and said nothing.

"Frank? To what do I owe…" She stopped then.

"Dot, I've got…"

"Oh, Jesus…It's Joshua."

I guess I need to go back to basic training, relearn that sympathetic but neutral cop expression we're supposed to use when we break the news.

"Is he...alright?" She finished the question though she already knew the answer.

"He's dead."

She took it better than I thought she would. No hysterics, no screaming. Her face sort of collapsed into its years. She turned away for a moment and rubbed a tissue across her eyes. I heard a couple of soft sobs but when she turned back she was calm.

"How did it happen? Some kind of accident?"

I didn't answer, somehow couldn't make my throat form the words and let them go.

"Not suicide?" Dorothy's grandfather had killed himself. It had almost destroyed her family and she lived in terror it might be genetic. She'd talked to a lot of doctors and even made Josh take screening but she never really believed their reassurances. Maybe that made it easier to tell her; maybe I thought murder would be a relief.

"Josh was killed. Someone murdered our son."

Her face hardened then and her eyes turned cold. "Joshua stopped being your son a long time ago."

I wondered when exactly that had happened. A long time ago I guess, just like Dorothy said. I remembered him when he was little, how much I loved to hold him and play with him, watch him discover all the things the world had to offer. Then I accidentally shot my partner during a botched operation, blew half his head off. After that, I spent eight years up my own asshole, going from work to counselling to bars. I finally kicked the counselling habit but by then Jack Daniels was my best friend and my little boy had grown into an angry teenager. And a few years after that, we decided to call the whole thing off.

And now, when I'd finally gotten well enough to want to have a family again, it was way too late for any of us. It was time for me to do what I do best and be a cop.

"I have a few questions. It may help with our investigation."

"I'm sorry I said that, Frank. Really, I..."

She probably was. But words are like bullets. Once fired, they can't be put back in the gun.

"Do you have someone you can call? Someone who can come over after we're done talking?" By the book.

"I guess, sure, I can..." She was starting to look a little confused.

"Put me on hold and make that call."

She stared at me, maybe wondering who the hell I was, then the screen went blank. A minute later she came back, under control again. She'd been a cop's wife for twenty years. She knew a little about this stuff too.

"Did Josh...Joshua have any enemies?" I asked.

"No. Everybody loved Joshua."

Obviously not everyone did but I let it go.

"When did you see him last?"

"Must be six months, no seven, he came down here for a long week-end. But I talked to him about two weeks ago. He had started a new job. Something to do with...oh, I forget. I have his work number. I'll flash it to you." She tapped a couple of numbers on the console and my phone pinged to indicate the number was now logged in memory.

"How did he seem?"

"Happy, excited, optimistic, the way he always was."

It wasn't how I remembered him but I took her word for it.

"How long had Joshua been a Borg?"

"My son wasn't a Borg."

I blinked. Had Chin been wrong about the nature of the crime, fooled by the mutilation and the body in the dumpster? Was it a copy-cat, or just a simple homicide that looked like one of ours? I felt a rush of relief. I could ship the case over to the newly minted Superintendent of Homicide, Willa O'Reilly, and get it off the books of the Special Detection Unit.

"I mean," Dorothy continued, "He was like all kids—enamoured with what was new and different. He hung with that dress-up crowd at college."

A wannabe, maybe, I thought. "So he hadn't had any...surgery?"

"Well, yes, he'd had one of those voice things done..."

"An augment or an actual vocoder?" I asked.

"The second, I think. And he was talking a couple of months ago about having something done to his hand. I'm not sure if he did it; I didn't pay much attention. I thought it was a fad, like when he spent all his money on those old comic books or wanted to try out for the space program because everyone else in his class wanted to, remember?"

I didn't but I nodded anyway.

"That doesn't make him a Borg, does it?" The door chimed behind her and Dorothy waved it open. I was oddly gratified when a woman came through it. We'd been divorced for seven years and we'd both moved on but you never actually want to see your replacement.

"I'll have a detective call you if we have any more questions," I said.

14

"If you need anything, well, you have my number."

She nodded absently and turned toward her friend, cutting the connection as she did.

I leaned back in my chair and stared up at the water stain patterns on the ceiling of my office. My ex might be in denial but I had no doubt that sometime in the last year my son had found enough cash to begin his transformation into something new and different. And that had made someone think he was a prime candidate for murder.

||||

I went down to the cafeteria for a cup of the sludge they call coffee. When I got back, the message icon on my phone was practically dancing. It was 6:02 so I didn't need three guesses to know who wanted my attention so badly. Chief Arsenault always started his day at six sharp. He wouldn't have needed a minute to decide I should be his first order of business.

The Chief and I were getting along better these days. Hard earned mutual respect will do that for you. We weren't exactly buddies but at least I didn't think of him as Chief Arsehole. Not often anyway.

Still, this wasn't going to be easy. I readied my arguments as to why I shouldn't be hauled off the Borg case now that I had a personal interest in the outcome.

I hit reply and the Chief's cherubic face popped into view as if he knew I was already at my desk and had been waiting for my response. Which was probably the case; the Chief kept a pretty close watch on his senior officers.

"Frank," he said, "I'm sorry for your loss. I always liked Joshua."

His usual warm smile had been replaced with a look of concern that might even have been real. I decided I needed to give him the benefit of the doubt. After all, he seemed to know no one called my son Josh anymore, which put him a leg up on me.

"Thanks, I appreciate that."

"I've been thinking of assigning this case to Superintendent O'Reilly," Arsenault said. "She does have extensive experience with the Borg."

I bristled at that, even though I had expected it. I had a lot of respect for Willa. More than that, our friendship had survived several years of butting heads at work and one night, six months ago, of bumping uglies at her condo when need overcame common sense. But the Borg murders were exactly the kind of cases the Special Detection Unit had been set up to handle.

"You're worried I'll lose my perspective," I said.

"Always," said Arsenault, still not smiling, "Besides I'd like you to focus on other parts of your caseload."

Okay, now I was thinking of him as Chief Arsehole. It always went this way. The Chief would assign cases to the SDU that no one else wanted. The Borg murders qualified in spades. Most cops are dedicated public servants who do their best in difficult circumstances but no one ever accuses them of having a deep tolerance for difference. Maybe different sounds too much like deviant.

I don't have much use for what passes these days as journalism but I'm not stupid. You don't survive very long as a Superintendent in the SDU if you don't read the newsfeeds and tap into the webcasts. The press was having a field day with the idea of a Borg serial killer, alternating between a sick fascination with the grisly details and vicious speculation on whether the culprit should be hunted down or given a medal.

Even the politicians had gotten into the act. The last election had left the governing Liberals in a minority. The New Unity Party had jumped from a single member to second place and while their leader, James Becker, always sounded reasonable, some of the members who had joined him on the opposition benches made the third place Conservatives look like communists. They were full of ruminations about "holy retribution' for those who had defiled 'God's sacred work.' Body modification had become the new evil in their eyes, though it didn't seem to stop any of them from participating in the other wonders of modern science to improve and lengthen their lives.

Arsenault didn't just listen to the news—he bathed in it. When the winds of political change blew, he bent like a willow rather than fell like an oak. Which, I guess, is why he's the longest serving Chief the Calgary Police Force ever had.

It's also why he wanted to move the Borg killings onto the back burner. But, damn it, this was the SDU's case. I'd turn the investigation over to Sanchez if I had to but I wanted it here, where I could keep my eyes on things.

I must have had a blank look on my face. At least I hope it was blank and not a reflection of my thoughts.

"All you alright, Frank?" Arsenault sounded worried now, not concerned about my dead son but apprehensive his most senior Superintendent was heading for the psych ward up at Ponoka.

"Never been better, Chief," I said. Probably not the best response given the circumstances. Arsenault looked like he was going to personally sign the committal papers.

"If I can be frank with you," I said, falling back on one of my oldest jokes, "Joshua and I weren't that close." Just close enough that his death was like a fist in my belly. "I can keep this in perspective. I have to, it's my job. We're not dealing with a single random murder. There's a pattern. The details aren't clear but they're getting there. And I have closer ties to the Borg than Willa ever will."

"You're staying connected to Wannamaker." A statement of fact, not a question. Chief Arsenault does like to stay informed.

"Yeah," I said. "We're like brothers."

Not exactly true but I wasn't going to tell the Chief that. He resented the fact that Buzz Wannamaker, Calgary's first Borg detective, had quit the very moment the going was at its toughest. Never mind he did so right before Arsenault could first fire and then arrest him. None of us were thinking clearly at the time—the Chief wanted to fire and arrest me—and the rest of the SDU, too. But only Wannamaker refused to come back when it was all over and done with. Forgive and forget wasn't a big part of his personality.

"Do you think he can or will help you?"

"Sure," I said, "we're in regular touch." Another white lie. I hadn't talked to Buzz in a month but I was in touch with Darwahl Singh, Buzz's partner in the detective agency they had recently set up, using Dar's money and Buzz's street creds. "I was heading out to see him when you called."

The Chief looked doubtful but he finally nodded. "Keep me apprised of developments. I don't need to tell you how sensitive this is." It was almost too easy.

The screen went blank. The absence of niceties to end the conversation was a little more typical of the Chief's approach and it gave me a sense of normalcy.

To the extent that having your world come unglued is ever normal.

There wasn't much point in going to Singh's office before business hours and we weren't so close that I wanted to drop by his apartment unannounced, so I lay on the couch to catch up on my report reading. Amazingly, I didn't fall asleep though I didn't get through many reports either. At 7:45 I gave up and checked Singh's agency address on my palmtop.

I pinged the other members of the unit to gather in the conference room at two that afternoon for a case review. I forwarded my phone to my cell, which, for once, I remembered to put in my pocket. As an afterthought, I took my service revolver out of my desk drawer.

I couldn't find my shoulder holster so I shoved the gun in the right pocket of my suit and headed out the door to see what Singh and Wannamaker had to offer.

I doubted it would bring me any joy.

Chapter 2

Buzz Wannamaker blinked on his internal clock. 05:32:21.

The girl wasn't coming. From the sounds of it, the party in the old warehouse across the road was beginning to wind down. He turned down the volume a notch on his enhanced left ear and sat staring out the windshield of his new car, or rather the Singh-Wannamaker Detective Agency's new car, contemplating his next move. The claws at the end of his right arm clicked absent-mindedly.

Cerise Kavanah had been missing from her home for nearly four weeks though she hadn't exactly disappeared. Not in the capital D sense at least. There were still traces of her here and there on Calgary streets, enough that the police had ruled out foul play. The girl was sixteen; she could legally do what she wanted with her life. As far as the cops were concerned, that took it out of their bailiwick and put it in the hands of social services. With the recent round of budget cuts, another black girl walking the streets of Calgary wasn't going to generate much action in that quarter.

Another runaway. Another casualty of modern times.

Cerise's family didn't buy it. So they had come to the small but stylish offices of Singh-Wannamaker to make their case. Only in business a few months, the agency had already developed a reputation for getting things done when the system couldn't or wouldn't act.

The Kavanah family wasn't middle-class though they had aspirations for their kids. The fact they came with the deposit in hand and in cash had impressed Darwhal Singh enough to take the case, even though Wannamaker doubted he really wanted to—it wasn't high profile enough for a guy who, until recently, had moved in the top echelons of the Calgary business community.

What had impressed Wannamaker was that they had all come together, mother, father and both brothers, a younger one in braces and an older one, wearing the surly expression young men use as armour against the world. People who stick together when it was all too easy and acceptable to fly apart had always impressed him.

Cerise wouldn't have run away, they claimed. She was a straight-A student at school, well-liked by both her teachers and her classmates. She had lots of friends but no boyfriends. She was active in the school drama club and on the basketball team. And, they said, she got along well at home, as well as a sixteen-year old girl with two brothers and a strict father could be expected to, at least.

A discreet background check had confirmed most of what the Kavanahs said, though a few of the girl's friends said she didn't get on with her father at all and that she often talked about how she couldn't wait to leave home when she went to university.

But the verdict was far from unanimous. And leaving home to go to school is a lot different than disappearing in the middle of Grade Eleven.

Wannamaker pushed the power button and listened to the faint click and fainter hum as the electric engine started up. He twisted his left earlobe to drop the volume further on his augment and put the car into gear. Time to follow up on his second—and last—lead.

"Take me to the Red Pomegranate in Kensington," he told the car and once the on-board had locked into the local traffic grid, he let go of the wheel and leaned back in his seat.

Cerise had left the house at about six in the evening to go to a friend's for an all-girl Valentine's dinner and pajama party. She never arrived. Cerise's family heard from the party's hostess at about seven and her father, Cris, had walked the eight blocks between the two apartments, looking for her. They called the police but were told they had to wait the usual twenty-four hours before the case would be treated as a missing person by the authorities.

Cris Kavanah spent the night and much of the next day covering the ground in ever increasing circles. He visited as many of her friends as he could and went to all her usual out-of-school haunts. The next day, the police covered all the same ground.

For a couple of weeks, the cops pursued the matter, which meant that a detective spent an hour every other day, following up leads. The beat cops in the area kept an eye out for a tall, pretty black girl dressed in a conservative sweater and dress outfit.

Then two of Cerise's best friends reported seeing her at a high-end mall, arm and arm with an older—meaning thirty-something—white man and dressed in a bright green dress that was anything but conservative. They had waved and called to her and she had smiled and waved back and said something to the man. He laughed and waved at Cerise's friends, too. But by the time they got to where Cerise had been standing, she and the man were both gone. Mall surveillance tapes were too fuzzy to even give a positive ID of the girl let alone her companion.

She was seen on the street the next day, again in the company of the same man or one who looked similar. The boy who spotted her, a classmate who didn't know her well, had even spoken to her, while she waited for the man to return from a public washroom. He said she was happy and laughed when he asked her if she was being held against her will.

The case went from active to dead faster than you could say 'teenage love affair.' The detective was reassigned to more urgent cases and even the local beat cop stopped answering the Kavanahs' calls after a couple of days. She was happy and unrestrained—that was enough for Calgary's finest. But Wannamaker knew as well as they did that there were at least a dozen drugs and several highly illegal neural implants that could have mimicked that condition, especially to a relative stranger.

After a week of getting the runaround from various social service agencies, they brought the case to the agency. For the last three days, Buzz Wannamaker had combed the streets of Calgary and trolled every social network site and virtual club for further clues to Cerise's fate. He'd even hacked into government and corporate surveillance sites and run image scans through hundreds of data archives looking for matches to the holo-photo her parents provided. So far, there had been no further sightings and only a few rumours about where she was, or in the case of last night's warehouse party, where she might be going. A couple of reports had put her outside the Red Pomegranate in Kensington. Wannamaker had his doubts but it was the only lead he had.

Cerise wasn't one of the Disappeared yet; her images and records still did exist in school and public databases. As long as they were there, there was a chance some cop or social worker would spot her and get her back to the loving arms of her family. Once they vanished, she would be like hundreds or thousands of other kids who had had their identities stolen away in the years since The Troubles ended and the new world disorder arose.

| | | |

The Red Pomegranate had started its life more than fifty years ago as a family restaurant, sitting on a busy corner where Memorial met 10th Street. The corner was still busy but not many families went to that neighborhood anymore, at least not the kind of families you wanted moving in next door. And the Red Pomegranate was usually the final stop before people crossed the line from 'in trouble' to 'beyond help.'

Wannamaker resumed control of the car and let it glide past the wide brass doors at the front of the club. There were half a dozen kids hanging around the entrance. One of the girls lifted her shirt as Wannamaker drove by, showing a pair of small heavily tattooed breasts.

He pulled the car into the alley behind the building. A few of the sleeping bundles stirred but nobody looked in his direction as he shut down the engines and climbed out of the vehicle. He keyed the security and watched the car fold up into a smooth metal and plastic ovoid. Two magnetic anchors attached to carbon fiber tethers crawled out of either end of the car, one attaching itself to a dumpster and the other drilling down into the ground, seeking bedrock or at least an old water main.

Satisfied that the car was safe from casual vandals and thieves, Wannamaker walked back to the front door. He scanned the faces of the two black girls among the crowd but neither of them looked remotely like Cerise. Turning down offers that ranged from the immoral to the criminally hazardous, he pushed his way through the double doors into the foyer. Another door, this one guarded by a small but dangerous looking Asian man, opened into the club, which despite the early hour was hopping. Of course, for most of the patrons it wasn't early but very, very late.

Wannamaker had been to the Pom plenty of times as a cop, walking past outraged bouncers without a second glance. But a P.I. license doesn't have the same cachet as a detective's badge and he had to slip the man fifty New Dollars to go inside and another fifty for the privilege of taking his piece in with him.

"Lights, camera, action," he whispered and took a deep breath. Like a lot of Aboriginals, he didn't like confrontation. Thinking he was in a movie helped.

The bouncer grunted. "The studio's upstairs. Rates are a hundred bucks a minute, two cast of your choice included. See Simba. She'll take care of you."

Wannamaker nodded, slightly embarrassed. *Everyone's getting augments these days*, he thought as he pushed into the main part of the club.

It wasn't a bar Borgs hung out in; they had their own bars on the other side of downtown in old Inglewood. Still, Borg weren't unknown and Wannamaker's appearance didn't warrant more than a casual glance as he strolled among the over-stimulated and under-dressed patrons. He wasn't sure what or who he was looking for but he was pretty sure he'd know it when he saw it.

What he didn't expect to see was Cerise Kavanah sitting beside an extraordinarily fat man at the main bar. The man had one meaty paw resting on the girl's thigh and the other was thrust deep into a high-end info cube, manipulating the holographic data structures with flicks of his fingers. From the way the man's head was twitching and nodding, the coder was inputting directly onto his retinas. Given the time of day and the type of 'businessmen' the Pom attracted, Wannamaker doubted he was a stockbroker trading in the Asian markets.

Cerise was sitting with her back to the bar perched on a stool with her long brown legs hanging down. She was wearing a dark shiny top that clung to her like a second skin and a skirt that was way too short. Every few seconds, she tugged at the skirt and shifted her legs in a vain effort to show less skin. She stopped when the fat man dug his fingers into her flesh. Her face was an expressionless mask but her eyes were wide and darting from face to face in a silent appeal for help. So far, no takers. Wannamaker avoided eye contact. He wasn't ready to make his move until he had a better sense of what was at stake and who the main players were in this little film noir.

The fat man was turned toward the bar so Wannamaker couldn't see his face but there was something familiar about him and not in any nice way.

He kept moving through the room, watching Cerise without ever looking directly at her. From time to time she glanced in his direction. He couldn't tell if it was because his enhancements—metal skull cap, artificial eye and ear and mechanical hand—had aroused her curiosity or if she was one of those natural talents who could always tell when the camera was on them.

Wannamaker began to watch who she was watching. There were two others beside himself and the fat man. One was a white man, about thirty-five, dressed in a loose-fitting linen suit. He had short black hair and a thin mustache, which pretty much fit the description of the guy Cerise had been seen with. He was with two other young girls, both wired on something, but he seldom took his eyes off the pair at the bar. Wannamaker figured him for a broker, here to sell Cerise to the highest bidder. That would be either the fat man or the other person Cerise kept glancing at, Candy Forbes.

Candy was the kind of person always referred to as 'of interest' whenever the police were investigating a particularly nasty occurrence in the unofficial red light district in Calgary's southeast. The courts had long ago lost interest in simple prostitution or pornography so unless someone was hurt and hurt badly, the cops pretty much let most of the city's sex merchants alone to police themselves. Kids under twelve— never mind the legal age of consent—and snuff films were about the only thing that would send a cruiser into the six-block area. Candy had twenty-two arrests and no convictions and, since the death of Gale Conklin, she had become the unofficial queen of western Canada's sex trade.

Wannamaker's eyes snapped back to the fat man at the bar. That's why he looked so familiar. The enormous bulk, the gleaming close-shaven skull, even the tailored silk suit. But Conklin had been reported dead, killed while resisting arrest in the great state of North California. Frank Steele had always claimed the report was bullshit; it appeared Frank's bullshit detector was fully operational.

If Gale Conklin was in the bidding for Cerise Kavanah, this might be her last night as fully human. Conklin would do things to the girl that Candy Forbes couldn't even imagine. It was his specialty, to wring the last drop of innocence from the human soul, to reduce a person to less than a thing, to make them disposable. Cerise was bright, gentle, pretty and, by all accounts, strong. By the time Conklin was done she would be none of those things. By the time he was done there wouldn't be enough of her left to beg for death. And that's when he would kill her, drawing one more drop of entertainment and pleasure from her lonely, bloody death.

But why was Conklin back in Calgary? He didn't exactly fit into the crowd. If word got around that he was back on the street it was only a matter of time before the full attention of the SDU was turned on him. Conklin had gone to a lot of trouble to fake his own death; whatever brought him back must be big.

Conklin shared Cerise's talent for noticing the spotlight. He slowly turned his head away from the data viewer, looked directly at Wannamaker, halfway up the stairs to the upper level, and smiled. It was the most frightening thing Wannamaker had seen in his life.

Chapter 3

I got out of the cruiser in front of the street-front office of the Singh-Wannamaker Detective Agency. I told the driver to circle the block until he spotted me back on the sidewalk. I didn't expect to be long.

I wasn't surprised to see that Singh was already in his office, or rather, in front of his office, talking to a pretty young thing at reception. He always was a hard worker, just one of the many things that annoyed me about the man.

As I watched him through the big window with the ornate lettering of the agency's name I had to admit, he was good looking. Tall, athletic and impeccably dressed, he was pretty much everything I had never been. He even had nice hair, though that was now hidden under a turban. Singh had grown a beard since I saw him last though it seemed too neatly trimmed to be regulation or kosher or whatever it was that Sikhs called it. Singh had recently rediscovered his heritage. I wondered how that was working out for him.

He spotted me watching him and flashed me a wide white grin and raised a carefully manicured hand in greeting. I sucked in my gut the way I always did when I saw Singh and went through the door.

"Frank," he said, crossing the room with hand extended, "Welcome to our new digs."

I shook his hand and we stood there, grinning and trying to break each other's knuckles, until by mutual consent we called it a draw. I resisted the urge to shake the kinks out of my hand and, instead, looked around the office. It was tastefully and expensively decorated and the reception desk looked state-of-the-art. I expected Singh's desk was one step past state-of-the-art. Rumour had it he had gotten a huge package when he left the National Asian Bank in exchange for an oath of secrecy about the circumstances that led to his departure.

Singh led me into his office and we sat on over-stuffed leather furniture and made small talk until the pretty young thing came with coffee for me and bottled water for Singh.

"Shade grown Kenyan," I said after my first sip. "Very nice."

Singh made an elaborate gesture and sipped his water. "How can I help you, Frank? Or is this a courtesy call?"

"There's nothing courteous about eight in the morning," I said. "I was hoping to see Buzz. Do you expect him in?"

Singh hesitated half a second. "Buzz is taking a few days off to visit his family up north. He should be back in a day or two."

There are any number of reasons why Singh might lie to me, most of which were none of my business. I wasn't going to call him on it. What good would that do? I still wouldn't get to see Wannamaker and Singh would be pissed for being caught in a lie. No point in burning your bridges until you had to.

This was a good lie though. Singh knew that I knew that Wannamaker never answered calls when he was up on the reserve; his parents had enough trouble accepting he was Borg without him talking to voices in his head.

"You have my number. Have him call me when he gets back to town."

"Sure, Frank," said Singh. "Look, I heard the early casts. Steele isn't that common a name. Any…?"

"My son," I cut him off holding up my hand, "We were…practically strangers." That was my line and I was sticking to it. I guess pretty soon I'd figure out if it was a line in the sand or a lifeline.

"I see. I understand how that can happen."

I looked in his eyes and saw a sadness that suggested maybe he did. One of these days I'd have to get him to explain it to me.

"If there is anything I can do to help…with the case," he finished lamely.

"Know much about the Borg?"

"Only what Wannamaker tells me," he said, "which isn't much. They hang out in Inglewood, I think." He shrugged.

I laughed. "You'll go far in the investigation business, Dar, I can just tell."

I stood in front of the agency until the cruiser picked me up. Then I called my recently assigned senior detective, Reno Sanchez, and told him to meet me at the Garry, the hottest Borg bar in Calgary.

Hard to know what we might find there this early in the day but I'd bet my badge on it being interesting.

|||

The Garry had started its life as a vaudeville house long before I was born; maybe even before my father was born. It had gone through plenty of changes since then, movie house, porn palace. It had its renaissance in the late twentieth as a live theatre under the guidance of one of Canada's greatest playwrights, Sharon Pollock.

Now it had undergone its most radical transformation, into the hottest bar in old Inglewood, catering to Borg and Borg wannabes from across the entire city. While its exterior displayed a classic theatre marquee, flanked by coffee shops, antique dealers and used book stores, the interior was considerably more dramatic, all steel and glass with lighting effects ranging far beyond normal human vision. Behind the storefronts, the entire block had been gutted to accommodate the two-story dance area and numerous side rooms for private functions.

Sanchez was waiting for me at the front entrance, doing a good job of blending into the street scene.

I still hadn't figured the man out, although he'd been under my command for nearly two months, ever since Willa had been promoted to the head of homicide. There was no doubt he was a good cop. His arrest record was impressive; his conviction ratio even more so. He and officers under his command had taken down some of the worst scum Calgary had ever produced. He'd even been seconded to the Denver police for a year and played a major role in breaking one of the toughest Spanish gangs in the American west.

Sanchez spoke well—in three languages—and the men and women serving under him all seemed to like and respect him. He had two degrees, one in chemistry and the other, earned at night while he was working his way up the ranks, in criminology. Only thirty-nine, he had made Inspector quicker than anyone in the history of the Calgary Force with the exception of Willa O'Reilly. The bright ones always want to try their hand at the SDU, which proved there really is a fine line between genius and madness.

Still, there was something about him that didn't quite sit right with me. His successes were many but his failures were notable. He'd spent three years in vice but had never laid a glove on Gale Conklin. He'd somehow screwed up the prosecution on Margo Falcone and she had walked even though everyone knew she was the trigger behind two very high profile political killings. Internal had cleared him but I still had questions.

Like they say, when life hands you shit, make shit-flavored lemonade. Sanchez was my 2IC and he'd demonstrated he could be a good cop. Maybe all he lacked was proper guidance. And I was just the guy to give it to him. Yeah, right.

Sanchez spotted the cruiser and raised his hand in greeting. He straightened up and took two steps toward the curb. He went from urbane stroller to hard-nosed cop in less than three seconds. The young couple who had been idly chatting to him, leapt away as if they had been stung.

Sanchez was wearing a pearl grey suit over a heavy white cotton shirt. He had matching grey suede shoes on his feet and a black trench coat slung over one arm. Casual and impeccable at the same time. He gave me a broad smile showing even white teeth that looked both perfect and real. It seemed everyone had a better dental plan than I did.

I climbed out of the cruiser, trying to smooth the rumples out of my suit, and dismissed the patrolman. I'd ride back downtown with Sanchez or take the bus home for a much needed nap. It had already been a long day.

I nodded at Sanchez and gestured to the entrance.

"Are you okay, Frank?" It seemed to be the question of the day.

"My back hurts and I've got the start of a headache," I grumbled, "but thanks for asking."

I made another move toward the door but Sanchez stepped in front of me.

"Are you sure you should still be involved in this case?"

It's one thing to have your judgment questioned by your boss, it's quite another when a subordinate does it. It was a natural question given the circumstances but it still pissed me off. The tight knot of anger that had boiling in my gut since I talked to Arsenault spewed out my mouth before I could stop it.

"Listen, you fuck, I've been doing this job since you were in diapers. I've had friends die, people under my command die and I have never, never lost sight of the target. I'm not about to start now. I know you young punks think Superintendents should sit behind their desks and shuffle paper. This case was important to me yesterday and what happened last night doesn't change a fucking thing. Now are you ready to go to work or should I get someone else down here to do your job for you?"

He took it well. He looked me in the eye and nodded. Then he led the way through the opaque glass doors into the Garry.

Wednesday morning wasn't the busiest time of the week but there were a dozen customers hovering around the edges of the main lounge, sipping coffee or something stronger. The big silver and glass bar at the far end of the room was closed but there were plenty of vending machines willing to take your New Dollars in exchange for every legal, and I expect a few illegal, stimulant under the sun.

I hadn't been to the Garry for a couple of years and it had been reno-vated again since my last visit. I stood there, gaping like a tourist from Topeka, until Sanchez pointed to an unobtrusive black door next to the bar. The word 'office' was stenciled in small dark red letters near the top of the door, barely visible in the ambient light, though probably not to enhanced Borg eyes.

The woman who answered Sanchez's light knock didn't look Borg until you looked again. Her clear blue eyes had a faint metallic glint deep inside them and her long blonde hair didn't so much float around her face as writhe. Her movements were quick but smooth and seemed oddly powerful for such a small woman. I expected there were plenty of enhancements hidden beneath her pale perfect skin.

"Como estás, Sanchez?" she asked.

"Muy bien, Angelita, y tu?"

"Cansada pero feliz. El negocio es bueno." She looked past Sanchez's shoulder. "Who's your friend?"

"Superintendent Frank Steele. This is Angel." No last name appar-ently.

Angel looked me over again, a bit more carefully this time.

"The famous Frank Steele. Your reputation precedes you."

I wasn't sure if that was a good thing or a bad thing. "You're a friend of Buzz Wannamaker, aren't you?" I asked.

"Don't see much of Buzz these days."

That made two of us. *Wannamaker should be here*, I thought. Sanchez was smooth but Buzz had the inside track when it came to the Borg. I could have used his advice on this case but it seemed he was avoiding me. I wonder what that meant.

"We're investigating a series of murders, involving Borg—"

"Really," Angel cut me off. "I thought you were here for our famous Wednesday morning breakfast."

"Depends," I said. "Can I have it with the sarcasm on the side? It tends to upset my stomach."

She gave me a slow smile and nodded. "Sorry, Superintendent. We're all a bit on edge down here. To tell you the truth, the community appreciates that you're giving it your personal attention. We know we're not Calgary's favourite citizens."

My direct involvement wasn't supposed to be a matter of public record. I glanced at Sanchez but he was ostentatiously watching the scattering of customers on the other side of the room.

"Are there any rumours as to who might be behind this?" I asked.

"Plenty of rumours," said Angel, "not much substance. I've seen the pictures, Steele. These Borg weren't shot, they weren't run over with cars; they were killed in hand-to-hand combat. Who could do that?"

"Another Borg," said Sanchez.

"Borg don't kill their brothers," snapped Angel.

Borg-on-Borg violence wasn't common but it wasn't unknown. The community was small and close-knit. I hadn't heard of a Borg killing another Borg but there has to be a first time for everything.

"What about Clean Boys?" Sanchez asked. I think Angel would have spat if she had been less of a lady.

"Those pricks," she said. "They may talk big on their side of the river about the new Master Race but they don't come over here except in daylight. It's not that they wouldn't kill a Borg if the opportunity arose but they'd need guns to do it."

Clean Boys was a generic name for several northeast 'social clubs' that drew their members from millenarian Mormons and other far-right sects. They didn't like being called street gangs and for the most part they avoided the usual drug and prostitution rackets. But they weren't above extorting protection money from local businesses and we'd convicted a few of them of money laundering and assorted acts of violence against those who didn't share their particular worldview. They opposed modification on religious grounds and considered the Borg as the spawn of Satan. I hadn't heard the Master Race bit before but it fit with their profile. But Angel was right; an unaugmented Clean Boy or even a whole gang of them would have no chance against a Borg in hand-to-hand combat. Except maybe one who hadn't mastered his modifications, yet. Joshua was the only victim who might fit that description.

"There was an altercation involving a Borg this morning over at the Red Pomegranate. Shots fired," said Sanchez. "Know anything about that?"

It was the first I'd heard about it but I'd been busy.

"The Pom's a dangerous place," said Angel. "Fights in bars aren't unusual. Even gun fights. Anyone killed?"

Sanchez shook his head.

Nice try, anyway. Can't catch fish if you don't put your line in the water.

Angel didn't have much to add after that though she did suggest a name for our Jane Doe, a Borg who had recently moved from Toronto but had dropped from view at about the same time the killings had started. Sanchez made a note of it in his palm and said he would check it out before our scheduled meeting that afternoon.

We asked around among the patrons but they either had nothing to add or nothing to say to a couple of cops. Two reporters from the crime desk of the local web caster came in as we left. I wondered if they'd have any better luck.

Sanchez offered me a lift back to HQ but I declined.

"It's a beautiful day and I need the exercise." What I really needed was time to think. I could always grab a cab if the six-kilometre hike proved too much.

Sanchez shrugged and almost avoided glancing at my spreading paunch. He pinged for his car and climbed in the backseat. That made me happier about walking. I hate riding in cars without drivers.

Chapter 4

Conklin raised his hand. He was still smiling, the filed points of his teeth gleaming wetly. A couple of thugs slumped in a booth on the far side of the room leapt to their feet. Two more came out of the women's washroom.

Showtime, thought Wannamaker. Singh insisted on top-of-the-line equipment for the new agency, including that installed in his partner's body. Not all of it was strictly legal. Carrying concealed was still an offence in Canada and these mods fit that definition.

Wannamaker flicked his wrist. The three claws that formed his right hand retracted. A shotgun barrel, loaded with a clip of thirty rubber slugs, replaced it. They might not take out any of the bruisers Conklin had brought with him but they should slow them down. He wasn't ready to use lethal force unless necessary. The targeting system had already overlaid the vision from his artificial right eye as the Stim kicked in. Everything slowed down.

He would pay for it later. Stim meant there would *be* a later. Unless of course, Conklin's goons were also on Stim.

The two in the booth weren't; they moved like they were swimming in molasses. No such luck with the other pair. They jerked down the hall like creatures in a stop-action animation film. Wannamaker fired off a half-dozen rounds in quick succession before they could get in the open. The slugs knocked the men on their asses. They were back up again in an instant. By that time Wannamaker had cleared the stairs and was across the room.

He heard the click of a hammer being drawn. He fired over his shoulder blindly, hoping his targeting could work from scattered reflections off the bottles at the bar. Even if they only ducked it would buy him a few seconds.

Conklin still had his hand gripped on Cerise Kavanah's thigh. Wannamaker brought the barrel of the gun up. Conklin's wrist snapped. He pushed the fat man away from the girl, surprised to feel hard muscle bunching under the flab, surprised too at how much weight the man was carrying. But the combination of Borg modifications and Stim were enough. Conklin rolled off the stool unto the floor.

Kavanah's face was a mask of surprise as Wannamaker swept her up in his arms. It would be easier to run if she were slung over his shoulders but he was expecting bullets before he got out of the room.

The bouncer obliged by opening the door to see what the commotion was. He got his answer in the form of a Borg straight-arm that sent him flying against the coat rack.

Someone was shooting. The low crack and hiss of gunfire cut through the shouts and screams of the bar patrons. One bullet glanced off his metal skullcap, making Wannamaker happy he had sprung for the titanium upgrade. A second drilled through the flesh of his shoulder. It thudded against the underlying mechanism supporting his artificial right arm. Something else he would pay for later, when the Stim wore off.

Then he was out, through the diminished crowd of street kids and into the alley. The car was completing its unfolding magic. Wannamaker dumped the girl in the passenger seat and sped down the lane, only his Stim-enhanced reflexes letting him avoid the trash, human and otherwise, that cluttered the way.

Once clear of Kensington, Wannamaker turned the car over to traffic control and ordered it to take them back to the agency office. Instead the vehicle pulled over to the side of the road. The console was flashing green, signaling it was ready for input, but refused to budge when he repeated his command.

Cerise had grabbed his right shoulder sending dull echoes of pain vibrating up his spine. He looked over at her. She was crying, slow tears forming at the corners of her eyes. Her mouth was open but all Buzz could hear was a low grinding sound.

Idiot, thought Wannamaker, *no wonder the car won't respond. You're talking too fast for its computer to recognize your voice. A simple fix if you ever get the time.* He had a momentary vision of what this must look like to the girl, like watching a movie on fast forward, his body seeming to jerk from place to place, the smaller motions of his hands and face nothing but a blur. No wonder she was crying; she's probably screaming too.

He couldn't afford to sit here on the side of the road with a girl having hysterics in the passenger seat. He had to move before Conklin's goons showed. He had no doubt they were on their way. Gale Conklin didn't take having his plans changed lightly. The broken wrist only increased his incentive. His men would have orders to bring them back, dead or alive. Wannamaker had no doubt as to which condition Conklin would prefer. The best bet was to get somewhere safe, somewhere the goons couldn't do a quick hit and run, somewhere revenge would cost Conklin more than it was worth.

Wannamaker triggered the pharmapack lodged in his chest, releasing the antidote for Stim. Payback was coming and it was coming soon. Hopefully he could get Cerise Kavanah back to the office before he wiped out. Singh had installed enough armour and weaponry in the walls to resist a small army. He could handle the goons if they came calling.

With any luck, he'd have the girl back in the loving arms of her family before the day was out. A few days or weeks in a safe house and Conklin will forget all about them. And if not, he'd review that movie when the lights come up.

The girl had stopped clutching his shoulder and was now staring in horror at the blood covering her hand. Tears still ran down her face but she wasn't making any sound, coherent or otherwise. The pain that had seemed a distant echo was now screaming loud and clear across his shoulder but he couldn't risk another visit to the medicine chest. He'd just have to deal with it.

He ordered the car back on the road and was gratified as it pulled into traffic and began the short journey to the agency.

"You're bleeding," said Cerise in a shaky whisper.

"Just a flesh wound," said Wannamaker, in a bad British accent.

Most of his non-Borg friends didn't get his jokes, let alone his obsession with classic film. Cerise obviously didn't get the reference but laughed anyway. *She's barely holding on*, thought Wannamaker. He slid his left hand to the door locks and keyed them closed to his command. He didn't want her to take it into her head to make a jump for it.

"Where are we going?" she asked, her voice a little calmer now.

"First to my office," he said, "then we'll get you back home."

"No, no, please."

"Don't worry," said Wannamaker. "We can protect your family."

"He said he'd kill them if I ran away."

"Conklin?" asked Wannamaker.

"Rickey," said Cerise. "The man who..."

The girl was blinking rapidly, her long thick lashes wet with tears. She put her hand to her mouth and shook her head. She was muttering something and Wannamaker turned up the gain on his ear to try and catch it.

"...three three tangent ka. Sprach slide four eleven over quesa machta Borg slin cha three three three tangent ka. Sprach..." She was repeating the same phrase over and over.

If Wannamaker had been driving, he might have veered off the road. Cerise Kavanah might be a straight-A student, but the last he'd heard they weren't teaching Borg in Calgary classrooms.

And it wasn't only that she was speaking Borg that shocked him— it was what she was saying, repeating a slogan of the Independistas that was seldom heard outside Borg safe houses. Why would a young woman from a working class neighborhood be calling for the creation of a Borg homeland?

"Where did you hear that?"

She looked at him with wide eyes.

"Was I talking?" A sickly pallor had spread beneath her chocolate skin and she looked like she might pass out. Wannamaker reached across his body so he could rest his paler brown hand on hers.

"We'll be at our office soon," he said.

"No, no, please," she said again. "Can't you take me someplace else? There's something…" She stopped suddenly, leaned forward and vomited onto the leather upholstery. "I'm sorry. Sorry."

Then she did pass out.

They were pulling up to the office. Wannamaker told the car to keep driving, to head southeast on a random pattern. It turned right past the gated Mount Royal neighborhood and began to weave its way toward McLeod Trail, one of the main arteries into the south of the city. He needed time to think.

Not that he had much time. He could feel the wave of dizziness building, like a tsunami in the deep ocean. Soon it would come crashing down on him and the car would be carrying two unconscious passengers until it ran off the grid on a deserted country road near Medicine Hat.

Something didn't add up. The girl had been scared back at the Pom but not out of control. Conklin would have wanted her clearheaded for the horrors to come. Whatever drugs Rickey had used to control her before—and Wannamaker had no doubt drugs had been used to keep her happy and laughing for the convenient witnesses in the mall—would have been washed out of her system before he took her to the market.

So why was she unconscious now? There was a lot more to Cerise Kavanah than met the eye. Maybe turning her over to her parents wasn't the wisest, or the safest, thing to do.

He could see the crest of the wave in his mind's eye. It was really high and it was going to hurt when it landed.

Why was she speaking Borg? More importantly, why was she speaking the closest thing to 'fighting words' in the whole damn language?

Wannamaker spoke an address at the car's computer.

Then the wave crested and he was buried under an ocean of pain.

Chapter 5

The walk downtown did me good. In a way.

A warm west wind was blowing out of the mountains, a Chinook in western parlance, and you could almost see the last dregs of winter snow evaporating before your eyes. It might snow again in a few days, though March snow had become increasingly rare in the last twenty years. For now, spring had sprung.

For a lot of people spring means renewed energy and the desire to throw off winter's shackles and get out into the great outdoors. For me, it meant that all the mold and fungus that had been growing under the snow banks could release their spores straight up my nose. Spring made me want to spend my days at my desk and my nights anywhere but outside. I did my best work under the influence of antihistamines.

I stopped for lunch on Steven Avenue Mall and then made my way the last few blocks to the aging tin box that served as police headquarters. By the time I got there, it was nearly two o'clock. I had time to drop my gun back in my desk drawer and pick up the data chips that had been dumped in my in-tray in preparation for the staff meeting. I preferred printouts but even dinosaurs have to compromise sometimes.

I walked in as the digital counter high on the far wall of the conference room clicked to 1400, which gave me the privilege of being the last to arrive at the meeting without technically being late.

I stood at the door and scanned the faces of the almost new SDU. Detective Sergeant Lily Chin and Constable Neil Lepinsky were old hands; they had been on board when I arrived nearly three years ago. They were sitting together on the side of the oak table farthest from the windows, comparing notes on their palms. Chin, as usual, had three units on the go, her eyes and stylus flicking from one screen to the next, even while she kept up a steady dialogue with Lepinsky.

Chin was scheduled to take her Inspector's exam in six months. She had failed it once before but I didn't expect she would let that happen again. She'd be moving on then, barring the unlikely departure of Reno Sanchez.

Constable Caleb Jones had been around for about a year but Constable Jim Phalen was a recent addition to the ranks. They were sitting along the sunny-side of the table, hoping the cranky air conditioning would compensate for the recent failure of the sun-sensitive window glass. Phalen's moon face was already beaded with perspiration though Jones looked cool enough. I wasn't sure anything could make Caleb Jones sweat.

Jones was studying his notes but Phalen kept glancing at Chin. I made a note to speak to him about 'The Rules,' the same ones Willa and I had violated a few months ago.

Sanchez was leaning back in his chair next to Chin watching the others and undoubtedly calculating who could best serve his ambitions and how.

Beside him was Dr. Vanessa Pham, a slight woman of Vietnamese origin. She had taken over from Cat Podnarski in the SDU's forensics lab. She was a by-the-book cop from Winnipeg who had taken leave to go to medical school in Calgary shortly after she turned forty. When she graduated four years ago, she decided to stay here rather than go back east. She was well into her fifties but her skin was remarkably smooth and her short-cropped hair jet black. Those kinds of mods are cheap and easy, but, given her political views, I didn't think she indulged.

Pham was more than competent but I didn't trust her instincts the way I had with Cat. I made a mental note to visit Cat again this weekend. Maybe this time she'd remember who I was.

That left Dmitri Yankovy, perched on the edge of his chair at the foot of the table. He had recently arrived from Moscow on a six-month exchange. He was the yin to Sanchez' yang, short and heavily muscled rather than long and lithe, his too long blond hair always in need of a comb. He grinned rather than smiled, his large crooked teeth stained with nicotine. He was always sneaking off to find someplace where it was still legal to smoke. Despite the recent advances in curing cancer, the non-smokers still refused to give up any hard-won ground.

Yankovy had a great career on paper but it was Russian paper and everyone knew what that was worth.

"Is average day," Yankovy was saying in his heavily accented English, "worse than yesterday, better than tomorrow!" He guffawed and the others joined in.

Silence fell as I took my seat at the head of the table and cleared my throat. They looked at me with expressions that ranged from sympathetic to cautious.

"Last night," I said, meeting their eyes one after the other, "Joshua Michael Steele was found dead in a dumpster. I expect you all know that and I expect you've all been talking about it. Some of you have even taken the trouble to talk to me about it." Chin smiled gently and Sanchez looked away.

"I discussed with Chief Arsenault the possibility of transferring the file to Homicide but we agreed that it was better to keep it here where it belongs. The Borg killings will continue to be our number one priority." Until the Chief explicitly orders me to the contrary, I added silently.

"This murder is not to be given any more or less attention than the others. They all had fathers and mothers too and I'm sure their families are as eager as I am to see the culprit or culprits brought to justice. Do I make myself clear?"

Like I said, the walk did me some good. It gave me time to practice that speech for one thing. I could tell not everyone was buying it so I decide to throw them a bone. I only hoped I didn't choke on it.

"I'll still be heading the investigation but I'm relying on you, all of you," I said, catching and holding each of them with my eyes, "to make sure the lines of the investigation stay clear, the evidence untainted. Josh and I—my son and I had grown apart but that won't cut it in court if the evidence isn't solid. Document everything and don't be afraid to speak up if you think I'm losing my perspective."

I must have sounded like I meant it because everyone, including Sanchez, nodded. Maybe I should take up improv theatre in my spare time. I took my seat at the head of the table and opened the palm that someone had brought down from my office.

"Alright, let's get started. Sanchez, give us an update on current caseload."

Sanchez nodded and checked his palmtop.

"The killing last night was the fifth of a Borg individual, the third male. If the pattern holds, the next victim will be female, probably within the next four days."

"Which means we have four days to solve this case," I said.

"Easier said than done, Superintendent Steele" said Vanessa Pham. "If you look at page three of my report…"

We all dutifully clicked forward on our palms. I adjusted the font to one I could read without glasses. The new medical plan was supposed to cover laser surgery but I wasn't blind enough yet to qualify.

Page three was filled with densely packed charts and footnotes. Everyone was supposed to have read these reports before coming to the meeting but it was obvious that I wasn't the only one who had failed to do their homework.

"Perhaps you could give us a summary, Dr. Pham." She insisted on the title. Pham was a stickler for formalities, yet another reason why I missed Cat and her easy-going farm-girl manner.

"Each of the bodies was found in a dumpster. We initially assumed that these locations were opportunistic, or perhaps ritualistic. However, I now believe the murders may have been conducted in situ. I reran toxicology and discovered minute traces of a substance which I believe may interfere with the relays between the Borg nervous system and their mechanical parts. We missed it the first time because it doesn't have easily detectable chemical properties. In fact, it is a fairly simple nano-particle that may mechanically block the transmissions."

I didn't like all the qualifiers. Most Borg technology was proprietary. As far as I knew those nano doodads were part of the package. But a possible clue was better than no clue at all.

"Why does that make a difference?" Sanchez asked.

"Maybe it doesn't but it would mean the Borg would be less…formidable. Of course, it's only a theory. I have to run more tests. But given that it is now abundantly clear the dumpsters were not chosen randomly—"

"How do you know that?" I asked.

"I raised the theoretical possibility in one of the footnotes to my report after the third killing…" Pham tapped a few keys and another report scrolled across my view screen.

"Facts not theories, Doctor," I said as if I actually read the footnotes to her endless reports. "You seem to be suggesting it's conclusive now."

Pham's face darkened. She looked down at her palm and tapped a few more keys. A list of the dumpster addresses and the companies that used them flashed up on the far wall of the conference room. Everyone swiveled in the chairs to take a look. Pham hit another key and several of the company names were highlighted in pale pink.

A brothel, a dental clinic, a day care, a medical lab and a hospice. What did they all have in common? DNA. Every one of the dumpsters had been filled with DNA traces, some from illegally discarded medical waste but most generated in the day to day operations of the businesses that used them. It had posed a problem right from the start as we tried to sort through the evidence—each dumpster had between fifty and a hundred individual codes. It had taken weeks instead of days to sort through the mess. We were still waiting for the final tally from murder number four.

We thought we had a suspect after the second killing when we found traces of the same DNA at the crime scene. No such luck. The suspect had been to both the dental clinic and the brothel in the days before the killing but had perfect alibis for the crimes themselves. And his DNA was nowhere to be found in the third dumpster. To make matters worse we had found samples of DNA from thirty known criminals, at least half of them with histories of violence. Phalen was spending most of his days trying to track them down.

"Based on what we have so far from the fourth killing as well as an examination of DNA traces on the body of the fifth victim, I feel it is probable there is no single killer despite the similarity of the methods used. We are looking at a group of killers."

"Or one killer who is extremely careful with his DNA," I said.

"That is the alternative hypothesis, yes."

I waited for a moment but Pham had nothing to add.

"Anything else?"

"I went to the last known address of…ah, last night's victim," said Lepinsky, "but he moved about two weeks ago. No forwarding address. Do you know…?"

"No," I said, "but I can find out for you." I didn't have a clue where Josh had moved from let alone where he had moved to, but I was sure Dorothy would know if anyone did. "I do have his work number. You can try there if I don't get back to you this afternoon. Let me know what you find out."

"I ran a check on the name Angel gave us," said Sanchez. "Looks like our Jane Doe alright. She hasn't been seen at her apartment or place of work since the killing. They weren't looking for her too hard. Her employers thought she might have left town but there's no record with any of the transit companies. I'll add her name to the file if you concur."

I nodded and looked around the table. Chin raised her stylus.

"Don't know if this is connected but I heard some rumours about an upsurge in assaults against Borg wannabes over the last few weeks. I checked it out this morning."

"Any pattern?" I asked.

"Not really. Assaults are up. A lot in fact. Over thirty percent in the last month. Some look like bar fights but nearly a third of them were carried out by Borg."

I raised an eyebrow at that. Borg on Borg wannabe violence on the rise; what did that mean?

"Another third were carried out by young white men in dark suits."

41

"Clean Boys," said Sanchez.

Chin nodded. "And those ones were more violent than the rest, some broken bones, a few internal injuries. Witnesses say the attacks were unprovoked and ended almost as quickly as they began. They just stopped beating on them and walked away. Some of the victims claim their attackers were wired on Stim—it all happened so fast. We've rounded up the usual suspects but no one has picked them out of the line-up. You know what they say…"

"Yeah," I said, "they all look alike to me. Keep on it. See if we can squeeze those cocksuckers a little to see if there's a connection between assaulting wannabe Borg and murdering the real thing."

Pham sighed. She didn't like it when I used foul language. Fuck her if she can't take a joke was my general attitude though I've tried to tone it down a bit. Harassment complaints seldom led anywhere these days but who needed all the paperwork?

"Why are you focusing on the Clean Boys?" she asked. "The Borg are more likely suspects. They're the ones who have changed, become more powerful. More dangerous."

I knew Pham was a supporter of James Becker and the NUP but then again who wasn't these days. According to the polls, Albertans were getting ready for one of those tidal waves that swept one party to oblivion and installed another in office for a couple of decades. The Clean Boys weren't officially aligned with the NUP but they were drawn from the same stock.

"I'll make a note of that." It sounded sarcastic so I decided to soften it. "Lily, see what's up with the Borg assaults, too."

I'd have been more than happy to wrap it at that. I could feel a blistering headache coming on, a product of too little sleep and not enough bourbon. But I was sure someone would report my lack of diligence to the Chief and I didn't need any more doubts about my competence being raised in those quarters.

"What else do we have, Sanchez?"

"Yankovy and Jones have some new insights into the last round of sabotage to the water system."

There had been three attacks on the water system in six months. The last had included fatalities. I looked expectantly at Inspector Yankovy. This would be his first report to a full staff meeting. I wanted to see how they handled it in Russia.

Yankovy leapt to his feet.

"Is okay? I think better on my feet." He started to pace. He patted his jacket pockets absently. I had a suspicion that if this were Moscow he'd have a cigarette clenched in his teeth. And probably a glass of vodka clutched in his hand. I made a note to apply for the international exchange program myself.

"My first thinking is, this is work of crazy person. Who would be poisoning own well?" He laughed. "I check for recent escapes from mental hospitals, maniacal laughter over radio waves. Like some American comic book, eh? No, no, don't worry, I am not myself a crazy person. Is Russian humor, is all."

Like I said, Yankovy had a good record on paper.

"Besides, we know who the culprits are. They leave calling cards. Messages. Whole thing." Yankovy pulled a file card out of his breast pocket. "Gaia Liberation Army of the West. GLAW. Must be real group. If it wasn't real, it would spell something."

I was having difficulty telling Russian humor from Russian logic. I was prepared to cut him some slack but my patience was wearing thin.

"Is this going somewhere, Inspector?"

"Da, da, sorry. Still, I don't know, why would they do this thing?"

I cleared my throat.

"To make long story short, I rely on classic Russian proverb. When faced with a mystery, ask yourself who benefits?"

I hadn't realized Cicero was a Russian. "So who benefits, Dimitri?"

The answer to my question was going to have to wait. The door to the conference burst open.

"Frank, Frank, I just heard. I'm so sorry."

It was my younger brother, Mike. He never showed up when he was supposed to and always did when he shouldn't. His face was redder than usual and he looked on the verge of tears.

"How did you get in here, Mike?"

"I told the desk sergeant I was your brother and they sent me right up. Probably figured you needed to be with your family right now."

I had left explicit instructions at reception never to let my family in without warning me first. I'm pretty sure they did it to annoy me.

"Mike, this isn't the best time. We're in a meeting here."

"Jesus, Frank, Joshua is dead and all you can do is have a meeting. Why aren't you, I don't know…investigating or something?"

"That's right, Mike, you don't know."

Yankovy had stopped talking and was looking from Mike to me and back again. The others were avoiding eye contact altogether. Well, I'd wanted to end the meeting anyway.

"Okay, fine," I said. "Carry on. Sanchez, Yankovy, see me in my office first thing tomorrow and we'll review the environmental sabotage and the rest of the cases then. Mike, you come with me."

| | |

Mike Steele was twelve years my junior. A gap like that doesn't do a lot to build closeness. Growing up, I more often felt like a babysitter than a brother and by the time he started to get interesting, I was already a cop and he wasn't sure if that was cool or revolting.

It didn't help that we had nothing in common, not even our looks. My hair was dark; his, blonde, though we both had blue eyes. I had a good ten centimetres on him and my broad shoulders dwarfed his narrower frame. Despite my current battle with the bulge, I was a bit of a jock in high school; no superstar but a solid first team player. Mike preferred academics and finished second when he graduated. He was a pudgy kid and a fat teenager, though over the years he's slimmed down a lot. These days he spends more time at the gym while I spend my spare time with a donut in my hand and my nose buried in a good book, that is, if Conan Doyle and Dashiel Hammett are your idea of great literature.

We did have one thing in common. We had both inherited our father's taste for hard liquor. I'd had my battles with Jack Daniels over the years but won more often than I lost. Mike wasn't so lucky. He fell into the bottle at University and hadn't crawled out again for nearly twenty years. He'd thrown away a promising academic career, a marriage and any semblance of a relationship with our parents. He and I had agreed to ignore each other's existence about fifteen years ago and we had pretty much lost touch until he showed up on my doorstep late last year, clean and sober and looking to make amends.

It hadn't gone well. Mike might be sober but he still had all the habits of a dry drunk—moody, unreliable and full of excuses. Still, blood is thicker than whiskey and I put up with him as best I could. It was all part of the new me.

"Sorry," he said, "I guess I shouldn't have barged in like that. I thought you needed to see a familiar face."

I grunted at that. I had barely gotten used to seeing his face at all. He wasn't the first person I thought of when I needed comforting. The fact that I couldn't think of who the first person was didn't make me feel any better.

Mike took a handkerchief out of his pocket and blew his nose loudly.

"Look," I said. "I appreciate the gesture. But I'm fine really."

Mike looked at me doubtfully. I gave him my best grin but it only seemed to increase his doubts.

"I know that you and Joshua weren't that close these last few years," he said, "but this must have come as a hell of a shock."

"Who told you we weren't close?"

"Joshua."

"Since when were you two intimate?" My gut was knotting again. I was having a hard time not grabbing Mike and throwing him across my office. And, for the life of me, I didn't know why.

"Well, I wouldn't call us that, but we've been friends, I don't know, seven or eight years."

Fuck.

"When did you see him last?"

"I helped him move about two weeks ago."

Fuck.

"Oh, and we had coffee in the Chinook Centre a couple of days ago."

Fuck.

Chapter 6

The call was waiting when Sanchez got back to his desk. He checked the weather report. The temperature had dropped ten degrees since morning and the wind had swung around to the north. There were flurries in the forecast for evening. Sanchez grimaced. Fifteen years in Calgary and he still couldn't get used to the weird weather. Why can't they have normal seasons like they do in Ottawa?

He pulled on his overcoat and grabbed a grey cashmere scarf from his wardrobe. He glanced in the mirror and then added a grey fedora to complete the outfit. Clothes made the man. People always treated you more seriously when you dressed the part.

It was all part of the game. A game Sanchez loved to play and loved to win. And if he couldn't win by the rules, he'd make his own rules.

He signed out an unmarked car and slid behind the wheel. No traffic control for this trip. He wanted no record of where he was going and who he was seeing when he got there. After a block, he pulled over and unsealed the hatch to the computer guidance system. He patched in his palm and hacked the GPS. If anyone did check later, it would look like he had made a few stops down in the southeast, following up leads on the Borg murders.

He resealed the hatch and headed west. After a few blocks he turned onto Crowchild Trail and drove north for thirty minutes. Just before Cochrane, he exited into one of the gated acreages favored by the rich and infamous.

The temperature had dropped another couple of degrees and Sanchez blew on his hands, wishing he had thought to bring gloves, while he waited for the computer at the front door to check his identification.

Someday, he thought, I*'m going to own one of these motherfuckers.* Not that he really liked the monstrosities that sprouted on the windswept bluffs like misshapen mushrooms. But it was the principle of the thing. These were trophies and he wanted one. Not that he would ever afford one on an Inspector's salary. But he had plans.

The door chimed acceptance and slid open. Sanchez took one last look around at the broad lawn and carefully cultivated pines separating the house from the one a hundred metres away. To the west, the snow-capped Rockies were rapidly disappearing behind scudding clouds. *We may have more than flurries before this night is over*, Sanchez thought, *crazy weather.*

"Come on in, you're letting in a draft."

Sanchez stepped into the wide marble foyer. He slipped his coat onto a hanger and bent down to take off his shoes.

"Never mind the shoes," said Chief Arsenault, standing at the top of a short flight of stairs. "The floors are self-cleaning."

"Nice place," said Sanchez as he joined Arsenault on the landing. The Chief didn't extend his hand. Sanchez took no offence; everyone knew of the Chief's aversion to being touched. They walked together down a broad hall into an oak-paneled library that was bigger than Sanchez's whole apartment. Rumour had it that Chief Arsenault had come back from his peacemaking mission to Africa with something a lot more valuable than an unhealthy aversion to germs. Either the rumours were true or the Chief was on the take big time.

"Excuse the boxes," said Arsenault. "I only recently moved. My office is an even bigger mess. I think we'll be more comfortable here."

Arsenault sat down in a black leather armchair and gestured Sanchez to the one opposite. Sanchez chose a hard-backed chair instead. He hated the feeling of being enveloped, held in.

"You took precautions."

Sanchez nodded. The Chief steepled his fingers in front of his face and peered at him through the arch his hands made. Sanchez waited. He was used to waiting. After a few minutes, Arsenault smiled.

"Good," he said. "Good. Do you know why I chose you for this job?"

It was Sanchez's turn to smile. "Because I'm bright and ambitious. And a beautiful dresser."

"You forgot modest." The smile was gone. "I chose you because you are a lot like me. Ambitious yes, but patient too. A man with a plan."

Sanchez felt suddenly warm. The Chief's words were too close to his own thoughts for comfort.

"And you have no illusions. Not like Steele. You and I know it's all a game. Sometimes you win and sometimes you lose. But you know that whatever you do, the game will never change. Because the world never changes. We know we can't fix it, just keep it running until our watch is over." Arsenault paused, holding Sanchez in his ice-blue stare. "The barbarians are at the gate. They've always been at the gate. Our job isn't to keep them out but to limit the damage they do when they get in."

Sanchez leaned forward. He could do business with this man. He wondered if Arsenault was going to ask him to join the Cadre, the force within the Force that answered only to the Chief. He wondered what his answer would be if he did.

Arsenault stood abruptly, his body moving smoothly like that of a young man and not like someone approaching eighty. Sanchez wondered what he'd paid for that facility.

"I've been a poor host," he said. "Would you care for tea, coffee, something stronger?"

"Water," said Sanchez. "Sparkling, if you have it."

"Frank must despair of you."

Sanchez shifted in his seat so he could watch Arsenault move across the room. *The man is testing me*, he thought. *Fine. I've always excelled at exams.*

Arsenault returned with two bottles of expensive water and glasses filled with ice on a tray. He sat one of each on the table beside Sanchez, who didn't offer to take it from Arsenault's hand.

Arsenault sat back down in the overstuffed chair and tilted his head back. He closed his eyes and said, "Report."

"Steele is still focusing all his attention on the Borg murders. I think the death of his son has affected him more than he's letting on."

"I'm counting on it."

"There are other cases that in my view are more important. The sabotage of the water system, for example."

"Who has Frank assigned to that?"

"The Russian transfer, Yankovy."

"Really. Interesting."

"Yankovy's a clown. I should be handling that investigation."

"Dimitri Yankovy is many things but he's no clown. I served under him in Africa, during one of those brief shining moments when Russia and the West were on the same side. Still, I was surprised when his application to serve here landed on my desk. He bears watching. Don't underestimate Inspector Yankovy. And don't underestimate Frank Steele. He's a blunt instrument but remarkably effective if you know where to aim him."

Sanchez licked his lips. Time for a gambit. "I think you should relieve Superintendent Steele of duty."

"I've tried that before. It only makes him worse." Arsenault smiled.

"It could jeopardize the prosecution. Even with third-party documentation, the courts will never—"

"Let's worry about that when—and if—he makes an arrest."

"But—"

"Frank is fine where he is. I'm quite comfortable with that decision. For now. Keep me apprised of developments and I'll let you know if I change my mind."

The discussion was over. Time to move on.

"Dr. Pham bothers me," Sanchez said. "Have you read her reports?"

"I oversee six hundred officers in twelve divisions. I have people like you to read the reports for me. What bothers you about Dr. Pham?"

"She's extremely conservative."

"Scientists should be."

"I don't only mean her work," said Sanchez. "I think she has an agenda."

"Don't we all?" Arsenault was looking at him carefully, his eyes glittering blue sparks in his pale face. Sanchez realized the last of the light had been wiped from the evening sky, the storm arriving ahead of schedule.

He had the feeling that Arsenault was toying with him, that he knew more about Pham than he was letting on. "I sometimes think she's working for the barbarians."

"Any particular horde?" Arsenault was smiling again.

"The New Unity Party." Sanchez wasn't partisan in any traditional way but he didn't much like the NUP. They were too certain of their morality for his taste. It limited opportunities for personal initiative and personal gain.

"Our soon-to-be political masters? Perhaps Dr. Pham is simply ahead of the curve. However, I do understand your concerns. Dr. Pham's a complex person. Even I don't quite grasp all her motivations." Arsenault sounded as if that wasn't a circumstance he was familiar with. "I have a backup agent in her lab. A Mr. Antoine King. Do you know him?"

"Black. Fifty something."

"That's the one. Talk to him. See if your concerns have merit."

"And if they do?"

The Chief smiled one more time, without a hint of warmth. "You're a man of initiative. I'll leave it up to you."

Chapter 7

Mike took me to a loft near the New Saddledome, the state-of-the-art arena where the NHL's Calgary Flames played. I could never figure out how we could find money for new arenas when we couldn't keep police stations open in the poorer part of town. But I guess that's why I'm a cop and not a politician. I told the officer who dropped us off to go get some coffee at the Tim's down the street; I'd call him when I wanted a lift.

It wasn't the nicest neighborhood in town but it wasn't the worst either. Halfway between downtown and old Inglewood where most Borg congregated, Victoria Park had hovered between gentrification and extermination for over fifty years. Newer, more expensive, developments encroached from the banks of the Bow River a dozen blocks north while the gradual expansion of the Stampede grounds, home of the 'biggest rodeo on earth' nibbled away from the south.

In between, Victoria Park remained what it had always been: a working class neighbourhood of low-rises and row houses, interspersed with marginal businesses, cheap bars and empty warehouses, many of which had been converted to loft apartments of varying degrees of quality. The local vegetation was sparse and looked on the verge of dying. When the wind blew from the south, as it was now, the air stank of sulphur and other, less identifiable, chemical smells from the industrial quarter of the city.

Josh's building—I still couldn't think of him as Joshua—was at the low end of the spectrum, about what you would expect for a recent university graduate who was spending all his available cash on body modifications. It was a three-story walk-up, clad in peeling green vinyl siding. There were rusting iron bars bolted over the lower windows and the glass front door had recently been replaced with a steel one, complete with a high-end security lock. I doubt any of it would have kept out a determined thief.

Mike knew the door code and had a spare key to Josh's place. When the door swung open, the sour reek of rotting garbage competed from the cooking odours of a half a dozen different cuisines. He led me up three flights of badly lit stairs and opened the sliding steel door into the spacious living room.

The building has nothing special but Josh had done a decent job of fixing up his unit—the furnishings were fairly new and better quality than the junk that cluttered up my place. And he must have installed an air purification system because the place smelled like rain on a summer day. Lepinsky hadn't reported back on Josh's workplace but whatever he was doing must have paid fairly well. The apartment was a full two-bedroom.

"You don't happen to know where Josh was working, do you, Mike?"

"He preferred Joshua," Mike reminded me, "but I guess that doesn't matter now. He worked for a place called Singularity House."

"What's that? Some kind of fusion restaurant?"

Mike laughed. "Good one, Frank."

Apparently I'd made some sort of joke.

"Joshua didn't talk a lot about it, except it was a great place to work and he really liked the people there. Their work is kind of hush-hush but I gather they were working on human-machine interfaces. Leading edge, according to Joshua. They snapped him up as soon as he graduated last year."

"They needed someone in their graphic design department?" I wondered if I looked as confused as I felt.

"Huh? I guess you really were out of the loop. Joshua quit fine arts after his first year, transferred to U of C and got a degree—two, in fact—in medical engineering. He was a real whiz kid."

They say you don't miss what you never had. So why did it hurt so bad to find out I never had a relationship with my only son? He had done so much while I was somewhere else.

"I guess it paid well," I said, looking around the combination living-dining room. A pale brown leather sectional divided the space into an entertainment centre, complete with wall screens and a small holo-projector, and an eating area. The dining room table against one wall was inlaid with dark wood and strips of reddish-grey slate. The four chairs also had stone inlaid into their back. I pulled one out and sat down. The table was bare except a couple of five dollar coins. I picked one up and absently began to flip it between my fingers.

"Decent, I guess," said Mike, joining me at the table, "though mostly they paid him in stock options and free medical treatments."

"Is that what this company did? Design Borg?"

"Not quite how it works, Frank. Nobody set about to create the Borg."

I knew that. Sometimes playing dumb is a useful way to find things out. Make stupid remarks and people feel an irresistible urge to share their superior knowledge with you. But sometimes it just gets in the way.

You could say the first Borg was built in the 1970s when they tried to implant an artificial heart in someone. Or maybe it was when dialysis machines were able to take over the function of failing kidneys. Or maybe it goes back to the first pirate with a peg leg or a hook for a hand.

But for a long time they were never more than second-rate replacements for the real thing. That all started to change in the early twenty-first century when they were able to devise prosthetics that would actually respond to the muscle twitches of amputated limbs. I remember there was a big controversy right before the Beijing Olympics in 2008 about the runner whose spring-loaded artificial feet gave him an advantage over able-bodied athletes. That same year a breakthrough in reading electrical impulses in the brain let a quadriplegic turn on the lights in his room just by thinking about it.

Not long after that, they figured out how to get a coherent signal from a neuron to a microchip and the possibility of constructing integrated human-machine combinations was born. All it took then was for people to begin replacing body parts—not because they had to but because they wanted to. Thus the Borg.

"Still doing magic tricks, I see," said Mike.

I realized I'd been palming the coin, making it appear and disappear. I put it back on the table and stood up. I took a peek in the kitchen. The appliances were all stainless steel. Cozy, if you were a Borg.

"Anyway," said Mike, "I think the owners of Singularity House were after bigger fish. From the little Joshua let slip, they were trying to get beyond simple nerve transmissions and actually merge human consciousness with computer systems to build a true thinking machine. That's why they called it Singularity House—once they achieved that kind of transcendence anything would be possible and nothing would be predictable, like the event horizon of a black hole."

"Right." On the other hand sometimes I really was dumb. I didn't have a clue what Mike was talking about but I made a note to find out before much longer. There were certainly people in this town who get mighty uncomfortable with unpredictability.

"Any idea why Joshua needed so much space?" In addition to the large living area and well-equipped kitchen, the apartment had two bedrooms, a small one off the living room and a larger one in the loft above the kitchen. There were bathrooms on both levels as well.

Mike looked embarrassed and got up from the table. "I guess he got tired of me crashing in his living room."

"You did that a lot?"

Mike shrugged. He never seemed to have that much trouble bumming off me. Why was Josh different?

"Not so much since I got my shit together. But sometimes, when things got a little rough and I was in danger of falling into old habits. When I first tried to get sober, Joshua was the guy who was always there for me. He'd had his own problems when he was a teenager so I guess he knew what I was going through."

Another revelation. I wasn't sure I could take much more of this.

"Joshua was really good to me. I'm going to miss him."

Mike's voice broke then and he started to cry. He didn't sit down or try to move toward me. Just stood there with his shoulders shaking and tears running down his face. And I stood there watching him, not knowing what I should be feeling but certain it shouldn't be jealousy.

"Sorry," he said, as if he was the one who had fucked it all up.

I finally couldn't take it any more. I grabbed a box of tissue and handed it to him.

"It's okay, Mike."

"Thanks," said Mike, blowing his nose. "He always told me I was his favourite uncle."

"You're his only uncle."

"That's what I used to say," Mike wiped his sleeve across his eyes. "He said that was what made me special. Family was important to Joshua."

Another body blow.

"Look, Mike," I said. "I appreciate you bringing me here and letting me in. It will really help our investigation. But could I ask you to leave?"

"Sure, I understand. You want to be alone with your memories."

"I want to carry out an investigation," I said. "I can't have you…"

"Right. Sure."

"Do you need cab fare? It looks like snow."

"No, I'll be fine. My bus stops right outside. I'll call you later."

"Great." I'd have to remember to forget my phone in the office.

After Mike left, I stood in the middle of Joshua's apartment, trying to regain my perspective. I had to treat this investigation like every other one I'd ever been involved with. No, I had to be doubly careful, taking extra precautions not to contaminate the evidence so when I caught the bastard that—I stopped, unsure what exactly I would do when I caught the person who did this to my son. Would I act like a cop then and arrest them or like a father and blow their fucking heads off?

I took out the one device I never left behind. I sat my personal documenter in one corner of the room where its multiple cameras could record my every move and turned the recorder on.

I had to treat Joshua's death like that of a complete stranger, another victim in need of justice. It shouldn't be hard. He was a stranger to me. He wasn't the little boy who used to laugh when I held him upside down in the playground, who used to cry against my shoulder when bad dreams woke him in the middle of the night. He was a stranger who had gone from dreams of being an artist to the reality of being a scientist, who had somehow along the way decided that the body he had been born with, that he had inherited from his mother and father, wasn't enough.

He had become a stranger to me as I had become a stranger to him. And I guess that was the way we both liked it. Otherwise we would have done something about it.

I climbed the stairs to his bedroom. Always start at the top.

The furniture was sparse but good quality. A king-sized bed was against one wall under a triangular window. A comfortable chair and a reading lamp sat beside a small bookshelf holding a couple dozen books, a mix of science and science fiction. There were also three multi-use viewers of different designs and a stack of memory cubes large enough to hold the book and film collection of a fair-sized public library.

The only other piece of furniture in the room was a small bedside table next to the unmade side of the bed. There was a small lamp, a clock, a glass of water going stale and a small collection of photos in plain silver frames.

His mother, his half-sister Amber, Mike and me. His family.

I was in full dress uniform, the day I made Superintendent. One of the last times I saw Josh that didn't end with a fight.

I sat on the edge of the bed, staring at my smiling face and wondering if I would ever smile again.

| | |

There may have been a dozen clues to the case, hidden in drawers or stuffed into books or lying in plain view on the floor but I didn't have the heart to look for them. I shuffled up and down the stairs a couple of times but mostly sat on the edge of the bed or in one of the chairs around the dining room table, staring at the clutter of things that had defined my son's home. In the end, I wanted nothing more than to go home, crawl into bed with a mindless mystery and three fingers of Jack. But I knew from long experience that wasn't going to help.

So I put some police tape across the door and an alarm on the lock and called for my driver. I had one more person to see before I could think of calling it a day.

Jim McConnaghey was one of the few guys in Calgary who had been on the force as long as I had. Jim and I had never been partners but we had formed a bond that was almost as close. He was the guy that helped me break that nasty counselling habit. He dragged me out of a bar one afternoon, hauled me into an alley and beat the living shit out of me, told me to grow up and stop letting the past govern the future or some such crap. He also told me if he caught me drinking on company time again, he'd make that beating look like a walk in the park. It wasn't the most effective alcohol treatment I ever got but at least I didn't have to go to a lot of meetings. Great guy, Jim.

Jim and I had lost touch after I made Inspector. He had never been ambitious that way; being the best cop on the beat had always been his goal. He only took a desk job and the Sergeant's stripes after a bank robber's bullet cost him his leg. But even behind a desk, Jim was more in tune with the streets than ninety percent of the force. Whenever I wanted a read on what was really going down, I'd drop by and have a cup of joe with Jim.

McConnaghey wasn't at reception when I walked into HQ. The officer on duty thought he had seen Jim walking into the ready room a half hour before. That surprised me a bit and I wondered what errand had required him to go in person. Jim had limited mobility on the cheap prosthesis the health plan provided and the ready room was two floors up. The building's elevators were slow and busy and Jim made it a point of pride to walk up anything less than three flights, grinding it out one step at a time, cane in one hand, banister in the other.

I on the other hand lost my pride a long time ago so I stood in front of the bank of lifts for several minutes, pressing the button from time to time as if that would speed up the service. An elevator door finally ground open and disgorged several tired looking cops heading home from their shift.

The doors were closing again when I heard a familiar voice call for me to 'hold that 'vator.' I stuck out an arm and Willa O'Reilly slipped in.

Willa and I had not spent more than a moment alone in several months, whether by good luck or good planning, but I still felt a tingle of desire when I smelled her perfume. We were officially over. In fact, officially, we never were. The force frowns on fraternization especially between Superintendents and their Inspectors. I had moved on to a new relationship of sorts and Willa had moved on to a new job as Superintendent down in homicide.

"Hey, Frank," said Willa.

"Willa," I said, hoping she wasn't going to ask me how I was doing. Lying to Willa was not something I wanted to start doing now.

She knew better. She didn't say anything at all during the time it took to ride up two floors. Willa knew what it was like to lose someone who should have been close but wasn't. When I got off the elevator, I looked back. She gave me a small soft smile and a slight nod that said I was going to make it. She must have known something I didn't. I smiled and nodded back. Maybe if I pretended she was right, she would be.

McConnaghey was in the ready room but he wasn't there on an errand. He was sitting on a bench, doing up his flak jacket.

"Just make sure you don't open your mouth before you know what you want to say and you'll do fine," he was saying to a young female officer. "And never draw your weapon unless you plan to use it."

"Yes, sir."

"Can the sir bullshit, Lisa. I'm Jim or Mac or you old fart," said Jim. "We're partners now so you better get used to it."

"Yes, sir, I mean Jim." Lisa smiled in my direction and shrugged her shoulders. She might not be up to Jim's standards yet but she knew well enough to vacate the room when a Superintendent showed up.

"Partners?" I asked, as I watched Lisa's trim backside disappear around a corner. "Since when?"

"Ever since yesterday when I went back on active duty status," said Jim, standing up. No groan and no effort, no need of a cane. He slapped his right leg.

"Buzz Wannamaker finally came through with that promise of an affordable prosthesis that actually works. He might not be cop anymore but he's still a right guy. Look at this."

Jim hopped from one foot to the other and finished with a little soft shoe. If I didn't know which leg he had lost, I could never have figured it out from that little demo.

"Works as good as the real one. I went in the clinic an old man and two weeks later they had me dancing the cha-cha. Best thing of all, no more phantom pain."

"That's a Borg leg," I said. Ordinary prosthetics didn't work that well and they didn't heal that fast.

"No," he replied. "It's a Jim McConnaghey leg and if you want to make something of it, well, I guess I can still haul your sorry ass into an alley and give you a whooping. No disrespect meant, Superintendent Steele."

"And none taken." I laughed. Whether Jim could help me out on the case, he'd already made me feel better than I had all day. Though even thinking that killed the mood. "Got time for a coffee, Jim?"

He glanced at the big digital clock on the ready room wall. 17:42. He nodded. "Shift doesn't start until six. We should be able to swill down a mug before then."

We walked down to the basement and grabbed a couple of cups of lukewarm sludge. We found a corner table and settled in. I could tell Jim was eager to hit the road and start his first day back on a regular beat.

"I won't keep you from Lisa. She's too cute to be kept waiting."

"Hey, that's my partner you're talking about," said Jim, "I don't care what she looks like as long as she covers my back."

No doubt true. Not every cop was as colour blind or gender neutral as Jim. But not every cop was as good a cop as Jim either.

"What do you expect to find when you get out there?" I never asked Jim a straight question. I let him tell me what was on his mind. Sometimes all I got was a rant; more often I got an insight as to what the street was thinking and doing.

"Not sure, really," Jim shook his head, looking genuinely puzzled. "If I didn't know better, naw, it's stupid."

"We're all crazy together, Jim."

"Okay, but don't laugh. You believe in ghosts?"

A chill ran down my spine. I don't believe in ghosts but I do believe that sometimes monsters come back from the grave.

"Because unless he's got a twin, Gale Conklin is haunting the streets of Calgary."

Chapter 8

Cerise Kavanah opened her eyes and wondered where she was. *I'm in a car,* she thought, *in a car with...*

There was a Borg slumped in the driver's seat.

The smell of vomit washed over her and she would have thrown up again if she had anything left in her stomach.

She tried the door but it was locked. She reached across the Borg's body, trying hard not to touch him but the mechanism was jammed. *Probably encoded,* she thought.

The car was moving slowly in the morning rush hour. She didn't recognize the neighborhood but they had to be on one of the main routes into downtown. Cerise pressed her face against the window though she doubted anyone could see her through the privacy shield. Most cars had their windows opaqued and the few drivers she could see were concentrating on the road or catching a few extra minutes of sleep.

Maybe I could shoot out the window, she thought. She looked at the Borg again. There had been shooting. She remembered that. Maybe he has a gun.

She leaned forward trying to see if he had a holster or a gun tucked into his waistband. Anything. She was still reluctant to touch him. He might wake up and then what would he think? What would he do?

Besides, she thought, *it's probably safety glass. The bullets would bounce around until they killed us.*

She looked at the Borg again. His head had lolled to one side and a little drool was leaking from his slightly open mouth. Gleaming chrome glinted where teeth should be. Cerise shuddered.

The Borg's skin was brown though not as dark as her own; more mahogany than chocolate. He had no hair; his skull was capped with more chrome. His cheeks and jaw were smooth and Cerise doubted he shaved often. His left eyebrow was dark with thick bristly hair and Cerise assumed the eye below it would be dark brown if it were open. The other eyebrow was a line of jewel-encrusted metal above an artificial eye that glinted like an emerald in the morning sun.

The car was moving faster now. It had left the main road and was moving through a part of town she did recognize though she couldn't remember what it was called or why she knew it. *Maybe I live near here. Maybe the car is taking me home.* The thought of home was a cold ball in the pit of her stomach.

He said he was taking me to his office and then taking me home. Going to an office sounded better but she wasn't sure what kind of office a Borg would have.

This Borg was dressed in an expensive tailored shirt under a suede jacket, not at all like the pasty-skinned, rubber-clad Borg she remembered from…dammit! From where?

He looked muscular, though whether from pumping iron or having it implanted in his body, she couldn't tell.

His left arm was stretched across his body. She had a sudden image of him reaching out to touch her hand. It hadn't been a bad thing. He had tried to comfort her, had reached for her with his real hand.

She looked at the three-pronged claw that extended from his right sleeve. That thing's real too, it's just not human.

Cerise shuddered again, not at the Borg's appearance but at her own thoughts. Everyone deserves to be judged on what they do and think and not what they look like. She knew that. But still…

The Borg had come for her. He had come to save her. She had been sitting at a bar with a man. A very fat man. He had held her thigh in his greasy hand, squeezed it until it hurt whenever she tried to squirm away. He wasn't doing anything else but something about him had made her afraid. She grasped at the memory but it slipped away.

What did they do to me?

My name is…I know this. She cried out in frustration. She remembered thinking her name a few moments ago but it was gone again.

Cerise Kavanah. It didn't sound strange.

He knows, she thought, *he can tell me who I am and how I got here.* She reached out to shake him awake. Her hand froze in mid-gesture.

There had been another Borg, like this one but different too. There was something about that Borg. Something that scared her.

She tried to remember but the image skittered away like a fleck on the edge of her vision. There had been…

Blood. A lot of blood. Cerise gagged and spat bile onto the floor.

The car turned off the street into the entrance to an underground parkade beneath a nondescript three-story building. The car stopped in front of a woman and two men. The woman looked normal but the men were even more Borg that the one slumped in front of the car.

One of them raised his arm and pointed a flashing red light at the car.

Chapter 9

I finally rolled home right before seven. Nancy, my latest try at romance, was sitting in my living room. That was when I remembered I had invited her over for dinner. It was officially our third date, the one where guys of my age make their first move. Of course, the fact that Nancy had made her first move two dates ago simplified things.

"Let me guess," she said, as I stood in the doorway, looking stupid. "We're ordering in Chinese."

"Sorry, Nancy," I said. "I forgot. It's been a hard day. Can we take a rain check?" I didn't want to get into why it had been a hard day. Nancy didn't know me as well as Willa but she wanted to. She wouldn't let it go at 'I'm fine.' She'd expect more. There'd probably be a fight.

I liked Nancy. I didn't want to fight with her. I wanted her to smile and say, that's all right, Frank. You look tired. We'll do this another day.

And maybe she would have said that if my ex-wife Dorothy hadn't chosen that moment to arrive unannounced at my still-open apartment door.

"Who's the bimbo, Frank?" asked Dorothy. She always knew how to win friends and influence people.

"Your younger, prettier replacement," said Nancy. She was no slouch either. I don't think she actually knew Dorothy was my ex but Nancy is a political reporter, used to taking shots in the dark.

It might have come to blows but Dorothy couldn't keep up the façade. She burst into tears and sort of tottered in place until I could get my arm around her and guide her to a chair. Nancy looked aghast and fascinated at the same time.

"Maybe I should go," Nancy said. She gave me a look that said we'd talk later. In detail.

"I'd appreciate it if you didn't." I knew I should be a man about this but I didn't want to be. Dorothy was in pain. Crying was the first stage; throwing things came later. She showed more restraint in company than when we were alone.

"If I'm staying," said Nancy, uncertainly. "Maybe you should introduce us."

Dorothy had stopped sobbing, still trying to be a good soldier. I handed her some tissues and she discreetly blew her nose with one and then dabbed her eyes with another. I realized then how on the edge my ex-wife was. No runny mascara. No make-up at all. Once Dot turned forty, she wouldn't take out the garbage without first putting on her face.

She stood and stuck out her hand.

"Dorothy Remington-Steele," she said. "Frank's wife."

"Ex-wife," I said, perhaps a little too hastily. "Almost ten years."

"How sweet, you remembered." Dorothy gave me a little smile that told me she was back and that I was going to pay.

Nancy gave me a sideways look. I knew what she was thinking.

"Dorothy and I both loved old detective shows," I said.

"Turns out it was one of the few things we had in common. Remington Steele was one of my favourites. Even after the divorce I couldn't give up the name."

Everything was going swimmingly. As long as Nancy was there we weren't going to talk about Joshua. That suited me fine. If I could get them to go off together and talk about my many flaws, the night would end perfectly. Me and Jack together again like old times.

No such luck.

"Nancy Whittington, I'm Frank's..." Nancy paused and looked at me.

Tricky question. Lover? Technically yes, but Dorothy didn't want or need to know. Girlfriend? Implied a commitment that I for one hadn't made.

"Date," I settled on. Should have picked something else.

"Date!" Dorothy practically spat the word. "You heartless cocksucker."

Dorothy normally wouldn't say shit if her mouth was full of it. But her son had been murdered less than eighteen hours ago. She had flown from Chicago to Calgary looking to me for answers, explanations, maybe a little comfort. This was not a normal situation.

"This was arranged days ago," I said. "I didn't have time to call and cancel. Nancy doesn't know what happened." We'd kept it out of the news all day, though I knew that wasn't going to last much longer.

It didn't help much. Dorothy collapsed back in the chair, not quietly crying now but sobbing, long loud wracking sobs that shook her body the way a cat shakes a mouse.

Nancy looked at me, too confused and shocked to formulate a question.

Be a cop, Frank.

"Last night," I said, "at about three o'clock in the morning, the body of Joshua Steele, Dorothy's son, our son, was found dead in a dumpster. He had been murdered."

"Oh, my God, who? Why?"

"We have no suspects. However, Joshua was Borg. We think…"

"My son," Dorothy's voice sounded like it was coming from the bottom of a well, "was not a Borg."

I shrugged and looked at Nancy, pleading with her to stay a little longer.

She must like me more than I thought.

"I'll make some tea," she said. "You do have some?"

I hate the stuff but I knew from our first two dates that Nancy liked it so I had bought some on the weekend. "It's in the cupboard over the sink."

I sat on the sofa opposite Dorothy and listened to Nancy bustling around the kitchen, making plenty of noise so Dot and I could talk in private. She had straightened up and her tears had stopped, but I could sense she was on a knife's edge. Maybe I should have held her. Maybe, but the river had long since washed that bridge away.

"I'm sorry," I said. "But you should have called."

"Your phone is never turned on."

I pulled it out of my pocket and looked at it. For once, it was on. I held it up.

Dorothy gave me a little smile. "Well, I assumed it was off."

"Where are you staying?" For a moment, I thought she was going to say 'here.'

She let the moment linger long enough to make me sweat.

"I've got a room at the Hyatt," she said. "What happened to our son?"

"It's still under investigation."

"Frank, please. You must know something."

"Dorothy, you were a cop's wife for nearly twenty years. You know I couldn't tell you anything. I can't even tell you if there is any thing to tell. You should have stayed in Chicago."

"Someone had to make sure Joshua was properly buried." Flat and cold. "Or were you going to handle that?"

Up to that moment I'd managed to put it out of my mind. No, more than that, I'd managed not to think of it at all, as if it wasn't going to happen. That somehow no one was going to have to make arrangements to put my son in a box.

Nancy walked into the silence that followed, sat down the tea tray on the table beside Dorothy and went back to the kitchen. Looking for cookies, maybe, or the back way out.

The phone I was still holding in my hand began to buzz. Not many people knew *that* code.

"I've got to take this," I said. Dorothy glared at me but said nothing.

It was Darwhal Singh.

"Frank, is this a bad time?" Darwhal didn't care but politeness was second nature to him.

"Could be worse," I said. "Have you heard from Buzz?"

"No," said Darwhal. "That's one of the things I'd like to talk to you about. And something else, something too delicate to discuss over the phone. Could you come over to my office?"

"Now?"

"That's what I had in mind."

I glanced at Dorothy who was still glaring at me. Nancy was standing in the kitchen doorway with a plate of very stale chocolate cookies, looking like she couldn't decide whether to cram them in her mouth or throw them at me. Now would be a very good time to leave.

"I'll be there in ten minutes."

"And, Frank, you may want to bring your gun."

I disconnected and shoved the phone back in my pocket.

"Sorry, ladies, but duty calls."

"You can't go," they said as if they had rehearsed it.

I grabbed my coat and headed for the door. I'd worry about how I was going to get to Singh's place once I was outside.

"Enjoy the tea and lock the door when you leave."

Something smashed against the wall as I ducked out. Whether it was the teapot or the cookies I couldn't say.

I called for a cruiser and headed down the three flights of stairs to the street. I stood on the curb, shivering in the sudden cold and waiting for my ride, hoping neither of the women would come out before it arrived. Getting another date with Nancy was going to put a major dent in my savings account.

Dealing with Dorothy was going to cost me a whole lot more.

But, right now I didn't care. Singh had promised me action and action was exactly what I needed right now.

Chapter 10

Ping.

Ping. Wannamaker swatted at the sound.

Ping. *I want to sleep.*

Ping. The sound of the multi-scanner lifted Wannamaker out of an ocean of pain and nausea. He opened his eyes.

The walls, floor and ceiling, as well as the heavy pillars supporting it, were uniform plasticrete grey with the exception of the complex designs painted along the central column that held the elevators and stairwells to the upper levels. Designs that only made sense when you could see beyond the visible spectrum. Borg designs.

The car had done its job. They were parked in the underground vault beneath the recently completed Borg fortress, officially known as the East Inglewood Community Centre.

Three Borg were standing in front of the car. He knew two of them. Angel and the Borg formerly known as Gamow, who now answered only to a complex string of Borg twitters and whistles, inaudible to anyone without an augment and indecipherable to anyone who didn't speak Borg. The third Borg, the one holding the scanner, he didn't know.

Beside him in the car, Cerise Kavanah was pressed back against the seat, her eyes wide with fear.

Wannamaker unlocked the doors. The girl looked around in panic.

"It's alright, Cerise, they won't hurt you," he said in a voice specifically designed to be soothing. The sub-harmonics did their job; the tension in her shoulders and neck eased.

"Are you sure?" she asked. Given all that had happened to her that day, her voice was remarkably calm.

"As certain as a summer sequel," said Wannamaker. "But we better keep our hands where they can see them, just in case."

He raised his hands and put them on the wheel. Kavanah leaned forward and rested hers on the dash.

The Borg with the scanner nodded an all clear and put the device away. Singh hadn't wasted his money. The weapon modifications were undetectable as promised, at least by low level scans. He wasn't sure he was ready to try to get on a jetliner anytime soon.

Wannamaker opened the driver-side door and tried standing. He made it on the second attempt, the muscles in his legs quivering as the remnants of several drugs sloshed through his system.

"You look like hell, Buzz," said Gamow, a fast burst of sound well above normal human hearing range.

"You're not up for any beauty awards yourself," replied Wannamaker in the same mode. He gestured to the girl and switched to regular speed. "She's had a rough time. Some of that may have involved Borg. Maybe we could confine ourselves to straight talk."

"Spee lar seven whisp bah!" said Gamow, this time not only at high speed but in Borg.

Wannamaker hadn't expected much else from Gamow. He was one of the intellectual forces behind the local Independista movement and made no concessions to unmodified humans. He spoke Borg or high speed English unless forced to deal with regular humans. Even then, he modified his voice with harmonics and sub-sonics, to reinforce aurally what his listeners could already see. That he was Borg and not like them at all.

"Maybe you should leave this to us," said Angel, placing a hand on Gamow's shoulder.

Gamow shook her off and glared from face to face as if cataloguing them for future retribution.

"Your time will come," he said, deigning to speak so everyone could hear. "Iron lungs." He turned and stalked off, deliberately letting his servos whine and growl.

Wannamaker watched him go. He had gotten used to the epithet but he hadn't grown to like it.

"Love the stereotype, baby!"

"That wasn't helpful," said Angel.

"It was all I had," he said. "The girl isn't the only one who's had a rough day. I need a flush and some rest and then maybe some food."

"Bjorn, get some help and a couple of gurneys," Angel said to the second Borg. "What the hell have you been doing, Buzz?"

"I've been mixing my drinks."

"What's with the girl?"

"I rescued her from a slave auction. And you'll never guess who the chief bidder was. Gale Conklin."

"I thought he was dead," said Angel. Her eyes had widened at the mention of Conklin's name. She knew what his return meant for the city.

"Not dead," said Kavanah, speaking for the first time.

"Definitely not dead," said Buzz, easing himself back into the car seat. He glanced over at the girl again. She was holding on, barely. Her skin was grey and her eyes so wide he could see white all the way around them. "Lay back and try to rest. Help is coming."

| | |

According to his internal chronometer, fourteen hours had passed since he lost consciousness in the garage. He was lying on his back between clean white sheets, his head resting on a standard issue hospital pillow. An IV tube led from a bottle of clear liquid into his left arm.

Cerise Kavanah was laying three beds down, propped up on several pillows and reading a graphic novel. She smiled at him uncertainly and he waved and tried to speak. It came out as a painful grind. Kavanah looked concerned and pressed the button above her bed.

A few moments later, a Borg in blue scrubs appeared in the doorway, followed closely by Angel. Angel was wearing a shimmery one-piece green coverall that on her looked sexy. *But, then*, thought Wannamaker, *what doesn't look sexy on Angel?*

"Where am I?" Wannamaker rasped.

"That's right," said Angel, "You haven't been here since we opened the clinic."

The doctor was adjusting Wannamaker's IV. He felt a sudden flush run though his body.

"Nothing but vitamins and electrolytes," said the doctor before Wannamaker could ask. "After the drugs you took, no stimulants of any kind for twenty four hours."

"I guess you'll have to leave the room, Angel," said Wannamaker, grinning.

She laughed—an always desirable result. "I can see you're on the road to recovery."

The doctor checked some of the devices plugged into the diagnostic panel on Wannamaker's arm and made a few notes on the keypad at the foot of the bed.

"Ten minutes," he said as he left the room.

"Aye, Aye, Captain," said Wannamaker. "Crank this thing up, will you?"

Angel pressed a button on the side of the bed and it folded into a more comfortable sitting position. She perched at its foot and rested her hand on the sheet over his leg. They had known each other for nearly a decade. He probably trusted Angel more than any one he knew, with the possible exception of his old boss, Frank Steele, and he was pretty sure she felt the same way about him. As for other feelings they might share, he couldn't say but he still had his hopes.

He glanced over at Kavanah. She was staring at them with obvious curiosity but turned back to her book when Buzz caught her looking.

I need to talk to Steele, thought Wannamaker, *he needs to know about Conklin. And about this girl.*

"How is she?" he asked, pitching his voice so only Angel could hear him.

"Fine, physically at least. She almost kicked Bjorn's head off when she woke up and found him leaning over her. She's a regular little tigress," said Angel, smiling over at the girl. She continued in a lower voice. "But she's having trouble remembering things. Even her name seems to come and go."

"Drugs?"

"There were traces but nothing in the last few days and nothing that would explain the amnesia."

"Trauma?"

"Again nothing physically, no evidence of a blow to the head, at least not in the last six months. She does have some old injuries that weren't properly treated but hard to say from what. How well do you know her?"

"Only what I read in her file. She was snatched about a month ago. Seems to come from a good family. She was active in sports at school. Might have got hurt doing that."

"The coach should be fired. At some point she had a minor fracture to her arm."

"Psychological? Hysterical amnesia?" asked Wannamaker. It wasn't as common as the vids made out but it did happen. Though memory loss tended to be more selective. "She's been in some bad places in the last month. Hard to know what she saw or heard."

Angel shook her head. "We think someone might have put a Bug in her head."

"Jesus, that's sick." Bugs were based on the same technology that allowed Borg modifications to work, translating neural impulses into digital code. The intent, so the official story went, had been to permit agents to transmit unbreakable identity code to protect secure installations from intrusions. The paranoid set assumed the government was working on a form of mind control or, at the very least, mind reading.

It turned out the brain was a lot subtler than the scientists or their bosses figured. Bugs could be used to soften people up for interrogation but drugs and old fashioned brainwashing worked as well or better with fewer downsides. The major downside was that if you didn't get what you wanted the first time, there sometimes was no second chance. Used inexpertly, and there were few experts outside dark ops military units, the Bugs could leave memory a jumble of disconnected images and emotions with little chance of recovery. That had become their main use: to wipe memories rather than read them. Bugs were illegal under the laws of most countries and banned by international treaties but that had never stopped the bad guys, or even some of the supposed good guys.

If someone had put a Bug in Cerise Kavanah's head, she might never reveal what she had seen.

Wannamaker looked over at the girl. She was still reading, her face a mask of youthful concentration, though Buzz suspected she was straining her ears to hear what they were saying. Bugs didn't affect the intellect but messed up its ability to access long-term memories or form new ones.

"Is there any chance you're wrong?"

"Sure. A Bug isn't the only thing that would cause her symptoms; it's not even the worst. There's no trace of the device itself but there was some bruising in the sinuses. That's the best entry point if you're going after something specific and don't want to completely fry the subject. And it doesn't leave external wounds."

Oddly that made Wannamaker more hopeful rather than less. There were easier and quicker ways to insert a Bug—through the ear, a tear duct or even the base of the skull—ways to use if you were in a hurry or didn't give a crap how much of the mind you destroyed in the process. Maybe Conklin had access to an expert. Or maybe they hadn't used a Bug at all.

"Would imaging show the type and extent of the damage?"

"It's the only way to be certain. But…"

"What?"

"Resources are limited and, well, frankly there are those who object to her even taking up a bed."

"Gamow."

"Among others." Angel looked away.

"The clinic is practically empty."

"That's not the point, Buzz, and you know it. I've called in some favours. She can stay for a day or two and we'll recoup what we can from the provincial government. But nothing extra. The Council decided—"

"Isn't my credit good? I can—"

"Stop it. People are spooked, Buzz. These killings have everyone looking over their shoulder. And your little escapade this morning hasn't helped. The press and police have been hovering around known Borg haunts all day. Even your old boss dropped into the Garry this morning. What's his interest in the Borg anyway?"

Wannamaker shrugged. He had always got along pretty well with Steele though he was still pissed that Wannamaker hadn't come back to the Force after the craziness of last fall had died down. But Steele's attitude could best be described as colour-blind; he didn't care where you came from or what you looked like as long as you did your job and played by the rules, or at least the rules as defined by Steele. He'd been burned by that approach a couple of times but he'd won a lot more often than he lost.

"I heard a rumour that his son was working in the field, even had some mods installed. Maybe Steele was trying to get some insight into…"

"His son was killed last night," said Angel. "I heard earlier today from…It was on the seven o'clock news. They're saying it's the same as the others."

I need to talk to Frank, thought Wannamaker. *He's going to need all the help he can get.* He activated the phone wired into the side of his head and dialed Steele's number. No answer. Not surprising. Steele was notorious for leaving his phone in his desk or turned off in his pocket.

Better call Darwhal and let him know what happened. He's probably running all kinds of film in his head wondering what happened to his partner, not to mention the agency's fancy new technology.

But Singh didn't answer any of his phones. And even his messenger was silent.

Chapter 11

Singh was waiting on the street outside his office, leaning against a black low-slung sports car. The man liked his cars. To me, they were a means of transport but he viewed them as a symbol of who he was. I've never really figured out how that works.

At least the snow had finally stopped, though a chill north wind promised more to come. We didn't waste a lot of time on pleasantries. The gull wing doors started to open before I even got out of the cruiser and Singh gestured me into the car. I think he liked to watch me try to fold myself in half.

If this car was a symbol of who Singh was, he was a narrow cramped man who spent his life way too close to the gutter, though I suspect that wasn't quite what he was trying to convey.

Singh slipped into the driver's seat and grinned at me. He seemed to have plenty of room on his side. Singh powered up the vehicle. It made no sound at all as we pulled away from the curve. He flicked on the music to fill the silence. Cool jazz with a hint of Asian rhythms. Not my taste but it didn't offend.

"Is this a date or are we working?" I asked after a couple of minutes. Singh seemed to be taking a roundabout route to wherever we were going. We'd passed the same row of restaurants twice. At least Singh was driving the car instead of letting the computer do it. Not surprising; he was a man who liked to be in control.

"Sorry, Frank. This is sensitive. I wanted to make sure no one was following us."

"If I wanted to be followed, don't you think I'd just wear a trace?"

"You might, though it wouldn't work in this car. Besides I'm not worried about the police. My client likes her privacy but the media doesn't often oblige. Nobody knows she's in Calgary but you can never be too careful."

"And why am I going to see your client?"

"As I said, it's delicate. But I think you'll find it in your best interests to see her. Though perhaps you should let me do all the talking. At least until she's comfortable with you."

I was still grateful for being rescued so I decided to play along. I crossed my arms and leaned back in the seat. Singh reached over and pressed a couple of controls. The car seat moved back and down and then squirmed under me. I suddenly had a lot more room and a lot more back support that I had thought possible.

I grunted my appreciation. I lay back and listened to the soft music and hoped like hell I didn't fall asleep.

I must have drifted off because the next thing I knew we were parked inside the walls of a small estate. From the size and age of the house and the maturity of the trees, I figured we were somewhere in the heart of Mount Royal, Calgary's oldest and most elite neighborhood.

Whatever else Singh's client might be, she was at least rich. Places like these didn't go on the market often. When they did, it was usually a major item in the gossip shows, either from the messiness of the domestic situation that led to the sale or for the sheer magnitude of the asking price. A hundred million wasn't uncommon, which even in New Dollars was not a trivial sum.

The car doors swished open and we clambered out. Singh's dark suit hung as if fresh from being pressed. Mine looked like I'd been sleeping in it for two days. Singh glanced at me critically and tried to adjust my collar. I glared at him and he stopped.

"Ah, well, at least you look the part," he said and led me to the front door.

We were clearly anticipated because the door opened as we mounted the verandah. It must have been the butler's night off because the foyer was empty, all polished marble and rich grained hardwood. A grand staircase led up into the darkness of the upper floors, lit only by a crystal chandelier that glowed dimly from high in the arched ceiling. The few pieces of antique furniture in the entrance hall were small but so elegant and perfectly chosen that it looked as if they had grown there instead of being placed by human hands.

Warm light beckoned from a half-open door at the far end of the hall. Singh swept towards it like he owned the place, which wasn't outside the scope of his ambitions even if it was beyond his current budget. I followed more slowly, like I was expecting that butler to show up any minute and throw me out on my ear.

Singh's client was sitting in a wingback chair next to an enormous fireplace. The metre-long lengths of hardwood crackling on the hearth were almost dwarfed by the massive stones. The chair was upholstered in pale flawless leather the colour of tanned blondes. The tanned blonde in question was curled up in the chair and gazing into the fire, a crystal goblet of amber liquid in her left hand. She didn't look up as we entered but gestured us to sit in two similar chairs gathered around a low stone-topped table. Two more glasses and a crystal decanter of the same liquid awaited us.

She was wearing one of those dresses that promised everything but revealed nothing, shimmering without being garish, something you could wear around the house or at the latest gala event. Nancy would look good in a dress like that. Maybe the next time I win the lottery, I'll buy her one.

The woman was striking rather than beautiful, eyes too far apart, nose and jaw a little too big, a woman you might not look at twice on the street. But if you did look twice, you might never look away.

I knew her, of course. Lady Natasha Redding had started her life as the second of three children of a lower middle class family from upstate New York. She'd been eighteen when the Troubles, as they were so euphemistically called these days, began in the mid-20s with a series of world economic collapses and an escalation of military conflicts that made the 09 recession look like a golden age of prosperity and the Iraq-Afghanistan war like a squabble in the sandbox.

A lot of people made bad decisions in those days, decisions that still haunted their families. A lot more had turned turtle, trying to salvage their little corner of the world while ignoring the bigger picture.

Not Natasha. She had reinvented social networking, merging it with viral marketing techniques and invasive worms that did no damage but reminded others of the damage they were doing, mobilizing over three hundred million people into a force for world peace. Towards the end, she was airdropping solar powered palmtops into every trouble spot on the planet. Computers that not only connected people but gave them a way to influence their political and military leaders. It was like the guy who had stood in front of the tank in Tiananmen Square all those years ago. Only this time, he was in front of every tank in the world and he looked like your mother or your best friend.

Some say she single-handedly stopped the escalation of the Troubles into a planet busting third world war. The good folks in Stockholm certainly thought so when they gave her the Nobel Peace Prize. Personally I'm not convinced. I think people all over the world, all nine billion of them, collectively woke up in 2029, looked at the smoking radioactive ruin that had been the Korean peninsula and said, 'Holy Crap! We need to take a step back.'

Not that my opinion matters much. The woman had figured out how to make a profit from world peace. But what do you do after you've saved the world and you're still not twenty-five? Most people would have taken their billions, bought an island and spent the rest of their lives cavorting with the rich and famous.

Not her style. She'd spent her money and a lot of the money of her rich friends rebuilding shattered economies. And when she bored of that, she had started a campaign to get people reading again, taking over a couple of moribund publishing companies and infusing them with new ideas and approaches that actually made them relevant to a wired and rewired world.

If they gave a Nobel Prize for Literature to someone who never wrote a word, she'd get one of those too.

Then three years ago, at the age of thirty-five she married Sir Jeffry Boynton, a British composer twenty-four years her senior, acquiring a Ladyship in the process, finally bought that island in the Pacific and dropped out of sight. To work behind the scenes and live happily ever after according to all media reports.

Of course, who trusts the media these days?

I looked at Singh with newfound respect. I knew he was connected in high places but this was stratospheric. He cocked an eyebrow and looked at the decanter.

I nodded. One couldn't hurt. It probably wouldn't help either given how long I'd been awake. But I suspected the contents of that decanter were way beyond anything I could ever afford. When opportunity knocks.

I was right. It was like swallowing a flame that warmed without burning, like listening to a complex symphony of sun-kissed fruit and gentle sea breezes, like looking into the face of a beautiful woman for the very first time. It wasn't Jack, but it was pretty good.

Singh watched me drink like the old General in *The Big Sleep* who couldn't drink himself but took his pleasure from watching others do it. I guess he was taking his return to the tenets of Sikhism seriously.

Lady Natasha was still looking into the flames.

"Who is this, Darwhal?" she asked, her voice sounding exactly like it did on the web casts, rich and low with only a hint of her New York origins.

Darwhal looked like he was going to string her some cock and bull story but he obviously thought better of it. This wasn't a woman who would take being lied to lightly.

"Lady Natasha Redding," said Singh, in case I didn't know, "may I present Superintendent Frank Steele."

I wasn't sure if I was supposed to bow or kiss her hand so I tipped my glass and nodded. She smiled and returned the gesture.

"A police officer, Dar? Are you sure that's wise?"

"Frank isn't your average police officer," said Singh. "I think you can trust him. I know I do."

This time it was my turn to raise an eyebrow. Singh returned my questioning glance with a steady gaze of his own, suggesting that maybe he was still sticking with the truth. I wasn't sure how I'd gained this trust but now I felt obliged to earn it.

"If you've committed a crime or are trying to protect someone who has, Lady Redding," I said, "the best thing would be for me to leave now. It may seem quaint but I take my oath of office seriously."

"My only crime is one of the heart," she said. She took a slow sip of her cognac and stared back at the fire.

We might have spent our evening in quiet reflection if Singh hadn't cleared his throat and broken the spell.

"Perhaps you should tell Frank about your little problem."

Lady Natasha put down her glass and rose in a single sinuous motion. She began to pace in front of the fire as if considering the best way to break the bad news—which words might keep me from bolting for the front door to flag down the nearest police cruiser to take us all downtown.

She stopped abruptly and turned her gaze on me. The fabric of her dress swirled against her slender limbs like sea foam against rocks. "What do you know about Borg politics, Frank?"

What did anyone know who wasn't Borg, I wondered. The community was deeply divided between those who wanted the Borg to be another distinct brick in the vertical mosaic we called Canada—or a unique flavour in the American melting pot—choose your metaphor— and those who wanted the Borg recognized as a new race, or even a new species, with their own separate country or institutions. But how deep those divisions went and how seriously the average Borg took them, I didn't know. And what they had to do with the price of coffee in Calgary, or more importantly with the life of the richest woman in the world was far beyond my area of expertise.

In any case, a response wasn't required. Lady Natasha continued.

"There are nearly two million Borg alive in the world today," she said. She had resumed pacing again, the transit of her body back and forth in front of the flickering flames almost hypnotic. "Most live in the West. But there are populations in nearly every major city in the world.

In some places they are merely disliked and feared; in others, the persecution is horrific."

"Life is tough all over," I said. "I'm trying to cope with what's happening to the Borg in this burg. I've got five dismembered bodies and no suspects in sight." I sounded like a bad Phillip Marlowe impersonator but I was tired and impatient with all this gentility.

I don't think she was used to being interrupted. She graced me with what the media called the Redding stare, icy green eyes under perfectly shaped brows and a frown that would freeze water. The reports were right; it did feel like having your skin flayed.

"Well, now you have six," she said. "There's a dead Borg in the back garden."

"Jesus Christ!" I leapt to my feet. The glass flew out of my hand and smashed against the hearth. Blue flames licked against the stone for a few moments as Lady Natasha danced out of the way.

Singh hadn't moved from his chair but I could see his shoulders tense. I'm not sure if he would have tried to tackle me if I headed for the door but I know he was thinking about it.

"You told me you committed no crime."

"I didn't kill him," she said.

"Failure to report a crime…" I started.

"But I have reported it," she said, "To you."

Technically true but it hadn't been her intent. She hadn't expected Singh to bring the police. I told her so.

She laughed. That laugh could mean she had expected me all along or that it simply didn't matter. This was a woman used to playing complex games with powerful people. I was out of my league.

"You know now. You would hardly have known any sooner if I'd gone through channels. I called Dar as soon as it happened."

"Ninety minutes ago, give or take a couple," volunteered Singh.

She was right. I'd probably still be on my way to the scene. I sat back down, signaling my willingness to hear her out.

"Who is he?" I asked. Somebody's son, a voice in my head whispered. I ignored it. For now.

She made a series of high-pitched clicks and whistles, a pretty good imitation of Borg as near as I could tell. As good as any one could do without the aid of a vocoder.

"I could never really pronounce it," she said. "I called him Dick. It amused us both." She sighed and went on. "He was a leader of the Independista movement in Brazil before the last Jesuit crackdown there. I met him in Geneva two years ago. I was fascinated with his intensity, his passion for his cause, his pure exoticism. We became lovers. I, for one, was in love. I suspect he saw me as an opportunity. No matter. The heart always makes excuses.

"We met in out of the way places whenever we could. I own a lot of property, very little of it in my own name. My husband, Jeffry, is an old fashioned man and a difficult one, prone to depression and anxiety. Drugs would cure him but he fears it would destroy his muse. I've stopped arguing with him, taking my consolation where I can find it. But it would destroy him if he knew and it would destroy me to hurt him like that."

Loving two people at once has never been something I've understood but I knew it happened.

"Jeffry thinks I'm at meetings at the United Nations, which in a few hours I will be. A tired institution but it still has its uses. I arranged to stop here on the way. Dick flew up from Los Angeles in a private jet. We planned to spend an evening together. Someone had other plans."

She stared into the fire for a few moments, gathering her thoughts. I'd seen this before. Witnesses to crimes able to talk at length about the events that brought them to the scene but then unwilling to describe the actual crime. I decided to give her as much time as she needed.

People like Natasha Redding operate on a different level from the rest of us. They don't spend their lives pondering what to do, they make their decisions in the blink of an eye and move forward.

"I turned the security off, shut down the house systems. Foolish perhaps, but no one knew I was here and what was the chance someone would wander into the heart of Mount Royal hoping to find an undefended home? Dick could no more be seen with me than I with him. A leader of the Borg independence movement couldn't have an affair with a woman famous for refusing modification even for vanity's sake."

"A bit like a televangelist being caught with a hooker," I said. I could see Singh wincing but Lady Natasha didn't miss a beat.

"He was to come as soon as it was dark and climb over the back wall. Someone followed him. Three someones in fact. They were on him before I could react. They were on him before *he* could react."

She let her last words sink in. Taken to the limit, body modification could triple or quadruple a person's speed and strength and at least halve their reaction time. Dick was sneaking into a house in the highest security neighborhood in Calgary. All his senses would have been on high alert.

"What the hell were they, ninjas?" I asked.

"Not human. No matter how you describe human. They tore him to pieces with their bare hands. He barely had time to cry out. By the time I turned the house back on, they were gone, and they took everything that made Dick a Borg with them."

Her voice finally broke but she wasn't ready to share tears with a stranger. She sat down and leaned back with her eyes closed.

"Were the attackers Borg?" I asked.

"I don't know. I have many talents, Superintendent, but seeing in the dark isn't one of them. They were fast and they were strong, inhumanly so, but they didn't move like Borg." She sighed. "But then I really only knew how one Borg moved." Her voice broke again and she clamped her jaw in an effort to retain control.

I wasn't sure there was a single way Borg moved, any more than there was a single way white men danced but maybe she was right. I'd seen goons on Stim move as fast as any Borg but there was always a hurky-jerky quality to their movements, the compression and release of human muscle rather than the machine smoothness of the Borg.

It was something anyway. They, whoever they were, Borg or something else, travelled in packs. But it left as many questions as it answered. Was it a crime of opportunity, hunters stumbling over their quarry in the night? Or had Dick been targeted and tracked from the private airport? And what about the political angle?

"I'm going to go now," she said. A statement not a request. "If you need anything more, Dar knows how to reach me. Good-bye Superintendent. And good luck."

She offered me her hand and I shook it. It was warm and dry and seemed remarkably small. I suddenly realized that her head barely reached the top of my shoulder. She had looked so much bigger pacing in front of the fire.

I suppose I could have made a fuss, tried to stop her. I expect it would have been like trying to stop the wind. I'd keep her out of it if I could. As for Dick, I doubt if he'd appear in any of our databases; the Brazilians weren't much into sharing these days.

Little steps as they say.

"You better go too, Darwhal. I'll call this in."

He nodded and followed Lady Redding out of the room. I'd figure out what to tell the response team when they came.

Then, maybe I could finally get some sleep.

Chapter 12

Cerise stood in front of the mirror in the small bathroom off the clinic staring at her face, trying to remember who she was and how she had come to be here, in a fortified warehouse full of Borg. The sand-coloured tiles were warm on her bare feet; the pale green porcelain of the sink cool where she leaned against it. The mirror was steamy from her shower and she wiped it with a towel to clear it.

"My name is Cerise Kavanah," she said. It sounded right; a big improvement over earlier in the day. She repeated it to be sure. "Cerise Kavanah."

She wondered if people called her 'Cherry.' Probably. She wasn't sure how she felt about that. Maybe they called her 'Cherry Baby.' She liked that better.

She turned sideways trying to see her profile out of the corner of her eye. She was wearing a blue t-shirt and grey sweat pants that the woman, Angel, had given her, a welcome relief from the outfit she had been wearing when Buzz Whatjamacallit rescued her from that bar. They felt more like her.

So at least I'm not a whore by nature, she thought.

A hot mouth on her neck and bare shoulders as she twisted and flailed to keep away the hard grasping hands. "Keep her clean," growled a harsh voice.

Cerise's knees buckled and she grabbed the sink to keep from falling. The image, and the wave of nausea it invoked, passed as quickly as it came.

How could he do that to me? Something seemed to crystallize inside her. Someone had betrayed her. Someone she trusted.

She banged her hand on the sink in rage. The sudden pain washed over her like a cleansing spray.

She didn't know who but it would come. It would come. And when it did, somehow, someway she would make them pay.

She looked in the mirror again, surprised to see the resolution that burned in her wide-brown eyes. What had Angel called her? A tigress.

She had a sudden memory of something she had learned in social history class. Native North Americans sometimes went on vision quests as part of growing up, as a way of finding out who they were. They could only come back when the animal that would be their totem revealed itself to them. So unfair!, she thought, that I can remember that when everything else is a blank.

She didn't know who she was, not yet. A name, Cerise Kavanah. Whose totem is tiger. It was something to hang onto, something to build on. It was all she had.

She tilted her head to one side and brushed her hands through her thick black hair until the curls and ringlets danced around her oval face like the mane of a tigress.

Tigers don't have manes, do they? she thought.

Whatever. It was her totem; it could have a mane if she wanted.

She tilted her head the other way and tried a seductive smile. *Too many teeth,* she thought and tried again.

"I will have my revenge," she said, her voice low and serious.

Then she laughed and shook her head. *Sure, right.*

She looked in the mirror again. *I wonder if boys think I'm pretty?*

Chapter 13

Angel sat on the end of Wannamaker's bed. Cerise had been taken to the dining room for lunch and they were alone in the ward.

"How are you feeling?"

"I'd feel a lot better if I knew what was going on," said Wannamaker.

"No one really knows what's going on. Not for sure. But you hear a lot of talk."

"*You* hear a lot of talk," said Wannamaker, "I only got back in town a few weeks ago and I've been busy."

After quitting the force, he'd headed north to spend Christmas with his folks and wound up staying for a couple of months, enjoying his first real winter in nearly a decade. People didn't exactly stare and point, that wouldn't have been polite, but his presence had created quite a stir.

At first, he'd resented the sideways glances and the whispered conversations that died away as he approached. Not that he couldn't have heard them if he wanted to but he had been raised to be polite, too, and he wouldn't embarrass his parents by intruding into their neighbors' thoughts like that. Besides, he understood their concerns. His people had taken a long time to find themselves again. It had taken generations to recover from the trauma of residential schools, children ripped from their families and culture, punished simply for being who and what they were, for even speaking their language.

It had been a long road to rebuild their culture and economy and to find a way to accommodate with a world they had never asked to join but was never going to go away. It must have been hard for them to see one of their best and brightest go away and then come back transformed in ways they couldn't begin to imagine.

So he had been honoured beyond belief when the village elders had come to him and asked him to stay on, to take over for the recently retired police chief, to be part of the community again as if nothing had ever changed.

But things had changed. He had changed. He was still Cree but he was something else too. He had made the choice to fulfill his natural destiny and he couldn't go back even if he wanted to. It wasn't easy to turn them down but his grandfather had taught him the words to use in

Cree that expressed both the honour and regret he felt.

When he got back to Calgary, the first Borg murder had already occurred though no one knew it was more than a random event. Singh's
offer had been waiting for him and he had spent most of the last few
weeks setting up the partnership or locked away in quick-cure cham-
bers recovering from the installation of his new mods.

The news of the murders had lurked on the edge of his consciousness like a dark beast but only now that he was back in the Borg
community, had they lurched into full view.

Wannamaker shook himself free of his memories. Angel was looking at him quizzically.

"What have you heard?" asked Wannamaker.

Angel glanced around before replying.

"I almost don't want to say, as if speaking it out loud might make it
true."

"If it's not safe to speak your mind here, where is it safe? We're all
Borg here."

"Are we?" she asked. "Not everyone agrees."

"No one questions your credentials." With the exception of her occasionally mobile hair, Angel had chosen to make her modifications
internal. Some Borg, like Gamow, argued if you were Borg you should
be proud to show it to the world. In fact you should shove it in the
world's face. But few had done more to advance Borg rights and to
promote Borg unity than Angel.

"I wouldn't be so sure," she said, "but I wasn't talking about me.
You know I've always tried to bridge the gap between Independista and
pan-humanist. Well, the gap has become a chasm."

Wannamaker had hoped that the death of two prominent
Independistas the year before might have calmed things down but Angel had told him that, instead, things had gotten worse, much worse. It
was as if the deaths had liberated the more radical members of the
group to ramp up the rhetoric and, some said, the violence. There had
always been tension between the Independistas and the Borg wannabes,
those who wanted to appropriate the hipness of Borg culture without
making the necessary personal 'commitment' to it. There had been an
increase in assaults on wannabes in the streets and bars of old
Inglewood and Angel was pretty sure the Independistas were behind
them.

"But what about the murders?

"I don't *want* to think so but really I don't know. You hear slogans, see them scrawled everywhere. 'Speak Borg or shut up,' and 'Borg purity is Borg destiny' or 'Live Borg or die human.' The Independistas call it standing up for the real Borg. I've heard others call it ethnic cleansing."

"And the people who were murdered?"

"Two had panhumanist leanings; the others were Independista sympathizers. None of them were activists. The deaths alternated like strike and counter-strike."

"It could be a coincidence," said Wannamaker.

"It could be. I...I don't think the police have made up their mind yet. From what I've heard." Wannamaker's spidey sense tingled at that. Angel knew something she wasn't telling him. But he knew better to push her on it. She'd tell him when the time was right.

"Besides it may not matter," said Angel. "I've heard some of the crazies on each side talk of the need to protect their people. And some have talked about retribution. And if that starts, there's no telling where it might end."

|||

Wannamaker extended his hearing to the limit. A Borg, recovering from minor surgery in the bed next to him, was snoring softly, the steady buzz of sedation.

Three beds down, behind a privacy screen, Cerise was mumbling in her sleep, something about being late for the dance. *Normal teenage dreams*, thought Buzz. He hoped she would recover, not only for the sake of what she knew but for her own sake. She had shown strength and resilience in the face of remarkable hardship as well as an innate cheerfulness and native intelligence.

Maybe I'm only reacting to her as damsel-in-distress but I think I like her. Buzz grinned and looked down at his clawed arm. *So does that make me a knight in shining armour?*

More distantly he could hear two people moving around, the night shift on duty. He should be able to avoid them. He had things to do and people to see that he didn't necessarily want to share with the whole Borg community—not yet, anyway.

He checked the heads-up display that overlaid the vision in his right eye. He had six of the heavy rubber slugs left as well as four rounds of birdshot. Not enough to win any wars but maybe enough to escape a battle if it came to that. He also had two doses of Stim and one dose of something even stronger in the med pack imbedded in his chest. The tech who had loaded the latter had called it Ultimate Rush and suggested he use it only if there was a good chance he was going to die anyway.

In his current condition, Buzz wasn't sure if he could even handle a double espresso.

His heart rate and blood pressure were running high but were operating 'within normal parameters' as they liked to say in all the sci-fi movies he had watched as a kid. His liver and kidneys were still a bit stressed but should be okay if he kept his electrolytes up. He made a mental note to ask Singh about those cutting-edge internal mods that would increase his ability to use Stim and other emergency chemical augments.

He put his servos on silent running and slipped out of the bed. Even he could barely hear the faint sigh and whirr of his modified legs. He looked down at his bare brown skin, at the faint tracery of scars around his knees and ankles, at the bulges where his human muscles connected to the underlying steel and plastic. Sometimes he wondered if he was still the same boy who played in the woods and fields that surrounded the cramped reserve where he had grown up, where he had gone hunting and fishing with his father and grandfather and listened to them talk in a language hardly anyone understood anymore. Was it possible to be many things and still one thing?

Time to think about that later. Now I better find my pants.

He pulled the small closet open, wincing as the hinges creaked. There was no answer of approaching footfalls. He retrieved his leather pants and shirt. He dropped the hospital gown on the floor of the closet and dressed quickly.

Wannamaker moved down the hall away from the clinic until he could no longer hear the sound of people moving around even with his ear on full gain. He planned to exit by a little used side entrance, where he might avoid the thickest layers of security. He wanted to keep his departure a secret, at least for a little while. There was little chance of reaching the garage undetected, let alone getting out with the agency's vehicle.

As soon as he felt he couldn't be heard, he tried to reach Steele's cell but had no luck. Singh wasn't answering his phone either but at least his messenger was running again. Wannamaker left a brief rundown of the day's events and told him where to pick up the car and Cerise Kavanah. He felt bad about leaving the girl behind but hopefully Singh would arrive before she woke up.

"And tell Frank Steele that we need to talk."

Wannamaker disconnected and headed toward the far side of the building. Before he reached the entrance he had another thought. He hadn't kept in touch with many of his old friends at the SDU but Lily Chin had sought him out a couple of days after he got back to town. They had coffee and she had given him her priority override number 'in case you ever need to hear a friendly voice.'

He hoped she hadn't already hit the sack and coded the number. She answered on the first ring.

"What can I do for you, Buzz?"

"This a good time?'

"Good as any," she said. "I'm pulling a little overtime down at HQ, trying to clear up some backlog. Frank's got me working on analyzing the sudden rise in assaults in the city."

"Not usual SDU fare. Things must be slow."

"We're looking for links to the Borg Butcher as they're starting to call it in the popular press."

"Have you heard from Frank tonight?" Wannamaker asked.

"He called in ten minutes ago about a body in Mount Royal. Not a lot of details. He only asked for a couple of constables but I'm going to head over there as soon as I'm done here to see if I can lend a hand."

Not normal procedure, thought Wannamaker. Sounds like I'm not the only one worried about Frank. "I may have something for you guys. Any chance you could pick me up?"

"Hold on." The line went dead for a few seconds. "Sure. Lepinsky can finish up here. Where are you?"

He gave her the address of an all night coffee shop a block from the safe house.

"I can be there in fifteen minutes," said Chin. "Ten if the traffic's decent."

"I'll be the tall good-looking guy sitting near the window, sipping a latte."

"Hey, I'd heard you'd had some more mods but those sound really rad."

Wanamaker laughed and disconnected. Five minutes later he had circumvented the side door security and was heading down the alley way to his rendezvous with Chin.

He wasn't halfway there when they hit him.

Chapter 14

Sanchez had eaten a leisurely supper at his favourite haunt on 17th Avenue. Wednesday was Cool Jazz Night at the Kaos Café and he had spent a relaxing hour over dessert and a glass of port, listening to a petite brunette woman sing the standards and considering the assignment the Chief had given him.

It had seemed clear enough at the time but as he drove back into town through the thick swirl of heavy snow it had become as blurred as the city lights beyond his windshield.

The Chief was concerned about what had happened with the water supply but not enough to overrule Frank's decision to put the Russian in charge of the investigation. He'd agreed with his own assessment about Dr. Pham and had told him 'to look into it' without giving clear direction as to how to proceed if his suspicions were correct.

Sanchez shook his head in frustration. There was something he wasn't seeing. It would come to him. The Chief knew what he wanted but he wasn't a free agent. He couldn't order Sanchez do something he couldn't later defend to his own superiors. But if Sanchez could make the connection on his own, the rewards might well be rich.

The Chief couldn't stay forever, no matter how often he passed the competency exams. Everyone knew his successor had to come from within. That was the way it worked. There were lots of Superintendents who wanted the job and several, like Frank Steele, who definitely didn't. But none were outstanding and none was a sure thing. Why not a bright young Inspector to replace the old warhorse? Sanchez knew he was dreaming in broadband but, hey, if you don't ask, you don't get.

It would come to him. Best to let it sit in the back of his brain until it did.

When the singer took her break, Sanchez shoved a fifty in her tip jar and headed for the exit. He nodded at Maurice, the bar's ancient owner. He looked sour but signalled to the waiter that the tab was on him.

Being a cop had its privileges and Sanchez took advantage of every one of them. *And why not*, he thought, *it's not like the public can afford to pay us a decent salary for keeping them safe*. Those who could afford it, the corporations and their shareholders, spent their money on private cops or high-tech security systems. Why protect the average Joe when you could get more bang for your buck by going private?

He'd probably be a corporation cop himself if circumstances had been different. It had even been his intention when he moved to Calgary at the tail end of the Troubles when everything had gone to shit back east. He had headed out to the land of opportunity with his credentials in hand looking to escape his former life.

But in the end he couldn't do it. Maybe it was the legacy of a father gunned down in the line of duty or maybe it just been the snotty-nosed attitude of the established corporate security companies. Whatever the reason, he'd signed on to the local force and fifteen years later, he was dreaming mad dreams of running the whole show. And if smaller fish like Maurice were willing to bribe him to do what he was sworn to do anyway, why should he insult them by saying no?

He shook his head. Every time you have a problem you're not ready to solve, it's the same old merry-go-round.

Introspection is for losers. I need some action.

| | |

By nine o'clock the Garry was usually hopping and tonight was no exception. Sanchez had stopped by his condo, only a few blocks from Kaos, to change into something more appropriate for a night on the town. He rifled through his wardrobe and settled on a black neosilk suit with metal threads embedded in the weave. In the shifting lights of the Garry the metal mesh would flicker and glow in counterpoint, letting him both blend in and stand out. The fact that they made the material impervious to knives and small arms fire was an added bonus.

Sanchez had found ways to make his work lucrative without ever *quite* violating his oath. It helped that his interpretation of its limits was more than liberal. But he had never done more than bend the law and he never had and never would put a fellow cop in danger. No matter how tempting it sometimes was.

Tomorrow he would tackle the problem of Vanessa Pham. Tonight he had another woman in mind.

Angel was waiting for him when he arrived and they slipped into her office for a quick glass of wine. She couldn't leave before eleven but he'd find things to keep himself entertained; the Garry held plenty of diversions for the Borg and non-Borg alike. For now, he was satisfied to watch her over the rim of his glass and contemplate the strange paths that life could take if you were only open to it.

It wasn't love but it was fun and they were both getting what they wanted. She pumped him for information and he pumped her for pleasure. He had never been attracted to a Borg before; he found all that metal and glass off-putting. But Angel was different. Smooth white flesh on the outside and underneath something unbelievable. The first time she had come to his bed had been a revelation and he knew that sex after Angel would never be the same. It wouldn't last, but while it did he planned to suck every drop of juice from the fruit.

Angel took a sip of the ruby coloured wine in her glass and said. "Gale Conklin is back in town."

Sanchez raised an eyebrow. "I thought he was dead."

"A popular misconception."

"I should let Steele know." So much for the sweet juice of love.

"That's what Buzz Wannamaker said."

"You've been seeing Wannamaker?"

"Jealous?"

"Hardly," said Sanchez. At least, he didn't *think* he was. He put his glass down on the arm of his chair.

"Buzz showed up at a Borg house this morning, juiced on Stim with an amnesiac black girl in tow. Claims he rescued her from Conklin."

"The shoot-out at The Pom this morning."

"No wonder you made Inspector so young. Nothing slips by you." Her soft smile took the sting out of her words.

"You think it's true?"

"Buzz has done a lot of things to me but he's never given me reason to doubt him." She was playing with him now. He liked it.

"The Pom is a known Clean Boy hang-out. Do you think Conklin's re-appearance has anything to do with the Borg murders?"

"I don't see how it could," she said. "Besides, the Clean Boys are your theory, not mine."

"What then?"

"You said it this morning. Borg are killing Borg."

Borg vocoders are designed to express what their owners wanted, not what they felt. Angel's voice didn't quaver when she said them but Sanchez knew her well enough to see the pain the words had caused.

He crossed to her and pulled her up into his arms. She let herself be held for a few minutes then pushed him away.

"I've got work to do," she said. "And so, I guess, do you."

"Right as usual Angelito. I better see if I can find Frank Steele."

Chapter 15

There were three of them, moving fast. Faster than Conklin's goons on Stim. Faster than anything Wannamaker had ever seen. He triggered the conversion from claw to shot gun and ramped up the range on his eye. The stereoscopic vision was off but at least he could see what was coming at him in the nearly dark alley. Almost. They were dressed in black with glints of metal at shoulder and hip. Their faces were hidden by molded plastic masks. The eyes behind them showed the flat sheen of glass lenses, either mods or the latest in vision enhancing goggles.

The first punch caught him at the base of his ribs just above his right kidney. Only the Kevlar sheath that protected his torso prevented the fight from ending then and there. Wannamaker dodged aside; a second glancing blow scraped across his chest, tearing his shirt and ripping the skin beneath. He brought up the shotgun and fired. His target danced aside like one of those improbable martial artists in Chinese vids.

The other two came in fast, one sweeping low to the ground in an effort to take out his knees, the other aiming a metal-clad fist at his face. Wannamaker jumped avoiding the leg sweep. The punch caught him square in the sternum, driving the air from his lungs. As he crumpled to his knees, he fired across his body, where logic dictated the puncher must be moving. He was briefly gratified to hear a grunt of pain. Then a boot caught him in the jaw. Teeth cracked and his mouth filed with blood. Another boot caught him in the chest. Darkness began to close in.

"Police! Freeze!" The cavalry, in the person of Lily Chin, had arrived. "I said, freeze, you motherfuckers."

Two shots. A yell of pain and anger. Then another. Then Chin's sudden cry.

Wannamaker pushed himself up to his feet, forced his eyes to focus. One of the attackers was rolling on the ground, clutching his thigh. Chin was down too, a dark figure leaning over her.

"Never mind her," said a deep growling voice. "Take out the primary target."

That would be me, thought Wannamaker. He staggered to his feet. The two remaining attackers were circling, moving fast. A car coming down the road caught one of them in his headlights. The car passed the alley without slowing but not before Wannamaker could clearly see that the man's left arm ended in both a human hand and a dangling Borg claw.

The wounded one on the ground had struggled to his feet. He advanced on Wannamaker, only slightly slower than before. Wannamaker figured two against one was better than two and a half and expended another shell. The man went down and didn't try to get up again. Wannamaker switched the magazine to birdshot. It had less stopping power but better spread. Any improvement in the odds was better than none.

"Leave them alone!" A woman's voice. Or rather a girl's. Wannamaker risked a quick glance over his shoulder.

Cerise Kavanah was standing at the far end of the alley, her tall slim body outlined in the faint glow of a streetlight.

If they went after the girl, he would use the drugs loaded in his chest to save her even if it meant his own life.

For a moment, it looked like it would come to that. Instead they swept up their wounded comrade and departed the field of combat at a dead run. Lily Chin barely rolled out of the way or they would have run right over her. She tried to get off another shot but it was too much for her. She slumped into unconsciousness.

Wannamaker's own vision was clouding. He needed to stay awake. Chin was hurt, maybe badly. Cerise was here but, in her condition, she might not know what to do. He let himself have a quarter dose of Stim.

He felt the chemical clarity take hold. It wasn't enough to overcome the pain in his jaw, chest and knees but it would have to do. Any more might shut down his systems entirely. He leaned against a dumpster. *The same dumpster they would have found me in if Cerise hadn't shown up.*

The girl walked slowly down the alley. She picked up a piece of wood and swung it in front of her.

"Buzz, are you there? Are you alright?"

He switched on the external speaker of his vocoder. Scary, perhaps, but better than trying to talk with a mouthful of blood.

"It's me," he said, his voice deep and metallic.

"It doesn't sound like you," Cerise said, uncertainly. She stopped moving toward him.

She could run at any minute, thought Wannamaker, *and I'm not sure I can chase her*. He tried triggering his cell but the damage to his jaw had knocked it off-line.

"You have to trust me, Cerise," he said. "There's a police officer at the other end of the alley. She's hurt, maybe badly. My phone isn't working. I need you to go down there and use hers."

"I don't know," Cerise said. "Those men might come back."

Wannamaker switched off the speaker. "Please," he said, making no effort to keep the pain from his voice.

Kavanah lowered the stick. "Should I call 9-1-1?"

"Too slow," said Buzz. He gave her the emergency, 'officer down' code and hoped they hadn't changed it. "The phone is linked to a universal GPS. They'll know right where to come. You just need to wait with her until they do."

Wannamaker slid down the side of the dumpster. He heard Cerise's footsteps go by but his vision was already going dark.

There was something he wanted to say.

Oh, yeah, don't forget to have them take me, too. He was never sure if he actually said it out loud.

Chapter 16

I had washed the glasses and put the cognac back in the liquor cabinet by the time the response team arrived. I sat in one of the big wingback chairs in front of the fire trying to round up enough energy to head home to bed.

I realized how tired I was when my cell rang. I'd forgotten to turn it off again after calling in the report.

It was Singh. Wannamaker had called in to Singh's messenger with a report. Singh had headed straight for the southeast address but by the time he arrived, Wannamaker was being loaded into an ambulance. The fact it was his partner hadn't made much difference to the cops on site but Singh did get the name of the hospital and the fact that a cop had also been wounded. He was on his way to Foothills Hospital and offered to pick me up on the way.

Before I could answer, another call came through on the priority channel. The wounded cop was Lily Chin.

Bed was going to have to wait.

| | |

Wannamaker and Chin were both listed in serious but stable condition. Lily had a badly broken left arm, extensive bruising and a mild concussion. She was under sedation and was scheduled to undergo surgery in the morning to repair the fractures. The doctor thought she might be off work for a week or two, depending on how well she responded to bone growth stimulants.

Wannamaker's injuries were, on the surface, less severe. He had three broken teeth that would have to be replaced with implants—no big deal for a Borg. He had a badly bruised sternum and severe contusions on his legs that would limit his mobility for a few days but the real concern was the stress put on his liver and kidneys from multiple doses of stimulants. They were keeping him under close observation in an isolation unit in case it had compromised his immune system.

No visitors allowed. At least until tomorrow.

I flashed my badge at the doctor but he wasn't buying it.

"But if you have to talk to someone," said the Doc, "there was a third patient in the ambulance. A girl named…" he checked his palm,

"…Cerise Kavanah."

Singh perked up at that.

"That's the girl Wannamaker was tracking," he said.

"She isn't physically hurt but she seems…disoriented. She needs some rest but I guess a few more minutes won't hurt."

March 16th was nearly over and I'd been awake for almost all of it. But I shrugged, bought some coffee from a vending machine and followed Singh to the fourth floor semi-private where the girl was bunked down for the night. The nurse at the station looked dubious but led us to the girl's room.

There was a cop on duty in front of the door and he didn't look too eager to let us by either, even after I showed him my badge. Not that I blamed him. Even the normally impeccable Singh was looking a little frayed; I probably looked like I'd been sleeping in an alleyway.

The girl was watching coverage of the Chinese Mars launch on the bedside terminal though she also had a palmtop displaying text and a picture of what looked like a tiger lying in her lap. She was dressed in a t-shirt and sweats that looked a size too big.

"These gentlemen are from the police," said the nurse, making it clear she didn't think gentlemen disturbed sixteen-year-old girls in the middle of the night. "If you need anything, anything at all, I'm right down the hall."

Cerise Kavanah pushed the terminal to one side though she didn't turn it off and set the palm on her bedside table. She gave us an uncertain smile, her eyes shifting from my face to Singh's before deciding I must be the one in charge. She turned to face me, sitting up straight with her legs folded underneath her.

"My name is Cerise Kavanah," she said, sticking out her hand. "Who are you?"

"I'm Frank," I said, surprised and strangely touched by the gesture. "Frank Steele. And this is Darwhal Singh. He's a private detective. Buzz Wannamaker the Borg you rode in with, is his partner."

"How is Buzz? They won't tell me anything."

"He had a bad beating but he's going to be okay. Did you see who did it?"

"It was pretty dark and they were all dressed in black," her brow furrowed. "There were three of them."

"Do you know why they were attacking Buzz?"

"I didn't see how it started. Maybe I should start from the beginning. If I tell you everything that happened, maybe it'll all make more sense."

This girl was full of surprises. I wondered if she was interested in a career in law enforcement.

"Go ahead," I said. Singh took out his palm and started making notes. One of these days my memory is going to go; until then, I prefer to listen first, record later.

Cerise explained that she didn't have many clear memories before today and those she did have were fragmentary and not very nice. She recounted the fight at the bar, how Buzz had rescued her. The description of 'the fat man with pointy teeth' left little doubt in my mind that Jim McConnaghey was right and that Gale Conklin was not only back from the dead but back to his old tricks as well. She told how they had arrived at the Borg 'hotel,' as she called it, and of the mixed reception they had received. I nodded when she mentioned Angel—I'd suspected she hadn't been telling me the whole truth this morning. Still, she seemed to be on the right side which was more than I could say for some of the other Borg Cerise described.

She described how she had woken up as Buzz was leaving and had decided to follow him. She returned to the garage, thinking he had gone to retrieve his car, but everything was locked up tight. She found a back entrance but it was sealed. She had been about to return to the clinic when the door had opened. That sounded odd and I made a mental note to check the security logs at the 'Borg hotel' in the morning.

Cerise heard the fight and came around the corner in time to see Chin go down at the far end of the alley.

"I yelled at them and they ran away," she concluded.

I'm sure there was more to it than that. Shots had been fired and forensics was on the scene right now to see what evidence might have been generated by that. Wannamaker and Chin could add details once they were well enough to talk. Until then, we could all use some sleep.

"We'll drop by again tomorrow," I said. "You should get some rest."

She looked too wired to sleep but I suspected it would hit her as soon as the adrenalin wore off.

"I'll contact the girl's family," said Singh. "I'm sure they'll want to know she's all right."

"No!" The word sounded like it had been torn from her throat. She was sitting rigid on the bed the blankets clutched in her clenched fists. The calm young woman had been replaced by a badly frightened child, her eyes wide and her dark skin turned grey.

I knew I should do something but the look of panic on her face froze me. Singh crossed the room and sat on the end of her bed and took her hands in his.

"It's alright," he said. "Everything's fine."

Cerise let out a low sob but seemed to relax.

"No it's not," she said. "I know I should want to see my family. My parents and…my brothers?"

Singh nodded. "Yes, your father, mother and two brothers. They all have been looking for you."

"No, I can't!" she said, her voice high to the point of breaking. Her eyes glistened with unshed tears and her mouth dragged down into the deepest frown I had ever seen. It hurt to look at it. I could almost see her trying to grasp at the fleeting memory. "I don't know. There's someone—. It's not safe there."

Singh looked doubtful but patted the girl's hand and nodded.

"Calling your parents can wait," he said, "until we know more about what happened to you."

I gave Singh a 'we need to talk' look. Something was niggling the back of my brain. I knew it would eventually emerge though probably not until I got some sleep.

The prospect of that seemed more and more remote. I had to report Conklin's return to Vice, or better yet, straight to Chief Arsenault. He deserved a midnight call for trying to convince me Conklin had been killed in North California. I didn't know what, if anything, Conklin had to do with our current caseload but his presence back in the city couldn't bode well for anyone.

Every detective had to have his Moriarty and Conklin was mine.

"Get some sleep," I said. "There'll be someone outside your door all night."

⏐⏐⏐

Not surprisingly, Arsenault wasn't available so I shunted the report to Vice.

I itched to go after Conklin myself but that's not how it works in the SDU. Until I could link him directly to one of our active files or until Arsenault specifically directed me to pursue it, my hands were tied. Besides with Chin out of commission for two weeks, I was short-handed; I couldn't spare resources for a wild sleazeball chase.

I was still sitting at my desk when Sanchez called to report the stunning news that Gale Conklin was back in town. He seemed a little miffed that I had already heard, so I told him details were still sketchy and anything he could add in the morning would be greatly appreciated.

The clock on the wall was crawling toward two when I finally gave up on the idea of going home. Maybe I was afraid Nancy and Dorothy would still be there trading war stories about life with Frank. Maybe I was afraid Jack would be waiting and calling my name. Maybe I was just afraid.

I lay down on the couch and closed my eyes. Josh's face loomed up out of the dark, not the face I had seen in the dumpster, not the damaged Borg face but the face I had seen at my promotion where that picture by his bed had been taken. Proud, angry, stricken. The face of a stranger.

| | |

The sound of the maintenance crew moving through the building woke me sometime after six. *Funny*, I thought, *for all our technical advances, we still need people to clean our toilets.*

Which reminded me. All that coffee was still sitting in my bladder.

The flat screen over the urinal was still covering the Mars mission. The Europeans had announced they were launching in three hours, two days early. The Chinese had beaten them to the moon; they were determined not to lose again. They didn't seem to think the American mission already a day toward Mars was competition.

Personally I thought we had enough problems on Earth without starting in on another planet.

Two nights without sleep were starting to take their toll. I wasn't a young cop anymore; this morning I couldn't remember ever having *been* a young cop. But duty called and when it did I almost always listened.

A shower and a shave later I felt a little better even if I still looked pretty much like what the cat refused to drag in. I'd rummaged through my locker to find some replacement clothes. They didn't exactly match but they hadn't been slept in. Not recently at least.

I've always believed breakfast was the most important meal of the day so I grabbed a coffee and Danish in the commissary and headed back to my desk.

Sanchez was waiting when I arrived. He'd been up all night checking into the Conklin rumours in every low-life dump in the city but he still looked better than I did. I'm really starting to hate people under forty. Though I had to admit I was starting to feel a grudging respect for his tenacity.

"Everyone says he's back," said Sanchez, "but nobody has actually seen him. No one who will talk to me in any case. A lot of speculation about what he might be up to but nothing concrete. The details are in my report."

"Yeah, it's hard to imagine a man that big could cast such a small shadow."

"There are a few trees I could shake," said Sanchez. "But I'll need back-up."

Every instinct told me to give him the green light, Arsenault be damned. I'd followed my instincts my whole career. But look where that had got me. Head of the Special Detection Unit—the only division that made Internal Affairs look good in the eyes of my fellow cops. "I'll pass on your report to Vice after I've read it. Keep your eyes and ears open but don't let it get in the way of your primary caseload."

Sanchez raised an eyebrow, then shrugged and headed back to his own office. I called the hospital. Wannamaker was out of isolation and awake so I called Singh and asked him to meet me there. It was time to get some answers straight from the Borg's mouth.

| | |

Buzz was more than awake; he was ready and raring to go. Unfortunately, the medical profession didn't agree. They insisted on keeping him for another forty-eight hours. Judging from the bruises I could see, I figured they were right though I doubted they could enforce their will if Buzz truly objected.

I had to give Wannamaker credit that the first words out of his mouth when Singh and I showed up were about the girl. He had been a good cop and it looked like his ethics were still intact now he was working the private side. He and Singh still seemed like an odd couple to me but stranger partnerships had worked in the past. Wannamaker only calmed down when we assured him the girl was safe and well. I promised him I'd have her come down and see him later.

"I don't know, Frank," said Wannamaker. "I'm worried about her. Something about that case doesn't add up."

"That's why I'm transferring her to a police safe house as soon as the docs say she's well enough to move."

Singh didn't look too surprised so I guess he'd reached the same conclusion.

"Get her a brain scan before she's released," said Wannamaker. "There's a chance someone put a Bug in her head."

"Fuck me," I said. That seemed to about cover it. I sent Singh to make the arrangements with a promise to keep him in the loop. He looked doubtful so I handed him my badge and told him to use it discreetly. The girl was technically old enough to consent to the tests—but barely. The badge might smooth the way if an overeager bureaucrat insisted on contacting her parents. For some reason I couldn't yet define I wanted to follow the girl's wishes on that.

Wannamaker confirmed that our good friend was indeed alive and kicking and back in Calgary. It didn't break my heart when he told how he took the girl right out of Conklin's grasp. I especially liked the part where he broke the fat bastard's wrist. I was sure it would all be fixed up pretty by now—private clinics catering to the evil rich had access to regenerative techniques that good cops like Lily Chin would never get in a public hospital—but it must have hurt like hell at the time.

That's right, Frank, keep thinking the positive thoughts.

"Any chance he's involved with the Borg killings?" I asked.

"Anything's possible, though I can't see the connection. The Pom is considered neutral ground but it's hardly a Borg hangout. Besides…" Buzz paused and looked away. I could see he was troubled by what he had to say, unsure whether he should say it to a cop at all, even his former boss.

"You think it might be Borg-on-Borg violence? Some internal settling of scores?"

Buzz nodded slowly.

"There's been growing rifts in the Borg community, not only in Calgary but right around the world," he said. "There are millions of us now, Frank, I suppose this was bound to happen."

"Yeah, it's not like you're part of a hive mind."

"No," said Buzz, "but that doesn't make us immune to group think. Do you know what makes us Borg, Frank?"

"I thought it was pretty obvious."

"Not really," said Buzz. "It's not the mods—or at least not the mods alone. Lots of people have artificial limbs, vocoders, artificial eyes or ears. To replace originals that failed. And plenty of people—the wannabes—have all the external decorations down pat though most of them don't have a clue how a true Borg even moves let alone how he thinks or acts. True Borg replace healthy body parts with mods because it makes them better, different."

"The NUP says it's an unhealthy lifestyle choice."

"The NUP says that about a lot of things. But Leviticus is remarkably silent about mods. We have our own language—one only Borg can truly learn. Language defines culture and Borg culture is all about the language only we can speak. Normals don't have the right equipment."

"So it's evolution?" I said.

"Maybe," said Buzz, "I call it a biomechanical imperative. We are Borg because something inside us makes us Borg. Some claim we are a new race of humans; others, a new species altogether."

"And what do you say? What does it have to do with these murders? The rift may be global but these killings are local. What's causing it?"

Buzz shook his head. "I don't have the answers to any of those questions, Frank, not even the first one. But civil wars have to start somewhere."

"So, you're sure your attackers were Borg."

"Would I swear to it in a court of law? No, I guess not. They weren't human. Who else could they be but Borg?"

Who else indeed?

III

By the time I left Wannamaker to get some rest, Singh had Cerise in the imaging lab undergoing a full body scan. There were supposed to be waiting lists for that type of thing but Singh had found a way around them. I put it down to his charm and winning smile, preferring not to think that doctors, like too many other underpaid public servants these days, were susceptible to bribes.

I joined Singh in the waiting room and we sat for a few minutes in companionable silence before Singh had to ruin it all by talking.

"She's quite a woman, isn't she?"

I was momentarily confused. Sleep deprivation will do that to you. "Who? Cerise?"

"She is an impressive girl but I was talking about…you know." He glanced around as if afraid that merely thinking about Natasha Redding would somehow reveal her secrets.

"Oh, yeah." I'd somehow edited last night's adventure into its most salient features—a dismembered Borg on a private estate—which didn't include one of the most important women in the world. People like that didn't concern people like me. It's not that I have an overdeveloped sense of deference. There are lots of people who have power or who exercise it for others but only a few are a power unto themselves. Lady Redding was one of those, a force of nature—like a summer storm or gravity—impartial in their effects on ordinary folk.

If anyone knew if the Borg were on the brink of civil war, she did. I tried replaying our conversation in my head. She claimed the attackers didn't move like Borg but, like Wannamaker, couldn't offer any alternatives. There used to be an old joke that if you put two Trotskyites in a room, you got three political parties. Radicals hate their enemies but they save their real vitriol for those they consider heretics and traitors to the cause. Love would be no excuse if his comrades thought Dick's affair with Lady Natasha crossed that line.

"Can you really contact her?"

He shrugged. "I have a number. If I call, she will call back. Eventually."

"How did you get to know her?"

Singh glanced around the waiting room again. He leaned forward and spoke so softly that I had to lean forward, too.

"Several years ago, she was part of an attempted hostile takeover of National Asian Bank. Very hostile. Some would say illegal even under our fairly forgiving current laws. I took measures. When she discovered what some of her partners were doing, she withdrew her support and the bid failed. After National Asian decided my services were no longer necessary, she offered me a job. But I wasn't prepared to leave Calgary. I have unfinished business here."

If Singh had something more to say, I'd have to wait to hear it. A middle-aged redheaded man in a white coat had emerged from the lab and was calling Singh's name. The expression on his face was more quizzical than concerned. I wasn't sure if that was a good sign.

"Ms. Kavanah's tests are inconclusive," the doctor said.

Foothills Hospital was supposed to have some of the most advanced scanning technology in Western Canada, even better than that found in some of the high-priced private clinics. They routinely found cancers that were little more than a collection of a few dozen cells. It seemed doubtful they would miss the traces left by a 'Bug.' Singh obviously agreed. He slung his arm around the doctor's thin neck and pulled him close.

"Listen, Doctor Angus. I paid good money, a lot of good money, to move to the front of the line. Do I need to apply for a refund?"

Singh's voice was so silky smooth; it took the doctor a few moments to realize he was being threatened. His already pale skin turned whiter, his freckles standing out like brown islets in a sea of milk.

"No." Angus tried to slide out of Singh's grasp but the arm around his neck only tightened. "We found something. I'm just not sure what it is."

Singh glanced at me and I stepped between the doctor and the door back into the lab. Singh loosened his hold.

"Go on," he said.

"We did full toxicology as well as a body scan," Angus said. "Never let it be said public health care isn't a bargain." He laughed nervously.

Singh narrowed his eyes and looked grim. I cracked a smile but only because the doctor couldn't see my face.

"Yes, well, the girl has taken a lot of drugs in the last few weeks," Angus said.

"Or been fed them," I interjected.

"I suppose," said Angus, "they certainly aren't the usual spectrum of recreational drugs. More like some kind of atypical anti-psychotic medication."

"Jesus," I said. "They gave her Thorazine?"

Like most people, even in our so-called enlightened society, my images of anti-psychotic treatments went back to old movies filled with shambling frozen-faced zombies locked away in psych wards.

"Nothing so primitive," said Angus. "This is much more specific, targeted. I think it may help explain her memory loss. As well as her delusions."

I exchanged glances with Singh. This didn't sound like the girl we had talked to last night.

"What delusions?"

"The usual, I suppose. A sense of being at the centre of some great conspiracy. Paranoia. A sense of estrangement from others. She was reluctant to enter the scan unit."

"Reluctant?"

"We had to sedate her. She was becoming quite hysterical."

Maybe it was the lack of sleep. Maybe it was something else. I grabbed Angus by the shoulder and spun him around.

"Where the fuck did you get your medical degree? From a box of corn flakes? That girl has been through hell the last few weeks and you think sedation is the right approach. No wonder they sent you down here to play with the machines. You're not fit to be around people."

We were starting to attract attention. I didn't mind the stares but several people were on their cells, calling the cops or, at least, hospital security.

"Sorry," I said. "Maybe you should tell us what you found without the editorial comments."

He probably figured discretion was the better part of valour. Hospital security would want their cut of whatever Singh had paid him.

"Advanced anti-psychotics, and these were very advanced—don't have the same range of side-effects as their predecessors. No involuntary repetitive movements, no muscular paralysis. They're designed to work their way out of the system in a few weeks, avoiding damage to the heart that so many second-generation drugs caused. I might not have spotted it at all but her insulin levels were off. Blacks are susceptible to induced diabetes from that class of drugs. I used the word 'delusion' earlier. It's more like when you have a particularly vivid dream and a few days later you aren't sure whether it was a dream or a real event.

"In any case, I don't think the drugs tell the whole story. The scan showed a contusion on the brain. It was small; at first, I suspected blunt trauma. But there was no trace of bruising under the skull. The contusion seemed to come from inside the brain. And when I looked deeper, the edges of the contusion became sharper, almost rectangular."

"Like a Bug," I said.

"Maybe. Except there was none of the neural disruption you normally see with those kind of devices. Usually there are patterns of ruptured neurons spreading far beyond the implantation. This seems benign by comparison." Dr. Angus looked furtive and I wondered exactly what kind of experience he had with Bugs. He went on. "I think the drugs were to…soften her up. They reduce the sense of awe, limit the ability to think reflectively, make you more susceptible to suggestion. Whatever device might have been there could then be used to selectively remove memories. Or add new ones. Except for one thing."

"And what would that be?"

"As far as I know, that technology is still five years in the future—as it has been for the last two decades."

Despite his concerns about her mental state, Angus saw no reason for Cerise to continue to occupy a scarce hospital bed and he released her into our care. If she was no longer his problem than neither were we. He did leave us with a ray of hope. Cerise's memory about the rest of her life might eventually re-emerge, though her recollection of the last few weeks, if it returned at all, would always be suspect.

We dropped her at one of the safe-houses the Force has scattered around Calgary. I picked one on the edge of the Tsuu T'ina reserve in the city's southwest. It was a long way from the trouble in the Borg part of town and even farther from where her family lived. If anyone caught a glimpse of her, she might stand out as the only black girl in the mixed white and Aboriginal neighborhood but no one was likely to be looking too closely.

Or so I thought at the time.

Chapter 17

Sanchez walked slowly back to his own office. He'd wanted Steele to authorize him to go after Conklin. Failing to make anything stick to him had been his one regret from his years in Vice. If he caught Conklin now it would be a major boost to his creds, nabbing the one the legendary Superintendent had let slip away. And if he didn't, it would still have given him something to hold over Steele for acting without the Chief's authorization.

One door closes and another opens.

Dr. Vanessa Pham had transferred from the main forensics unit to run the SDU lab. Some said it was a punishment; others that she had requested the job. Either way, it marked her as a loser in Sanchez's eyes. His transfer at least offered a chance at future promotions.

Arsenault was concerned about Pham, though not for the same reasons as Sanchez. That alone was reason to doubt she had been dumped in the SDU to rot.

He thought of what Yankovy had said in yesterday's staff meeting. When faced with a mystery, ask who benefits? So who benefited from having Dr. Vanessa Pham heading up the SDU's scientific arm? It wasn't her, so who was it? Or maybe she benefited in ways that had nothing to do with the usual incentives of career advancement.

The world was full of hidden and sometimes not so hidden agendas. He knew Pham was sympathetic to the causes espoused by the NUP, though as Chief Arsenault pointed out, maybe she was just ahead of the curve. But even if she was providing her political friends with insider dope on the actions of the Special Detection Unit, it hardly mattered. Unless of course they were somehow involved in the crimes the SDU were currently investigating.

That might be worth following up, Sanchez thought. *Our current lines of pursuit aren't yielding much. Maybe thinking outside the box— way outside in this case—might lead to something, a new perspective if nothing else.*

The question was—how to pursue that line of investigation? James Becker, head of the NUP claimed to be a firm supporter of law and order but Sanchez suspected he wouldn't welcome an interview with a Calgary cop asking whether his party was connected to a series of Borg murders. Sanchez doubted there was a direct connection anyway—that would be too convenient. Besides, the Borg killings were only the lead case the SDU was following. What about the attacks on the Calgary water supply?

That didn't seem likely either. The NUP was big on the environment—in a weird quasi-religious way. 'Restore the land and restore the people' had been one of their slogans in the last campaign. Suitably vague to win votes from the rural right and the urban environmentalists. But Sanchez could remember when people claimed the initials of the New Unity Party stood for 'Nature-Unity-Purity' with a frightening emphasis on the purity part.

Sanchez hated this kind of work. Sometimes, he wondered why Arsenault had pegged him for the job. He was hardly the Internal Affairs kind of guy. Hell, he was more likely to be investigated *by* Internal Affairs.

The simplest thing might be to just go to Pham and ask her what her game was. Yeah, that would work.

And why not? Not directly of course. But Pham wrote endlessly detailed reports, knowing full well that most cops, himself included, wouldn't read past the executive summary and data highlights. Frank Steele never would and even Lily Chin had her limits.

That reminds me, he thought, *I better send her a card and some flowers—it never hurts to be considered a caring colleague.* He flipped open his palm top and logged the request into his personal shopper application; it would research Chin's tastes and send exactly the right message and gift to generate the maximum in warm and fuzzies.

But not wanting to wade through technical garble wasn't the same as not being able to. He keyed open Pham's latest report to see if the good doctor's motives could be uncovered in the quagmire of her turgid prose.

|||

Four hours and three cups of tea later, Sanchez leaned back in his chair. It was all there, hidden in the mind-numbing charts and obscure hyperlinked footnotes. She had been careful. The data was valid and complete, if you knew where and how to look. Fortunately he did. *Nice to know that graduate methods course last fall was actually worth all the pain*, he thought.

Even her conclusions were carefully worded to suggest they were, in her considered opinion, the most likely explanation of the evidence rather than absolute certainties. Alternative theories were either poorly articulated or relegated to complex discussions of scientific process in lengthy appendices.

But what it came down to, in Sanchez's view, was a deliberate attempt to throw the SDU off the trail of the real culprits and onto radical elements within the Borg community.

Take for example, her theory that the nano-particles found in the murdered Borgs' blood were a subtle poison designed to slow and weaken them. The flip side of that was it didn't require their killers to be anyone special. A weakened Borg, taken alone, might well be vulnerable to a well-armed and well-prepared gang of normals. He or she would certainly have no chance against a Borg who hadn't been slowed by poison.

Pham claimed the nano-particles acted to block signals flowing from their nervous system into their mechanical limbs. She backed that up with a detailed Appendix that described several possible mechanisms for the blocking action. She had even run a few experiments on a Borg who had died of natural causes—if being hit by a bus could be deemed natural. As she put it, not definitive but indicative.

It was only in footnotes that she raised doubts about her own theory. The nano-particles were concentrated around the area where the modifications had been removed rather than spread throughout the body. Moreover, while they appeared in every Borg, they didn't appear to the same degree, nor did they appear anywhere except in the extremities. There were no particles, for example, near where an artificial eye or ear had been removed.

When he followed a link to an external source article about the use of nano-technology in the implantation of augments, doubts about Pham's interpretation became certainties. The article described research nearly a decade old. It took that long for proprietary medical information to seep into the journals. Still, it described how nano-devices were used to integrate nerve fibers into augments—technology way beyond the simple neural interfaces that allowed amputees to use artificial limbs by taking advantage of the 'phantom limb' phenomenon. The devices were designed to do exactly what Pham described—block the rate of neural transmission—but only in the initial stages of integration until the neural nets were fully established.

The article was less informative about what it called 'breakthrough' applications of nano-machines in augment technology, all of which enhanced the performance capabilities. Of particular interest were new ultra-smooth particles that would improve the operation of joint mecha-nisms. The details of the actual process were sparse but it was clear to Sanchez that these were what Pham had found. Particles designed to improve flexibility and strength in mechanical joints had been released when those joints were shattered during the attacks.

The conclusion Pham should have drawn was not that the Borg vic-tims were weaker but the assailants were as strong or stronger.

But who would be stronger than a Borg but another Borg or a group of them? It's not impossible that a sufficiently large gang of unmodified humans, sufficiently well armed might have gotten lucky with an un-wary Borg. It might have even happened twice but once word got around that Borg were being killed in such a spectacular way…it seemed unlikely.

Anyway he cut it Pham's report seemed to implicate Borg for these murders. If the Borg were weakened by the particles, they were killed by other Borg or by gangs of their unmodified enemies, of which there were many possibilities. But if they weren't weakened, they had to be killed by their fellow Borg.

Unless you thought outside the box.

Witnesses to the attacks on Borg wannabes, claimed the attackers were either Borg or Clean Boy gangs hyped on Stim. If the latter, given the frequency of attacks, there should have been an up-tick in reports of Stim overdose. A quick check of medical databases showed no such thing.

If not Stim, what else would give unmodified humans—if that's what they are—the power to take on a Borg? Were the Clean Boys secretly going against their own stated beliefs and getting internal modifications? Or was there something new in town that gave them all the benefits of Stim and none of the drawbacks?

Conklin.

Sanchez had wondered why Gale Conklin would return to Calgary. By all accounts he had an iron-tight alibi that exonerated him from all past and future crimes. Being dead was the best alibi of all and with his enemies on both sides of the law ready to accept his demise, Conklin would have a free hand to recreate his criminal empire somewhere else or, for that matter, retire and enjoy his ill-gotten but certainly well-laun-dered gains at leisure.

It must have taken a major incentive—money or power or both—to tempt him into blowing his cover by returning to the one place he was practically a public figure.

Mix money and the quasi-independent principality of North California and you got only one thing: the bio-engineering labs of Sonoma Valley. Almost every innovation—good or bad—in the area of medical and biological science these days came out of a sixty kilometre stretch of former wine country.

A lot of people's lives had been improved as a result of the centre of innovation and excellence that had been created when North California more or less seceded from the Union during the height of the Troubles. Washington made a lot of noise about sending in the troops at the time but found itself with other fish to fry when things really fell apart. Once the inventions started flowing, the talk turned from bringing NoCal home to building partnerships and free trade arrangements. It suited puritan America's interests to have an enclave permitted to do research forbidden mainstream Americans. Not surprisingly, scientists and entrepreneurs of all stripes had flocked to the valley to set up shop.

Was Conklin peddling a new version of Stim? But if so, why was he being so subtle about it? It was hardly his style and it probably didn't need his presence. There had to be something else at stake.

"Well, I'm not going to get any answers sitting behind this desk," said Sanchez to no one in particular, as he shut down the program and shoved his palm into his jacket pocket.

Sanchez hesitated, debating whether to call Steele with his suspicions about Gale Conklin and the possible link to the Borg murders. It was exactly the kind of connection that would let the Superintendent go after the fat bastard. Facts not theories. That's what Steele had snarled at Vanessa Pham at the staff meeting yesterday. And so far that was all he had, a theory. And one with a lot of holes.

Was Pham working for Conklin, misdirecting the SDU's investigations away from the possibility of a new 'superman' drug—for want of a better term? Or was the misdirection a result of another agenda, the desire of the New Unity Party to blame society's problems on degenerate secular rationality, made flesh in the bodies of the Borg?

Either way, she had some explaining to do.

Right, thought Sanchez. *A few questions for the good doctor and then I hit the streets.*

The SDU had its own lab on the fifth floor but Vanessa Pham wasn't there. Sanchez headed for the elevators that would take him to the basement to the main forensics lab, where according to her pager he would find the scientist. He flipped open his palm and keyed in the override codes the Chief had provided that gave him access to the personal records of everyone in the Department below the rank of Superintendent. It wouldn't hurt to see whom he was up against.

Sanchez knew vaguely Pham had been a cop before taking a leave of absence to return to medical school. He understood why he didn't have more than that vague impression when he discovered she had spent most of her career in Winnipeg, where the Troubles had run deeper and lasted longer than in the rest of Canada. He wasn't sure what he had expected to find, but it wasn't six citations for bravery and a Cross of Valour given for 'acts of the most conspicuous courage in circumstances of extreme peril,' the highest civilian honour awarded by the Governor General of Canada. He copied the citation into his personal log for later reading. She only started with the Calgary force after she finished her medical degree, working as assistant director of forensics before taking the SDU job.

Pham hardly seemed the type to work for a scumbag like Conklin but the devil was in the details. He's seen good cops go bad—he'd come close to the line a few times himself; some would say he crossed it. Still, she might be the idealistic type—driven to wrong things by the certainty they were doing right.

Or maybe she was just lousy at her job.

Apparently the old saying was true; there was never a cop around when you needed one. Vanessa Pham wasn't in the lab, though her pager was, perched on a shelf above her desk. In theory, the Force required their officers to keep the locater with them at all times but the rule was observed more in the breach. The Chief had even floated a proposal to make implantation mandatory—as a safety measure, of course. No cop without back-up, was the way he put it. The union had seen it differently—as no cop without surveillance. They didn't win a lot of battles these days but so far they had won that one.

Sanchez understood completely. Some meetings needed to be kept off the record for everybody's benefit. That wasn't easy to do if someone could check your whereabouts whenever they wanted.

That didn't stop him from being annoyed. He needed to know what side of the street Pham was playing on before he took the risk of walking down it.

Sanchez was staring at the pager, contemplating his next move when a soft voice broke his reverie.

"Vanessa hasn't come back from lunch yet."

Sanchez turned to find Antoine King, the Chief's man, at his shoulder.

"It's after two o'clock," said Sanchez.

"Is it?" said King. "I hadn't noticed. Time flies whether you're having fun or not."

"Does Dr. Pham always take a late lunch?"

"This one is not so much late as long. But no, she usually brings her lunch and eats at her desk."

The faint chemical smells of the lab had already put Sanchez off the idea of grabbing a bite in the cafeteria himself. "She must be very dedicated."

King shrugged. "Everybody's dedicated to something."

King seemed to want to say something more.

"I haven't had lunch myself," said Sanchez. "Care to join me? I know a nice Cajun place on Steven Avenue Mall."

"I know the place myself." King removed his pager from his belt and dropped it in the drawer of a neighboring desk. King glanced at the open drawer and Sanchez added his to the pile.

| | |

The two men made small talk through their entrees—Jambalaya for Sanchez and blackened snapper for King—rating the chances of the Flames to make the hockey playoffs and discussing the growing unpredictability of Calgary's weather. Yesterday's snow had been replaced with temperatures stretching toward twenty Celsius with no certainty of what tomorrow might bring, other than change.

Over coffee and generous servings of pecan pie topped with dollops of real whipped cream, the conversation turned to Vanessa Pham.

King barely tasted the rich confection before pushing his plate to one side. He sat for a minute as if assessing the situation. Sanchez returned his steady gaze. King had one of those faces that made it hard to guess his age—fifty-eight according to the file Sanchez had checked while King was in the bathroom—sienna skin stretched over high cheekbones and a broad forehead. Lines were lightly etched around his mouth and eyes that suggested the man liked to laugh but Sanchez had seen little evidence during lunch. His close-cropped hair was still mostly black.

"She doesn't talk about it but I gather her time in Winnipeg was pretty God-awful," said King.

No doubt, thought Sanchez. You don't get too many opportunities to win awards for bravery when things are going well. The Government had maintained martial law in Winnipeg for six years and information, even in the age of spy satellites and personal broadcast stations, had

been sketchy at best. When it was over, the population had been literally decimated with ten percent of its citizens dead and another ten
"missing"—fled, dead or Disappeared.

"Her record was impressive," said Sanchez, "A half a dozen bravery awards before she turned thirty."

King nodded. "She's pretty unflappable. Some of the things we get
in the lab these days would shake a stronger man than me. It's why I
don't work overtime anymore. You can only take so much horror. But
it's like water off a duck's back to her. It's why she transferred to the
SDU, for the challenge."

"I'd wondered about that," said Sanchez.

"That and the fact that Rodriguez signed up for another ten years.
No room for advancement in the main lab but the SDU might open
things up with the Horsemen or with that new provincial police force
James Becker promises to create when the NUP wins the next election."

"If they win."

"Sure," said King, smiling.

"Is she any good as a pathologist?"

"She's cautious and she has her blind spots but, yeah, she's as good
as they come. Not instinctive, the way her predecessor Cat Podnarski
was, but more thorough, more professional."

Probably why Frank Steele didn't like her much, thought Sanchez.
For all his derision of theories, the man ran on instinct and guesswork.

"You've read her reports on the Borg killings."

"I did half of the background research," said King. "Though she's
pretty jealous about final authorship. The conclusions are hers not
mine."

"I take it you don't agree."

"Are we still having lunch or is this getting official?"

"I haven't finished my pie yet," said Sanchez, smiling. He wondered
what game King was playing. He might be the Chief's back-up but that
didn't mean he didn't have his own agenda.

King interlaced his fingers as if he were about to pray and stared up
at the tin-tiled roof. "There is nothing inaccurate about what's in those
reports. It's what's not in them that's the problem. There are hints and
clues, bits and pieces, that taken one at a time don't amount to much—
but taken together, may amount to a hell of a lot."

"Like what?"

"That whole thing about those nano-particles being an inhibitor on the Borg metabolism to start with."

"The public record…"

"…supports it as well as it supports any other theory. We both know that when it comes to leading edge technology, the public record is useless. Pham knows it too. She even knows local people who could, privately, give her more recent information. She chooses not to talk to them."

"Why?"

"Like I said she has her blind spots," said King. "You ever hear the expression 'the real McCoy?'"

"Sure."

"Some people say it comes from Elijah McCoy, a black Canadian inventor from the nineteenth century. He invented a railway lubricant that lots of people tried to copy—so his was referred to as the 'real McCoy.' The real point though is the fact that most people at the time wouldn't give credence to his brilliance for one simple fact—he was a black man. The world isn't perfect but at least most of it has moved past that foolishness."

"Are you saying Pham is a racist?"

"I don't know if that's the right word for it. She's never been anything but completely fair with me. Or to any, well, *normal* human for want of a better word. But for some reason, she doesn't like Borg and pretty much anyone she could talk with to find out the real McCoy on those nano-particles just happen to be Borg."

"A lot of people don't like Borg."

"True. But not everyone hates them. I've watched her face during autopsies. People shouldn't enjoy their work that much."

Sanchez put the last piece of pie in his mouth, savoring the rich caramel and the mealy crunch of the roasted pecans. Pham's hatred of the Borg was a revelation but he wasn't sure what it changed. He knew she supported the NUP, hating the Borg probably came easy especially if she had some personal reason for it. He wondered what had really happened all those years ago in Winnipeg.

King glanced at the chronometer tattooed to his wrist.

"Looks like lunch is over. I have to get back. I'm only a working stiff, as we like to say in the morgue."

"I still have questions," said Sanchez.

"And I have answers. Tonight is my darts night. Drop over to the Naked Onion. Buy me a beer and we can talk some more. I think I've got some useful stuff for you."

"Which you'll trade me for a beer?" Sanchez grinned. He figured King was looking for a lot more than a couple of pilsner. Now it's a matter of negotiation. "And how much cash should I bring to cover the round?"

"Fuck you, Inspector," said King. "I'm not in this for money or for career advancement. I could do a hell of a lot better in a private lab. You can still come over tonight and I'll still talk to you because that's the job I promised to do. But I'll buy my own fucking beer."

Christ, thought Sanchez, *all this moral indignation is getting up my ass.* "Sorry," he said, 'no offence intended."

King stood up and threw a couple of bills on the table. "That should cover my lunch." He turned to go, then turned back. "There's one other thing that hasn't shown up in any of the reports—not the ones anyone reads at least. Everyone knows about the dead Borg but there are a bunch of other bodies that have turned up in places they shouldn't be. Disappeared. More than a dozen of them. And no real good explanation as to why they died. You might want to look into that. If you got the stomach for it."

Sanchez sipped the last of his coffee and watched as King, back ramrod straight despite his nearly sixty years, strode out of the restaurant. He'd wanted King to make things clearer. If anything, it had all gotten murkier.

|||

Sanchez stopped at the lab on his way back to his office but Pham still hadn't returned. King was nowhere in sight either so Sanchez retrieved his pager and headed back upstairs. He wasn't sure where he would find the reports that 'nobody reads,' but he found King's assertion disturbing if only because it jibed with his own conception of how society, including his police colleagues, ignored the plight of those who most needed their attention.

There had always been those too poor, too isolated, too marginal to make an impact. Prostitutes, drug addicts, runaways from dysfunctional homes whose deaths, often at the hands of others, were deemed somehow their own fault. If they were black or Aboriginal, too, they became almost invisible. Sometimes the outrage or the guilt in mainstream society became enough to galvanize change but all too often, when the story fell out of the media spotlight, things slipped back to the way they'd always been.

The National Data Bank was supposed to fix those problems, give everyone, no matter what their status in life, something to hold on to, something to affirm that they, too, existed and mattered. For some it only became one more road to oblivion.

Those who failed to register or who were somehow removed—identity theft at its most complete—became invisible in the eyes of the state. The Disappeared didn't exist as far as the government was concerned but like most cops, he'd seen too many pretty but vacant eyed youths in the sex shops. The Disappeared supplied their bodies and sometimes their body parts to men like Conklin who sold sex and replacement organs to the highest bidders. And somehow the cops and courts found ways, profitable ways, to let them get away with it.

That, Sanchez told himself, is my own line, the one I'll never cross. Everybody needs to make a living, everybody wants to get ahead. He'd taken incentives to be a better cop but never to be a bad one. That's why he hoped Pham was an idealistic fool rather than a crooked cop. The former he could deal with; the latter he'd have to bring down no matter the cost to his own career.

He had only begun to search for King's elusive reports when Lepinsky poked his head in Sanchez's office.

"Hey, Inspector, you been following the news?"

"We live in a global fishbowl, Neil, which news do you mean?"

Lepinsky looked at Sanchez like he was from outer space, appropriate given his next words.

"The Mars mission."

Sanchez shrugged. Unlike most people his age, Sanchez had never liked being constantly connected, his attention scattered by a dozen inputs all struggling for his attention over the constant hum of music from his personal library. When he was working, he turned everything else off, relying on his assistant to filter and summarize what he really needed to know and present it in one fast fifteen minute burst at the end of the day.

But he also knew that you didn't rise without the support of those beneath you so he followed Lepinsky down to the ready room where half a dozen uniforms and a couple of detectives were huddled around the media centre watching a scattering of screens all displaying essentially the same story.

The American mission to Mars, launched two weeks early to get the jump on their Chinese and European rivals was in trouble. Less than thirty-six hours after leaving Earth orbit, a small explosion had lead to a cascade of system failures. None of the crew had been hurt but the ship could neither continue its mission nor return to Earth. Emergency power was sustaining life support but no one expected it to last more than a week.

Black banners scrolled across various plasma screens decrying the lack of a backup-up plan to rescue the stranded astronauts while several engineers vainly tried to explain to journalists why a rescue mission wasn't feasible. The lone holographic viewer was tuned to a real time simulation that showed how the trajectories of the three competing Mars missions were diverging. The Chinese and European ships were following similar paths but the explosion had nudged the American capsule off course. It wasn't much but the gap grew with each passing hour.

Sanchez watched his colleagues watching the unfolding disaster for a few minutes, then shook his head and turned away. People were always willing to worry and speculate over things over which they had no control rather than act to change things they could.

Before he reached his office, he ran into Dmitri Yankovy coming down the hall. Yankovy was looking down at his palmtop and muttering something in what Sanchez assumed was Russian and nearly ran Sanchez over.

"Careful, big guy," said Sanchez, glancing down at the palmtop. A steady stream of Cyrillic characters scrolled across the screen.

"Sorry, sorry, am preoccupied." Yankovy tried to step past Sanchez.

"Following the Mars' fiasco, Dmitri?"

The Russian's brow furrowed. "No. I am working on case for Superintendent Steele. Have you seen him?"

"Not since this morning," said Sanchez. "Have you tried calling him?"

"Calling, paging, messaging, alerting, visiting office. Soon I will use bloodhounds. He asked me to report this morning but now he is nowhere to be found."

"Frank's been a little preoccupied, too."

Yankovy frowned, the expression of sadness echoing in his large brown eyes. "Yes. Yes, it is a hard thing. I lost both my boys during the...Restoration."

Sanchez nodded sympathetically. The Russian Restoration was rumoured to have cost over three million lives.

"My condolences."

"Is long time ago. But..." Yankovy shook his head. "Is not your problem. I need to find..."

"Are you any closer to cracking the water plant case?"

"Closer, yes, but not there yet. Soon. And when I do, you will be second to know." Yankovy stepped around Sanchez, clearly in a hurry to be somewhere else.

"Look, Dimitri, I've got a feeling that something big is going on—bigger than any one individual case. It's only a hunch but…"

The Russian turned and stared at Sanchez, his eyes narrowed and his lips pursed.

"You may be right, Inspector Sanchez," said Yankovy, his accent faded to a bare hint. "We are all pawns in the Grand Game. Only the playing board changes. How did Clausewitz put it: 'war is politics by other means?' It may seem we are in a war, Inspector Sanchez, but to the shadowy Players it is only politics."

Chapter 18

Cerise turned off the monitor and flopped back onto the narrow bed. The news anchors had run out of anything new to say about the disaster in space and were merely finding new ways to say the old stuff.

She knew she should care more about the eight people now trapped in a tiny capsule, hurtling through space without any hope of getting home or reaching their targeted destination. The accident had happened during the last minutes of the ship's final burn and it was now destined to miss Mars by a few hundred thousand kilometres. Not that it would matter to those aboard. They would be dead long before their ship sailed past the Red Planet.

She knew she should care more and, in an abstract way, she did. But they were far away and she was here, trapped in her own tiny prison far from home, uncertain whether she would ever get home or would recognize it if she did.

She didn't even know if she wanted to go home. Everything had changed. The world was scarier than she had imagined. She had always known that bad things happened to people but believed that she herself was safe, insulated by her family and school, protected by her friends.

But none of them had come through for her. Someone she loved and trusted had betrayed her. She could almost remember, could almost see his face. It was a male face, that much she was sure of. Her father or one of her brothers. Or maybe a friend from school or church? *If he could do this to me, he could do it to anyone,* she thought. If she was in danger, what about her mother? What about the innocent members of her family?

Cerise groaned in frustration. She could remember so much—the order of the planets the Mars capsule would pass on its way out of the solar system, the lyrics to Denny Dalmonico's latest love ballad, even the algebra she'd struggled over last semester. But she couldn't remember her mother's face or her brothers' names.

Cerise rolled onto her stomach and clutched the thin pillow in her arms, willing herself not to cry. The pillow smelled of bleach and must. Like everything in her life, clean and unclean at the same time.

She squeezed her eyes tight and pressed her face into the rough cloth. Images—ugly, confusing, frightening—swirled in her mind, threatening to overwhelm her.

Breathe, girl, just breathe.

She listened to the sound of the air in her throat, concentrated on the steady beat of her pulse the way she had been taught. She vaguely wondered who had taught her as she drifted into sleep.

| | |

It was nearly dark by the time Cerise started awake from a jumbled and frightening dream. For a moment, she lay in the dim light, scarcely breathing, trying to hold on to the stark dream images before they slipped away.

There was music playing downstairs, the low thump of the bass vibrating through the floor boards. Someone was cooking, the smell of roasting meat made her stomach grumble. She hadn't eaten since Superintendent Steele had dropped her off. She had felt dizzy from the round of early morning tests; too tired and nauseous to eat when lunch was offered. Now she was starving.

She went to the windows and peeked through the heavy green drapes. Most of the houses were dark, their occupants at work or unwilling to waste costly electricity on unneeded lighting. No one was walking in the street, though as she watched a small car drove slowly by.

It had the same deserted feel that morning when she arrived. The Superintendent delivered her himself though he had stayed behind the tinted windows of the unmarked car. A young woman, Cathy, dressed in jeans and heavy denim jacket, her smile bright in her light brown face, took her into the house and introduced her to the four other occupants as Denise, the name she was to use while she stayed here. Cerise had been wearing the sweats Angel had given her the day before covered by a light parka, the hood pulled up and drawn tight to hide her face.

She had glanced from side to side but all the houses looked much the same, worn two-story wooden buildings, painted in fading pastels. The few trees showed no signs of impending spring and the grass had only the barest hint of green among the brown remnants of winter. Behind the house an empty field, still clotted with dirty snow, stretched unbroken except for a few lonely buildings in the distance.

Cathy had given her a small parcel of clothes, the only ones they had on hand that were close to her size. She promised they would get some new ones if Cerise's stay extended past a couple of days. Cerise hoped that included underwear and bras; the ones from the hospital were functional but wearing them made her feel like she was on her way to a religious colony.

Most of the pants were too big. She squeezed into some black chinos that looked good but made breathing an adventure. She took them off and reluctantly pulled on the smallest of the jeans that she cinched around her waist with a silver-studded black belt. The tops were closer to her size and she picked out a tight turquoise top and an even tighter faux-leather jacket adorned with dozens of zippers. Most were decorative but six led to pockets of various sizes. It had probably belonged to a Borg wannabe. *Either that or a sex dream girl*, thought Cerise, but she didn't care. It made her look older, more dangerous. It wasn't her—she knew that as soon as she slipped it on. It felt like a costume for a play.

But maybe it was the way she needed to be right now, the way a tiger needs its stripes so it could hide in the jungle until it was ready to pounce. What did they call it—protective colouration?

She debated going downstairs to see what was being served for supper. But she decided they would probably call her when it was ready and she wanted time to think before having to join the other occupants of the house.

She wondered who they were. Police officers for sure, working under cover, and people like herself who were being kept hidden for their own protection.

Cerise sat on the bed. She wondered if there was anything new on the Mars mission but she didn't turn the monitor on. *This is what I do,* she thought, *when I don't want to face a problem.* The sudden insight made her feel better.

She closed her eyes and tried to recall the fragments of the dream. There had been a Borg. Not Buzz Wannamaker but another one, one she couldn't remember seeing before. He had been young, only a half-dozen years older than she was. His right hand had been replaced with a mechanical device but otherwise he looked human, though when he spoke she could tell he had a vocoder implanted and one of his ears looked funny. His expression had been gentle and his face reminded her of someone she knew, though she wasn't sure who.

They were together in a white room, a hospital or a lab, and he had seemed concerned or puzzled at her presence there. He kept telling her that everything would be fine and that he would find out what was happening.

Then he was gone, simply disappeared the way people do in

dreams. She was still in the white room, stretched out on a table, paralyzed. No not paralyzed, strapped down, she remembered now. She was strapped on a table and two people were leaning over her. She couldn't tell if they were men or women because they were gowned and masked, like surgeons in a web-cast.

Her face was numb as they leaned over her. One of them had a long metal instrument with a tiny pod at the end. He shoved it up her nose.

Cerise suppressed the urge to laugh. It was both funny and disgusting but she knew she had to concentrate. This wasn't a dream, it was a memory, she was sure of it.

Too late. The last images were slipping away. A fleeting feeling, not physical, but a sense of being connected to someone, or more, something, cold, inhuman. Machine.

Cerise shuddered.

She wasn't safe here, despite what Superintendent Steele thought. She picked up the emergency phone he had given her. It was keyed into his personal pager but she knew ways around that. Getting access to the web was a little more difficult but not impossible. Math had never been her strength but code seemed more like language, more natural.

She flipped on the monitor and began searching for her mother's phone number.

Chapter 19

After I dropped Cerise at the safe house, I headed back down town and checked in at the office. Yankovy had left several messages for me, including one taped to my office door but when I tried to reach him, his messenger said he was out to lunch. Somehow that didn't surprise me. I tried Nancy to see if she was free for supper but all I got was her assistant. I hate those things so I hung up without leaving a message.

I started flipping through the endless stack of reports that never seemed to disappear from the corner of my desk no matter how fast I dealt with them. I suspected if I dumped them in the shredder they'd all magically reappear by morning. I started slogging through them and by the time I looked up again it was well after two o'clock. My stomach suggested lunch so I headed down to the commissary to grab a sandwich.

Vanessa Pham was coming out of the SDU lab but darted back inside when she spotted me. I thought I'd done enough to placate her at the staff meeting but apparently not. When your staff try to avoid you, there are only two things you can do. Get new staff or nip the problem in the bud. I wasn't ready to start another staffing process yet so I stuck my head in the lab. She was standing right inside the door and blushed slightly at being caught.

"Got a minute?" I asked, pretending not to have noticed her duck and cover.

She nodded, pretending she believed me, and gestured to the chair beside her desk.

"I wanted to tell you that I appreciate the thoroughness of your reports," I began in the style they taught in the yearly management seminars the Chief made us attend. "It's a significant contribution to our work."

She nodded again and gave me a small smile that said she recognized the bullshit but appreciated the effort.

"We haven't really had a chance to get to know each other," I said. That much was true. I remembered her as shorter and slimmer. Maybe she had been working out.

"And you still compare me to my predecessor," she said. "Negatively in most respects."

She had me there. Cat Podnarski, before she went off the rails, had been exactly the kind of forensics specialist the SDU needed, one who relied as much on her gut instincts as her considerable scientific skills. She provided insight as well as information. She had never been afraid to take risks and make guesses. And she'd been right a hell of a lot more often than she'd been wrong.

No matter. Vanessa Pham was sitting right in front of me. You have to work with what you've got.

"I'm sorry if I've given that impression," I said. And I was. Resentful employees who feel unappreciated never give you their best work. Maybe that was why she was such a tight-ass all the time; she was afraid I'd never think she was good enough. I think it was Karl Marx who said sincerity was the key to success: if you could fake that you've got it made. Or maybe it was Groucho. In any case, it was time for a little white lie.

"Ms. Podnarski was a valued member of the SDU but she didn't have your medical qualifications and she had never been a cop. It's clear to everyone in the department that the SDU is better because of your presence." Everyone except me but I only had to run the place.

Pham looked almost embarrassed by what was by any standard faint praise. She nodded again and this time her smile was a little more genuine.

"My door is always open," I said. "If you ever feel you want to explore a theory or make a suggestion, even before all the facts are in, don't wait for a staff meeting or for a formal report."

"I'll do that, Superintendent."

"Please call me, Frank."

"Sure, Frank, I…" She hesitated as if she had something else to say but then abruptly stood up. I resisted the urge to look at her feet to see if she had started wearing heels. "I have a meeting."

"Don't let me keep you," I said, standing myself.

She still hesitated and we stood there for several seconds, staring at each other, neither quite willing to make the break for the door.

"You worked with a Borg, didn't you? There was one in the SDU."

"Buzz Wannamaker," I said.

"I understand he quit the force. During a particularly difficult time."

"That's the generally accepted version of events,"

"But not yours?"

"I can't go into details," I said, maybe a little too stiffly. The Canadian Security and Intelligence Service had exercised a little known law to make most of the details illegal to go into.

"You can't rely on them, you know."

This wasn't quite what I had in mind when I asked Pham to share her innermost thoughts. I'd dealt with my share of bigots but I didn't much like them working for me. Maybe it was time to start another staffing process after all.

"I know what you're thinking, Frank. But I'm not prejudiced, merely…experienced. The Borg are like any closed community. They're clannish. They stick together, protect each other. And if push comes to shove they choose clan interests over those of the wider community. And if they have a problem they deal with it themselves rather than using the rules and institutions of the bigger society."

"So that's why you think Borg are killing Borg? Because they're dealing with clan business?" It was a reasonable theory, at least if your experience with the Borg was limited. But it didn't apply to Buzz and I didn't think it applied to a lot of the other Borg I'd met over the years, like Sanchez's contact, Angel.

"Yes," Pham said. She stepped past me but stopped before she got to the door, her back to me, rubbing one hand back and forth on the black surface of a lab table. "And I think they are deliberately trying to throw suspicion on the Clean Boys."

"The Clean Boys are no friends of the Borg."

"But none have ever actually killed one."

"Not in Calgary." Though not from lack of trying.

"Has Antoine King spoken to you?"

"Your assistant?"

"He has a theory about a rise in deaths among the Disappeared. I have an alternative theory. I think those dead children were not so-called Disappeared but Clean Boy recruits, newly arrived from the religious colonies south of Calgary. They have no public records, either."

"And who do you think are killing them?"

She turned to look at me with a broad smile on her face. "The same people who are killing the Borg. I can't prove it. Yet. But maybe after this meeting."

Before I could ask her who she was rushing off to see, she swept out the door and was gone.

|||

I took my sandwich back to my desk and got through another half dozen reports before giving up and calling Singh to see if he wanted to go over to visit Joshua's employer with me. I would have preferred Buzz or even Chin for this job but Singh would have to do. His experience with corporate systems still made him a better choice than anyone else in the SDU. I had a feeling the good people at Singularity House weren't going to be easy to work with. As usual I let him drive.

Despite its name, the building that held Singularity House didn't look very home-like. It was a low metal-clad structure with a slightly peaked metal roof. It was about three times as long as it was wide and generally rectangular except for a small jut at the far end where two heavily armoured cargo doors allowed access for delivery vehicles.

The building was windowless and unmarked with only one other visible entrance. A small sign at the curb and a smaller one on the door gave the lone indication of the occupants.

A pair of fences surrounded the entire structure, the outer one made of heavy chain link, interlaced and topped with razor wire. The inner fence consisted of half a dozen strings of barbed wire and had large 'High Voltage' signs spaced at regular intervals. A kind of airlock penetrated the fences in front of the main entrance and heavy gates with a manned station blocked access to the cargo doors.

Heavy security isn't uncommon around research labs but most places were a little more subtle. At least there were no machine gun towers.

Singh pulled into an unpaved lot across the road from Singularity House. The wind had picked up again and we stood for a minute letting the dust fill our mouths and eyes while we assessed our likely welcome.

"Let's hope we don't have to break in," said Singh.

I gasped in mock alarm. "Are you suggesting a sworn officer of the law would commit simple burglary?

"Knowing your methods, I'm sure there would be nothing simple about it." Singh lifted the collar of his trench coat up around his ears. "Let's get on with this. I'm getting cold."

I pressed the button on the intercom but there was no reply. On the third attempt, I held the button down until someone poked their head out the door and told me to stop. I took my finger off the button and the screen lit up. A somewhat flustered young woman was replaced at once by a grim-faced older man showing several days of salt and pepper stubble.

"What the fuck do you bozos want? This is a private facility and visitors are not welcome."

I pressed my ID against the pick up, so close that all they would see inside would be a blurred full-screen version of my badge.

"Calgary police. Do want to let me in to answer a few quiet questions or do I need to get a warrant to come with a full squad of bozos to trash the place?"

The screen went black for a ten count. I was about to try to make good on my empty threat when it lit up again. Flustered Girl, looking a little calmer now, reappeared.

"Please enter the lock when you hear the buzzer. Make sure the outer door is fully closed before trying to open the inner one. Wait for the chime."

Since I expected the inner door was as electric as the fence it passed through, I followed directions to the letter. The door to the facility swung open as Singh and I approached it. Flustered Girl smiled wanly as we entered. Not exactly welcoming but it was better than Angry Man, who was nowhere to be seen.

"I'm Sally. Sorry for that. Mr. Baxter can be a little, um, abrupt."

The reception area was as attractive as the exterior had been utilitarian. The floor was carpeted in an abstract pattern of greens and browns that reminded me of the last time I had been in a forest. The look was amplified by the numerous large plants and the floor to ceiling screens on two walls, one depicting a quiet glade complete with grazing deer and the other a crystal pool fed by a small waterfall.

Sally led us to a small sitting area, which despite having the appearance of being carved out of deadfall was quite comfortable. There was a silver coffee urn and an assortment of drinks on the table, along with china cups and crystal glassware. Sally urged us to help ourselves.

"Dr. Grigg will be with you momentarily."

Grigg was listed as head of research. Not the top dog at Singularity House but the one who sniffed his tail.

Grigg's moments stretched to several minutes. I kept myself from losing my temper by watching the forest scene to see if I could tell when it looped. As near as I could tell it didn't and I had about decided it was a live feed from some unspoiled paradise when Grigg showed up.

Grigg was medium height and medium build, good looking in a nondescript sort of way. The kind of guy people have trouble picking out of a line-up. He looked about thirty though the company bio had said he was forty-eight, so I figured head of research must pay well enough for frequent rejuv treatments. I doubted his hair was really that shade of gold but they had done such a good job matching it with his eyebrows and skin colour that he could get away with it.

He flashed me one of those too-white smiles that people of fifty still thought of as Hollywood perfect. That gave away his age—real thirty-year-olds were into a more natural look or else had a mouth full of chrome and jewels.

"Dr. Grigg?" I stood too quickly and a faint blur of dizziness washed through me. "This is Darwhal Singh. I'm Frank Steele."

The smile was replaced with what I assumed Grigg meant to be a sympathetic expression as he shook my extended hand in both of his.

"Superintendent Steele, we're so sorry for your loss. Joshua was a fine young man."

"Good. Then you know why I'm here."

Grigg glanced over his shoulder at Angry Man—Baxter—who had reappeared and was standing near the entrance to the main lab at the far end of the reception area, taking up a good part of one wall.

"No. Not really."

"Joshua Steele did work for Singularity House."

"He wasn't an employee, per se. He did some contract work for us from time to time."

Not what he had told Mike but maybe he was trying to assure him that his life was going better than it was. Or maybe Dr. Grigg was lying to me.

"Did he work on-site or from home?"

I don't think that any company that surrounded their building with razor wire was going to let anyone take their laundry off-site, let alone any work files of significance. But I wanted to see how far Grigg was willing to go to keep me away from Josh's work station.

Grigg glanced over his shoulder again. I couldn't see any puppet strings but I assumed it was Baxter, Singularity House's Head of Security, who was calling the shots. Angry Man didn't budge and I couldn't see his lips move, but you can do wonderful things with implanted electronics these days.

"Almost exclusively from home," said Grigg.

Apparently he, or his puppet master, was prepared to go pretty far but I made a note to have Josh's home computer sent to the lab in case there was some nugget of truth in Grigg's assertions—though it was probably too late to recover anything useful. Singularity House would have taken measures by now to protect their proprietary interests.

I should have come here yesterday. There are a lot of things I should have done.

"Still, he must have dropped by, spoken to people?"

Grigg was starting to look uncomfortable.

"I'm sure he came by to pick up assignments or deliver work that couldn't be sent electronically."

Singh had been silent until then. Now he did an exaggerated eye roll and sighed loudly. "Really, Dr. Grigg, do you expect us to believe that?"

Grigg looked back at Baxter but he was already on his way across the lobby.

Singh took a device out of his pocket. There was a row of lights flashing down one edge. They were all red.

"Do you know what this is?"

Grigg shook his head, but judging from the look on Baxter's face, he did. Which put him one step ahead of me.

"Perhaps you should return to the lab, doctor," he said, laying a massive hand on Grigg's shoulder. "I'll handle these gentlemen."

A step up from bozo, at least.

Grigg nodded, clearly relieved. He took my hand again and shook it. "I really am sorry about Joshua. You have my deepest sympathy."

It sounded a lot more genuine in the singular.

"Thanks," I said, though my throat threatened to close around the word.

"I think Dr. Grigg answered all your questions," said Baxter.

"I take it you're not inviting us on a company tour," said Singh.

"I think I mentioned before—we don't welcome visitors. Especially ones who try to probe our security."

"This?" Singh smiled and pocketed the flashing gadget. "I'm always looking for new clients. But I can see you're not in the market."

Baxter looked like he wanted to wipe the smile off Singh's face. Darwahl sometimes had that effect on people.

"I can still get that warrant," I said. "This is a murder investigation."

"Joshua Steele was a low-level contract employee of this company. He did his work from home. He had no relationship to this building or anyone in it."

"That's your story," I said. "A judge might…'

Baxter smirked. I liked his angry look better.

"A judge already has. Our lawyers got an injunction while you were standing around yapping. You can try to fight it if you want but you know as well as I do you're going to lose."

I guess what pissed me off the most was the fact he was right. I'd have to prove probable cause and if it came down to my hunch against his word, I didn't have a chance. By now their accountants and lawyers would be busy rewriting any records that contradicted the official line.

"We'll see about that, Baxter." It sounded lame and he obviously thought so too. His smirk grew bigger as he gestured to the exit, which was already standing open.

"Come on Frank," said Singh. "It's time to go."

I probably should have left it at that. I'd learned a long time ago not to let my personal feelings get in the way of my work.

But isn't that what you're doing, Frank. If Joshua was a complete stranger, wouldn't you be pushing this prick against a wall, demanding straight answers instead of this bullshit? I was still trying to figure that one out when Baxter decided he needed to have the last word.

"You're a relic, Steele. Cops like you should stick to trying to make the street safe from shoplifters and bicycle thieves and leave the important work to those qualified to handle it. People like me and Singh."

The prick was trying to goad me into taking a swing so he could lay a thrashing on me. It might have worked, if Singh hadn't beaten me to it. His fist cracked Baxter's jaw below his left ear. The big man crumpled like a paper doll, unconscious before he hit the floor.

I looked at Singh. He shrugged.

"I never asked to join his club."

|||

I asked Singh to drive me to Josh's flat, hoping against all expectation that Singularity House hadn't beaten me to it. He parked across from the warehouse loft and got out when I did.

"It's okay, Dar, I can handle it from here."

"I doubt that." Singh took the gadget out of his pocket and checked a reading in the small screen at one end.

"What is that thing anyway?"

"Something Buzz put together for me," said Singh. "You know how good he is with machines."

"Professional courtesy."

"It's a combination security scanner and jammer."

I'd used a similar device on Singh the first time we met. He'd offered to buy it from me at the time but I'd declined. This one looked a bit more complicated than mine but I recognized the family resemblance now that Singh had pointed it out.

"These lights down the side…" The ones that had been flashing back at Singularity House. "…give you a reading on the type of security systems in play. At our last stop, they were all red. Without getting into the details, Fort Knox is probably easier to penetrate than Singularity House's lobby."

I hoped Singh was exaggerating because I'd already decided to ask him and Buzz—when he was free of the hospital—to do exactly that.

"What does it say about the top left apartment?"

"I'd have to go inside to be sure, but there is a steady stream of data being transmitted so I assume someone has bugged the place."

"Care to lend me that?"

"Not really," said Singh, slipping it back in his pocket. He gave me one of those annoying smiles and leaned back against his car with his arms folded.

For some reason, I didn't want him to see Josh's apartment, the unmade bed, the pictures on the table. It felt like a violation of intimacy to let strangers poke around.

Get a grip, Frank, you're practically a stranger yourself. I nodded for Singh to follow me.

The yellow tape and alarm were still in place though Singh's device said it had been tampered with. That became apparent as soon as I opened the door. The crew who had searched the place were professionals. If I hadn't spent an hour there yesterday, doing nothing but staring at the objects that cluttered the rooms, I wouldn't have known they'd been there.

The place was still cluttered but not the way a place that has been lived in looks. Everything had been gathered up and examined and then artfully arranged to give the appearance of casual living. But chaos has its own essence and no amount of planning can quite capture the spore left by a particular human being.

I had no way to inventory my son's possessions, especially those that had remained hidden in drawers or behind cabinet doors but my instincts told me things were missing, that someone had stolen away precious memories. With every moment, Josh was slipping farther from me.

The computer was still there but I didn't need to send it to the lab to know that whatever it might have held was long since wiped away using electromagnetic pulses or viral worms that could re-write memory or software or even infiltrate the hard coding of secure discs. I expected if I tried to dig too deeply the unit would self-destruct.

Upstairs the bed had been carefully stripped, re-made and unmade. They had even made it look like someone had slept in it. The body impression in the sheets was no longer my son but some stranger. Even that had been taken from me. Anger threatened to choke me; sorrow, to drown me.

Singh stayed by the door, leaving me the bitter privacy I craved. Good man that Singh. Wannamaker's device whirred and buzzed comfortingly, blocking out transmissions from pinpoint cameras or dust mote microphones.

Eat static, you bastards.

I was pretty sure there were fewer memory cubes than before and suspected the ones that remained were either wiped or had been replaced with harmless dummies. I hoped there was nothing illegal on those that remained. Corporate cops can be malicious pricks, sometimes.

I rubbed my hands across my face, feeling the rough stubble of two days growth and the soft pouches of flesh that had appeared beneath my eyes. I needed sleep and food and time to think. I had done everything wrong since the moment I had first looked into Joshua's dead face. It was time to start doing things right.

My body suddenly shook like a dog coming out of a cold river. People used to say it meant someone had walked across your grave—the place you were going to be buried.

Part of me was always going to be buried right here in the last place my son had lived. I went to the top of the stairs to see if Singh was willing to drive me back down town. I'd wait until we were safely away from here and any possibility of being heard before I broached the idea of breaking into Singularity House.

I looked down at Singh blocking the door. Mike was framed in the archway, looking scared, embarrassed and determined all at the same time.

"What are you doing here, Mike?"

Singh looked at me quizzically but stepped aside to let my brother step into the flat.

"Sorry, Frank, sorry. I know you didn't want me hanging around, getting in the way."

"You're here now." He took another step into the flat.

You probably have as much right to be here as I do, I thought, *maybe more*. I came down the stairs and motioned the others to join me at the dining room table.

"After I left, I didn't go home. I had things I wanted to say to you. I waited around outside but when you came out, you were so…" He paused and I wondered what exactly I had looked like in that moment when I thought I was alone, unobserved.

"I followed you for a few blocks but never got up the courage to interrupt your thoughts."

If my brother could tail me without me noticing, maybe it was time to take my pension. I could always sell pencils on the street corner to make ends meet.

"Anyway, I started to go home. But then, I don't know, I had a hunch I should come back here and keep an eye on the place. Must run in the family, huh?"

"Yeah. You stayed here all night?"

"In the alley across the street. It got pretty cold but that helped keep me awake. I pulled some cardboard over me. No one notices you when you're sleeping in the street."

It sounded like he was speaking from experience. More information about my family that I didn't need to hear.

"About three in the morning, a black van pulled up and three guys got out and went into the building. I didn't think anything of it until I saw the lights go on in Joshua's apartment. The driver stayed with the van so I couldn't get closer but I was able to get some pictures with my phone."

He projected four dimly lit photos on the wall. The van's license had been covered and there was nothing distinctive about the vehicle. Mike had gotten a couple of shots of the driver but the face was mostly obscured by the tinted windshield. The lab might be able to worm enough details out of it to make an identification but I doubted it.

The final shot was of the three searchers coming out of the building. Two men and a woman judging from the cut of their body suits. The woman was pulling off her ski mask but the others already had theirs off. Only one face was clearly visible though—our good friend, Baxter.

"Nice work, Mike," I said grudgingly.

"Are you going to arrest them?" Mike looked so pleased with himself that I hated to break the news to him.

"No. I've got no basis to arrest anyone—and certainly not this particular crew."

"But they were breaking into Joshua's place, interfering with an investigation, all that stuff."

"We only have your word these photos were taken in front of this building—all these warehouses look pretty much the same and the street number isn't visible. And none of the photos show them in the apartment anyway, so it's your word against theirs." I didn't bother to go into the kinds of questions their lawyers would raise about a civilian—one related to both the victim and chief investigator—undertaking an unauthorized surveillance. Mike looked crestfallen so I added. "But it helps me. It confirms certain…hunches of my own. And it shows me a possible way forward."

"Frank, I know I've been a disappointment to you…"

"It's okay Mike." I didn't need to air my dirty laundry in front of Singh.

"I think I'll make sure we're still clean," said Singh, taking out his scanner and moving back to the door. I didn't remember Darwahl being that sensitive but I guess people can change if they really want to.

"Mike, I appreciate you keeping a watch on this place but you've got to stop getting in the way. It's…it's dangerous. Josh was murdered. I don't know if these people had anything to do with that but even if they didn't, they wouldn't be happy if they found out you were watching them." I wanted to tell him I was worried about him, that I couldn't stand losing someone else, especially someone I still had a chance to be close to. Instead I said. "I can't afford the resources to protect you and I can't have you fucking up my investigation. I want to punish the people who hurt Josh. I can't risk you screwing up my case."

Mike nodded and put his hand on my arm.

"Whatever you say, big brother. But if you need anything from me, anything at all, well, you got my number."

He stood up and took a long look around the apartment as if trying to memorize every last detail.

"Hey," he said, "I almost forgot."

He reached into his pocket and took out a data cube.

"Joshua loaned me some movies when we had coffee on Tuesday afternoon." Mike paused as if realizing for the first time that he may have been the last person to see Joshua alive. "This must have got mixed in with the pile. I've been carrying it around in my pocket, meaning to give it to him the next…" His voice broke. "Maybe you should have it."

"What is it?"

"Joshua's personal journal."

Chapter 20

Wannamaker leaned back against the hospital bed. The private room Singh had paid for was quiet but he could still hear the steady bustle of the afternoon shift wrapping up their business outside his door. Four programs were running simultaneously on the wall screen, three versions of the Mars mission disaster and a recent romantic comedy Wannamaker had already seen twice. He waved his hand over the remote and the screens went blank.

The more Wannamaker thought about it the more uncomfortable he was with his last conversation with Frank Steele. The idea that Borg were systematically killing other Borg didn't just seem wrong, it seemed impossible.

There were less than twelve hundred true Borg in Calgary and barely twenty-five hundred in all of western Canada. It seemed unlikely that a secret clique of Borg assassins was operating without someone knowing who they were. Gossip and rumour were the lifeblood of the Borg. Some said it was what made them who they were.

He had told Frank the Borg were driven by a biomechanical imperative, an urge to modify themselves in a quest for endless improvement, a quest for perfection.

It was, of course, a Borg joke.

The shambling cyborgs of *Star Trek* had been driven to assimilate other societies in their quest for perfection. They were the ultimate mash-up of flesh and metal, the subjugation of personality into the group mind. The True Borg—as they called themselves in the secret language that only Borg (and dogs) could hear—were something far more complex and far more human.

We are driven, he thought, *not by the desire for physical perfection but by the quest for perfect communion.*

When he was a boy, it had seemed to him that he could never express all the ideas and emotions that flooded his mind, that poured like a river from his tongue. It is not our people's way, he had been told, to burble like a brook, to express our every thought and feeling. It had been that more than anything that had driven him off the reserve—the need to find minds and spirits that ran the way his did.

Borg minds did not work better than those of normals, but they often seemed to work faster. Wannamaker supposed there had always been people like that—people whose brains produced thoughts and emotions faster than words could express them. But with vocoders and artificial ears and the high speed visual processing of optical implants, it had finally been possible to share everything in real-time.

The rest had come after. The arms and legs, the skeletal enhancements, the body armour and organ augments—they were the logical extension of the Borg desire for family and community, the visual markers that set them apart for the rest of the world. But it had been communication that created the first Borg. And the goal of that communication had never been the creation of a group mind but the full expression of each individual within a shared perspective.

The difference was not subtle but seemed lost on anyone who was not Borg.

No. It was impossible that a community built on the continuous sharing of thoughts could ever harbour a secret cabal of killers. He had always known the name of every Borg who crossed the line. It had been one of the toughest challenges he had faced when he had become a cop, balancing his duty to the Force with his duty to his family. He would know if any Borg had set themselves apart as judge and executioner of their brothers.

He had talked about civil war but never really believed in it. *We are too close,* he thought, *brother might turn against brother but never Borg against Borg. At least, I hope not.*

Wannamaker activated the cell implanted within his artificial ear and coded Angel's contact. There was no answer, unusual but not unknown, though the fact her messenger didn't pick up bothered him. It was already getting dark so he tried the general line at the Garry but the assistant manager, a recent Borg convert with the unlikely name of Krakatoa, hadn't seen her for several hours. He seemed worried.

He was about to try the not-so-safe house where he had last seen her when Singh called. Wannamaker wasn't sure if he really wanted to stay in the agency but until he made up his mind, the man was his partner.

"You got me," he said.

"Good," said Singh. "Can you meet me in an hour?"

The doctors had insisted on another night of observation but they couldn't make him stay.

"Sure," he said. "What did you have in mind?"

"Not sure yet," said Singh, "but I think it'll be fun."

132

Chapter 21

By the time Singh dropped me back at HQ—after a brief side trip to take Mike home—it was nearly four in the afternoon. I didn't broach the subject of a Singularity House break-in though I hinted I might have a job for him and Buzz. I needed to think it through a little more. The early morning sun had given over to a dull overcast making the day seem even shorter than it really was.

The SDU seemed unusually quiet, everyone off pursuing leads or skiving off early while the boss was away. Only Constable Phelen was in his cubicle, going through the reports on the Borg wannabe assaults, doing a favour for Lily Chin. I stopped by and asked him how it was going and he told me he was starting to see some patterns and should have something for me first thing in the morning. The workstations at Jones' desk were also lit up but he was nowhere to be seen. I thought Sanchez might be in his office but I had no desire to talk to him.

I went down the hall to my own office and closed the door behind me. I'd stopped keeping a bottle of Jack in my desk drawer since one of my colleagues had been suspended for celebrating his birthday with a glass of champagne during working hours. I made it a rule never to drink at my desk but I used to like to think that I could if things ever got bad enough.

Today probably would have been the day.

I put the data cube in the middle of the desk and stared at it for a few minutes, the way I used to stare at the bottle on dark days. It was a non-standard unit, nearly four centimetres on a side and a bright electric blue. There were three data access ports—one of which fortunately fit my standard-issue reader. Finally I picked it up and slipped it in a multi-reader.

It was worse than I thought. Josh had recorded his journal holographically so I had to watch a 3-D image of my son, staring straight at me, talking earnestly as if in a confessional.

Treat it like evidence, Frank. Keep your distance.

I really needed that bottle of bourbon.

I took out my documenter but turned the visual recorder off. I really had no idea how I was going to react and didn't trust Internal to keep the film secret.

The first entry was from more than a year ago, dated January 2nd, 2043, before he had begun the process of becoming Borg, and as near as I could tell from looking at the index, he seldom skipped a day. Though he wasn't working from any kind of script—too many hesitations and corrections for that—it was clear he had thought through what he wanted to record before he turned the camera on. Each entry started with a brief 'our topic for today' introduction and he mostly kept to his subject only deviating into new areas towards the end of each recording. Sometimes, it seemed he was addressing a specific audience and I suspected those entries had later been uploaded for his friends to see and hear. Others seemed too private and unrehearsed, often too painful for public consumption. I made a note to do a search of social networking sites to see if I could separate the public from the private Josh.

It's all about patterns in the end.

At first, he mostly worried about his coming finals and wondered whether he should continue on at university or take a job for a few years so he could start enjoying the 'good life.' He talked about the difficulty of maintaining friendships when people were always on the move and right from the start he talked about family and about the person he wanted to become.

| | |

"Meant to start this cube yesterday but I was way too busy. Not hungover. My fifth New Year without a drink. Go me. That's what I want to talk about today. Not sobriety. No boring AA lectures. Promise. No this is about family and about growing up.

"Let me start again. New Year's Eve. I was planning on heading down town to take in the First Night Festival. Lame I know but I kind of like it. All the families and their kids, skating and laughing and eating cotton candy and fried bread. Then fireworks at nine for the kids and again at midnight for the adults who hang around. It's a Cowtown tradition.

"Anyway, I watched the early show and was about to head down to the Garry to see what was happening in Borgville—I feel more comfortable every time I'm there—when my cell buzzed. It was Uncle Mike. He'd been drinking—not too heavy yet but he was on his way. I'm his buddy, the guy he calls when things get out of control.

"It was a drag but I agreed to meet him. By the time we hooked up he'd had three or four more drinks and was in pretty bad shape. I brought him back here and talked him through it. It took most of the night. Mike has a good heart but he's a Steele, just like me.

"I got my first genetic scan when I was seven years old. My mom has always been worried about what I might inherit from her side of the family—but that kind of craziness doesn't comes from your genes. No my inheritance came from the Steele side. So I knew from a very young age that I should never take a drink. Not that I needed a lab coat to tell me. I could see what it had done to my grandfather; I could see what it was doing to my father.

"When I was fifteen and everything had really gone to shit with my parents and my dad was suddenly almost sober again, I went off the rails. I figured if that's what it took to be a man in our family, I'd show them. And I did—not that anyone noticed. My parents were…so…"

Josh rubbed his hands across his face and turned away. The image skipped and then came back on again.

"To conclude. No one noticed. At least at first. I had pretty much hit rock bottom when my Uncle Mike showed up. I hadn't seen him in years. No one had. He still won't talk much about where he was or what he did but he'd drifted back to Calgary seven or eight years ago."

I'd had no idea Mike had been back in town all that time. He only got in touch with me last January, a few days after this recording was made.

"He was no role model. Alcohol, drugs, gambling, sex, if there was an addiction going, Mike was going with it. But like me, alcohol was the worst. But he was trying. He's still trying. And he got me to try too.

"I had my last drink eight days after my nineteenth birthday. More than five years without backsliding. I wish I could say the same for Mike. Maybe he has bigger demons to wrestle than me. Mike came through for me, restored my faith in the power of family. I've been closer to my mother since then, even started spending time with my half-sister, whenever she comes back to Canada. My Dad is my next big challenge. Not sure when I'll have the strength to climb Mount Frank, but someday I will.

"In the meantime, I've been thinking a lot about family and a lot about destiny. I overcame my genetic programming to become the person I am right now. Maybe it's time to carry that process a step further.

"I've spent a lot of time in the Borg community. It started off because of my studies. But I've never felt more at home, more with family, than I do with them. We talk endlessly but I never seem able to say everything I want. I've been saving my shekels and I'm scheduled to have a vocoder and ear installed—the first step on my journey to become Borg."

|||

I watched the first dozen entries, each running three to five minutes, in their entirety. Sometimes he seemed happy, almost giddy; in others, his misery was palpable. He second guessed himself, celebrated triumphs at school, wondered if he would ever find true love, talked confidently about his plans for the future, despaired of ever resolving his differences with his mother and, especially, me. In other words, he was his father's son.

After an hour, I was no closer to understanding what had driven my son to become a Borg, let alone how that choice had led to his murder. I looked at the index again. There were over four hundred entries, more than twenty-six hours of recordings. I'd barely scratched the surface. As much as I wanted to wallow in every painful moment, I didn't have the time or emotional energy. But I couldn't bring myself to turn it over to Lepinsky or Jones, either.

It's only evidence, Frank. Yeah, right.

I finally ran a key word search, isolating only those sections where Josh talked either about the Borg or about his job at Singularity House. That got it down to under five hours, mostly Borg related.

I copied the Borg material onto a separate cube, to watch whenever I could grab a spare couple of minutes. Maybe I was being vindictive but my gut told me it was those pricks at Singularity House that had led my son to his death, even if they weren't directly responsible themselves.

I watched the seven remaining entries—the ones that mentioned Singularity House—several times. They didn't tell me a lot. Sometimes Josh referred to his job, sometimes to his contract, so whether he was a full-fledged employee as Mike claimed or merely a contractor as Baxter said remained unclear—and whether it mattered even less so. The work paid well and the contract came with a modest benefit package—some medical coverage and the opportunity to buy non-voting stock. He thought the latter was pretty funny but made full use of the former to help pay for his second Borg modification—though most of the cost came out of his pay.

There was no question, however, that he did the bulk of his work at the main office of Singularity House. He was forbidden to take anything but the most mundane work home and he was careful not to reveal too much about what he was working on. Only one entry stood out— the last one—dated Monday, March 14th, 22:33. A little more than twenty-four hours before he died.

|||

He was sitting on the end of his bed, staring into the camera. He reached out with his right arm, his Borg arm, and adjusted the controls. He looked agitated. If I hadn't known of his struggles, I might have thought he was a little high.

"There's something odd happening at work. Erich came into the office today. First time in two months."

Erich Carpentier was the founder of Singularity House. He had been the one to hire Josh last May but his own involvement in the business had declined after that. He spent more time out of the country than in, raising money or recruiting scientists for the company.

"He had a couple of guests. I didn't get a good look at either of them but, from the quickness of his movements, I think one was Borg. The other, I'm not sure, but I think I've seen his picture on the web-casts. There was a girl too. Young. Black. They all arrived in an armoured car and came in through the loading doors. Baxter met them himself and took them straight downstairs to the labs. I'm used to the security at SH but this was something special. It seemed like Baxter was giving the orders and Erich was going along with them.

"The labs downstairs are all pretty hush-hush. I probably shouldn't even be mentioning them. But nobody is going to see this 'cast, except me and maybe…"

He hesitated and glanced over his right shoulder. I couldn't tell what he was looking at.

"Yeah, that might be the ticket to the top. It's where they do the really interesting work. The Project. It's a lot more than simply an enhanced interface, no matter what the prospectus says. This is bigger than nano, bigger than quantum computing. All the scientific pipedreams wrapped into one. Ponce de Leon would be proud.

"And it should be all cool. It's what everyone has been dreaming about. It's what—he made a series of high whirrs and buzzes, a Borg name—says we're striving toward, where evolution must ultimately take us.

"But there's something else going on. Something not cool at all. That girl isn't the only one. There have been others—kids or a little older. At least she came out again. The others…"

A chime rang from somewhere in the apartment.

"Shit…" Josh stood up and moved out of camera range to the right.

I could hear him talking but his voice was muffled, the words indistinct. I tried to enhance the sound but I still couldn't make it out. There was no answer. Maybe he was talking on a cell, maybe on his intercom. Maybe the person he was talking to had nothing to say. After a few minutes, he came back and sat on the bed. He wiped his hand through his hair. There was a sheen of sweat on his face.

"Okay, I wasn't going to put this on the record. But what I just heard, I…Dr. Grigg asked me to run a couple of tests on…doesn't matter. The instruments weren't in his lab so I went downstairs to central stores. The door to the Project lab was open. I couldn't resist. I had to look inside. At first I thought it was empty. I don't know where Erich and the rest were. But then I saw the black girl. She was in a hospital gown, sort of huddled in a chair in the corner. She kept trying to get up but I could see she had been strapped in the chair. There was a gurney in the room, surrounded by a lot of instruments, some I recognized and some I didn't. But I knew they were going to use them on her. I tried to talk to her, tell her everything would be okay but then I heard them coming back so I had to take off. I tried a trick I learned from Angel— I hope it pays off. A couple of hours later they all left again. They took the girl with them but they had to half carry her. Baxter saw me watching and got mad as hell.

"I know what the Project is and it isn't cool at all. I don't know who is really behind it all. Not Dr. Grigg. Maybe not Erich. Baxter, yeah, probably, but he's not the brains behind it. That's someone else, someone I don't think I've ever met. This is way bigger than me, bigger than anyone I know, even—he said the Borg name again—or Angel. Someone else has to deal with this."

Josh hesitated for a long time, staring hard into the camera lens as if it might give him the answer he was looking for. He reached out once, twice to turn off the recording. Then he said:

"If you're watching this Dad, it means I'm dead. Find the bastards who did it."

Chapter 22

Who the hell is Dmitri Yankovy and what's he doing working for the SDU? Sanchez leaned back in his chair and stared at the water stains on his office ceiling then turned back to the file the Chief's overrides had provided. To call it meager would be an insult to minimalism. There was no mention of his tour in Africa and few details of his career before his appointment to the rank of Inspector for Moscow's foreign sector. He had served with distinction during the Restoration though the file was unclear with which army—presumably the winner. In the convoluted world of Russian politics that was by no means certain.

Chief Arsenault had seemed sanguine enough about Yankovy's unexpected request to participate in the international officer exchange. Maybe he had something on him from their days together in Africa and figured he could control the man. Or maybe he knew full well why Yankovy was here. Maybe he had even recruited him for his own larger purposes. The Chief worked in mysterious ways.

And he had his own agenda. Sanchez wondered if, even at eighty, the Chief harboured higher ambitions. And why not? If Yuanchao could still be running China with an iron fist at ninety-three, anything was possible.

Yankovy was playing at something—of that there was no doubt. The exaggerated accent, the country bumpkin routine, all part of some scheme. But why drop the routine and why to me?

He had talked about the Grand Game and the shadowy Players. His tone of voice had left no doubt they were meant to be proper names. The Great Game was what the English called the strategic rivalry and conflict between the British and Russian Empires for control of Central Asia during the nineteenth century. The Russians had called it the Tournament of Shadows.

Was there some new competition between superpowers? It seemed unlikely that any self-respecting superpower would care about events here in Calgary. Even the most ardent booster of the city or region didn't aspire for them to be players on the world stage, let alone in the Grand Game, whatever that was.

And who qualified as a superpower these days? Certainly not England or Russia. China, Europe, the United States were in the running.

India and Brazil had aspirations but still lagged behind. The Troubles had brought ruin to most people's dreams, including those of even the most powerful and prosperous nations. Besides, real power no longer lay with governments but with corporations. At the turn of the century, the biggest of them were richer than half the countries in the United Nations. Now it was rumoured that half a dozen of them would rank in the world's top twenty if they were countries instead of companies.

It was only a rumour of course. No one had the authority to reveal how rich any of the corporations or the small cadre of men and women who controlled them were. *Fortune Magazine* might still publish its famous lists but not for public consumption.

The meaning of Yankovy's words was less important than the way they had been delivered or the fact they had been spoken at all. It was bait, of that Sanchez had no doubt. But what kind of bait? Bait you used in a trap or to hook a fish? Or was it the kind of bait you used to lead someone down a particular path, the way he had recently lured a family of raccoons out of their den beneath his garage. Was Yankovy trying to trap him or was he trying to set him on the path to enlightenment?

He certainly wasn't going to find out sitting at his desk reading nearly empty files. Constable Jones had been working with Yankovy on the water system case. He would be a good place to start. If he was still around.

Shift change was at five and it was now several minutes past. The city had stopped paying overtime after the Big Crunch of '32, the last gasp of the Troubles that had rocked the world for nearly a decade. The police pension fund had gone belly up at about the same time, putting most cops between a rock and a hard place. The union made a lot of noise but in the end there wasn't much they could do. Eroding property values meant the city depended on service fees to operate. Most corporations had opted out of police coverage in favour of their own security forces especially after the constitutional amendments of 2036 which, among other things, enshrined property rights in the Charter.

Most cops voted with their feet—either moving over to private security if they had enough seniority and skill to grab the few jobs that paid well or by moonlighting. Which meant most constables and not a few detectives disappeared when the whistle blew.

Jones appeared to be an exception. He was still in his cubicle, poring over reports displayed on a half dozen small screens on his desk and the wall above it. *Maybe the rumours about his wife's trust fund are true*, thought Sanchez.

"Working late, Caleb?"

"Hmm?" Jones looked up from his desk, though his fingers kept working the multiple keyboards. "Is it late already?"

"Past five."

"Hmm, I'm almost done with this report for Inspector Yankovy."

"This have something to do with the sabotage of the water system?" Sanchez asked. There had been three separate attempts to damage the Calgary water system in the last six months. The first had been rather harmless—the introduction of a fast growing red algae that mimicked the appearance of red tide but without its toxic effects. The City had been on bottled water for three days until they cleaned it up.

The next two had been more serious. A chemical agent had been used to cause widespread gelling of water entering the filtration plant. It cost nearly fifty million New Dollars to fix the problems and there had been several weeks of water rationing. Then, a few weeks ago, an explosion at a pumping station killed two workers and injured another. The cause of the explosion was still unknown.

The Gaia Liberation Army of the West had taken credit for all three attacks—apparently in retribution for Calgarian's profligate use of water while unnamed others were dying of thirst—but no one seemed to know who or what GLAW was, other than a vague connection to an ecoterrorist group in Oregon.

"It must have—it's the only case he's working on," said Jones. "But damned if I can see exactly what."

Sanchez glanced at the screens surrounding Jones. "What is all this?"

"I don't really know, Inspector."

"Call me Reno. You don't know?"

"Well, I know what it is, uh, Reno. But I'm not sure what it means. Inspector Yankovy asked some pretty specific questions and gave me a few suggestions where I might find answers." Jones gestured at a couple of unlined hand-written sheets spread across his desk. Yankovy's writing was unexpectedly neat, nearly straight with perfectly formed letters that resembled stylized printing. The sheets contained a numbered list of questions and a half-dozen web-addresses, not all of them on the publicly-accessible net. "He told me 'to let my spirit soar free.'"

"So where did you fly off to?"

Jones laughed. "You name it, Inspector, umm, Reno, and I've pretty much been there. The first question looks pretty simple, doesn't it? Do the following companies have operations in western Canada? Followed by eleven names, well, nine names and a couple of numbered corporations. Some I could answer without looking. I bank at National Asian and Biocore was implicated and later cleared in an organ harvesting case a year ago—one of the first things I worked on for the SDU.

"Some of the others are pretty obscure though the web addresses helped. Most of them are double-encrypted and password protected but Inspector Yankovy made me memorize a bunch of codes that gave me free access. He said he'd help me forget them later. I assume he was kidding though he seemed pretty grim when he said it."

"It's the Russian way." Sanchez was pretty sure Yankovy was at least half serious. The Russians had pioneered 'Bug' technology and it was rumoured that their psychotropic drugs were state of the art. Not that Sanchez had any intention of letting Yankovy use them on a fellow cop. "What else did you find?"

"It took me half the day but it seems that all of them do have local operations or at least investments—all but this one." He pointed to the next to last company on the list. Boynton Biotronic Systems, Inc.

Where do I know that name from? thought Sanchez.

"What I should say," said Jones, "is that I can't find an answer one way or another. I assume it exists but there's no record of that name anywhere I can find. Plenty of businesses with the name Boynton, from a used-car dealership owned by an ex-hockey player in Florida to a string of British-owned music stores. They even have a store here in Calgary. But nothing remotely connected to biotronic systems—whatever those are."

"What kind of operations are we talking about?"

"It was hard to see a pattern, though I'm pretty sure there is one. Maybe if I could track down that last one it would all fall into place."

Frank Steele was pretty particular about who got to work for him. At least when he had some choice in the matter. Sanchez had been surprised to find that ninety percent of his people were promoted within four years of coming under Steele's command. It was one of the reasons he had pursued an SDU position himself.

People were always trying to dump their deadwood on the much-hated and more-maligned SDU but Steele had a way of deflecting the worst into other divisions. The losers he had to accept usually found it in their best interests to straighten up if they could and get out if they couldn't. Jones had been here for more than a year—which meant Steele thought he had potential.

"What's your theory?"

Jones flushed and glanced around. "Inspector Yankovy asked me not to discuss the case. 'Premature speculation is both embarrassing and messy', is the way he put it."

Sanchez raised an eyebrow at that—Yankovy was not at all who he appeared to be. "We're all friends here, Caleb. I'm sure Dmitri wouldn't mind."

"About half the companies are based in North California. National Asian is HQed right here in Calgary. The others operate under 'flags of convenience.' Which means they're involved in things most of the world prefers not to know about. Neural manipulation, human cloning, personality enhancement, chimeras. That kind of thing."

"Pariah companies. Until they provide some miraculous breakthrough."

"You got that right. Though there are those who make a habit of resisting temptation. Or blowing up the source before it becomes too tempting."

"So what has this got to do with the Calgary water supply?"

"Maybe nothing," said Jones. "But, imagine this. Suppose you've developed something radical, or given the speed of innovation these days, a dozen radical things all at once. It's all working in the lab but you want a field test."

"There are lots of places where that would be easier to do than here. Most of Africa, all of Australia, Alaska."

"Those would all be on my A-list," said Jones with a shit-eating grin. "But maybe they don't simply want guinea pigs, disposable humans trapped in an anarchic environment. Maybe they want to test themselves against a place where law and order still has a fighting chance, where people still have some say over what corporations can do to them. There are places that have done a better job at keeping the barbarians at the gates but not many."

Barbarians at the gates. The Chief's metaphor, thought Sanchez. *How deep did his fingers reach?*

"So you think someone is running an experiment, or a series of them, to see how far we can be pushed?"

"Well, it's not so much a theory as a guess."

Sanchez nodded encouragement. Jones glanced around and lowered his voice.

"It's all these questions that Inspector Yankovy had." He gestured to sheets on his desk. "At first, I didn't really notice where they were leading. I'm too linear—that's what Superintendent Steele says, anyway—

143

and I got focused on the first search without really paying too much attention to the rest. But look at this."

Jones pointed to three questions grouped together at the bottom of Yankovy's list.

Has there been an increase in Russian tourism to western Canada?

What Calgary facilities are available to treat severe brain damage?

Chart unsolved deaths among the lumpenproletariat versus water contamination exceeding acceptable standards.

"I had to look up 'lumpenproletariat;' it means…"

"The social underclass," finished Sanchez. "Habitual criminals, drug addicts and sex trade workers. The Disappeared."

"Some theorists include the unemployed but the original definition only meant those who had given up on employment, beggars, swindlers and the like."

What is Yankovy looking for? wondered Sanchez. And why would a police officer from the restored Russian Empire be using Marxist theory to crack an eco-terrorist plot in southern Alberta?

"Anyway," said Jones, "I decided to try to approach it laterally." He tapped a few keys and a holographic display appeared in one corner of his desk filled with a dozen globs of different colours and a series of single or doubled headed arrows connecting them.

"I inherited Buzz Wannamaker's old computer," said Jones, "This software was already installed. It's pretty nifty once you figure out how to use it."

Sanchez nodded. The display was impressive although it was not immediately obvious what it represented. It took him a minute to realize Steele used a similar program himself—though his display was produced with paper and pencil and was based more on intuition than hard calculation.

"It's a little confusing at first because it's a three-dimensional plot of nearly a dozen variables. It gets a little clearer when you add a fourth dimension." Jones tapped a few more keys and the globs and lines began to shift through space.

Clearer wasn't the term Sanchez would have used but he could see that something was happening. The shifting lights and structures looked right somehow, like a pattern seen through fun-house mirrors and distorting lenses. The meaning was elusive but it *was* there.

"These ten blue ones," said Jones pointing to a group of ellipsoids in a rough line, "represent the ten companies I could identify. The size reflects the dollar value of their known investments in Calgary. At first, they were all over the place but when I postulated an eleventh, they got more orderly. Once I determined it had to be the third largest, they more or less became linear. You can see the gap in the line."

Once pointed out, the missing data point was obvious. Boynton Biometrics had to exist and had to be a considerable player in the Calgary economy—not as big as National Asian, to be sure, but big nonetheless. Yet it was completely hidden.

"When I run the data over the last six months, you see two things. First, the size of the investments has increased for all eleven companies—assuming the graph stays linear. But the growth isn't steady. It increases in steps and, depending on the company, each step occurs three to eleven days before each of the three attacks on the Calgary water system.

"And these two data structures—the green represents the presence of Russian passport-holders in Calgary based on airport arrivals and departures and the red the deaths or hospitalization of, well, lumpenproletariat, where the cause of injury or death was head trauma. They both rise and fall in relation to the three attacks. The green—Russian arrivals—swells about two weeks before each incident and falls dramatically the day after and the red—head injuries—peaks in the three day period after each attack before falling back to normal levels."

"Good work, Caleb. Anything else?"

"Not directly related to Yankovy's questions. But I wondered about all those head injuries. It turns out they doubled about eight or nine months ago."

Sanchez shrugged. "Could be we've got something new and dangerous being peddled on the stroll. People are always looking for something to give them an extra thrill—and some of them don't care what it does to their heads. Send the data to Vice and see if they have anything. In the meantime, keep working on Yankovy's questions. When are you meeting with him?"

"We have a meeting scheduled for ten," said Jones.

"I'll see you then."

He walked slowly back to his office. Yankovy was looking for something but Sanchez doubted it had a lot to do with protecting the good people of Calgary from having their water poisoned. The regular rise and fall of Russian nationals in the city suggested he was working to someone else's agenda. The Russian Empire was not what it used to be but its new Tsar had ambition.

He opened Yankovy's file again. There was nothing there to suggest he was more than he appeared to be; a simple police inspector looking for international experience. M*ore international experience*, thought Sanchez. He had served in Africa. Chief Arsenault had served with him. No, not with him, *under* him.

Either Yankovy had been demoted after the Restoration or he was a lot bigger player than he or anyone else was letting on.

I need to talk to Arsenault, thought Sanchez. *Something is not right here.*

His palm chimed. The Chief's private line. *I swear to God the man's a mind reader*, thought Sanchez.

"Sanchez here."

"Inspector," said Yankovy, "I promised you would be the second to know."

How in hell did he get this number? thought Sanchez. *Unless the Chief gave it to him. Careful, now.*

"What do you have?"

"This line is private but certainly not secure. Do you recall the lunch we had a few days after I arrived?"

"Sure, it was—"

"Never mind. Do you remember what I ordered?"

"Yeah," Yankovy had ordered a thousand gram pseudo-steak with all the trimmings. By the time he had finished it they were all late getting back to the office. Sanchez remembered wondering what the man ate for supper if this was what he considered lunch.

"Then you will know where it came from."

Proponents claimed that eventually everyone would be eating meat grown in vats without the benefit of animals but for now the only local producer was a small operation east of the city.

"Meet me there in an hour."

Yankovy didn't wait for Sanchez to reply.

Chapter 23

Josh had known he was marked for death.

If only he had come to me, I thought, *if only he had told me.*

He did tell you, Frank. In the only way he could. He recorded this message and then deliberately gave it to Mike, knowing that if he was wrong he could always get it back. And if he was right, it would eventually come to me.

Deep under the layers of pain and anger, I felt…relief? Almost happiness? Josh had reached out to me in the only way he was sure would work. He trusted me to solve his murder, to bring his killer to justice, maybe, even to solve and stop the bigger crime he had witnessed. The one that had lead to his death.

I may have been a lousy father but I'd always been a decent cop. Even at my worst, I had always done my job, my duty. Maybe this was Josh's way of telling me he knew that. Maybe it was his way of telling me it almost made up for the rest.

I made a copy of his last entry and backed it up in as many ways as I could think of—my palm, the central police server, even my cell phone. I sent encrypted and date-locked versions to my most trusted colleagues on the force, that is to say, Willa O'Reilly and Jim McConnaghey, as well as Darwhal Singh and a couple of old cop friends now serving in other cities.

I had no doubt that the people who had killed six Borg and who knew how many other innocents wouldn't draw the line at disposing of a pesky Superintendent if that was what it took to protect their dirty little secret.

I sat at my desk for a few minutes, contemplating my next move. I heard Sanchez talking outside my office door—one side of a cell conversation. He was the one I should turn to; he was my second-in-command. But for some reason, I still didn't trust him. Arsenault had seemed too pleased when I announced my decision and, even if Sanchez wasn't reporting directly to the Chief on the SDU, he was too ambitious and way too slick for my liking.

Maybe given time and experience he would be the guy I turned to but for now I needed to rely on people I was sure I could trust. People who trusted me.

I was only mildly surprised to find myself dialing Singh's number and asking him to meet me at a little café we both liked, halfway between my office and his.

| | |

Singh was waiting for me when I arrived.

"We've got to stop meeting like this," he said, as I slid into the booth opposite him. "People will start to talk."

"Let 'em, sweetheart," I said, doing my best Humphrey Bogart. The reference was clearly lost on Singh. He leaned back in his seat and raised an eyebrow at me.

"You still got that little gadget handy?"

Singh brought his hand above the table. The device was cupped in his palm, flashing away.

"You're getting paranoid in your old age, Frank."

"Me? You're the one with his jammer in his hand. Sometimes paranoia is just clear thinking."

"Yeah, yeah and just because you're paranoid doesn't mean people aren't out to get you."

It was the kind of familiar banter people use when they don't want to get down to the business at hand.

"You didn't come here to repeat old jokes," said Singh. "Feel free to talk. My little buddy doesn't only jam transmissions it sends out fake ones. Right now we're talking about the prospects of the Flames winning the Cup."

That was a joke. I was a Leaf's fan. Me and Saint Jude, patron saint of lost causes.

"There's something I'd like you to do for me,"

"Break into Singularity House."

I blinked. "Am I getting that transparent?"

"The train of logic isn't that complex. We get lied to by Grigg and Baxter who, we discover, have been breaking into Joshua's apartment. If nothing else, we owe them a return visit. Add to that the fact I get an encrypted message I can't open for a week and an urgent request to meet after you've spent an hour with your son's private journal. I figured it wasn't because you can't get enough of the vanilla cappuccinos."

"Have you ever thought about opening a detective agency? You've got a real knack for it."

Singh grinned. One of these days, I'm going to have to ask him who does his dental work. "What am I looking for?"

I gave him the edited version of Josh's last journal entry.

"You're probably going to want Wannamaker's help on this," I said.

"Way ahead of you, Frank. I called Buzz while I was waiting for you. No details of course but he said he could be out of the hospital within the hour. You think the black girl is Cerise Kavanah?"

I nodded. It seemed to fit. "Maybe I'll head over there and see if I can jog her memory."

Singh reached across the table and put his hand on my forearm. "Frank, you look like you're ready to fall over. Go home, get some rest, it can wait until morning. Or at least until Buzz and I report back."

I pulled my arm away. "I'm fine."

"You're not but that's not the point. A woman came into the café about thirty seconds after you. I'm pretty sure it's the same one from Mike's photo - the woman who broke into Josh's house."

Jesus, I was getting old. I'd had no idea I was being tailed.

"Don't let it spook you," said Singh. "Baxter probably has five or six operatives tag-teaming you. You, of all people, know how that works. It was only luck the one who came in here was someone I'd recognize. Which also means they don't know of your brother's involvement."

Singh was right. Otherwise they would never have used an operative we could make. The muscles in my neck relaxed a little and the knot in my gut seemed a little smaller. At least Mike was still safe—though for how long…I put that thought out of my head.

"Go home, eat something, maybe take a nap. It might throw them off the scent."

I nodded and smiled. Singh turned off the jammer. I told Singh an old joke. He laughed. Make them think this was two old friends meeting for coffee, nothing more.

After a few minutes, we got up. I slapped Singh on the back and headed for the door, leaving him to pick up the tab. The woman didn't look at me as I passed but I was pretty sure Singh was right.

I spotted her replacement as soon as I left the café. I took a long circuitous route home, picking up a few things at a couple different stores. By the time I got there, I'd made all of Baxter's team.

| | |

I tried getting back into the Sawyer novel but I was too frazzled to give it the attention it deserved. I lay on my bed for twenty minutes trying to will myself to sleep but Josh's final words rumbled around my head like the last night train from downtown.

Finally, I got up, took Jack out of the cupboard and poured myself three fingers in the last clean glass in the kitchen. I set it on the table and stared at it for a moment until the smoky smell reached my nostrils. I cupped my hands around the glass to warm the whiskey, the familiar comfortable ritual that prepared me to slide off the wagon. This time I might slip right under the wagon's wheels.

I raised the glass to my lips, then put it back on the table without tasting it.

I searched my kitchen drawers until I found the funnel and poured the bourbon back in the bottle. 'Waste not, want not' has always been my philosophy.

I went to the window and stared down at the street three floors below. The burly black man who had followed me home had somehow acquired a car and was half-hidden by its open hood as he did a fair imitation of auto repair. I expected he had a mini-cam mounted somewhere on the car and was watching my window for signs of life. I resisted the urge to wave.

It looked like I was stuck here for the long haul. I couldn't read or sleep and didn't want to drink.

Well, I wanted to but I wasn't going to.

Nothing on cable or the web-feeds appealed to me—it was mostly about the Mars mission. I'd watched every movie in my collection at least a dozen times. I took the hundredth anniversary edition of *Casablanca* off the shelf. The cube came with the option of adding sub-plots or programming alternate endings. You could even substitute your favourite actor for the original. I'd tried that once. Casablanca with Leonardo Dicaprio in the Rick role and the latest net sensation, Amanda Whelan, as Ilsa. It was okay I guess but I preferred the original. I put the cube back.

What can I say? I'm an old-fashioned kind of guy.

Which reminded me—I still owed Nancy supper. I wasn't sure if she still wanted to talk to me after last night but it was worth a try. It would give the black guy something to tell Baxter. Steele may be a relic but he has a hot girlfriend.

Nancy answered on the second ring. She sounded like she'd been asleep but she always sounds that way on the phone, her voice husky and slow like syrup being poured over ice cream. She didn't seem too upset with me.

"You owe me big time," she purred. "And I intend to collect."

I liked the sound of that. She said she'd be over in half an hour. I asked her if she was hungry and she said she was—and she wouldn't mind having supper too.

Maybe I'm shallow but I felt my spirits rise as I clattered around the kitchen, trying to figure what I could whip together out of the odds and ends of last weekend's grocery run. I settled on a frittata, the one dish you can serve morning, noon or night, depending on what you chop into it. Asparagus, peppers, chorizo and shredded jalapeño cheddar made it supper. Served with salad and a glass of white wine under the light of a couple of cheap candles might even make it a romantic supper.

Nancy arrived almost exactly thirty minutes later—another one of her virtues. She was wearing a little red number and a pair of fuck-me pumps that showed off her long legs and suggested all was indeed forgiven. I thought I showed great restraint by still insisting on supper. She looked doubtful when I presented her with an omelet but her attitude changed once she bit into it. I really only cooked four things well and frittata was my specialty.

After I poured us a second glass of wine, we retired to the living room sofa for a little preview of the main event. Nancy is a pretty good kisser and I like to think I'm no slouch either so it was a few minutes before we came up for air. I was ready to move on but I could tell from the expression on Nancy's face that she wanted to talk.

I wasn't sure how I felt about that. I was pretty sure she didn't want to discuss the weather, the décor of my bedroom or the latest Hollywood holo-flic. She probably wanted to discuss what happened last night with Dorothy. Though that wasn't the worst possible topic.

"Tell me about your son, Frank."

That was.

I sort of grunted and looked away, hoping she would figure out Josh wasn't something I wanted to talk about right now. She likely knew that but thought it would be good for me. People always think they know what's good for me. They're usually right but I never let that influence me.

"Dorothy said you and Joshua didn't get along."

I knew better but I was desperate.

"I can't discuss Joshua Steele with you. He's part of an active investigation."

"Jesus, Frank, that's cold. You're his father."

"I'm also the cop in charge of that investigation."

"Don't be a cop, Frank. Not now. Talk to me. I want to help."

I liked Nancy but I hardly knew her. Not really. Maybe if it had been Dorothy I could have done it. Stammered out my pain and anger. Found some way to express the loss I felt, the love I felt. Not that Dorothy would have asked, not after all we'd been through.

"I can't. Please, I can't." I couldn't look at her, didn't want her to see the tears that were starting to blur my vision.

"You can," Nancy said. "Talk to me, Frank. I'm a good listener."

"That's what reporters do, right? They listen and then they report."

Words are like bullets and these ones found their target.

"Thanks for dinner, Frank." Her voice wasn't husky and slow now but quiet and brittle. "I can find my own way out."

I sat on the sofa with my head hung down over my folded hands and listened while she left.

"Don't call me," she said from the door of my apartment. A pause. "Don't call me until you're ready to stop being a cop and start being a man."

Words are like bullets.

| | |

I thought of giving Jack another try but decided drinking alone at home was not a good choice right now.

Drinking alone in a bar wasn't much better. But it might lead to better things.

David Ross—for whom I'd recently secured a posthumous Medal of Valour—used to have a needlepoint on his wall that said 'Arbeit macht frei.' I don't think David ever got the reference—I'd had to look it up myself. But this was a Hammer Ross kind of moment and maybe work *would* set me free. Something had to.

I threw on a black leather jacket that had been my father's. It was warm enough for March and was wind and water proof if the weather should change, which in Calgary was a regular occurrence. Besides it was a little big on me and didn't show the bulge of my shoulder holster. I'm not really a big fan of guns, given my history but wearing one had started to seem like a good idea lately. Who says a dog can't learn new tricks? I jammed my cell—in silent mode—in my pocket and headed down the stairs to the street.

Black Burly Man seemed to have fixed his car and driven off but it only took me a moment to spot his replacement, a tall skinny white man with bad skin and worse posture.

I walked briskly to a bar a few blocks from my apartment, quick enough that Mr. Pimples had a hard time keeping up without blowing his cover, not so fast he would call ahead for a replacement. Not yet.

The bar was called McCharles Place, no apostrophe, sort of an upscale Irish pub if that isn't an oxymoron. It wasn't a place where I normally drank, on those rare occasions I drank in public, but they knew me. Well enough not to ask questions or tell tales.

I didn't turn into the bar until I was almost past the door and once inside, I breezed through the lounge and into the kitchen. I nodded at the chef and ducked out of the back entrance into the alley. There was another restaurant across the alley, its back door ajar to let out the heat. They didn't know me there so I dug out my badge and flashed it at a couple of surprised looking cooks as I practically ran across the kitchen and through the swinging doors into the dining room. Luckily, there wasn't a waiter coming through from the other side.

My luck held as I came out of the restaurant. A cab was pulling up front. Before the couple waiting for it could board, I stepped in front of them and flashed them the badge I was still holding in my hand.

"Police business," I grunted. The guy wouldn't let go of the cab door. Maybe he was trying to impress his date or maybe he had no respect for the law. I showed him the inside of my coat and while he was staring my gun, I gave him a short jab to the solar plexus, not enough to knock him down but more than enough to take the fight out of him.

"Sorry," I said and gave him my best in-the-line-of-duty smile. Before he could reply, I slipped into the back seat and slammed the door. He was smart enough to remove his hand before I did.

The cab was one of the automated ones that had taken over most of the transit business once the city had finished the grid ten years back. It wouldn't go to some of the more colourful parts of town but I figured I'd had enough colour for one night anyway. Fortunately, this one took both cash and credit so I didn't have to worry about Baxter's men being able to trace my ID from my bank card.

I slipped a couple of fifties into the bill reader and gave it an address. The exercise had dulled my thirst. Maybe work was a better idea after all.

I leaned back in the seat and relaxed as the cab whisked me south and west to where Cerise Kavanah was waiting to answer my questions.

|||

I had the cab let me off a couple blocks away from the safe house. I wanted to make sure Baxter's people hadn't followed me despite my precautions. I took a circuitous route, keeping to the shadows as much as I could. Besides, I needed some time to think. Time to rebalance my inner detective.

Maybe Nancy was right. Maybe I needed to act more like a father than a cop. Maybe I would if I knew how. I don't think I was that great a dad even when we were a family and now seemed a little late to learn. Being a cop was all I had right now and for now it would have to do.

It would be time to be a father soon enough.

Barely two days had passed since I'd found my son in a dumpster but I'd been working on the case for more than three weeks. Six Borg dead during that time with the time between each death shrinking, typical profile for a serial killer. The first death had occurred roughly twenty-four days ago, with two more spaced eight days apart. The fourth had come four days after the third and Josh had been killed two days after that. The next day, Natasha Redding's boyfriend bought it up in Mount Royal.

There was something not right about that sequence but I couldn't quite see what it was. Other than the fact there should have already been another Borg death. Maybe there had been and I hadn't heard about it yet. But I doubted that.

Where did the attack on Buzz Wannamaker fit in?

Besides, there were too many things that didn't fit the profile. It was almost certainly true that we weren't looking for a single killer. The one eye-witness account we had—the attack on Buzz—said there had been three perps and Dr. Pham's analysis suggested that the other murders involved more than one attacker even if the killers were Borg. Lady Redding also thought there were multiple attackers. Serial killers occasionally had sidekicks, psychopaths insufficiently crazy to kill on their own but more than adept when teamed with another. The Bernardo-Homolka case from when I was a kid or the Xiang-Kauderer one ten years ago in Seattle came to mind but neither seemed a model for what I was seeing here.

Although stripping the bodies of all modifications might be considered a form of trophy taking, it was too systematic, too inclusive a fetish to ring true. I had dismissed the serial killer theory almost as soon as it was raised, if only because it was so popular with the press.

The two theories we'd discussed at the last staff meeting still seemed equally possible. Either we were witnessing a civil war among the Borg or their gang rivals, the Clean Boys, had acquired the means to carry out these attacks.

If it was the Borg, the motivations were political. Certainly, Redding's lover had been a high flyer in international Borg politics. But there was no indication that the others were more than minor players. Josh knew something of Borg aspirations and had cited one Borg leader in his last journal entry. I'd have to ask Buzz or Angel who that was. All Borg names sounded alike to me.

Still, Josh was new to the Borg community, an unlikely victim in an international political battle. None of the others had registered high on the activist scale, with some deaths on both sides of the fence. The exception was "Dick," as Natasha Redding called him, a leader in the more radical separatist movement in Brazil before the Jesuit crackdown. Of course, each murder might have been revenge for ones already committed. It was possible one group of Borg could have duplicated the method of killing carried out by another but I doubt they could have done it without inside info.

Leaks had always been a problem with the SDU. But why would the Borg bother being clandestine? If anything, a rival group would want their response to be open and obvious.

Or Dick's murder could have been by his own side who viewed his dalliance as the act of a traitor. But somehow that didn't add up.

No, I preferred the one set of killers model.

The Clean Boy theory wasn't any easier to accept. They had plenty of motive but, unless something had dramatically changed, never the means. They made lots of threats but, as Angel had pointed out, had seldom shown any real inclination to carry them out. The Borg gangs weren't very big but what the gangs lacked in size they more than made up for in terms of fire power and ferocity. The occasional incursion of other criminal elements into Borg territory had been met with swift and certain reprisal.

The Borg never took over the local underworld because most of the Borg had no interest in or involvement with criminal activities. If anything, despite the public fear their appearance seemed to generate, the Borg were less involved in crime than most sub-sections of Calgary society. Certainly none of the victims had obvious gang or criminal connections.

A general vendetta against all Borg elevated the matter out of simple gang rivalry. Not self-interest but ideology. The brutal removal of all that made a person Borg certainly had the marks of being a political statement.

What had changed in recent months that might have given the Clean Boys the upper hand?

Gale Conklin had returned to town and a secret project at a high tech firm had made my son afraid for his life.

And what connected those two events together?

I couldn't be certain but my instincts told me it was Cerise Kavanah. The answers to my questions were right around the next corner.

Then I heard the sound of gunfire.

Chapter 24

Getting out of the hospital had been easy though the doctors were surprisingly determined to keep him there. They seemed to think he was under arrest for some reason and had even called security. One guard tried to block his way, wielding his electroshock device as if it were a real gun. Three others bulked behind him, clutching their batons and trying to look like cops. It's surprising what some guys will do for fifty bucks an hour.

Tazers hurt, but Borg technology is well shielded so the jolt didn't even slow Wannamaker down.

He took a couple of quick steps toward the cluster of security blocking the exit to the ward, his arm extended, pincers clacking.

With his vocoder augmenting his voice into both the sub- and supersonic ranges, he said, "Prepare to be assimilated."

To give them credit, they hesitated, exchanging glances, while their leader pumped charge after charge into him. It was getting annoying so Wannamaker plucked the wireless electrodes from his chest and crushed them in his clawed hand. He let the mangled metal clatter to the floor and took another step.

"Holy shit!" said the guard bringing up the rear. His voice had the flat twang that marked him as a recent arrival from one of the religious enclaves from near the Alberta-Montana border. "They don't pay me enough to become no freaking Borg." He bolted back down the hall.

Their leader pulled the now useless trigger a couple more times. The broken electrodes on the floor sparked and jumped against the tile.

Wannamaker took one more step with arm extended.

"Resistance is futile," he said.

The three remaining guards scattered, running in every direction.

Wannamaker suppressed a laugh. *They probably won't stop,* he thought, *until they're safely back in their mothers' basements.*

Getting out of the hospital was easy. Getting into Singularity House was going to be another matter entirely.

Singh was waiting in front of the hospital, slouched behind the wheel of a low-slung vehicle almost invisible in the dim light between the street lamps. Wannamaker wasn't sure if he would have spotted him at all except for the white of his turban against the darkness.

"Was there a problem?" asked Singh as Wannamaker slid in beside him. The lights on the fourth floor were flickering red. A police cruiser pulled up in front of the main entrance to the hospital, its lights flashing but its engine and siren silenced.

"A slight misunderstanding," said Wannamaker. "We should go."

Singh adjusted some controls on the dash. The windows turned grey. A second later, the exterior view returned as an augmented digital display. Singh pulled the car into the street and slid into traffic. No one turned to watch them go.

"This new?" asked Wannamaker.

"It was delivered this morning," said Singh, grinning broadly. His teeth were whiter than his turban. "Full stealth technology. Shielded electric engine, sound absorbers in the tires, two-way projectors on the windows, light bending and radar absorbing exterior. I have to leave it on the grid and only partly masked when we're in traffic but once we're off the main road, we're practically invisible. Cost a bomb, but it's worth every penny."

Wannamaker had to think for a moment what that meant. Pennies hadn't been manufactured since before he was born. It was funny how some expressions; some scraps of culture persist long after the meaning is lost. Probably none of those guards could name a single one of the captains of the Enterprise but they all remembered the Borg. Race memory, or in that case, racist memory.

Singh exited the Deerfoot two ramps before the one that led to the industrial park that held their target. He removed the car from the grid and took them in a roundabout route to within two blocks of Singularity House. Singh touched the blue gem in the centre of his turban and the headgear went from white to dark grey. He grinned at Wannamaker and gestured for him to get out. Then he pulled into an alley and parked tight against the wall of an abandoned warehouse.

Singh dug a couple of coveralls and a suitcase out of the trunk of the car. He pulled on one pair and handed the other to Wannamaker who looked at it dubiously. Singh unloaded the weapons from the case, handing one to his partner and shoving the other three in his own pockets. He replaced the case and put the car into lock-down. When it was finished, the car was indeed practically invisible, bending the light from objects behind it so it seemed they were looking at nothing but pavement and brick walls.

"You can still see it in the UV end of the spectrum," said Singh. "And of course someone might walk into it, though they'd feel it more than hear the collision."

Wannamaker knew Singh had gotten a big buy-out from National Asian when he was asked to leave. At times like these, he was surprised they hadn't simply paid a pro to kill him. It would certainly have been cheaper and they wouldn't have had to worry about him ever revealing corporate secrets.

He must have a guardian angel. Wannamaker felt a pang. He had tried to reach Angel on the drive down. Still, no response. Still, no messenger. It wasn't like her; it wasn't like any Borg, to be out of touch for so long.

He should be looking for Angel. And he would be, if it were only Singh who wanted him to do this job. But this was for Frank. This was for Frank's son.

Singh adjusted the tabs on his coveralls and they shifted from dull green to a spackle of light and dark grey that shifted as he moved. They had some version of the same technology that was masking the car. Singh wasn't quite invisible but he had a tendency to slip from view unless you were looking right at him.

Wannamaker grunted and got dressed. Singh showed him how to initiate the camouflage system and operate the built-in communication device.

"It's tight-band line-of sight transmission. Almost unbugable. There's a backup radio in case we get separated but only use it if you have to and then only in short bursts. It's encrypted but detectable," said Singh, as he adjusted the mike against Wannamaker's throat. "It will pick up sub-vocalizations and deliver them here." He tapped the bud in his ear. "No sound leakage so you don't have to worry about being overheard."

Wannamaker nodded and inserted the speaker into his unaugmented ear. He adjusted the range of his artificial one, high enough to prevent surprises but not so high as to be distracting. He shifted his right eye into the infrared and the street flared into sudden visibility. Singh showed as nothing more than background radiation.

They walked the last few blocks to Singularity House, seeing no one and, hopefully, not being seen. The exterior of the building was dark though both the front door and the loading dock were lit. Half a dozen vehicles parked in the lot across the street from the front entrance suggested the building wasn't completely unoccupied, despite the fact it was now after ten o'clock.

There was a guard in the station near the loading dock but he appeared to be asleep or deeply engrossed in the screen flickering in front of him. If there were any other entrances, they weren't immediately obvious.

Wannamaker extended his vision far into both the ultraviolet and infrared ranges. In theory, his optical unit could detect both microwaves and X-rays but he'd never been able to figure out how to interpret the data it fed into his visual cortex. Mostly it gave him a headache. Singh was scanning the building with the device Wannamaker had designed, running it on its lowest setting so as not to be detected by the building's security.

They both spotted the back door at the same time. It showed as a faint outline in the low infrared, only half a degree warmer than the ambient temperature of the wall. The scanner showed low level emissions from across the EM spectrum, about what you might expect from a lab with a wide range of electronic devices in play.

The door was located on the south wall about halfway between the loading bay and the front of the building. It was narrow, slightly over half a metre, and only two metres high. An emergency exit, in case of an accident in the labs. Wannamaker signalled for Singh to stay put while he checked the north side of the building.

"There's another door on this side," he whispered over the comm. "No guard post to deal with."

Singh grunted acknowledgment and joined Wannamaker in the shadow of a dumpster. The stink of several days' garbage threatened to overwhelm them.

"What do you think?" asked Singh, his voice whispering in Wannamaker's ear.

"Shick spratz three ^—#," Wannamaker said under his breath. "Sorry, I said, I think on the whole I'd rather be in Philadelphia."

"I don't know what that means," said Singh, "but I think I agree."

"We can either both go this way and cover each others back," said Wannamaker. "Or we could each take a door and meet in the middle."

"There is safety in numbers," said Singh, "but I think we're way past playing it safe. I'll take the south side. You go in this way."

"What about the guard?"

"You of all people should know, you have to trust your technology." Singh pulled the hood of the coverall over his head and sprinted toward the fence. He was invisible against the lines of light and dark that striped the street.

Wannamaker watched him for a moment then followed, his mods on full silent mode. Singh jumped when Wannamaker appeared beside him and rested his hand on his shoulder. The scanner indicated a signal running along the outer fence and together they connected two adjacent fence poles with a wire and modulator so the signal would appear unbroken when they cut through the fence. Singh pulled the chain link together and Wannamaker ran his pincer from top to bottom, shearing through the metal like scissors through lace. The faint ping of parting metal barely rose above the noise of the traffic from the nearby highway.

The second fence had no security channel running through it. They must have figured fifty thousand volts was security enough. Only three of the six lines of barbed wire were juiced. It was easy to tell the live ones by the faint hum they gave off. Installing a bridge was a little trickier but only because making a mistake wouldn't set off an alarm; it would throw them across the street.

Singh had five metres of light weight cable with high-tension grips at either end slung over his shoulder. He pointed at the middle wire and then counted down from three but Wannamaker kept his eyes on Singh's wrist, releasing his own grip in time to the movement of the other man's muscles. They made the connection without a single spark. Wannamaker clipped the single live wire and the dead ones on either side of it and the two men slipped onto the grounds of Singularity House.

Singh gave the 'eyes open' gesture as if he were the star of some old spy movie and sprinted around the front of the building, avoiding the well-lit front door as best he could.

"See you on the inside," he whispered, before disappearing around the side of building.

I guess we have to get in, thought Wannamaker, *before we can break out*. He slipped through the darkness to the faint red outline of the door.

| | |

Getting in undetected was easy compared to staying that way once inside. Wannamaker crouched at the top of the stairwell which, according to the information Frank had passed on to Singh, led down to the lab where 'The Project' was being carried out.

He adjusted the pick-up on his Borg ear, tuning out certain frequencies and raising the gain on a few narrow bands. The sound of footsteps and breathing flooded his aural centres. There were eight, maybe nine, people moving around in the lower level, plus two more, probably security guards, pacing through the upper one.

"Chief." Wannamaker risked a quick burst on the radio.

"Yup."

"Nine down, two up."

"Go," said Singh, confirming that he too was in position to enter the lower level.

Wannamaker reset his ear to normal plus and started down the stairs, pulling the access door tight behind him. They hadn't planned on the facility being this busy. Fortunately, the traffic seemed to be at the far end of the building from the lab he and Singh had come to search.

The door at the foot of the stairs was equipped with magnetic locks and a security keyboard. Wannamaker pried the panel loose and inserted a probe. A scanner, similar to the one he had built for Singh, was embedded in his arm and it only took a few moments for it to identify the six digit code to unlock the door. *Maybe we should try to get a security contract with these guys when all this is done*, thought Wannamaker. *They need a serious upgrade*. The door locks released. Wannamaker replaced the security panel and slipped through into the hall beyond.

Singh was a faint blur smeared across the wall outside the Project lab. Not exactly invisible but a preoccupied scientist might not notice until it was too late.

"So far so good," Singh's voice whispered in his ear.

"Isn't that what the optimist said halfway between the bridge and the water?"

Like most people, Singh didn't appreciate his humor.

"Do we have company?" Singh asked.

Wannamaker gestured for Singh to be quiet and twisted the control on his earlobe. Beneath the sudden roar of the ventilation system, he could hear the cacophony of voices arguing and the jangle of routine work. He lowered the volume to alert levels.

"Sounds like a staff meeting going on at the far end of the building. Two people are working in the lab two doors down. This one sounds clear."

Singh tried the door but it didn't open. Singh inserted a thin wire into the lock. There was a soft whirr.

Wannamaker looked up and down the hallway. Nothing had changed. He followed Singh into the lab.

Singh had described the lab based on what Frank had told him. It looked much the same, minus the presence of a young black girl. There was still a chair in the corner, one of three scattered around the room. The gurney was now shoved against one wall but the instruments were still gathered around the place it must have been when Joshua Steele had seen it.

At one end of the lab were several rows of computer towers, sheathed in coolant blankets. They had to be nano-chips if they were running that hot or maybe even optical processors, enough of them to run a small country. Wannamaker stretched his perceptions to the edges of comprehension. Faintly glowing ionized gas showed a maze of high energy lasers connecting the stacks in a complex web. If this was what he suspected it was, Joshua was right. This was bigger than people imagined.

No, that wasn't quite right. Plenty of people had imagined it. These people had built it.

His mind raced, following all the paths of possibility, both for good or ill. A hundred scenarios played themselves out, a hundred more died still-born.

This information wanted to be free. Wannamaker felt a nearly over-whelming urge to liberate it, to broadcast what he had seen and guessed as far and as wide as his built-in transceiver could reach. Someone would hear.

People needed to know, that was true. But not now, not from here. This was not the time. It could not lead to a positive result, not for him, not for Singh, maybe not for anyone. Wannamaker took a deep breath and willed his mind to stop racing, invoked the mental disciplines he had learned as an adult that his childhood self had rejected.

Singh kept watch on the door unaware of the myriad thoughts and feelings that had raced through Wannamaker's mind. He had an electroshock device in one hand and a gun in the other. Wannamaker wondered how he would decide which to use if someone walked in on them.

Wannamaker left the computers and went to the circle of instruments that had almost certainly been used on Cerise Kavanah and maybe on others as well. He wondered how many had suffered on that gurney and what had happened to them after.

Wannamaker had seen a lot during his eight years as a cop, a lot of which he preferred to forget. These gadgets would help with that. Some of the machines were standard medical remotes, designed to perform surgery under the guidance of absent doctors or sophisticated software. Others were more sinister.

Wannamaker ran his artificial hand along the length of one stainless steel armature, resisting the urge to crush it in his pincers. It was the delivery arm for a Bug, more delicate and sophisticated than any he had seen before but there was no mistaking the basic shape or the nature of the electrodes at the end of the tapering arm. This had been used to insert a patch into the brain of Cerise Kavanah, possibly damaging her for the rest of her life.

But there were other devices he didn't recognize, which, for a Borg, was disconcerting. They were less polished in design, appearing almost makeshift or jury-rigged. They had probably been built on-site, Singularity House's contribution to the break-through that had been both long-sought and much-feared.

One device was a square box with a flexible arm extending from either side. At the back were several data ports, designed for optical transmission, probably similar to the laser links between the computer stacks. One of the arms ended in a number of instruments that appeared to be standard life sign monitoring devices. The other had a football helmet attached to it, with half a dozen fiber optic cables penetrating the shell. The entire thing was sheathed in the same liquid helium coolant blankets that wrapped the computer towers. It looked like a combination of an early portable magnetic resonance imager and a superconducting quantum interference device. Wannamaker had seen both an MRI and a SQUID in a science museum when he was a boy but this combo was both more compact and more sophisticated than either.

The interior of the helmet was lined with a fine metal mesh of what looked to be platinum. Layered over the mesh, a pale fog of nano-chips and optical diodes surrounded a few dozen thin metal probes. Each contained a small laser device and was tipped with a surgical drill.

They hadn't used this device on the girl—there had been no holes drilled into her skull—but he was sure it had been used on someone. Whether or not that use had been successful was the billion dollar baby.

"Incredible, isn't it?"

The Borg must have been working in an adjacent lab. He was in silent mode, with audio dampeners on full and EM shielding in place. Any sounds he had made as he glided in behind Wannamaker had been masked by the gentle hum of the lab equipment.

He was the most modified Borg that Wannamaker had ever seen. Both arms had been replaced with multi-tool devices and his legs ended in curved back steel springs. His torso bulked thick with armour or augments or both. Both eyes and one ear were Borg and a chrome skull cap had been fitted over his cranium. Only the lower half of his face, of the same brown hue as Wannamaker's own though considerably more lined, remained unchanged. This was not a Borg Wannamaker had met or even heard of in the tight-knit Calgary community. He was either a newcomer or had lived his life in seclusion.

Singh was turning, the arm holding the real gun coming up fast. *I guess that's how he decides,* thought Wannamaker, *shocks for normals, bullets for Borg.*

"Please don't," said the Borg, his vocoder stripping all hint of emotion and accent from his voice. An accompanying pulse of highly compressed code vibrated Wannamaker's transceiver: facts, opinions, layers of emotions, speculations, hard truths, identifiers, diagrams. It was more data than he could process immediately but he got the gist of it at once.

"Dr. Siqueira Silva is not a threat to us, Darwhal," said Wannamaker. Singh's finger loosened on the trigger, though he kept the gun pointed at Siqueira Silva's head.

"If you say so, Buzz," said Singh. "Doctor Sick…?"

"You can call me Silva, if that's easier," said Siqueira Silva. He smiled broadly, revealing a jumble of tobacco-stained teeth. His modifications didn't run to dental work. "We don't have much time. The guards will make their rounds in six minutes. If you are not gone by then, they will kill you." He glanced at the surrounding medical equipment. "Or do something worse."

"They can try," said Singh. He pocketed the electroshock device and produced a small rocket launcher from inside his coverall.

"Impressive," said Siqueira Silva. "Mr. Singh, isn't it? Between your armaments and Mr. Wannamaker's arm, you make a formidable team. However, the guards here have advantages of their own and, frankly, they are better equipped. Now, listen. I've already given your partner as much information as I can, but it will take him some time to process it. We now have five minutes."

Singh nodded. Wannamaker resisted the urge to delve into the information Siqueira Silva had sent him. He needed all his senses on full alert.

"I was hired," said Siqueira Silva, "by the founder of this company, Erich Carpentier, to work on a project. It was a project near and dear to my heart and to the hearts of many Borg. I have been a Borg for a long time, for almost as long as there have been true Borg. This project was to be the next step in my evolution.

"But Erich lied to me. Perhaps he had been lied to by someone else. It doesn't matter. This Project, of which my work was a small part, is a subversion of all I believe in. It is not being pursued for the greater good but for the interests of a selfish few."

"Welcome to the twenty-first century," said Singh.

"Spare me your cynicism. My generation invented it." Siqueira Silva gestured for them to follow him. He led the way behind the computer stack into a small adjacent lab. There were no other exits. Singh hesitated at the entrance. "If the guards come early, they may not discover us here. In any case, you will be no worse off."

"Maybe you should run the final reel, Doctor," said Wannamaker. He glanced around the lab. It was mostly empty, other than a set of metal and glass cylinders on the work bench closest to the entry. Cables ran from them through the wall into the other lab.

Siqueira Silva paused, then nodded.

"I was not kept 'in the loop' as we used to say in my day," he said. "None of us were. Not even Grigg knew all the details. We all worked on our own separate piece of the puzzle with little communication or collaboration. That was how they could do what they did."

"How did you get into the loop?" asked Singh.

"Joshua Steele," said Siqueira Silva. "He stumbled on part of the truth, figured out most of the rest. He was a very intelligent young man. He left me a message."

"How and what?" Singh had told Wannamaker about the journal Steele had kept but somehow he doubted Siqueira Silva had been watching a holo-projection.

"As to how, I'm not entirely sure. I went to bed early on Tuesday night. I was awakened shortly after midnight by a particularly vivid dream. If I had been awake it would undoubtedly have taken the form of a visual hallucination—a bi-product of direct EM stimulus of the optical implant. I had never been in this lab before—my work is carried out in a separate section of the building—but I suddenly knew of its existence and what it contained. And I knew that soon, someone would be coming to investigate. I had been sent a message in a way that only a Borg could receive it. Though at the time I had no idea who had sent it. So I've been coming here as often as I could to discover what I could in hope of your arrival."

He gestured at the six metal and glass cylinders. They looked identical, about sixty centimetres high and thirty in diameter, made of stainless steel and translucent crystal panels. Lights pulsed in seemingly random patterns behind the crystal of four of the cylinders. The other two were dark. There were no controls or instruments on the outside of the cylinders, only a single cable coming out the back and a pair of optical ports in the front. In the centre of the workbench, a black box squatted, adorned with half a dozen knobs and as many dials.

"These are storage devices of a sort, though unlike any you will find on the market. They operate using high energy lasers traveling along nanometer sized channels. They encode using photons rather than electrons. The advantages in terms of data compression and the complexity of interconnectivity are enormous. Each of these units is capable of storing all the information contained in the human brain, with capacity to spare. They don't have its real-time processing power, of course, but they don't need it to achieve their purpose."

"Why are you telling us all this? I thought we were under a time constraint here," Singh said. He had put away his weapons but now took them out again.

"Yes. The two minute drill. As I said, Wannamaker already has the details. I don't know what the first three of these devices hold but the fourth contains information, information uploaded by Joshua Steele at great risk to himself."

"He was murdered for it," said Wannamaker.

"There are worse risks than death," said Siqueira Silva. "It is not information as you normally think of it—facts and figures. It contains those, of course, but much more, feelings, fragments of personality, bits of Joshua himself, uploaded directly from his brain. Stored there now, the only thing left of him in the world.

"To answer your question, Mr. Singh. They murdered Joshua Steel, they murdered—a burst of Borg-speak—and others, too, I know now. This was not meant to be about death but about life."

"Life everlasting," whispered Wannamaker.

Siqueira Silva didn't say anything for a long moment. "I can only decipher part of it from here. To do more would require risks I'm not quite ready to take. And I am afraid it would destroy the record he left. But it was enough. They must be stopped. I don't overestimate my own abilities in that regard. I will do what I can from here. You must do the rest. Now go."

Too late.

"What the hell?" boomed a voice from the main lab.

Chapter 25

There weren't a lot of Kavanahs listed by any of the Calgary search engines, only twelve sets of listings in all, and Cerise soon had them displayed on the monitor in her room. There might be some unlisted ones but this was a start.

Most people these days had their own personal call number but some people had more than one. Mr. Singh had told her that she had both a mother and a father plus two brothers. So the family cluster should contain at least five numbers, unless her brothers were too young to have their own.

Three sets of listings had at least five numbers, a total of nineteen, but she didn't recognize any of the names, and some of them were only listed as initials anyway. Why hadn't she asked Mr. Singh her mother's name?

She hesitated for a long while before trying them. It would be so embarrassing to call complete strangers and ask them if they remembered having a daughter. Not that there was likely to be anything wrong with their memories. Just hers.

Don't be such a girl, Cerise thought, *you're a tigress. Tigers don't get embarrassed, or if they do they never let it stop them.*

"Dinner will be ready in fifteen minutes," called a voice through the door. "Get washed and come down to the dining room when you're ready."

It was now or never.

One of the names, Sonia, clearly belonged to a woman and another, Lawrie, could be either gender. She knew that women were more likely than men to list their names as initials—that added five more possibilities. That would be a good start. She started with Sonia.

She had already reprogrammed the phone to by-pass the security protocols. She adjusted the settings for narrow visual broadcast. The recipients would be able to see her face but little else.

She dialed Sonia's number. A few seconds later a white woman with shockingly red hair answered. She stared at Cerise suspiciously.

"Who are you and what do you want?" she asked, her voice raspy.

"Sorry," Cerise said. "Wrong number."

It *was* embarrassing.

Lawrie's number was no longer in service.

Cerise looked at the five remaining numbers. Maybe she should go down to dinner. Mr. Singh or Superintendent Steele must know what was best when they put her here. Maybe she should call and ask them to contact her mother.

She punched in another code. The one for B Kavanah.

A black woman answered the phone. Cerise didn't recognize her face, though it seemed the right age and shape.

"Hello...Oh, my God! Cerise, honey baby, is that you? Oh, my God!"

"Mom?" Cerise asked.

"Where are you, darling?" the woman—her mother!—asked.

"I don't really know, Mom." She hadn't paid much attention on the drive from the hospital, too wrapped up in her own misery to care.

"Now, you must have some idea," said her mother. There was someone moving around in the background but her mother had her phone on narrow view too. Cerise couldn't tell who else was there.

"In a police, um, house. Somewhere south of downtown." Cerise hesitated. She couldn't be sure who was with her mother. Maybe it was the person who had betrayed her. "Maybe southeast."

"I see. And are there police officers there too?"

"I guess. A couple. Superintendent Steele dropped me off himself. He said I'd be safe here."

"Of course. We all want you to come home, Cerise."

Cerise wasn't sure if that was true. Someone close to her had betrayed her. She was sure of that at least. "Soon, Mom. I'll be home soon. I wanted to see your face. Wanted to let you know I was okay. Maybe I can call you later. When you're alone and have time to talk."

Her mother nodded. "I think I understand. Yes, I think I do. Is there a number I can call you?"

"No, this cell only makes outgoing calls," Cerise said. *It wouldn't be hard to change that setting, too, but I don't know who else might be there*, she thought. *If they knew how to reach me they might figure out where I was.*

"The boys are going to a hockey game tonight," said her mother. "Call me after eight. We can talk for a—"

The line cut off. She checked the battery but it was still fully charged. Maybe she had missed one of the protocols. Maybe someone in the safe house had detected the call and cancelled it.

"Seven o'clock. Dinner's ready," said a male voice through the door. "Get it while it's hot."

Her stomach growled again. She needed food if not the company that went along with it. She erased the immediate evidence of her web search from the monitor and replaced the security protocols. Years of hiding her diary and netchats from snoopy brothers had made her quite adept at covering her tracks. She restored the CNN feed. The Americans had asked the Chinese and Europeans for help but neither had yet replied.

The phone was another matter. If they knew she was making unauthorized calls, they might take it away or reduce its functionality. Of course if the call had been interrupted by automatic systems no one would know until they checked the logs. She looked around the room but there was no place to hide the phone that couldn't be uncovered by the briefest of searches.

Maybe I should keep it with me, she thought. She shut the phone down, disabling all functions so it wouldn't show up on security scans. The zippers on the jacket would mask the phone from metal detectors. The cell was one of the ultra-thin models but still showed as a bulge in the tight side and breast pockets. There were also pockets in each arm right below the shoulder. The arms and shoulders were padded, which she hoped might disguise the bulge of the phone. But the pockets were a centimetre too shallow; when she tried to force the phone into the narrow space in the left arm she heard fabric ripping.

"Crap!" she said under her breath. She reached into the pocket to see how much damage she had done. Someone had replaced the bottom of the pocket with a thin strip of Velcro. She pried it apart and found a second larger pocket hidden in the shoulder padding. She slid the phone inside and then pressed the Velcro closed again from the outside. *There,* she thought, *my guardians won't be able to find it without an X-ray.*

There was a soft tap at the door. "Are you alright, Denise?" asked Cathy. "We're waiting supper for you."

Cerise slipped her feet into her sneakers and opened the door.

Cathy's eyebrows rose a bit when she saw Cerise and she gave a lopsided grin.

"I'd forgotten that jacket," she said.

"It's really sprag, isn't it?" If she was going to look like a wannabe, she should talk like one too.

"Hmm," said Cathy and led the way downstairs.

There were five people sitting at the dining room table, four men and a woman. She had met the woman, Olivia, an Asian woman in her thirties or early forties, and three of the men, Parker, a rugged looking white man, who, she was pretty sure, was also a cop, as well as fellow guests, Taroc and Matt, both white and under thirty. The fourth man, heavyset and light brown in complexion, was introduced as Whiteduck.

No one, it seemed, had last names and, of course, like Denise, all the names could be false. But Cerise felt happy to be able to look someone in the face and call them by name. She hadn't been able to do it with her mother. All she knew was that her name started with B.

Cerise felt a wave of sadness and anger crash over her. Why had they done this to her?

"Are you all right, Denise?" asked Whiteduck, his voice soft and low.

"Hunger pangs," she said, as she slid into the only empty chair. "Sorry to keep you all waiting."

"Yeah," grunted Taroc, reaching for one of the covered pots in the middle of the table.

Whiteduck cleared his throat and Taroc sighed but pulled back his hand. The older man bowed his head. Without thinking, Cerise bowed hers as well and reached out to take the hands of Cathy and Matt who were sitting on either side of her.

"We give thanks to the Creator who made us all and in whose gaze we are safe," said Whiteduck. "Let us welcome Denise into our new family by breaking this bread and sharing this water." He paused for a moment.

It wasn't the prayer that echoed faintly in her own thoughts but it felt right, it felt normal.

"Amen," said Taroc.

"Amen," echoed the other voices around the table. Whiteduck smiled softly and nodded at Taroc.

Supper consisted of pot roast, cooked in red wine with potatoes, carrots and onions. There was also plenty of green salad and a heaping bowl of steamed rice. A vegetable and cheese casserole had been prepared for Olivia and Matt, who didn't eat meat, though everyone else was welcome to a small portion of what was left after the two vegetarians had loaded their plates.

"Enjoy your one free meal," said Taroc. "Tomorrow you go on kitchen detail with the rest of us."

Cerise took a small serving of everything on offer. The food smelled delicious and Cerise's stomach suddenly rumbled, loud enough for everyone to hear. She felt her face grow hot.

"As chief cook and bottle washer," said Whiteduck, "I take that as a compliment."

Everyone laughed gently and Cerise felt a wave of gratitude to the older man for deflecting everyone's attention from her.

She didn't remember ever feeling this hungry. *Of course,* she thought, *it's not like you can remember all that much anyway.*

But that wasn't true. She remembered lots of things. It was the pattern that was missing, the narrative of her life. She remembered the taste of beef perfectly well. The taste and the smell and—

It was her father's favourite. Roast beef was her father's favourite food. Although they lived in the middle of cattle country, they couldn't afford beef often, but once a month her father would bring home a small roast and cook it himself. In the traditional style, he used to say, laughing, complete with gravy and Yorkshire pudding, just like they used to serve in Bermuda when I was a boy.

Her father's name was Cris and he was always laughing. And every night he came into her room before bed and told her how much he loved her, how proud he was of her, his shining star. Her father would never have let anyone hurt her. He would never betray her.

Her father's name was Cris and her mother's name was Bea. Her father loved roast beef and was always laughing. He would carve the small roast and serve it up to them one at a time, first, to her mother. She could see him do it, see him pass the plate to her mother, see her take it, see her face as she smiled up at her father.

Her face. She could see her mother's face. And it wasn't the face of the woman on the phone.

Cerise stood up from the table. A wave of dizziness carried her to the floor.

When she woke up, she was lying on her bed, fully clothed, except for her jacket which was nowhere in sight. The clock over the desk said nine-ten. She sat up on the bed. She had to call Frank Steele.

Then an alarm went off. Seconds later, gunfire crackled and someone in the house below cried out in pain.

Chapter 26

Sanchez preferred to work alone. It kept his options open. But there was something about Yankovy's careful circumlocution that generated a frisson of—not fear, exactly, but its close cousin. He walked back to where Caleb Jones was still struggling over Yankovy's research project.

"Are you up for a drive in the country, Caleb?"

"Is that a rhetorical question or a direct order, Inspector?" asked Jones.

Sanchez smiled. "Think of as an invitation to test your theories in the field."

Jones shrugged. He shut down two of the computers and coded security locks into the other four, leaving the programs running with the displays turned off.

Jones grabbed his cell and gun from the desk drawer and took his police jacket off the hook on the wall.

"You have any street clothes?" asked Sanchez.

"In the ready room."

"We need to stop there anyway to pick up some armour," said Sanchez.

Jones raised his eyebrows at that but unhooked his badge from his jacket and clipped it to his belt.

Sanchez traded his trench coat for a slightly bulkier model lined with woven plastisteel, that ran from his shoulder to halfway down his thigh. Not as effective as close fitting armour but more stylish.

Jones opted for a heavy vest cinched tight against his torso. It fit easily under the fur-trimmed leather coat that he pulled from his locker.

"Nice coat," said Sanchez.

"Russian army surplus," said Jones. "Inspector Yankovy told me where to get it. Said it made him feel more at home."

"What are you carrying?" asked Sanchez.

"Standard issue .45"

Sanchez carried one of those himself as a backup strapped to his leg. He had an old Walther P99 in a holster on his hip. His weapon of choice was an Israeli-made 9mm with computer-assisted aiming and accelerated armour-piercing rounds. The gun was barely legal in Canada; the ammo definitely wasn't—illegal and untraceable according to his supplier. In Sanchez's view the law of the jungle superseded every other jurisdiction.

He went to the arms cabinet, keyed in his authorization and then leaned forward for a retinal scan. He selected a high-powered Beretta, three ammo clips and a couple of concussion grenades. He handed them to Jones.

"The countryside can be a dangerous place."

Jones didn't reply. He shoved the Beretta in his holster and put the .45 and the grenades into one of the coat's deep pockets.

Sanchez requisitioned an unmarked car from the garage and it was waiting for them in the parkade when they stepped out of the elevator. It was hardly a thing of beauty, a low-slung dirty-grey sedan with more than a few dents and dings, but it had bullet-proof side-panels and windows and its battery was fully charged. There were a couple of heavy-duty slug-throwers in the trunk in case things got really rough.

He thought of signing out something more formidable but decided he was letting his natural caution get the better of him. Yankovy had given no indication they were driving to a fire fight. But he had been careful not to say where he was even over an encrypted line.

He waved Jones away from the driver's side and climbed behind the wheel. He'd let the grid take them to the edge of the city but would take over himself once they hit the highway north. Past Airdrie, he would take highway 72 east until he reached the 9. A few miles south of that was the pseudo-meat factory where Yankovy presumably was waiting for him. It wasn't the most direct route but, given the Russian's caution, maybe directness wasn't a virtue.

Forty-five minutes later, they turned down a narrow paved lane that led to the Eco-Carne plant. According to the brochure he'd downloaded into his palmtop, the operation was almost completely automated. 'The succulent pseudo-beef is produced free from contamination in immaculate stainless steel vats, untouched by human hands.' The Cattlemen's Association had been fighting a five-year battle to keep the adjective 'pseudo' as part of the product's name even though genetically the meat produced was identical to the cattle they raised in the massive feedlots that dominated the east and south of Alberta.

There would only be one or two technicians on duty along with a well-armed private patrol that protected the plant from those whose abhorrence of 'franken-foods' motivated them to do more than simply sign petitions and carry protest signs during Vegan Day at the Stampede.

The plant was a four-story metal clad tower, flanked by a couple of taller silos containing the feedstock for the vats. Several two-story attachments housed freezers and warehouses for the final product. A wide lane led up to a large set of loading doors. Sanchez stopped in front of the chain-link fence that surrounded the entire operation. The buildings and yard were well-lit by several banks of flood lights. The city by-laws against light pollution obviously didn't extend to the surrounding counties.

The gate to the complex was wide-open and the guard house beside it appeared empty.

"This doesn't look good," said Jones.

Sanchez agreed. He slowly got out of the car and retrieved one of the shot guns from the trunk. He slipped a pair of thin carbon filament gloves on his hands, protection against both injury and identification. Jones followed suit.

"Cover me," he said, handing the shotgun to Jones.

Jones crouched behind the car while Sanchez ran to the corner of the guard house, bent low to present the smallest target possible.

If the empty guardhouse had looked bad, the two bodies spread on the ground behind it looked worse. Both were wearing full body armour but it hadn't done them any good when they were shot in the head. Someone they trusted or, at least, knew. Or perhaps a marksman hidden somewhere in the dark. Sanchez resisted the urge to rub his head. It wasn't like you could feel a targeting laser anyway.

Sanchez signalled for Jones to join him.

The younger cop didn't say a word. He pulled a pair of goggles out of the other pocket of the leather coat and clamped them on his head. He squatted with his back to Sanchez scanning the dark prairie landscape. After a moment, he turned and adjusted the settings on the goggles.

"There's nobody behind us for at least a kilometre," he said, "unless they're fully insulated and lying flat on their bellies. There's another security guard near the front door. I can't be sure from this distance but I think it might be Zerger from Vice. He moonlights with this outfit."

Sanchez nodded. Now he knew what Steele saw in this officer. Professional, cool under pressure, takes initiative, too. Sanchez hadn't had a regular backup for nearly three years. Maybe it was time to change that.

"Thoughts?" he asked.

"Could be Yankovy. I've got a feeling he's not exactly what he appears to be. Might be connected to the water supply case. It tastes like eco-radicals. Life is sacred and they don't care who has to die to prove it."

"In which case Inspector Yankovy could be in big trouble."

"Should we call for backup?"

"Wouldn't get here for twenty minutes. Besides we're out of our jurisdiction. Let's move."

Sanchez started forward. Jones stopped him with an arm on the shoulder.

"Got a flash. Top of the silo on the left." He handed Sanchez the goggles. There was someone there, barely visible in the shadow of the curving silo. He had a rifle. Sanchez pulled out his 9mm Special. A red dot appeared on Jones forehead. Sanchez pushed him aside; the soft whoosh of a passing bullet, followed by the smothered report of the gun. He pointed in the general direction of the shooter. The gun was a bit like a cursed sword; it couldn't be drawn without targeting the nearest human in its general line of sight. Sanchez pulled the trigger as soon as the computer-driven guidance system locked on. His gun barked and a moment later the figure flicked off the silo's wall and fell, twisting, onto the roof of the tower below.

"Nice shot," said Jones.

"I cheat," said Sanchez, already sprinting for the door of the complex.

He stopped to check the body spread-eagled in front of the entrance. It was indeed Zerger, still alive though his breath sounded ragged and thin. He had been shot twice, in the right leg above the knee and, more seriously on the right side of his neck. The bullet had entered from above, shattering his collarbone and lodging deep in his torso.

Shit. Life would have been simpler if Zerger was dead. He took out one of the disposable cells he always carried for moments like these and dialed the Royal Canadian Mounted Police dispatch. He reported shots fired at the Eco-Carne plant and hung up when they asked him his name. Then he triggered Zerger's emergency beacon and shoved the disposable phone in Zerger's vest pocket. Let the Horsemen figure it out.

Sanchez checked the time on his palm. 21:57. He set an alarm for thirteen minutes. He intended to be long gone by the time the Mounties arrived.

The door to the complex was ajar and he cautiously pushed it open. After a moment, he edged around the corner and scanned the interior. The door opened into a standard reception area, with a large desk in the middle and a small seating area to the right. There were doors in the rear wall, probably leading to offices and another to the left, giving access to the main plant. Both doors were closed. A thin line of light seeped under the plant entrance. Sanchez signalled the all-clear to Jones, who dashed across the compound to join him.

With Jones guarding the entrance, Sanchez worked his way to the door on the left wall. Before he could open it, Jones yelled. From outside came the low hum of an accelerating car and the hiss of tires spinning on gravel. By the time Sanchez got to the entrance, a black SUV was flying toward the main gate. He squeezed off a couple of rounds but they seemed to have no effect on the fleeing vehicle.

"Do you think there's any more of them inside?" asked Jones.

"I doubt it,' said Sanchez. "They've probably done whatever they came to do. But keep your head down anyway."

He and Jones moved to either side of the plant door and Sanchez pushed it open with his foot. Light spilled through the doorway. When it wasn't followed by gunfire, Sanchez rolled through the door while Jones covered him. He came out of the roll behind a stack of boxes.

"Police! Nobody moves, nobody gets hurt."

A security guard was lying in the middle of the floor in a large pool of his own blood.

On the side of one of the vats someone had scrawled in yellow paint the words, 'Soylent Green.' Sanchez typed the words into his palmtop and grimaced when the reference came up.

One of the technicians and what was left of the Russian were stacked at the base of a ladder, leading up to an open hatchway. There was a lot of blood but no sign of a second technician or of Yankovy's legs and right arm. Both men had been shot point blank in the heart with a small caliber revolver. The gun, along with a bloody fire ax, was beside the bodies. Sanchez doubted the weapon would be traceable. They might have better luck identifying the gunman on the roof, though that seemed doubtful as well. None of the evidence at the other environmental crime sites had led anywhere either.

Sanchez glanced up at the open hatch. He doubted he would be trying Eco-Carne's products any time soon. If the company survived the scandal. He suspected there would be a bunch of Mounties driving new cars by the morning, if the media hadn't intercepted his call to dispatch. He considered calling corporate PR himself but decided the payoff wasn't sufficient for the trouble of explaining his presence this far outside his jurisdiction, let alone his choice of weaponry.

He knelt by Yankovy's body and began to go through his pockets, starting with the remnants of his blood stained pants.

"What are you looking for?" asked Jones.

"I'll know it when I see it," said Sanchez.

The wallet held the usual identifications, a couple of credit chips and about a thousand dollars in Canadian cash. Walking around money. There was also about ten thousand in New Rubles. About a month's wages in the Russian Empire, though they wouldn't buy a cup of coffee in Calgary. There was a business card for Boynton Music Shoppe with a phone number on the back. Sanchez pocketed that and put the rest back in the wallet.

The other pants pockets held an assortment of coins, an unopened pack of gum and a set of car keys with a Calgary Police Department tag attached. He put those back as well and started on the jacket.

Inside pockets held a pair of reading glasses, Yankovy's passport, a silver flask that sounded half-full when he shook it and a coppery metal cube, less than a centimetre along each edge. It had no visible port and looked too small to fit any data reader Sanchez was familiar with but the lab might turn up something. Sanchez put it with the business card and replaced the rest.

Side pockets contained a pack of cigarettes and a disposable lighter, a clean handkerchief and a small coil notebook with a pencil shoved into the coil. Yankovy's neat script covered about six pages but it was in code, or more likely, Russian. Sanchez pocketed the notebook. He started to replace the other items but then opened the cigarette pack on a whim. There were six filtered smokes in one foil pouch, a single one with the filter broken off in the other. Sanchez carefully broke apart that cigarette. There was a thin silver wire hidden inside. He took an envelope from his own pocket and put the wire in it.

The breast pocket of both the jacket and shirt were empty, as was the hat that still perched on his head. Sanchez inspected Yankovy's throat and the area behind his ears for implants. If there were any they were too small or buried too deep for discovery by such a cursory inspection. Sanchez had no intention of further desecrating the man's body with impromptu surgery. Yankovy wasn't a friend but he was a fellow cop.

"Try his mouth," said Jones, "The Russians often put electronics in their bridgework."

"You're a wealth of information,' said Sanchez.

"It was something Inspector Yankovy said. Maybe he foresaw this moment."

Sanchez shuddered involuntarily. He pried open the dead man's mouth and tilted his head back so the overhead lights shone into the cavity. Yankovy's teeth were in pretty good shape for a Russian of his age, but the upper right side was solid metal. Sanchez grimaced but put his fingers into Yankovy's mouth and pried until the bridge came free. He was no expert but he didn't think dental work usually had serial numbers imprinted on their underside. He dropped the device in his pocket.

Sanchez stood up as the palmtop alarm went off.

"Time to go."

Three RCMP cruisers, an ambulance and a media van passed them barely a kilometre after they turned back onto the highway.

Chapter 27

I came around the corner at a dead run, pistol in one hand while the other fumbled for my pager. I pulled up short and ducked behind an old oak tree when I spotted the black van pulled up opposite the safe house where I had parked Cerise Kavanah. Baxter's crew had driven a black van but so did a lot of other people.

I jabbed the 'crime in progress' button on the pager and then thumbed the 'officer down' one for good measure. It wasn't technically true but might be by the time help arrived. If I was lucky and there was a car hanging around the community police station a few blocks away, it could be here in two minutes. More likely, I was looking at ten.

There were three of them, pouring round after round into the front of the safe house from a variety of high-powered weapons, including a Kalashnikov Mark VII. I had one of those myself and I knew the damage it could do.

It might have been a trick of the light but they seemed grotesque somehow, outsized and lumpy as if they had sacks of rocks strapped under their black suits. When they moved, it was jerky and fast, like stop-motion photography, not the smooth speed of the Borg.

Thugs on Stim. Conklin's goons.

Or worse. Not Borg but the killers of Borg.

There was answering fire from the house, the pop-pop-pop of small arms. I saw one of the attackers jerk and I was pretty sure he had taken a slug to the shoulder but it didn't seem to bother him much, only made him madder. He was either well armoured or impervious.

Great. Frank Steele against the Man of Steel.

There was a cry of pain from inside the house. Two of them ran for the front door while the one with the Kalashnikov laid down covering fire, holding the rifle with one hand, braced against his belly as if it had no recoil at all. In his free hand, he was holding a big silver revolver, maybe to take out anyone who tried to run. The other two moved faster than I thought humanly possible, sprinting the dozen metres to the house. They each grabbed one side of the door frame and tore it right out of the house.

There was still no sign of backup so I stepped from behind the tree and walked toward the guy with the assault rifle, squeezing off a round with every step. I was trying for head shots but either I needed to spend more time on the firing range or his skull was made of steel, too. He hardly glanced in my direction but flicked the revolver at me. I saw the muzzle flash before I felt the impact.

I don't know what ammo he was packing but it wasn't small. The last time I got hit that hard was my final game as a high school quarterback. Fortunately the Kevlar vest I'd taken to wearing a couple of months back provided better protection than my football jersey.

The slug threw me onto my back about six feet away. My chest hurt like hell but I didn't think anything was broken, though maybe I'd find out different once I was able to draw a breath again.

The shooting had stopped by the time I struggled back to a sitting position. The approaching sirens were still six blocks away. I'd dropped my gun somewhere so all I could do was watch as the two thugs came out of the now silent house. One of them had a body slung over his shoulder.

Between the speed they were moving and the lights dancing in front of my eyes, I couldn't be sure but it looked like Cerise Kavanah.

Chapter 28

Sanchez and Jones didn't talk during the drive back into town, both men lost in their own thoughts. Sanchez let the car drive while he watched the scroll of reports from dispatch. It was turning out to be a busy night though there was nothing about the assault on Eco-Carne. The Horseman didn't have the authority they once did but that didn't stop them from thinking they were better than other cops. They would only call on the local force as a last resort.

They had almost reached the city limits when the 'officer down' call came in from Frank Steele's pager. The GPS said he was somewhere in Calgary's southwest.

"Should we respond?" asked Jones. The man sounded bone weary but willing.

Sanchez considered it for a moment. The SDU survived in the Force by protecting each other. Finally, he shook his head. "There are already three units on the way. By the time we got there it would be all over."

Jones looked doubtful but nodded.

"Do you need any help back at headquarters, sir?"

Sanchez shook his head. He was beginning to trust the man but wasn't quite ready to take him completely into his confidence. If need be, he could override the security codes on Jones's workstation.

"Take your time coming in tomorrow," said Sanchez. "And if you need to talk about what went down tonight, call me." He gave Jones his private access code. "Do you need a lift home?"

Jones was stripping off his body armour, placing it and the requisitioned weapons in the back seat. "Thanks, no, drop me at the next C-train station. I'll be fine."

Sanchez doubted that was entirely true. Good cops are never really fine with death—especially that of a colleague—but it wouldn't help if he pushed the matter.

||||

Headquarters was largely empty this time of night. The civilian staff was long gone and the cleaners wouldn't arrive for hours. Most of the on-duty cops were patrolling the streets, part of the Chief's new "Visible Presence, Rapid Response" approach to policing. Viper, as it

182

was known, was popular both with the press and with the rank-and-file cops. More importantly, it was popular with the politicians who had seen a reduction in both crime and cost. Of course, measured against the unprecedented spike in violent incidents the year before, maybe Viper was doing less than it appeared. Numbers said what you wanted them to say.

Sanchez took the stairs two steps at a time, trying to burn off nervous energy from the night's activities. The SDU's outer precincts were dark when he entered them though there was a light on in Steele's office. The door was open but Steele himself wasn't inside. Someone must have been there recently though—the maintenance computer was programmed to turn lights off if an office was vacated for more than five minutes.

There was a faint aroma of perfume in the air. Not a cop then, or at least not an on-duty one. The Calgary Force was officially odour-free. Sanchez wondered briefly if Willa O'Reilly had dropped by to visit her old boss. There had been rumours about them before she was promoted. *None of your business, Reno,* he thought.

He went into his own office and closed the door. He turned on his desk lamp but left the overheads off. He was less likely to be disturbed that way. Besides he felt more like a detective working in a pool of soft light while shadows gathered around him.

Dispatch had little more information about the situation in the southwest. There had been an attack on a safe house, two casualties, one of whom was an officer. Not yet ID-ed. Sanchez entered the incident code so his palm would interrupt him as more news came in.

Sanchez laid the four items he had taken from Yankovy's body in a line across his desk. He was, of course, guilty of removing evidence from a crime scene but he didn't let it bother him. He had done worse in the pursuit of justice. He expected he would do worse still before he was done. There were times when he wished he lived in gentler times, when there was some hope the system would protect the innocent and punish the guilty. If it had ever existed, that system had been swept away during the Troubles when the only law was the law of the jungle. Things were better now, at least here in this corner of the world, but innocence was still threatened and guilt met with reward as often as punishment.

What bothered him more was that there was a witness. Jones had a weapon to hold to his head now; one he might never use but its very existence changed their relationship, for good or ill. It had been his decision to take Jones along. He could have met Yankovy alone though chances were he'd be dead now and not worrying about things that might never happen.

If he had judged the man right, Jones wouldn't see these events as an opportunity but as a defining moment. Sanchez had been wrong before about whom he should trust, in one instance disastrously so. The memory of the mistake that let the assassin Margo Falcone walk free was still bitter. But he didn't think he had been wrong about Jones.

Only time would tell.

Sanchez stared at the four items, notebook, implant, wire and cube, as if his gaze alone could command them to speak. They were all that were left of Yankovy now. Any words of wisdom he had still to impart about what was happening were locked in these four things.

The notebook would be quickest to reveal its secrets, provided the lines of print were Russian and not some elaborate code using the Cyrillic alphabet. He scanned the six pages into his palmtop, then fed it into two of the resident translation programs. The first would provide a literal transcription into English; the second, a more literary translation. Neither would really represent Yankovy's thinking but comparing the two might provide him with the necessary insights.

The task completed icon blinked. The transcription showed a jumble of English words, interspersed with clusters of the original letters. Either the untranslated words were obscure or slang or the letters spelt out nothing at all. The translation program showed even less. The few expressions it did provide read more like lines from Carroll's "The Jabberwocky" than a police report.

Code, then. Probably a simple substitution code but whether the symbols stood for English letters in English words, Cyrillic letters in Russian words or something else altogether was impossible to guess. The palmtop didn't come with a code-breaking program so he instructed it to find one on the Net and try all possible variations on English or Russian coding. If Yankovy had decided to try his hand at French, Canada's other official language, well, *il traverserait ce pont quand il y est venu*. And if it was more complicated than that, what was another dead end among dead friends?

Sanchez took a magnifying glass from his desk drawer and examined the silver wire. Even cranked to maximum power the glass revealed little other than a few notches engraved randomly along its length. He had thought it might be some type of Russian memory device but by all appearances it was exactly what it looked like—a wire made of steel or some other silvery metal with half a dozen nicks carved into it. Sanchez put it back on the desk and picked up the hunk of metal he had pried out of Yankovy's mouth. It was as wide as a molar and somewhat less than five centimetres in length.

If Jones was right, the bridgework was packed with Russian electronics. *Must be built tough,* thought Sanchez, t*o withstand chewing through a kilo of pseudosteak.* It could be a cell or some sort of homing device or even a self-destruct mechanism, though if the latter Yankovy had failed to activate it before someone began to carve him up. Most Borg had cell implants complete with answering systems; some cops had gone that route too despite what the union said. They were usually placed behind one ear with a mike wired into the jaw or even the throat to allow them to pick up sub-vocalizations. Maybe Yankovy didn't want something that permanent.

A cell might contain a record of outgoing and incoming calls. It might even have some messages stored in its memory if Sanchez could figure out a way to access them. He examined the device under the magnifying glass, turning it this way and that in the dim light of his lamp. If not for the serial number and the hint Yankovy may or may not have given Jones, he would have taken it as nothing more than a second-rate dental appliance, about what you might expect from a backwater like imperial Russia. He was about to drop it in an envelope and send it down to the lab when he spotted the tiny circular indentation.

Sanchez picked up the silver wire and compared it with the device from Yankovy's mouth. It was about five millimetres longer but its diameter was almost exactly the same as the indentation. He held it under the glass again. The nicks started a little more than a centimetre from one end and continued almost all the way to the other. He held the smooth section between thumb and forefinger and pressed the notched end against the indentation. A concealed trap slid aside and the wire slipped easily into the device. A previously invisible panel popped open on the top of the device. Underneath were two small buttons, one red and one green, and a small square grill. Not a cell then but possibly a recording device, though there was no visible way to turn it on and off. Maybe it was in another tooth.

Green means go, thought Sanchez. Or does it? Maybe it means go to hell. It would be embarrassing to be killed by booby-trapped dental work stolen from a crime scene. Sanchez didn't mind dying but he hated being embarrassed.

A *spy might use reverse logic,* thought Sanchez. I suspect the green button so I press the red one but the spy knows I'll suspect the green button so he makes the red one the self destruct. Even if it doesn't make it explode, pressing the wrong button might erase whatever's stored in memory. Or maybe you have to press them both, multiple times and in the proper sequence. Or, whatever.

No guts, no glory. Sanchez snatched a pencil off the desk and jammed its point firmly onto the green button.

Well, at least it didn't explode. In fact, it didn't seem to be doing anything.

A few seconds later, Yankovy's voice, tinny and distant, emerged from the grill. He was speaking in Russian of course. Sanchez hit the record button on his palm. He could translate later when he had it all on file.

"Turn it off."

Sanchez jumped. He hadn't heard his door swing open. Chief Ron Arsenault was standing in the doorway. That, in itself, was unusual. Arsenault seldom came to police headquarters anymore, preferring to work from his duplicate office buried, it was rumoured, in an armoured sub-basement of his house. As far as Sanchez knew, he hadn't been to the SDU offices for more than a year. The fact he was here without his normal gang of bodyguards, the infamous Cadre, as they were known, made the visit unique.

"Turn it off," said Arsenault, again. Sanchez poked the red button with the pencil and the voice stopped. "Now erase the recording on your computer."

Sanchez did as he was told. The Chief stepped into the office and closed the door. He pointed to the device with a gloved hand and Sanchez slid it across the desk. Arsenault picked it up and dropped it into a plastic bag, which he sealed and put into the pocket of his great-coat.

"The notebook, too. And please erase any copies you may have made. I've already dealt with Constable Jones' research."

Jones must have called Arsenault as soon as I dropped him off, thought Sanchez bitterly. He tapped a few keys on the palmtop under Arsenault's watchful eye. The Chief might be old but he had a reputation for being a technical whiz; Sanchez didn't bother trying to fool him.

"Jones is a good man, very loyal in his limited way," said Arsenault. "I knew he was doing research for Yankovy. As soon as I heard from the

Horsemen, I called him and got the codes to his computers. He didn't say a word about you though, but the way the situation went down at Eco-Carne had a certain flair. I assumed your involvement."

Arsenault didn't have to tell him that and he felt surprisingly grateful to the man. *That's how he stays Chief,* Sanchez thought, *even when he's taking things away from you, he gives something back.* Arsenault hadn't mentioned the small metal cube. Either it wasn't important or he didn't know about it. Sanchez resisted looking at it; tried not to even think of it.

"I'm sorry, Sanchez," said Arsenault. "I know what it's like to be shunted aside by higher ups."

Sanchez didn't reply but stared steadily at Arsenault who didn't seem to want to meet his eye.

"I don't owe you anything," said Arsenault.

"No, sir," said Sanchez, "but what about Yankovy?"

Arsenault sighed and his shoulders slumped. He removed his coat and hung it on the back of the door. He kept his gloves on. He wiped Sanchez' extra chair with a handkerchief and sat down. Sanchez felt mildly insulted—he kept his office immaculate—but he let it pass. Arsenault fiddled with a pin on his lapel until it flashed green.

"Dmirti was…not my friend exactly. We didn't like each other all that much. But we had a bond, the kind of bond men and women make in combat. I told you we served together in Africa. He was technically my commander but our relationship was more complex than that."

Arsenault leaned back in his chair with his eyes half-closed. His voice was soft, almost gentle. Sanchez leaned forward to catch every word. He had no idea where the Chief was going with this but he was ready to go along.

"We had taken a small force into Madagascar trying to root out a particularly nasty bunch of the ARIC. Our intelligence was faulty and we were badly outgunned. What was left of the unit fled south along the Onilahy River to Toliara. By the time we got there, ARIC was already in the outskirts of the city. Half the population was dead and half the rest were dying. We boarded a refugee ship. It was a twenty-metre sailing sloop, all that was left in the harbour by then.

"When we were discovered, the crew tried to remove us. We had failed to defeat the ARIC but we had gathered information that we thought would change the course of the war in our favour. As it turns out we were right. Perhaps that justifies what we did, the information we had and what it led to. We commandeered the boat, though we had to kill most of the people on it to do so. We planned to sail south and east around the Cape of Good Hope and rejoin the main force in Namibia.

"Have you ever been on a big sailing ship, Sanchez?"

"No. Maybe my next vacation." He wondered why the Chief was telling him all this. The man wasn't known for his warm personal anecdotes.

Arsenault laughed. "This was no vacation. We were barely out of port before we hit a storm, coming down out of the Indian Ocean. The Captain tried to run south but the winds and the waves followed us, pushing us almost all the way to Antarctica. At the bottom of the world.

"They say the ice is not as thick or plentiful as it once was but there was plenty enough for me. The waters calmed but still the ocean was filled with ice, great islands of the stuff banging together and cracking apart. Anyone of them would have crushed our hull. Only luck and the deft hand of Captain Pham saved us. It took three days but we finally hit open water."

Pham? thought Sanchez. That's more than a coincidence. And this story is more than an anecdote.

"Then we hit another storm. It made the first look like a summer squall. Waves twenty metres high. It was like sailing through canyons of water. We were all crew then, doing what we were told by Pham and her first mate. We had no thought of the war or even of our mission. We were only trying to stay alive, keep our one small corner of the world, that ship, safe. We had no desire to disappear from the face of the earth.

"That's where we are now Sanchez. On a ship at sea. In a storm. This is bigger than you and me, bigger than the Force, bigger than the whole damn city. There is an international game going on. People more powerful than most countries are involved. It's no place for sailors like us. We have plenty of little barbarians to keep us busy. And we have to use whatever tools we have at hand, even flawed ones and ones of uncertain provenance.

"But Inspector Yankovy and his mission here are no longer our concern. I have my orders and now you have yours."

"What am I supposed to do," asked Sanchez, "sit at my desk and twiddle my thumbs?"

Arsenault stood up and put his coat back on.

"What you do with your thumbs is your own concern, Inspector," Arsenault said, smiling faintly. He paused with his head cocked, perhaps wondering who else might be listening, perhaps not trusting his lapel pin to block all possible surveillance. Then he turned his head and stared fixedly at a point on the desk. Sanchez followed his gaze. The Chief was staring at the small metal cube.

"You have your orders Sanchez," Arsenault said. "I suggest you follow them. But it's late, why don't you go home or maybe go visit your lady friend at the Garry. I'm sure you'll find that...satisfying after the night you've had."

Sanchez stared at the Chief's departing back. For the first time he thought he saw the signs of age in the man's slumping shoulders.

Christ, does he know everything about me?

Sanchez didn't hear the outside office door open and close or the clunk the elevator door always made when it opened on this floor. *Maybe he walked through the wall,* thought Sanchez, *or was teleported away by some strange alien ship.* Anything seemed possible today.

Sanchez sat at his desk, feeling a strange mixture of anger, disappointment and relief. *What the hell was that about anyway?* Chief Arsenault appearing out of the night like a ghost, all to confiscate a bit of evidence. *Evidence I shouldn't have had in the first place.* There were plenty of people in the Force who could have run that errand, no questions asked, especially if it meant discomfiting a member of the SDU. *Hell, a phone call would have done the trick,* he thought. *I'm not crazy enough to disobey a direct order. At least, he hadn't sent the Cadre to deliver his message. That would have been unpleasant.*

No, the Chief felt he had to do this job himself. Sanchez glanced back at the metal cube. The Chief had left him that, plus, he now remembered, the business card still stuffed in his wallet. He hesitated, unwilling to pick it up. A micro-camera could be anywhere; even the daily sweeps he did were no guarantee of privacy. Not in police headquarters. He let his eyes continue to the pile of flimsies in his inbox, the summary reports on the Disappeared that Antoine King had suggested he look at.

Arsenault had said something about disappearing, about not wanting to disappear from the face of the earth. An odd way of putting it now that he thought about it. And he said the Captain was called Pham. What would a Vietnamese captain be doing in Madagascar during the height of the Ebola Wars?

Apparently Dmitri Yankovy wasn't the only one who could communicate in code. Whoever had captained that ship through Antarctic waters, Sanchez was pretty sure her name wasn't Pham. Arsenault meant Vanessa Pham—a flawed tool of uncertain provenance.

Sanchez thought about the conversation he'd had with the Chief, was it only yesterday? He had referred to it all as a game. Not a great game, perhaps but a game with players. The barbarians are at the gate, he said. Our job wasn't to keep them out but to limit the damage they did when they got in.

Arsenault didn't come here to order me to drop my investigation; he came to tell me to tackle it at a different level, to limit the damage the barbarians could do. And somehow, Vanessa Pham was going to help him do that—even if he had to commandeer her to the task.

But first he was going to follow Arsenault's advice and go see Angel.

Sanchez picked up the flimsies and examined them briefly. He threw them back on the desk and folded his arms with what he hoped was a look of disgust on his face. For the cameras, if there were any. Then he sighed and swept them up again, palming the cube as he did so. He dropped both flimsies and cube into his briefcase. He downloaded the detailed reports onto his palm and put it into the case with the rest. They could wait until he reached the privacy of Angel's office. He doubted if anyone could secretly spy on a Borg stronghold.

But when he called ahead to let her know he was coming, she wasn't there and the Borg who answered the phone sounded worried despite the neutrality of his vocoder.

Sanchez dropped a couple of extra clips of ammo in his jacket pocket and headed for the Garry to see what was up.

Chapter 29

"What the hell?"

Wannamaker slipped into silent mode. The servos in his artificial limbs made little noise in any case unless he chose to have them whirr and clank. *Another Borg joke,* thought Wannamaker; *we're natural born comics.* Now those faint sighs were eliminated by the noise dampeners scattered throughout his body. Even his footsteps and his heartbeats would barely register on all but the most sensitive of listening devices. Siqueira Silva followed suit and Wannamaker gestured for Singh not to move.

There were two of them beyond the adjoining door and if what Siqueira Silva said was true, they were both heavily armoured and armed and quite possibly augmented as well. For all he knew they were pulling an EM pulse generator—tasers for Borg—in a wagon behind them.

Wannamaker made the silent transition from claw to shotgun. He didn't want to use Stim so soon after getting out of hospital from his last overdose but he would if he had to. There was now a lot more at stake than his life. He moved to one side of the entrance.

Siqueira Silva shook his head. He fired a few milliseconds of laser light into Wannamaker's modified eye. It wasn't the best method of communication the Borg had ever devised, since it left the recipient momentarily blind, but it was effective. It was fast and almost impossible to detect, let alone intercept. The message length was limited but Siqueira Silva didn't have a lot to say.

You can't win a gun fight. Not here, not now. Let me handle this.

The older Borg shut off his audio dampeners and even added a few sound effects for good measure, so that he whirred and clanked like a robot from a 1950s movie. *Yup, Borg love a good joke*, thought Wannamaker, watching the reddish blur move across the room.

Siqueira Silva didn't hesitate but entered talking. Singh took advantage of the noise of his passage to assume a position on the opposite side of the entranceway. He had a small pistol in one hand and the rocket launcher in the other. Wannamaker doubted either would be effective against armour and augments.

"Thank goodness you're here," said Siqueira Silva from the next room. His voice was pitched high, almost hysterical.

"This is a restricted area," said booming voice.

"I know, I know. I was working in my lab and I thought I heard something at this end of the building. I should have called you, of course, but I've been having trouble with my audio implants. Didn't want to trouble you for no reason." Siqueira Silva was babbling now, and quite effectively, sounding like a character in a bad movie. "I've been meaning to have them…"

"Get to the point, doctor." The second guard spoke for the first time, his voice soft and slightly nasal.

"I knew this lab was home to some top secret work so I checked it first. I was surprised to find the door unlocked. I looked inside but there was no one here. Then I heard voices in the corridor so I slipped into the lab next door, only to find it had no other exit. Fortunately, they didn't come in. Maybe they already had what they were looking for."

"Is there anything missing?" asked booming voice.

"How would I know?" asked Siqueira Silva, "I've never been here before."

"Do you know which way they went?" asked soft voice.

"Towards the front of the building, I think. You must have just missed them."

"Let's go," said soft voice. "You, too, doctor, for your own protection."

As soon as they left, Singh held up his hand and counted down five with his fingers. He was headed for the exit but Wannamaker put a hand on his arm.

"Wait a second," he whispered. He slipped a small hinged ring from the pocket of his vest. The cables from the memory storage boxes connected into a black box in the main lab. A single line came out the other side and hooked into the mainframe. Wannamaker slipped the ring over that cable and snapped it closed. He slid it tight against the back of the computer where the cable connected. He made a few adjustments. When he was done, the ring looked like part of the machine. It would pass close inspection by anyone who hadn't had a hand in building the thing.

"We'll be able to get in without actually having to come in again," explained Wannamaker.

Singh flashed one of his trademark grins and ushered Wannamaker to the door. By the time the external lights came on and the siren sounded, they were halfway to Singh's car.

| | |

Wannamaker didn't relax until they were safely in Singh's hideaway, a bachelor flat located above the agency offices on 17th Avenue. Singh poured himself a small brandy and tilted the decanter at his partner.

Wannamaker nodded and Singh poured him a couple of fingers. As a rule neither of them drank, Singh for religious reasons; Wannamaker for political ones. Tonight they both must have felt they earned or needed it.

They sat for a few minutes in the overstuffed brown leather chairs which, with the narrow bed at the far end of the room, made up the bulk of Singh's furniture. They'd been partners for a couple of months but this was the first time Singh had invited him into his pied-à-terre, let alone to his main house on the western edge of the city. Wannamaker sipped the sweetly aromatic liquor and observed the other man over the rim of the crystal goblet that held it.

Singh hadn't taken a drink yet, satisfying himself with the fumes that filled the bowl of his glass. Maybe he thought he could stay alcohol free if he gave it enough time. *Singh is a complex man*, thought Wannamaker, not for the first time. He has plenty of money and connections. He could do better than this if he was willing to leave Calgary behind.

Maybe it has something to do with his return to Sikhism, some mission he'd set for himself as a penance for his years of apostasy. Still, there was something about the guy that elicited trust. He had 'It' as they used to say about movie stars of the early twentieth century—a kind of charisma that transcended the physical.

Wannamaker had plenty of doubts about the Singh-Wannamaker Detective Agency. But about Darwhal Singh, he had no doubts at all.

"So what did Siqueira Silva tell you?" said Singh, breaking the comradely silence at last.

"Do you know what the Singularity is?"

"As in Singularity House?"

Wannamaker nodded and took another sip of his brandy.

"If I remember my high school physics, it's a black hole, right?"

"Close enough. It's the event horizon of one—the point were gravity is so strong that nothing can escape. That was its original meaning in any case. About sixty years ago, a mathematician and science fiction writer, Vernor Vinge, coined the term to mean the tremendous change that would be caused by a huge increase in machine intelligence.

Others, like Ray Kurzweil, believed that Moore's law made it inevitable that artificial intelligence..."

"Moore's law?"

"Based on an observation that computing power seemed to double at regular intervals. Anyway, the idea was that eventually technological progress would advance so fast no one would be able to predict what was going to happen, a kind of event horizon on the future. It didn't work out quite that way. Moore's law failed when they reached the limits to miniaturization imposed by quantum effects. And artificial intelligence has yet to produce a machine that can outthink a human. Out compute one, no problem, but thinking is not computing. But if the people at Singularity House have indeed solved the problems of photonic circuitry, then Moore's law starts up again."

"And makes us all obsolete?"

"That has been one fear people have expressed," said Wannamaker.

Singh finally took a sip of his brandy. From the expression on his face, it was something he missed.

"The Singularity has been called the Technological Rapture," Wannamaker continued. Singh looked confused.

"From Christianity, the moment when God takes the blessed up into heaven. The Borg have taken that quite literally. At least some of them. It's the closest thing we have to religion, I guess. They see it as the final destination of our biomechanical destiny, when our human biological consciousnesses are uplifted into computers, or even into the Net itself. Freed from both flesh and metal we would become transcendent." Wannamaker grinned. "Your results may differ, check package for warranty."

"That's what Siqueira Silva thought he was working on."

"Right the first time. But that isn't what they're doing at all."

"Then what are they doing?" asked Singh.

"I think they're copying people's brains and storing them in those boxes."

"Wasn't that what we were talking about?"

"No," said Wannamaker. "This isn't an upload of consciousness. They have the storage but not the processing power of a human brain. I doubt they've solved the programming or interconnectivity problems. A lot of people now think they're insoluble."

"What then?"

"Joshua Steele figured it out. Some very rich, very powerful, and probably very old, people are planning to have their brains copied and the copies downloaded into other brains, younger brains that have been wiped clean using advanced Bug technology stolen from the Russians. If it works, it's the ultimate rejuv treatment—new brains and new bodies for old."

"To quote the immortal Frank Steele," said Singh. "Fuck me."

"Siqueira Silva thinks they've worked out the last of the glitches. He thinks they're ready to make their first download. And I think, Cerise Kavanah was meant to be the first donor brain."

"To paraphrase our friend Frank, fuck that."

"My sentiments exactly. Do you want to call him or should I?"

"You do it," said Singh. "There's someone else I need to reach. Someone rich enough and powerful enough to lend a hand."

"Sure, I'll try to reach him on my way to the Garry. I think Angel may be able to help us, too. There's a lot more to her than meets the eye."

"I'll join you there as soon as I can. Hopefully, I'll have re-enforcements in tow."

Chapter 30

I watched as they loaded Cerise Kavanah into the van and drove away. I tried to get up, tried to make one last futile effort to stop them. But I couldn't. I had neither the strength nor the will. For the first time in my life I felt old—not 'getting older'—but old. My years pulled me down the way the heavy wet snow of early winter pulled down trees.

By the time backup arrived, the van had long disappeared from view. The four cops who jumped out of the armoured jeeps were in full battle gear and armed with assault rifles. I wasn't sure if they would have been a match for the goons in the van but it might have been a fair fight. I wanted to call out to them that it was all over but the shouting but I didn't seem to have the energy.

I watched as they entered the wounded house, two of them taking point as the others provided cover from the safety of the jeeps. They stepped gingerly around the shattered door and secured the entrance before waving their comrades forward to investigate the interior.

The back of the house burst into flame. A hunched figure was briefly outlined against the orange light before running down the alley and out of sight. *I don't blame you*, I thought, *you're probably safer on your own than under the protection of the police. Than under my protection.*

I watched and, for the first time since I had seen my son's face staring up at me from a dumpster, I cried. I had let two people under my care, two people I was sworn to protect, be taken asway from me, one through neglect and one through weakness. I had failed as a father and I had failed as a cop.

Stop your fucking whining, Frank. You still have things to do. Crying is for...crying is for later. Yeah, there would be plenty of time for crying later.

I levered myself to my feet and walked over to the house, identifying myself in a loud voice, holding out my badge while keeping my other hand in plain view. I had no desire to be added to the list of casualties.

They had already laid one body on the lawn and covered it in a white sheet. As I approached, they put another one beside it. He was an older man, native-looking. They covered him in a sheet, too.

"Any sign of a young black girl?" I asked Inspector Derek Künksten, the officer in charge.

He typed his overrides into his palm. "Cerise Kavanah?" He pronounced it Sar-ah-see but I knew who he meant. "No, she's among the missing. Her and some kid named Taroc Smith." He gestured to the two white shrouded bodies. "Constable Cathy Louis and Chief Roddy Jules, also known as Whiteduck. He was being kept under wraps in advance of a trial next week and she was protecting him."

Taroc Smith was a refugee from the Angels of God. He was supposed to be the key witness in a triple murder they had pulled last year in Lethbridge. The Crown prosecutor was going to be pissed about losing him. I didn't know Jules but I'd sat on the Board that had hired Louis out of the Sarcee Reserve. She was a good cop. Had been a good cop.

The losses kept piling up.

"Anything else?"

"Detective Parker Atwood is wounded but he'll be fine. Our two other guests are scared but uninjured. I've got an ambulance and a caseworker on the way."

Another cruiser arrived about then, lights flashing but siren silent.

"Send me a copy of your report when it's done. The SDU has an interest in this."

Künksten grunted, whether in assent or derision I couldn't tell, and went back to work managing the scene. The fire suppression system had pretty much doused the flames in the kitchen but there was still plenty of steam and smoke swirling around. As usual, people had appeared out of nowhere and were milling about getting in the way. One of the officers was trying to establish a perimeter and I gestured for one of the arriving constables to give him a hand. The other I commandeered to drive me back downtown. Rank hath its privileges.

| | |

Headquarters was buttoned down for the night and I was able to slip through the parkade entrance without seeing anyone I knew. I didn't feel much like talking. The lights in the SDU were mostly off though there was a dim glow coming from under Sanchez's door. I didn't check to see if he was actually there or if it was a glitch in the computer management system. If he was working late, he probably didn't want to be disturbed. Man—the rationalizing animal.

I knew I should be working more closely with the guy. He was my second in command, after all. Sanchez worked hard, he wasn't afraid to tell me when he thought I was wrong but he still did what I asked of him. I even trusted him to the extent I trusted most of my colleagues. No, a lot more than most of them. But there was something about the man that made me uncomfortable. It was something I was going to have to deal with soon. But not tonight.

My own office was dark but I knew right away it hadn't been for long. The faint aroma of perfume hung in the air, a smoky sweetness like honey and musk. Dorothy. Even after all these years I still remembered her smell. I felt a tingle along my spine and down into my cock, sexual desire that both surprised and shamed me.

I sat at my desk in the dark with my face in my hands, breathing in, breathing out, trying not to think or feel. Soon, I would have to do both and then turn thoughts and feelings into actions. But for now, I needed the dark and the quiet and the steady sound of my breathing to remind me that life continues. Pain stops and life continues. Someday.

After a while, five minutes or fifty, I really couldn't say, I heard someone, Sanchez I suppose, open and close a door and walk down the hall. The outer door opened and closed and I finally looked up. A message icon was blinking on my desk console, not urgent but insistent. It hadn't been there before; it must have come in while I was sitting there. I hadn't even heard the tone.

"Return the call," I said and the computer entered the code.

Jim McConnaghey answered on the first ring.

"Frank, good to hear your voice."

I glanced at the display from dispatch. Künksten's report hadn't arrived yet and the preliminary report said one dead cop. Nice of Jim to think of me.

"What can I do for you, Jim?"

"Ah, well, Dot's here. She was waiting in your office but I thought it would be better if she had some company. We're at the east end of the cafeteria if you want to come down."

Jim had always liked Dorothy. I thought he had a thing for her, maybe more than a thing during the last dreg ends of my marriage. That's what dealing with criminals all your life will do for you, make you think the worst of even the best of men.

Turns out, Jim was one of those rare and special people who could like both halves of a couple for themselves and not as part of a unit. We weren't as close as we used to be but I knew I could still count on him as a friend. And so could Dorothy.

The last thing I wanted to do was to spend time with my ex-wife but maybe it was the first thing I had to do.

"I'll be right down."

| | |

Dorothy was doing better. She had on a new outfit and her make-up was impeccable. She was laughing at something Jim had said, with her hand resting on his arm, flirting in that meaningless way some women do without even being aware of it. She was still a beautiful woman and the smile took ten years off her face. If I hadn't known her so well, I might have been tempted to ask her out.

I felt a pang of guilt when I thought of how things had gone with Nancy. Which seemed unfair given she was the one who had told me to take a hike.

"Is this a private party or can anyone join?"

Dorothy looked stricken, caught in an oasis of happiness surrounded by the desert of her grief. She pulled her hands into her lap and sat for a moment, eyes downcast, trying to compose herself.

Jim McConnaghey looked like he wanted to be anywhere but sitting between the two of us but to his credit he didn't budge.

"I wonder if I could trouble you for a coffee, Jim. It's been a long day." I said as I eased myself into the chair opposite my ex-wife.

Jim looked so grateful that I changed my order to a latte. I don't really like that much milk with my coffee and the ones they made here were particularly bad but it would give Jim a few more minutes away from us.

"How are you, Dorothy?" I said once he was out of earshot. It was a dumb question meant to fill the void that lay between us. She treated it as such, staring at me with a strangely unreadable expression. I thought after all this time I knew all her looks but this was a new one to me. "Look, I can only stay a few minutes."

"We need to talk. We need to talk about…" She put her hand to her mouth, unable to finish the sentence.

"Joshua's funeral."

"Yes. I was thinking Saturday."

I wasn't ready for this. I felt a surge of panic. I wanted to tell her it was too soon but I couldn't. The autopsy was over; no more evidence could be wrung from his flesh. I had no reason to keep his body in a freezer in the morgue. But I wasn't ready to put my son in the ground, not yet, not before I could find the ones who did this to him. I wasn't ready.

"Sunday would be better," I said. It would give me two full days and what was left of tonight. It gave me breathing room. "More people could come on Sunday."

Dorothy nodded. "I could stay until then."

I suddenly realized how hard this was for her. I had my work, my own place, all the bits and pieces of my life. Dorothy's life was back in Chicago. There, she had her career, her friends, maybe a lover; here, nothing but an ex-husband and a dead son.

"Where should we hold the service?" she asked.

I had somehow become responsible. That seemed only fair. I had ducked my responsibilities to my son for most of his life. Maybe in death I could make up for it.

I didn't know how the Borg grieved their dead, whether they had a religion of their own or if they had given up on faith in the pursuit of their biomechanical destiny. Dorothy was Unitarian which meant her prayers were directed 'to whom it may concern.' I wanted more than that. I wanted the weight of the ages to bear my son home.

"There's an Anglican chapel in Bragg Creek. I know the priest."

I'd met Father Blake last fall during a hellish investigation. He was a good man, maybe even a holy one; he'd gotten me on my knees for the first time in thirty years. He was retired but I thought he'd do this for me.

"Give me his name and number and I'll make the arrangements."

Maybe she needed something to occupy her time, give meaning to the next few days. Or maybe she still remembered what it was like to be married to a cop obsessed with an investigation. I didn't care. I felt relief at having made a decision and gratitude to her for taking the details off my hands.

Jim was back with the coffee. He put it on the table in front of me and then stood there, awkwardly shifting from side to side, wondering what else might be expected of him.

I took a sip of the slop they had the nerve to charge thirty-five dollars for, just to be polite.

"It's okay, Jim," I said. "I'll get Dorothy back to her hotel."

I'd like to say I took her home and left her at her door with a handshake or a kiss on the cheek. But it wouldn't be true.

We had been married for seventeen years, seen each other through the purest ecstasy and the darkest despair. We knew each other better than we would ever know anyone else.

We hardly said a word. There was nothing to say and the few platitudes we managed were smothered by lips and tongues. We fucked hard and fast with our clothes barely off and then made love slowly, gazing at each other through curtains of tears. We slept for a few hours, entwined in her king-sized bed.

At about four, I got dressed and left her there. Time enough to deal with this later. Now I had to get to work.

Chapter 31

Cerise kept her eyes closed, pretending to be unconscious, just as she had pretended to faint when the huge man first burst through the door of her room. She had seen at once she couldn't resist and thought they might let something slip if they thought she couldn't hear them. She had read that 'knowledge was power' in one of her school assignments and, though she wasn't quite sure how that worked, she knew she'd need all the power she could muster if she was going to get out of this alive.

He seemed to buy it. Men can be pretty stupid about girls. He seemed to accept she would faint dead away faced with his masculine glory.

Or maybe he decided it would be easier to just carry her.

The fight hadn't lasted long. Even through the walls of the house the gunfire from outside sounded louder than that from inside. She had seen enough webcasts to know what that meant. The bad guys always had the bigger guns, at least in the first half of the story. She hoped there was going to be a second half.

She strained her senses to build a picture of what had happened. The alarm had shut down and, after the roar of the guns, the house seemed strangely quiet, like the calm after a storm. Beneath the sharp tang of gunsmoke, there was a faint whiff of something burning. The air left a bitter taste in her mouth and she resisted the urge to spit it out.

The man's footfalls were heavy in the hall and on the stairs and glass crunched under foot as he moved. He lurched more than walked, seeming to leap forward in quick jerks rather than with the rolling rhythm big men often had, and Cerise hoped she wouldn't get sick from the motion. His shoulder felt odd beneath her body, his muscles moving beneath his skin like lumps of stone.

There were two people crying softly at the foot of the stairs, a woman and a man. She thought the woman was Olivia but she couldn't tell who the man was. Farther away, she heard low moans of someone in pain. She hoped it wasn't Whiteduck; he had been so kind to her.

There was a cold draft and they seemed to be moving toward it. She guessed the front door must be open. The air outside still smelled of gun smoke but a soft west wind was rapidly clearing it and Cerise risked a few big breaths to clear her lungs. The man carrying her didn't seem to notice. It was cold and she missed the jacket though not as much as the phone hidden inside it.

Several sirens were approaching, their rise and fall muted by distance. The man didn't seem to notice that either, his pace unchanging. Maybe he knew they wouldn't get here in time or maybe he didn't care, hoping for another fight he was certain to win.

He lifted her off his shoulder and laid her on a hard metal floor. He said something then, but his voice was so deep and ragged it sounded like the growl of an animal, though Cerise was sure it was English. There was an answering growl and then the door of the van slammed. A few seconds later they were driving away. She risked cracking her eyes open but there was nothing to see but the dancing lights of utter darkness.

|||

She tried counting to have some sense of the passage of time, but after she reached five hundred realized it was pointless. She didn't know how fast they were moving or even in what direction so knowing how long the journey took wasn't going to help, other than to draw a big circle of possibilities with the so-called safe house at its centre. And she had no way to tell anyone anyway.

The counting at least had kept her from thinking about what was happening, what had already happened back at the house. People had been hurt, maybe killed, and all because of her. What made her so important to these men? There was nothing special about her, was there? Wouldn't she at least remember that—if she was some sort of genius at school or an exceptional athlete? She knew she was pretty but not like a web-star or a fashion model. Besides, beauty was so easy to manufacture these days.

She was a virgin, a source of both pride and embarrassment, and she had read of men who were willing to pay a lot of money to do it with a virgin. Still, despite all the bragging of boys at her school, she knew there were plenty of virgins, maybe even more than there used to be with all the religious groups that insisted on it. It was hard to believe anyone would take these kind of risks for something that only had a one-time value.

The van was one of the old gas-electric hybrids so the engine wasn't completely silent and she could tell when they suddenly picked up speed. The hum of the tires grew louder, too, and she thought they must be on one of the major cross-city connectors, either the McLeod heading north or the Glenmore taking them east. North would take them deep into Calgary's bedroom communities while east could take them downtown or into the industrial southeast.

She had a sudden sharp memory of being driven to a building in the southeast by the fat man with the pointy teeth. She remembered looking out the windows as they drove past rows of factories, each surrounded by high wire fences. There was a curious flatness to the memory as if she had been disinterested in her surroundings or in what was happening to her.

Someone had given her drugs. That was how it had happened.

She had been walking to Becky's place for the party. She had been excited; Becky gave the best parties. All her friends were going to be there. It was a party for Valentine's Day but with no boys allowed. What did they know about romance anyway? They were going eat chocolate and play games. Aleah was going to read the Tarot and then they were going to watch movies.

She was about halfway there when she suddenly felt dizzy, not the way you got from a carnival ride, but confused the way you get if you go down the wrong corridor at the mall and nothing looks quite right. Disoriented and a little afraid. A car had pulled up beside her. She knew the driver. It was…nothing. A blank where his face should be. Then later she had been with Rickey, the dark haired man who made her dress like a slut, though she hadn't seemed to care at the time. But he wasn't the one who picked her up. If only she could remember.

The hum of the tires changed pitch. They had left the high-speed connector and were back on local streets. There were no speed bumps so she guessed they weren't in the suburbs; the lack of traffic sounds ruled out downtown even at this time of night. They were somewhere in the industrial sector of the city. A shiver of fear slid down Cerise's spine. Were they taking her back to the lab? Something terrible had happened to her there.

The van made a sharp turn and the tires crunched on gravel. The engine died and for a few moments she lay in the silent dark waiting for the next thing. She was tired of being treated as baggage. Even Buzz the Borg and Superindent Steele hadn't really thought she was anything more than a victim. She heard the front doors of the van open. The van rocked as the men got out. There were at least two of them, she knew, maybe more. No matter. They would find out what it was like to deal with a tigress.

She twisted until her feet were pointed to the back of the van, on her back with her legs raised and her hands held in front of her face like claws, the way they had taught her in self defense class. The door opened. The sudden glare of a street light almost blinded her. She lashed out with both feet at the indistinct bulk that filled the opening.

It was like kicking a wall. He barely grunted when her shoes slammed into his chest. An instant later he grabbed her flailing legs and hauled her out of the van and held her upside down, her head at the level of his knees. She punched him as hard as she could between his legs. He grunted a little louder but didn't do any of the things men were supposed to do when hit there. He shook her hard and then let go of one her legs to reach down and slap her lightly across the face. Her jaw cracked from the impact and lights danced in front of her eyes.

"Settle down," he growled, his words scarcely intelligible. "Next time, I hurt you."

"Restrain her anyway you like, Amos," said an oily voice. It was the fat man they called Conklin. "But don't hit her. She is of no value to us if she's damaged."

The huge man, Amos, said something else then but Cerise couldn't make it out. It was as if his mouth and throat were full of rocks and the words were crushed before coming past his lips. He slung her across his shoulder and ignored her further efforts to punch and scratch him. Cerise decided to save her energy. She might have a chance to use it later on.

"Where did you find her?" said Conklin as they walked across the gravel to a low metal-clad building. It wasn't the lab. There was no double metal fence here. Cerise felt oddly relieved. More and more of her memory was coming back. Maybe soon she'd be able to remember everything. If she lived long enough.

The man carrying her, Amos, said something in return. Maybe she was getting better at interpreting it or maybe he was making more of an effort to be clear. She heard the words, 'house' and 'dead cop.' A hard lump formed in the pit of her stomach. They had killed Cathy. Then she heard the name, Jarrod.

Her older brother. He was the one. She remembered now. Jarrod had been acting strange all winter. He was involved with some group, a group her father didn't approve of. Her mother had said it was politics, nothing serious. It didn't affect her. He was Jarrod, the older brother she loved to tease, the older brother she loved and respected more than words could tell.

Before she left for the party, he had offered her a drink of guava juice from his own personal store. It was all the rage, though hardly anyone she knew could afford it on a regular basis. But Jarrod was always working at something, always seemed to have money.

He had offered to walk with her to the party but she preferred to go alone. But when the drugs, the drugs he had put in the juice, took effect, he was there. She hadn't even wondered where he had gotten a car as she got in and let him drive her away from everything she knew.

Her brother had sold her to Rickey and he had sold her Conklin. And when she called from the house, he had intercepted it. He had been the one in the background while she talked to the woman pretending to be her mother.

Cerise had to bite her lip to keep from crying out, had to clench her stomach to keep from throwing up. She wanted to purge herself of the bitterness of her recovering past, the bitterness of her brother's betrayal.

They were inside the building now. Amos dropped her on a sofa against one wall. He pointed one bulky finger at her and said, "Stay!" He grinned at his own cleverness, his mouth a jumble of large crooked teeth. There were braces across his smile but the metal was bent and twisted with bits of wire hanging loose, as if his jaw and teeth had somehow grown too big for the steel to hold them.

Cerise shivered. She was surrounded by monsters. She pulled the blanket covering the sofa around her and clutched it tight. She wanted to bury her face in its scratchy warmth. She wanted this nightmare to end.

Instead, she forced herself to look around. Knowledge was power. And tigresses don't hide under blankets.

The building had been a factory at one point. She could see the grey hulks of unused machines lurking at the edge of the light. They were cloaked in layers of dust. Whatever they had made here had been forgotten by the world. Like her.

No, she thought, *I haven't been forgotten.* Superintendent and Buzz and Angel and, what's his name, Singh, were out there right now, looking for her. They would help her if they could but, in the meantime she had to do everything she could to help herself.

Most of the building was in darkness. That might help if she could slip away. Where she was sitting was the best lit area though it was still fairly dim. There was the sofa she was sitting on and two more as well as several chairs, both stuffed and hard-backed, arranged in a rough semi-circle around a large low table. The table was covered in dirty dishes and the half-empty containers from a dozen different take-aways. The entire area hung with the sickly sweet smell of rotting food.

The only one who seemed to notice was Conklin. He was sitting in a chair as far away from the table as he could, holding a handkerchief to his face. She couldn't see his mouth move but she could tell he was on a call by the way his eyes were staring up and away into the vacant space of the shadowed roof.

The others, Amos and two more who looked enough like him to be his brothers, were sitting together at the far end of the table. Every once in a while one of them would say something. Sometimes another answered; sometimes they laughed. Amos kept looking in her direction with a vacant hungry expression. His deep-set eyes were cobalt blue and cold like frozen pools of water.

They did look like monsters. All three of them were more than two metres tall with barrel-like torsos. Their gleaming bald heads squatted on their shoulders, their lumpy skulls looking as if they had been molded from clay. The muscles on their arms and legs were twisted masses of rope and steel that bulged and jutted at odd angles. She had seen the body builders at the gym where her brother, her betrayer—her mind spat—went. They were gross and disgusting but this was unnatural. It was obscene.

She turned her attention back to Conklin. It was sick to think that he was the only one who stood between her and Amos. He wasn't her idea of a guardian angel. He had finished his conversation and was gazing at her speculatively, his tiny black eyes barely visible in the folds of flesh on his face. He smiled when she looked at him; his front teeth had been filed to points. No, not an angel at all.

They were all monsters. And they were going to kill her.

She wanted to scream but she knew no one would answer. She wanted to run but she had seen how fast Amos could move, despite his ungainly body. She took a deep breath. That's right. *Breathe girl, just breathe*. She wanted her voice to be calm and strong.

"What do you want from me?"

Conklin licked his lips.

"Oh, darling, you don't want to know what I want. I saw you shiver when Amos looked at you. But I'm the one you should fear. His hungers are simple ones. Not like mine at all."

He got up and moved toward her. Cerise felt herself pull back against the sofa and forced herself to sit up straight. He wasn't like Amos in other ways. Her feet and nails could hurt him.

"Not that I can afford to indulge. My clients want you. Unsullied. The sacrifices I am forced to make in the name of commerce." He sighed theatrically.

Cerise shook her head. This really couldn't be about her virginity, could it? No, he had told Amos not to damage her. This was about all of her.

"Don't fight me girl," said Conklin. "I have ways to hurt you that won't leave any marks. Not on the outside anyway."

He sat beside her on the sofa and brushed the back of his hand across her face. It made her skin crawl.

"Buzz found me before, he can find me again."

"Oh, I hope so," said Conklin holding up his other hand. A thin flesh-coloured cast sheathed his wrist. "I owe him for this. You may have noticed. I've upgraded my protection."

He glanced over at the three behemoths, clustered together like boulders.

"Doctor," he said. "It's time."

A woman had been sitting on one of the big armchairs halfway between Cerise and where Amos and the others were sitting. The chair had been turned away so Cerise hadn't noticed her before but she must have been there the whole time, watching and listening. She was Asian, a little taller than Cerise and quite muscular. Cerise thought she looked the same age as her mother, about forty or forty-five, but it was hard to tell in the dim light.

Amos grunted and stood up. He picked up a small black leather case and snapped it open. He took out a bottle and a large hypodermic needle and handed it to the woman. The doctor as Conklin had called her.

Cerise shrank back into the corner of the sofa, her eyes darting frantically, looking for a way out. But the needle wasn't for her. Amos sat beside the other two men and the doctor injected each of them in the neck, plunging the long needle deep into their flesh.

"It's not safe to share needles," she said, inanely parroting one of the school's constant safety messages.

"My boys are clean," said Conklin, giggling. "They don't need to worry about things like that."

The three men tilted back their heads and roared, their voices ripped with pain and rage. Their bodies shook like dogs when they get wet and their eyes rolled back in their heads. The woman stumbled backwards, getting out of reach of their flailing limbs.

Cerise tensed. It was now or never.

Conklin's hand closed on her arm.

"Don't," he said. "I don't want to hurt you but I will if you run again. I'm tired of chasing after you."

Amos and the others had fallen onto the floor. Their bodies convulsed and they cried out again and again. Their voices had changed. There was another sound underlying their groans. Cerise had never heard noises like that but she thought it might be the sound of sexual pleasure.

"Amazing, isn't it?" said Conklin, his voice low and husky. "Watch now."

It must have been a trick of the light, an illusion created by the shadows and the shaking of their bodies but the men seemed to get even bigger, their muscles bulging in new directions, even their bones shifting and changing under their mobile skin. It couldn't be real, could it?

"What's happening to them?" Cerise stared in horror as Amos clambered to his feet. He looked different as if his face had become less distinct, as if fingers had reshaped the clay of his flesh, making him less human.

"Magic," said Conklin. "The magic of modern science. Are they finished, doctor?"

Amos lurched toward them, moving in sudden rapid jerks, like a stop-action film. His face was contorted, filled with animal rage. Conklin stood and slipped his hand in his pocket. Amos stopped.

Conklin smiled. He tilted his head to one side and the muscles in his thick neck twitched. His smile broadened.

"Our clients have arrived," he said. "Time for Miss Kavanah to meet her destiny. Amos, you come with me. Timothy, Saul, create a distraction, will you? Something splashy. Doctor Vanessa, you have your assignment."

Amos scooped her up in his arms before she could move. The other two were already out the door. The woman picked up the leather case and followed more slowly.

"Where are you taking me?" Cerise asked, though she already knew the answer.

"You've been there before, though you may not remember it," said Conklin. "We're going to Singularity House, where you are going to make history. And I am going to get richer than even I have ever dreamed."

Chapter 32

I went back to my office. The few hours sleep seemed to have done me some good. Or maybe it was the sex. I felt energized and alert. Deadlines affected me that way.

A little more than forty-eight hours ago, life had been simple. Heading the SDU wasn't easy but the work seemed worth doing. I'd figured a few things out about life and was trying to put the lessons into practice by starting a brand new relationship, one that didn't involve either co-workers or co-dependency. My ex-wife was in my past and the future held real possibilities. I'd even thought I might be ready to make another go at being a father to my children.

That had all ended with a phone call and a quick trip across town to look at a body in a dumpster.

Maybe I was crazy to think I could solve this in the next two days, that I could somehow bury my guilt and frustration when I buried my son. But for the first time in two days I felt I was back on track. All I had to do was ignore the grief and pain that lurked on the edge of my consciousness like a great black beast. All I had to do was set aside my anger and my fear and be a cop.

Self-delusion can be a wonderful thing.

So what did I have?

My desk had all the latest gadgets. There was a messaging system that answered the routine calls for me and flagged the rest in order of urgency based on my own programmed set of rules. It had two red blinking lights and four amber ones but for now I ignored them. There was a voice activated terminal with holographic display, which got upgraded twice a year as new models came out, and a dispatching slave that would let me track and direct every officer in my command and, in certain circumstances, call on half the force for backup. I could directly access police databases from over a hundred countries and could even initiate research with a dozen contractors who were available on a 24/7 basis. Rank indeed had its privileges.

But my favourite was a large pad of blank sheets and a dozen coloured pencils. I picked a blue one and held it poised over the centre of an expanse of white. Blank sheets could be daunting; the first mark set the pattern for everything that followed. Choosing what constituted the centre of the problem often determined the kind of solution you found.

In small block letters I wrote 'Joshua.'

It was a good beginning and it was the centre of *my* problem. To one side I wrote Singularity House and above that I wrote Cerise Kavanah. That led me to Gale Conklin and Buzz Wannamaker and through him to the whole Borg community, which led to Natasha Redding.

If my son had been murdered because he had seen Cerise Kavanah in a lab at Singularity House, did that mean Gale Conklin was responsible for Joshua's death and for the spate of Borg eviscerations over the last few weeks?

I hoped so. I always wanted to kill that fat cocksucker.

Natasha Redding bothered me. She didn't fit into the puzzle. She was too big, a whole puzzle unto herself. Lions don't concern themselves with what jackals do. If her presence in Calgary was more than a coincidence, if the death of her Borg-friend more than an accident of being in the wrong place, then that changed the whole picture. If she was somehow directly connected, this was no longer local but international.

Yankovy was from Russia. That was as international as it got.

I looked at the few connected circles on the diagram. It seemed sparse. I wrote Angel beside Buzz. Beside her name I wrote Sanchez. There had been something about the way they had looked at each other that suggested there was more than a cop-informant relationship. And where did Sanchez lead? And why didn't I really trust him? Was it paranoia or insight?

Insight. He reminded me of Chief Arsenault. The way he walked, the way he talked, maybe even the way he thought. But Sanchez wasn't Arsenault. Maybe it was time I stopped treating him like he was.

I needed to call together the troops. The last staff meeting had ended in turmoil and loose ends; maybe it was time to tie them altogether.

I initiated the calendar function on the slave and set a priority one meeting for seven a.m. It would be sent to everyone connected to the SDU including Vanessa Pham. I sent a copy to Singh and Buzz. They didn't work for me but I wanted them there anyway. Screw protocol.

Two red message lights were still winking at me.

I looked back at the diagram but nothing else came to me. Maybe I didn't have all the facts. I had spent too much of the last two days wandering around in a fog, sticking my nose in where it didn't belong, instead of sitting at the centre and drawing all the pieces of other people's investigations together. Wasn't that what Superintendents were supposed to do? Yeah, so how come I can never remember to do it?

Maybe those lights held the facts I needed.

My hand hesitated over the activation panel. I wasn't sure my brain could process any more information. Or, perhaps, I wasn't ready for any more bad news. In my experience red lights always meant bad news.

I leaned back in my chair and rubbed my face with my hands. I needed a shave. Hell, I needed a lot of things.

I flicked on the news. At this time of night it often covered the bizarre and obscure. In the past, I'd sometimes found the weird conjunctions triggered different ways of thinking about problems.

CNN still had nothing but the failed American Mars mission. The Chinese had offered their sympathies but declined to abort their own mission to launch a rescue. The Europeans promised to give it serious consideration and promised an answer by noon. As the spokesman from NASA pointed out, by then it would be too late.

The Americans had admitted they had cannibalized every piece of launch equipment they had in order to get the ship on its way; no rescue was possible from that source.

So much for the unifying perspective of looking down on our blue and white globe from space, I thought. So much for the family of man.

I skipped through the other news channels but they were all carrying much the same stories. I was about to turn it off when the BBC announced breaking news. The Indians had offered to divert the scheduled re-supply of their moonbase to attempt a mission. They had determined that the risk to their base crew was 'acceptable.' The rescue would be manned by volunteers, which suggested where the real risk lay. Maybe there was a family of man after all.

It wasn't what I had been looking for but it was what I needed to hear. No problem was too big that it couldn't be solved. All it took was for the right person to make the right decision.

The first urgent message was from dispatch. Dmitri Yankovy had been murdered. His partially dismembered body had been discovered by the RCMP after an anonymous tip led them to the Eco-Carne meat factory east of the city. One of the assailants had apparently been badly wounded but had escaped. DNA evidence at the scene was linked to an unidentified individual who had previously been implicated in a series of assassinations carried out by a radical eco-terrorist ring out of Oregon.

I found myself standing at my desk, my flight or fight response pumping adrenalin into my already over-stimulated body. I forced myself back into my seat. The second message was from Ron Arsenault. As usual he was way ahead of me. He ordered me to leave Yankovy to the Horsemen. He went on to say he was personally escorting 'his old friend' back to Moscow and that Superintendent O'Reilly was Acting Chief in his absence.

Fuck. I had nothing against Willa but, since Matt Moore retired, I was senior Superintendent on the force. Not that I wanted to be Chief. But it's nice to be asked. Fine, Willa was Chief. I could ignore her as well as I ignored Arsenault.

I was on a roll now. I decided to listen to the four amber messages and, if those didn't give me satisfaction, every other message that didn't warrant its own light, until I found one that made me tingle.

The first message was from Buzz Wannamaker, telling me that he and Singh had been to Singularity House and had a pretty good idea who was behind the Borg murders and why. It was linked to Cerise Kavanah, details to follow. Buzz had always been reluctant to say too much on the phone. He knew how easy our security systems were to crack.

The second call was from someone called Taroc Smith. It took me a moment to place him as the kid who had run away from the safe-house. I'd talked to him a couple of times about a separate investigation involving the Angels of God. He hadn't been very helpful but I had left him my private number in case he thought of something. Still, I wasn't sure why my messenger thought he deserved an amber light until I heard the contents.

He actually apologized for running away as if he was a choir boy who had missed rehearsal. That wasn't the amber part of the message. He said he was sorry about my son and that he was pretty sure he knew who did it. The Angels who pulled the trigger down in Lethbridge had also helped bring Gale Conklin back across the border. Given how they felt about that shitbag, there must have been a lot of money involved. The rumour was, Conklin was back in Canada to field test some new drugs, drugs designed to work with the body's natural systems to make you a better, stronger, faster you. He'd been delivered to a local Clean Boy leader named Amos. They were the ones killing Borg, using nothing more than their own bodies.

That gave me pretty much all the satisfaction I could handle, but I listened to the last two messages anyway, in case they too held some hidden treat.

Next up was Vanessa Pham informing me she was tendering her

resignation. Her voice has harsh, like a metal file grating across stone. I'd heard a woman sound like that before—right after her husband tried to strangle her. Pham was in trouble. She might be quitting on me but I wasn't quitting on her. I put out an APB and played the final message.

It was Buzz again, though I barely recognized his voice either. He had gone in search of Angel but she hadn't been at the Garry all night. When he went back to her apartment it had been torn to pieces, the door ripped from the wall as if it were made of tissue paper. And there was blood and Borg parts scattered everywhere.

Chapter 33

Angel still hadn't arrived at the Garry by the time Sanchez got there, though the Borg at the bar said she was expected any minute. He let himself into her office and lay down on the red leather couch that had provided both of them so much pleasure during previous visits.

After a few minutes, he stood up and began to pace the narrow office. *Maybe I should head up to her apartment,* he thought. *Though I'd likely pass her on the way.* He sat at Angel's desk and flipped open his palm top.

He'd accumulated a lot of material over the last few days even after the Chief had made him erase what he'd gotten from Yankovy. He'd already scanned through the executive summary of King's report and didn't feel the details were going to shed a lot more light on that situation. There had been an upswing in the number of unexplained deaths of the Disappeared, unexplained in the sense that the explanations attached to the file—suicide, overdoses, accidents, homicide by person or persons unknown—were seldom more than unsubstantiated guesses. And there had been an unprecedented number of head traumas.

King had made a special effort to show that these were Disappeared and not simply people who didn't have files in the national data bank for legitimate, usually religious, reasons. A few had been positively identified by workers on the stroll. For the others, there had been no inquiries or complaints from parents or community leaders, bodies had gone unclaimed, that sort of thing. His rigor suggested that someone, perhaps Vanessa Pham, had suggested an alternate theory.

Sanchez still had Pham's personal file. Maybe it was time to learn a bit more about the good doctor.

Before becoming a doctor and coming to Calgary, she had spent a number of years as a cop in Winnipeg. By all accounts she had been a good cop, though records were a bit spotty. Winnipeg, like Milwaukee and Chicago to the south, had a particularly rough time during the Troubles. Accidents of history put the wrong people in the wrong place when it all went to shit. Military units in both the Canadian and US army had mutinied and for a couple of years, during the worst of the southwest droughts, had tried to establish a separate country whose wealth was based on supplies of fresh water in Lakes Superior and

Winnipeg.

The fighting to restore national control had been brutal, almost door to door. Most places fell into chaos, especially the bigger cities.

Only those neighbourhoods where local police had kept true to their oaths had survived. Pham had served in a station house in south Winnipeg and, with a dozen other officers, had fought the barbarians who poured through the gates and forced them back step by step, reclaiming their city until order could be restored.

The last fight had been against a squad of augmented soldiers, part of the group that had been defeated in Chicago. Borg-like if not truly Borg, the soldiers had been both desperate and dangerous but Pham had, almost single handedly, held them off until the Canadian military arrived to finish the job. She'd saved nearly sixty people from certain death though two of her fellow officers, including her partner, had been killed. That was why she had received the Citation of Valour, for bravery in the face of overwhelming odds and personal tragedy.

Bravery in battle is one thing, he thought, but it leaves scars. No wonder she's suspicious of modified humans. One of them killed her partner.

There was something odd about the way the Citation read. Sanchez went back to the beginning of Pham's personal file. Marital status. Widow. He dug deeper—into the parts of the file marked Personal and Confidential, the parts no one was supposed to look at even if they could—until he found what he was looking for.

He leaned back in the swivel chair and stared at the ceiling. Steele needed to know this.

The door to Angel's office burst open. It was the Borg from the bar.

"The police scanner reports another dead Borg," he said. "The address is Angel's apartment."

Sanchez' guts twisted and, for a moment he thought he was going to vomit. He staggered to his feet, his palmtop clattering on the floor. *I should have followed my instincts*, he thought, *I could have saved her. Or, at least, I could have died trying.*

Chapter 34

Wannamaker stood at the entrance to Angel's apartment, staring at the devastation. He'd walked into worse movies during his brief career as a cop but this one involved a friend, maybe his best friend. Maybe more than a friend.

He coded Frank's number without thinking. If anyone would know what to do next, it would be Frank. Still no answer. He left another message, in his human voice. This was no time for Borg neutrality. But it was time for calm. He released a mild sedative, tailored to still his emotions while leaving his thinking clear.

He stepped through the hole in the wall and began to catalogue the damage.

A Borg had died here. Maybe more than one. It was different from the other murders, at least different from what had been reported in the media or discussed in Borg circles. The mods weren't missing but scattered around the living room like the broken pieces of a child's toy. Two mechanical legs, an arm and part of an internal skeleton augment. The head had been separated from the body and crushed beyond recognition but it was clear that one eye and both ears had been replaced as well as the skullcap. A vocoder was still sticking out of the top of the torso.

A forensics team would have had to resort to DNA testing if they hoped to identify the victim but Wannamaker was Borg and knew the members of his community intimately. These parts belonged to Gamow, the Independista. Wannamaker wondered what he had been doing in Angel's apartment. They weren't exactly friends. But Angel was the facilitator, trying to bring the two sides of the Borg family together. Maybe that explained it.

The door to Angel's bedroom was hanging by one hinge. He hesitated, unwilling to witness what he might find in the next room. He took a deep breath and crossed the threshold. The room was torn to shreds but there was no blood, no Borg parts. Wannamaker was doubly glad of that. Angel's mods were internal, buried deep within her body and head. Her death would have been especially grisly.

The bedroom window was smashed. There was a glitter of glass on the outer sill and more scattered in the alley one floor below.

Angel had been here but had escaped, at least temporarily. Gamow had bought her time to do that.

Where would she run? The Garry was out of the question. There were too many innocents there; Angel wouldn't risk them, no matter how scared she was. One of the things that made Angel special. The clinic was out for the same reason. If it was the same gang who had attacked him, they knew where it was. But she wouldn't want to remind them of that. Wannamaker had a feeling the situation had changed. The other murders had been private affairs, carried out in lonely alleys and vacant lots, far from surveillance cameras or crowds. Angel's apartment wasn't exactly Olympic Plaza but it wasn't isolated either.

So if not her usual hangouts, where? He had given her the key to his place. That's where she would head.

He tried Frank Steele again. This time he actually got him.

"I'm heading for my place. Care to join me?"

"I thought you'd never ask," said Steele.

Chapter 35

By the time I got to Buzz's place in the northwest, he and Angel were already there, sipping tea and discussing Borg politics as if it were a Sunday social. I was long past the tea stage but knew better than to suggest bourbon. I listened to them talk for a couple of minutes to be polite. After all, they had lost someone too though from the sound of it he wasn't as close as Joshua had been to me. In other words, hardly even a friend.

There seemed to be something they were deliberately not saying, almost defining the topic by the edges of their avoidance. I really didn't have time for this. And neither did Cerise Kavanah.

I told them what Taroc Smith had reported.

"That sounds about right," Angel said. "I caught a glimpse of them on the security scanner when they came through the front entrance of the building. They came out of a black van, moving so fast their arms and legs were blurred. They had to pause to smash through the entrance but they still looked blurred, their features indistinct as if they were in a constant state of flux, shifting because the bones and muscles underneath were moving, growing. And they were huge. I've never seen people that big."

"What would do that?" I asked.

"Gamma radiation?" said Wannamaker, making some reference I didn't get. "Seriously though it sounds like someone has perfected Dr. Jeckyll's formula. Probably some sort of nano-device. One that works on the body's own systems or at least starts with that."

"But why go to all that trouble?" I asked.

"That's the only way the Clean Boys would accept it. I don't care much for their politics but at least they're consistent. No unnatural modifications for them."

"The end result sounds pretty unnatural to me," I said.

"Change is a slippery slope," said Angel.

"Yeah." I looked at her. Still looked like her name, despite the night's events. "Why did they come after you?"

She and Buzz exchanged glances.

"I guess you're going to find out sooner or later," she said. "I've been working with Inspector Yankovy."

"He's dead."

I guess it wasn't widely known. Her hand flew to her mouth and her eyes widened. I watched her closely. You could tell a lot by the way people reacted to bad news.

It took only a few seconds for her to pull herself together but a lot passed over her face in those moments. She had genuinely liked the Russian. It was clear she considered his death a real loss, both personally and to the cause that had brought them together, whatever that was.

"What do you know about the Russian Tsar?" It wasn't the first thing I'd expected to come out of her mouth.

"Not much," I said, "other than they say he rules with an iron fist. Nothing new for Russian leaders I guess."

She actually laughed at that. A hard bitter bark. "There's more to that expression than you think. Tsar Nicholas is a Borg. Of course his iron fist is beneath a glove of flesh. He's a Borg the way I am, preferring to keep his changes hidden away from the world. But a true Borg nonetheless."

I'd seen a few vids smuggled out of Moscow by some enterprising paparazzi—the Russian royals weren't big on public relations—but I would never have guessed. I was willing to take her word for it.

"Not many people know, not even among the Russian aristocracy. Yankovy wasn't simply an inspector general in Moscow, he was *The* Inspector General for all of Russia, the Tsar's right hand man. The person Nicholas turned to when he couldn't turn anywhere else."

"So Yankovy was here on a mission for the Tsar?"

"He didn't tell me all the details," she said, "It was always on a need to know basis. But he came bearing a Borg ID cube. It was enough for me."

"To do what?" asked Wannamaker.

"Listen mostly. To people who wouldn't have talked to him," said Angel. "I've always stayed in the middle of Borg disputes. I take a lot of criticism for that but that also means I hear a lot of talk. Not just from Borg but from the Wannabe community."

"What did he tell you?" I was getting restless. I knew that feeling. It usually came right before I completely lost it.

"The Empire is unsettled. There are forces both within and without who want to overturn the monarchy. Russia lags behind much of the world in technology. The one area where they do excel is in the science of interrogation and brain manipulation. Someone stole their most advanced Bug—one that wouldn't simply probe and edit memory but one that could wipe a personality clean while leaving other parts of the infrastructure intact."

"What would be the value in that?" asked Wannamaker.

"Yankovy didn't say but I can imagine."

So could I. A spy with all his contacts and passwords intact but his personality replaced with a few simple directives—assassination was the nicest of the possibilities.

"And that's the Bug they used on Cerise Kavanah."

"She wasn't the first," said Angel. "Not by a long shot"

That sent a chill down my spine. If Bugs were being used in Calgary, it was something I should have known about.

"Who?" I asked, though I already suspected the answer.

"Disappeared. People nobody notices, nobody cares about. No families. All their friends in the same boat. Yankovy was having some research done but he thought it might be more than a dozen. A lot of people come to the Garry. Some become regulars but for some it's just one stop on the road to nowhere. Yankovy asked me to watch where they went and who they went with."

"Conklin?" I asked. That fat bastard had been trading in human flesh for longer than I could remember.

"Not necessarily," said Buzz. "Or at least not exclusively. Lots of others picked up the slack in his absence. Candy Forbes comes to mind."

That made sense. Kids drifted into town, runaways or throwaways, and had to wind up somewhere. Some of them managed to get jobs, create lives for themselves. Others got sucked into the dream trade, sex and drugs without the rock and roll. Candy Forbes and people like her scooped them up, used them up and then passed them on. Bodies, still living, sold to medical science.

"If they're using Disappeared, why are they still after Cerise Kavanah?"

"Because the others didn't work," said Angel. "Trauma changes the brain. We've known that for years. Physical, sexual, emotional, it all builds up. Add heavy, repetitive drug use to that and the changes are pretty extensive. They could wipe their brains but the infrastructure left behind…"

"Looked pretty much like city streets in springtime, broken and full of holes," I finished for her.

"But weren't they using drugs on Cerise?" asked Wannamaker.

"According to Doctor Angus at Foothills, they were designed to have short term effects and then disappear," I said.

"And she wasn't on them for long," added Angel.

"So from their point of view, she was the perfect starlet for their horror film," said Wannamaker.

"She was unblemished," I said, feeling the anger start to swell in my gut. I understood shitbags like Conklin. He only valued human life for the cash and the kicks it provided. Even hardasses like Baxter made sense to me. There were plenty of guys who are 'only following orders.' But people like Grigg or the other scientists and doctors at Singularity House. How did they justify it? And what about the people paying for this? The so-called movers and shakers in the world, people we were supposed to respect, people we were supposed to follow. They couldn't all be psychopaths, could they?

It all came down to who you thought of as being part of your family, you and those like you or the family of man. Us and them or just us. Hadn't that really been the great achievement of history, the gradual widening of the circle of those we consider part of us? I don't know when it had peaked but I did know that in the last twenty years it had been steadily shrinking.

But why should I be surprised at that? Hadn't I let it shrink in my own life?

"She was an unblemished human being," I repeated, "and they're going to turn her into a tool for their own selfish ends."

"It's worse than that," said Wannamaker. "There's more involved than the Russian tech. They aren't stopping at implanting a few directives. They're planning on implanting an entire new personality. They intend to wipe Cerise away and use her body and brain to house someone else. It's like another remake of *Night of the Living Dead*."

"Who?"

"There are hundreds of people in the world," said Angel, "old enough that even rejuv and organ replacement can't keep them going. Or sick with the dozen or so diseases that we still can't treat let alone cure. Some are rich enough to pay whatever price Singularity House is asking."

"So Singularity House is behind this, what's his name, Erich Carpentier? He's the master mind that set this all in motion?"

"We're not sure, Frank," said Angel. "He certainly developed some of the tech but Yankovy didn't think he had the contacts to steal the Russian Bug or to bring Conklin on-board to provide the muscle. There were bigger players. Rupert White's name came up."

The mysterious Mr. White seemed to have it in for our part of the world. I'd run into the results of his efforts before though I'd never run into him. Maybe I'd have to try to fix that. Right after I fixed Gale Conklin.

I stood up.

"Where are you going Frank?" asked Wannamaker.

"I'm going home," I said. It was at least partly true.

"And then you're going to Singularity House," said Angel, which was completely true.

"This isn't a problem that can be solved with a Kalashnikov," said Wannamaker.

"Wanna bet?"

"Frank, you don't have all the facts."

"And you do?"

Wannamaker and Angel exchanged glances. Maybe they exchanged more than that. They were Borg and could do lots of things I'd never catch. It was really starting to piss me off.

"Listen, Frank…"

"No, you listen, Buzz! Someone butchered my son. They didn't just kill him; they carved away everything he wanted to be. For all I know they even wiped his brain before they did it. Maybe it wasn't Carpentier and the rest of his mad scientists at Singularity House that did the actual deed but they were behind it. I don't give a shit what happens in Russia or anywhere else. I only care what happens here, in my town. It's my job, it's my fucking duty as a cop and as a father to deal with this. And that's what I'm going to do."

"Nice speech, Superintendent," said Angel. "But this has nothing to do with your job or your duty. It has to do with vengeance not justice. Joshua wouldn't have wanted…"

"Don't fucking try to tell me what my son wanted. You didn't know my son or…"

"I knew him better than you did."

I wanted to hit her then—wanted to slap the grim determined expression off her face. I would have too, except she was right. Joshua had chosen his family. He had chosen the Borg; hell, he had chosen my brother Mike over me. Maybe, if he had lived, I'd have had my chance. But he was gone. Gone forever and all I could do was to try to do the right thing, try to do what would have made him proud. I didn't think storming a factory in the middle of Calgary, with no regard for innocence or guilt, qualified.

I unclenched my fists and then I unclenched my jaw. I wanted to unclench my heart too but there would be no coming back from that. Collapsing in tears didn't qualify either.

"So what would Joshua do?" I asked.

"He'd want you to catch the people who killed him and the others,' said Wannamaker. "That means Conklin and the three monsters he's created."

"Three?" said Angel. "There were only two at my apartment."

"Which means Conklin still has the other one with him," I said. "And that's assuming he stopped at three."

"Why would he split them up?" asked Wannamaker.

"I'm not sure," I said. Conklin might be evil but he didn't do things without a purpose. Maybe he was trying to create a distraction or maybe there was something more sinister involved. "Whatever his reason, I can't take the chance of letting them run amok. This city has enough monsters running loose as it is. I'm going to have to tell Chief O'Reilly what's going on."

"Chief *Willa* O'Reilly?" Wannamaker's metal eyebrow arched.

"Arsenault works in mysterious ways," I said. "What else do I need to tell the Chief?"

"Conklin is probably taking Cerise Kavanah to Singularity House though we don't think he's done it yet," said Angel. "Look, three of the scientists at Singularity House are Borg, so they may be in immediate danger. I know two of them and I've met some of the other scientists, too. They would be horrified by what is going on, at how their research is being perverted. We need to find some way to get them out or at least warn them that a police raid is coming."

"Or to get them to help us,' said Wannamaker. He explained about Siqueira Silva and the information he'd provided on the secret project. "Funny thing is," he concluded, "they expected Cerise's memory wipe to be permanent. Something must have interfered with that."

Another Borg from Brazil. I wondered if that was a coincidence. Maybe someone else was taking a hand in these matters. Someone with as much money and power as Rupert White but working for the other side. For my side.

"There's something else I think you need to know, though even I don't know what it means." He hesitated. I had a feeling I wasn't going to like what he was about to tell me. As it turned out my instincts were right. And wrong.

"Joshua somehow hooked himself up to the equipment in Singularity

House."

I was confused. "He tried to wipe his own memories?"

"Not the Bug," said Wannamaker. "The upload device. He uploaded part of himself into one of the storage devices in the lab."

"Why would he do that? Surely he didn't want to transfer his mind into..."

"No," said Wannamaker, "he wanted to stop that from happening."

"I'm not sure if I'm following you. He said he only had minutes alone with the girl. He couldn't know how long the process might take, could he?"

"It was his field. At the very least, he figured out what it did and how he could use it. He may have been able to access the system after he left the lab. Either from his work station at Singularity House or later somewhere else."

"Mike said he was brilliant." I wish I had known that before but maybe it was enough that I knew it now. "But why?"

"I think he sent an idea, a wish, into the computer and then used the field it generated to send a message. The range wouldn't be great but it reached Siqueira Silva. I think he left as many messages as many places as he could to try to get people to act if he couldn't himself."

"Like the journal he left with Mike."

"Those thoughts and desires are still there, stored in the photonic memory. I left a device in place linked to that memory and, if it's still there, we can use it to reach Siqueira Silva and the others."

"Wouldn't their security systems detect the signal?" asked Angel.

"Not if we did it the same way Joshua did."

Now I had another reason not to storm the barricades at Singularity House. A part of my son was stored in a box, not quite alive but not quite dead either. Maybe there was some way still to touch him.

"Alright," I said. "Set it up. I'll go see Willa. Meet me at headquarters at 7 a.m. Both of you."

| | |

It wasn't six yet but Acting Chief Willa O'Reilly was already at her desk, or rather the desk in Chief Arsenault's little-used downtown office. My visit was more than a courtesy call. I needed to know exactly where things stood not only with the Department but with Willa.

I've never had a problem reporting to women, especially competent smart women I respected. But less than six months ago, Willa was reporting to me. We crossed the line in more ways than one and we'd kept our distance ever since. I wasn't sure how we'd deal with this new relationship. At least, it couldn't be worse than the way I was dealing with my new relationship with Nancy.

"Sit down, Frank," she said, after the uniform in the outer office ushered me into her inner sanctum. "Coffee?"

I nodded and sat in one of Arsenault's famous leather chairs while she played mother. When she handed me a cup, I sniffed it appreciatively.

"Mountain grown Kona," I said. It was an old game we played.

"You're amazing, Frank." She sat behind Arsenault's desk rather than beside me on the other chair.

"How much do you know about what's going on at Singularity House?" I asked.

"I know exactly as much as the Chief decided I need to know."

It was going to be like that.

"They're killing street kids. They're involved with the Borg murders. They're behind the theft of Russian technology."

"I see," said Willa. "Do you have evidence? And by that I mean legally obtained evidence that will convince a judge and jury."

Josh's journal might qualify but would hardly stand up against a concerted defense. He made allegations against Singularity House but little more. We might be able to get Doctor Siqueira Silva to testify but first we'd have to get him out alive.

When I didn't answer, Willa nodded.

"I understand how you feel, Frank, I really do. But I think you need to concentrate on the task at hand. I believe you have reason to think Gale Conklin is involved somehow in the Borg killings, perhaps in league with one of the Clean Boy gangs."

I wasn't sure how she knew that. I hadn't shared my suspicions with Arsenault's office though I'm sure he had his own sources in the SDU. Maybe Willa still did, too.

"Yeah, but Conklin is…"

Willa held up her hand. "…a known racketeer with dozens of outstanding warrants to his name. I suggest you make finding and stopping Gale Conklin your number one priority."

"Sure," I said. I didn't have to be hit in the head with a baseball bat to understand we were playing ball. "But that could be dangerous."

She was way ahead of me. Willa handed me a letter on the Chief's stationary.

"Gale Conklin is wanted on suspicion of murder and is armed and dangerous. This letter authorizes you to take whatever measures you consider reasonable and prudent to apprehend him. I've downloaded an electronic version to your palm and registered it in the appropriate databases."

In other words, do whatever you want in the pursuit of Gale Conklin wherever that leads. Including Singularity House. And if you fuck up, it'll be your ass in a sling. Fair enough. I was getting tired of this job anyway. At least I now knew where I stood. On my own.

I took the letter, folded it twice and slipped it into my jacket pocket. I gave Willa my best regulation salute. Anyone who didn't know us would have thought I was pissed off. But Willa and I were family and families have their own language.

Hayden Trenholm

Chapter 36

Sanchez's heart leapt when he saw Angel outside the SDU board-room, talking to Buzz Wannamaker. He had spent the entire night searching the city for her, after the police forensics' unit had assured him she wasn't anywhere in her blood-spattered apartment. Without thinking, he swept her up in his arms and held her close.

"I thought I'd lost you," he whispered into her hair. "I think I love you."

Angel didn't say anything but kissed him hard. Actions do speak louder than words.

Wannamaker cleared his throat.

"Maybe you guys should get a room," he said.

"I wish," said Angel, grinning.

Sanchez looked at Wannamaker. He knew the two of them went a long way back. But Wannamaker smiled and clapped him on the shoulder.

"I hate to break up this love-in," said Frank Steele as he stepped out of his office, "but we have work to do." He gestured them into the meeting room where Lily Chin, looking bruised but determined, was waiting with the other members of the SDU. Notably absent was Dr. Vanessa Pham, her place at the table taken by a wary-looking Antoine King. Sanchez had forgotten all about him and their scheduled rendez-vous in the madness of the previous night's events.

Steele took his seat at the end of the table and took a letter out of his jacket pocket. He unfolded it and put it on the table in front of him. Steele looked tired, as if he hadn't slept for three days, which Sanchez thought, is probably not far from true. The man looked every one of his fifty-seven years but there was fire in his eyes when he raised his head and took in the room. He held each of them in his gaze, stopping long-est when he came to Sanchez. Sanchez held his gaze, suddenly wanting nothing more than to find acceptance in his commanding officer's ap-praisal. Steele finally nodded and addressed his team.

"We have our marching orders," Steele said, smoothing the letter with one hand. "Gale Conklin has become public enemy number one as far as the SDU is concerned. He is our target. We think he may be connected to the recent Borg murders, possibly assisting a Clean Boy

228

gang with some form of performance enhancing drugs. Dr. Pham thought the attacks on Borg are in retaliation for a number of deaths among Clean Boy recruits."

"That's one theory," said Antoine King, his voice quavering, though whether from anger or nerves, Sanchez wasn't sure.

"For those of you who don't know yet," said Steele, "Dr. Pham has resigned her position. Under duress, I think. Mr. King is acting in her place."

"There's something you need to know about Vanessa Pham," Sanchez said.

"Speak."

"She received the Citation of Valour while serving as a cop in Winnipeg during the Troubles."

"Yeah," said Steele, "she's a fucking hero. Tell me something I don't know."

"During the incident that earned her that Citation, her partner was killed by a gang of US military augments."

Buzz Wannamaker said something high and fast. Angel laid her hand across his arm.

"Her partner was killed by Borg?" asked Steele.

"Modified soldiers are not Borg," said Angel.

"But close enough that real Borg might bring back bitter memories," said Steele. He smiled and looked at Sanchez. "Prejudice against the Borg is not uncommon. Pham is a professional, she wouldn't let it bias her work."

King shook his head but said nothing.

Steele wants something from me, thought Sanchez. *Maybe it's time I gave it to him.*

"I think your respect for professionals is admirable," said Sanchez. "But a little...naïve."

Steele raised an eyebrow at that. "Go on, Inspector. You have my attention"

"There's more to the story. Things were bad in Winnipeg. Cops were killing cops. The normal command structure had broken down and the police were more like a group of loosely connected gangs, not always working for a common purpose."

"Yeah," said Steele. "I've experienced something similar myself."

"Then you know that sometimes boundaries get crossed. Cops were working with people they trusted. Vanessa Pham's partner was also her husband."

He had their undivided attention now. The only sound in the room was the faint sigh of the ventilation system.

"And her husband's name was David Conklin."

"Fuck me," said Steele.

"And her next of kin is listed in her personal file as G. Conklin."

| | |

Steele had wasted no time after that. He clearly knew what he wanted and had a pretty good idea how to get it. He upgraded the APB for Vanessa Pham to a warrant for her arrest. He wanted to give her the benefit of the doubt—the SDU stuck up for their own even when they were traitors—but he wasn't going to let her continued freedom become a liability.

Sanchez and Jones were assigned a tactical team, headed by Jim McConnaghey, and sent to investigate known Clean Boy hangouts. They were to report back to Lily Chin who was still not fit enough for street duty. She didn't look ecstatic about being given the desk job but gave Steele a sharp salute and headed for dispatch. *She'd be the right choice even if she weren't injured,* thought Sanchez. *She's the only one in the SDU the rest of the force actually likes. That would come in handy if this turned into a serious shooting war.*

Lepinsky was assigned to investigate the Angels of God connection, while Phalen was sent to the new Borg safe house and medical clinic to get suggestions on how to deal with Conklin's creations.

Steele didn't say what he would be doing while the rest of the SDU fanned out across the city but Sanchez knew it involved Angel, Wannamaker and from what he overheard Steele say to the two Borg, Wannamaker's new partner, Darwhal Singh, as well. He felt a sharp ache at the thought of being separated from Angel and wondered whether he would go rogue himself if something happened to her during the operation.

It bothered Sanchez that Steele was using civilians instead of calling in departmental backup. He'd only used Sergeant McConnaghey because they were old friends and Steele trusted him implicitly. *Once people stop trusting the system,* thought Sanchez, *it was only a matter of time before the moral code cops used to interpret the rules replaced the rules altogether.*

Ottawa, where Sanchez grew up, had suffered less than most places during the Troubles. Maybe it was the culture of bureaucratic caution or maybe it was the fact it had snowed almost every summer during the

20s but people there had mostly followed the rules and done what they were told. Still, he had heard his father debate with his fellow cops what they would do if things fell apart the way they had in Toronto or some of the big American cities. His father, who had emigrated from Colombia at the turn of the century, always argued for the rule of law but he was often in the minority.

Jones was driving the armoured personnel carrier Steele had requisitioned for them. McConnaghey was riding shotgun while Sanchez sat in back with the seven tac-officers. Given what he had heard about the Borg-killers, he would have preferred one of the Department's two tanks but they were only available if martial law was declared. Sanchez had abandoned his suit for body armour though he covered it with a knee-length black cloak and he eschewed a helmet in favor of his favourite fedora. Being safe didn't have to come at the cost of looking good.

The grid had cleared a path through most of the traffic between headquarters and the Kensington area that marked the edge of Clean Boy territory. Those drivers bold or stupid enough to risk high-speed downtown driving off-grid either got out of the way or had their systems overridden and their vehicles sent to the impound lot, with them still inside.

Kensington had once been one of the trendier areas of town, home to gourmet coffee shops, repertory cinemas and university professors. Now the academics lived in the secure towers on campus, their houses cut up into apartments or sold to lower middle class families for whom this was a way station on the way to better things. The shops and cinemas had been replaced with a weird mix of churches, bars and sex shops. And, of course, Clean Boy clubhouses.

Like most groups, the Clean Boys had both good and bad among them. The term itself wasn't even their own but one the media had started to use when the first big influx of young men and women had arrived from the religious colonies south of the city. Those self-sufficient and well-armed colonies had prospered and grown during the Troubles and, when the Troubles ended, decided to send their surplus population into the city to separate the heathens from their money. Most of them were hard workers earning honest livings at whatever jobs they could find, living frugally and sending their earnings home. They kept to themselves and might not have been noticed at all if not for the multitude of their churches and their uniform look. The men wore dark suits and were mostly clean-shaven, though some groups sported closely trimmed beards, and the women, when they were seen in public at all, wore dresses that covered their limbs and bonnets tied tight over their hair.

Others took a more liberal view of their mission. They avoided sin themselves but saw nothing wrong with profiting from the sins of others. They ran gambling houses and sex dream shops, peddled drugs or bootlegged booze. It was rumoured they traded in stolen human organs, too, though none had ever been convicted of it.

Those were the ones Sanchez had been sent looking for. They had a list of nine clubhouses to check, all associated with Clean Boy groups who had known criminal connections. Sanchez put the three implicated in the organ harvesting at the top of the list. They were the ones Conklin had most likely approached first when he came back to town. If you could believe that stealing organs from heathens, killing or at least maiming them in the process, could somehow fit within the Ten Commandments, you could also buy that taking drugs that turned you into Borg-killing monsters didn't cross the line either.

McConnaghey insisted on doing things by the book. Go in fast and hard, knock down resistance before it could get organized. Secure the perimeter and the exits before starting negotiations. Sanchez wasn't sure it was the best approach in this case but Steele had made it clear that, while Sanchez was in charge of the investigation, he was to defer to McConnaghey in all matters tactical.

The first clubhouse on the list was on Kensington Avenue, not more than a block from the bar where Wannamaker had found Cerise Kavanah in the company of Gale Conklin. Added to its past associations with parts of Conklin's empire, that made it the most likely culprit according to departmental intelligence.

Half of McConnaghey's team poured out the back of the APC as soon as they crossed the bridge, two of them heading for the back of the building, while the other two took up positions on nearby rooftops. Jones hit the accelerator and the vehicle's backup propane engines kicked in as they rocketed around the corner and pulled up in front of the clubhouse main entrance.

The building had once housed a cinema and the marquee still arched over the now-armoured front doors, but instead of advertising films, the plasma display ran animations of biblical torments alternating with simple text messages inviting new recruits. Half a dozen young men were lounging around the doors, smoking clove cigarettes and calling out insults to passersby.

McConnaghey and the three remaining team members were out of the vehicle before it rolled to a stop. Two of the men made a dash for the entrance while a couple more fumbled inside their jackets for weapons. All four of them were on the ground within seconds, twitching and jerking from the effect of shock devices. McConnaghey fired a couple rounds of Nausene through the front entrance before those inside could get it shut.

In the distance, Sanchez heard the soft thump of shaped charges as the back entrance was blown open. The occupants at the back of the building were undoubtedly getting their own taste of the vomit-inducing gas.

In less than thirty seconds, the front doors flew open and the remaining Clean Boys staggered into the street, the faces pale and their clothing stained with the remains of their breakfasts.

It was a nice neat operation. Unfortunately it was the wrong house. There was no sign of Conklin, his transformed warriors or of Vanessa Pham.

Sanchez sat in the back of the APC with McConnaghey, going over the list of possible targets. The next target on the list, not more than three blocks away, would be more than ready for them.

"Maybe we should skip them," said McConnaghey, "and hit number three. They're on the other side of 16th Avenue. They might not have heard about this raid." He sounded dubious.

"Intelligence said this Club was nearly 60% likely to be the place. Number two on the list is rated in the thirties. Number three, less than five."

"You know what they say about police intelligence."

"It's an oxymoron."

McConnaghey grinned. "Naw, they say they're fucking idiots."

Sanchez laughed and looked back at the list displayed on his palmtop. Maybe they were looking at this all wrong. The list was comprised of known Clean Boy organizations; groups with criminal connections that Conklin might have had arrangements with. But what if Conklin had hooked up with a previously unknown sect? Steele's informant, Taroc Smith, had said the Angels of God had helped bring Conklin back across the border. Like the Clean Boys, the Angels had arisen out of the millenarian movements of the late twentieth century and both had close ties to the colonies that had proliferated on both sides of the Alberta border during the Troubles. They had their religious differences, often violently expressed, but Sanchez could imagine situations where they might be willing to work together, especially if it helped hurt their mutual enemy, the Borg.

"If you wanted to launch attacks on the Borg, Sergeant," Sanchez asked, "where would you set up base?"

"Not here," said McConnaghey. "We've increased monitoring along the river in the wake of the problems last year. It's not exactly a no-go zone but we pretty much know who's coming and going, both Clean Boy and Borg. I think it would have been pretty difficult for a trio of seven-foot monstrosities to slip back and forth unnoticed."

"Why didn't you mention this before?"

"No one asked me. First rule of a long and happy career, don't volunteer information." McConnaghey laughed. "Pretty much the same rule applies to marriage."

"I'll keep that in mind." No wonder Steele trusted McConnaghey. They could be twins separated at birth. "Where then?"

"Southeast. Someplace with a lot heavy industry or warehousing where public surveillance is limited. And I sure as hell wouldn't pick someplace like this." He waved at the now darkened marquee. " No, I'd probably have three or four places, well separated, with little traffic between them. Operate in cells. Something like that."

That made sense. Southeast Calgary was almost a separate jurisdiction, with limited City infrastructure or control. The larger corporate entities kept industrial compounds covering a dozen city blocks. The streets inside were private and were patrolled by corporation security forces. Corporations didn't much care about the law as long as order was maintained. For the right price, they'd have no problem turning a blind eye to someone like Gale Conklin.

Hardly anyone lived between Glenmore Trail and the edge of the industrial district south of 100th Avenue. Nobody, including the Borg, would be expecting attacks from that quarter and small groups of Clean Boys, no matter how grotesque they had become, might well be able to operate from there with impunity.

Sanchez called up a map of the area on his palmtop, a square nearly forty blocks per side. The prospect of tracing even one of the cells McConnaghey postulated seemed daunting.

But sometimes you get lucky.

Jones leaned into the back from his place in the driver's seat.

"I've been tracking progress on the search Superintendent Steele had me set up. There were four black vans in the area of the safe house but only one had a destination in the southeast. We've got an address."

Chapter 37

The black cargo van was gone when they came out of the warehouse, taken by the woman and her two monstrous companions, but a smaller silver van with tinted windows waited in its place. Amos thrust Cerise in through the side door and then crawled in through the double back doors, bent almost in half to make his massive frame fit. His misshapen head hung over the back of the seat and Cerise could feel his breath on the back of her neck as she cowered against the far side of the cab. It was oddly sweet smelling and faintly spicy like a mixture of cinnamon, honey and lavender. But beneath it lurked the metallic musk of his body.

Conklin slammed the rear doors shut and squeezed into the front seat beside the pale, ginger-haired driver. The trip to Singularity House took less than five minutes. They passed two police cruisers on the way but no one was looking for her, or at least, they weren't looking for her in a silver van. Cerise knew screaming would do nothing but anger Amos. She didn't want to see him angry.

The van pulled through the rear gate and backed up to the loading doors. Amos lifted her over the back seat and carried her in one arm into the building, down a set of stairs and along a hall to the all-too-familiar lab. She saw no one other than two burly but otherwise normal-looking guards who refused to make eye contact with her.

Amos dropped her in a chair and stood by the entrance, staring at her. There was no one else in the lab. Conklin had continued down the hall when they entered it. Several minutes passed and she tried edging off the chair. Amos grunted and took a step in her direction. His swollen purple tongue slid back and forth over his lips and he reached down with right hand and began to rub his crotch. He took another step and Cerise shrank back in the chair.

"Call off your dog, Conklin," said a tall man, standing in the doorway, almost filling it. Cerise remembered him. Baxter. He was dressed in a dark rumpled suit and hadn't shaved in several days, though that didn't hide the bruise on the side of his face. His voice sounded fierce but his eyes kept shifting from side to side as if he were hunting for a way out.

"Amos," Conklin said softly, almost as if he were addressing an animal rather than a man.

Amos shook his head and took another step, reaching for Cerise with his left hand. Conklin took a small device out of his pocket and pointed it at the lumbering form. Amos shuddered and took another step. Drool was running down his chin. The front of his trousers tented forward. Cerise was a virgin but she still knew what that was. It both fascinated and horrified her.

"Amos," said Conklin, louder this time. He adjusted the setting on the device in his hand. Amos barked with pain, his head thrown back, his hands flailing, but he stopped moving forward.

Slowly, he turned to face his tormentor.

"Kill you," he growled.

Conklin's expression didn't change. He pointed the device at Amos and pressed its trigger repeatedly. Each time, Amos' body jerked as if he had been hit by a massive fist, his head snapping from side to side. Howls of anger and pain shook the room. But he kept moving toward Conklin, one small staggering step at a time as if he were pushing through surging surf.

Baxter backed away, drawing a revolver from behind his back.

"Jesus Christ, Conklin! What the fuck's going on here?"

Conklin adjusted the device again. In the sudden respite, Amos lurched forward. Baxter emptied his pistol, the report deafening in the enclosed space. Amos swatted the air in front of him as if he were waving away flies. He had almost reached Conklin when the fat man triggered the device again.

The giant's head snapped from side to side and he arched backward so fiercely that it carried him off his feet. His legs and arms whipped through the air. Cerise was sure she heard his bones snapping. Amos fell onto his back, twitched several times and was still.

Conklin stepped forward and prodded the still form with the point of his shoe.

"Is he dead?" asked Baxter. He had retreated through the door and was now flanked by the two guards, their rifles unslung and pointed in the direction of the fallen monster.

"Quite," said Conklin.

"What the fuck was that about?" asked Baxter.

"They get like that after awhile. Fortunately I had the foresight to install my little leash." He slipped the small box back into his coat. "The more powerful they become, the less rational they are. We don't know why yet. It's been a major disappointment to my employers."

"Your problem is, you have too many employers."

"My services are in much demand. What's a fellow to do? Speaking of which, I believe the arrangement was cash on delivery."

"Fifty million has already been transferred into your off-shore account."

"Fifty?" said Conklin, frowning.

"The other fifty is contingent on the transfer being successful," said Baxter. "That was the arrangement."

"Yes," said Conklin. "I suppose it was."

"You paid one hundred million dollars for me?" said Cerise. "That's crazy."

Baxter looked at her for the first time, his eyes flat and expressionless. "That's what *I* said. Cunts like you are a dime a dozen."

"Your employer didn't think so. His specifications were…quite specific." Conklin tilted his head and his eyes briefly unfocused. "Hmm, it seems another warrant has been issued for my arrest."

Baxter laughed. "I'd think you'd be used to that by now."

"It seems this one is a little open-ended. I think I'll have to trust you for the other fifty. Pressing business, you know."

"You can leave with me, Gale. I have a jet waiting to take both of us to NoCal." Cerise jumped at the sudden voice from behind her. She twisted in her seat. Three men had appeared, seemingly out of nowhere. One of them was a Borg she had never seen before. But the other two had been there the last time. Carpentier and the man who had spoken, whose name she had never heard.

"Sprach slide four eleven over quesa machta Borg slin cha three three three tangent ka," she said, almost without thinking. The last of her lost memories fell into place. There had been a Borg, not this one but a younger, less modified one. He had shone lights in her eyes and said this to her, told her to repeat it to any Borg she saw. She had said it to Wannamaker in the car, after he rescued her. He must have hypnotized me, she thought.

"What did she say, Doctor?" said the nameless man.

"It is an Independista slogan," said the Borg. "I can't imagine where she heard it."

"I can."

"What's he doing here?" asked Baxter.

"Dr. Siqueira Silva has shown such an interest in our little project that I thought I'd let him stay and watch."

"I don't like it,' said Baxter. "This operation works on a need to know basis, Mr. White."

White looked around the room, pointedly staring at the two armed guards. "And every one needed to know my name?"

Baxter blanched.

"Oh, don't worry, Baxter. I'm sure I can trust that *your* men won't say anything. And Dr. Siqueira Silva will be coming on the plane with Gale and me. Though he won't be going all the way to San Francisco."

Conklin laughed. It was an ugly sound.

"What are you going to do to me?" asked Cerise. She didn't think it had anything to do with her virginity anymore. She almost wished it did.

"Don't worry. You won't feel much pain. So they tell me anyway. And it's not as if you'll remember it." White gestured at Carpentier, who began moving equipment into the centre of the room.

It was now or never, thought Cerise. Baxter still stood in the doorway, the two guards stationed behind him. But there must be a door in the other wall, maybe behind that rack of computer towers. She leapt to her feet and ran for her life. White tried to grab her and she brought her knee up hard the way she'd been taught at school. He twisted but she still made solid contact with his thigh. She pushed hard and he fell to the floor, grunting in pain as his shoulder slammed into the ground. She danced by him and dashed for the bank of computers. The Borg moved faster than she thought possible and pulled her against him, pinning her arms to her sides. His breath was warm against her face, smelling faintly of tobacco.

"There is no escape through there," he whispered in her ear. "Not for either of us. I will do what I can."

White got to his feet. His face was flushed and his mouth twisted in an angry snarl. He glared at Cerise and she thought he was going to hit her. Then he took a deep breath, smoothed down his suit and smiled as if nothing had happened.

"Wasn't that exciting?" he said. He looked at her, his icy blue eyes above his calculated smile dead and flat.

Cerise remembered an expression her preacher sometimes used. The banality of evil. She had never really understood what he meant until this moment.

White looked harmless, normal. He was a few inches taller than average and was showing the beginning of a middle-age spread. His pale face was clean-shaven and round, almost plump. His brown hair was conservatively styled. Only the blueness of his eyes seemed out of the ordinary and, then, only when he stared at you. His suit probably cost a fortune but it didn't look much different than one he could have bought in any clothing store. He looked like a hundred other business men she might pass in the mall without a second glance.

No tail, no horns, no glowing red skin. But so casually evil in his thoughts and actions that he made Conklin and his creatures seem like cartoon copies. When Baxter said his name it was like calling down a curse.

"What are you going to do to me?" she asked again.

"Unlike Gale, I've never seen the point of causing unnecessary fear or pain. There's no profit in it. But in your case I think I'll make an exception. Besides I've had a slight change of heart about your fate.

"We were going to wipe your memory clean. We've already done a little test run in that regard. You responded exactly as predicted."

Cerise realized they didn't know her memories had all come back. Maybe that was something she could use. Though she didn't know how yet.

"Tabula rasa, a blank slate, ready to have a new mind inscribed upon it. A copy of that mind sits waiting in the next room, all that remains of the woman who was courageous enough to be the first of the new pioneers."

Cerise wondered how much courage it took to steal someone else's life.

White continued. "She died waiting for us to find you—determined not simply to be reborn but to be reborn into a body and brain as closely resembling her own young self as was currently possible. It took seven months and the good offices of our friend, Gale, but here you are."

"Why not use a clone?" Cerise asked.

"Good god, what do they teach children at school these days? Cloning is fine for organ transplant but has serious limits when it comes to complex organisms. They tend to die young, you know."

"I'm ready here," said Carpentier.

"Not yet," said White. "Cerise must learn not to attack her betters."

"I thought she was to be untouched," said Conklin. "If I'd only known there was some latitude in that."

"I have no intention of harming this perfect receptacle. No, I have a better idea. We have to drill through her head for the download anyway. Why not kill two birds with one laser beam. We have spare capacity. Let's make a copy of this sweet girl and when I find a suitably aged, suitably diseased, and suitably disgusting host, we will bring her back. If only briefly."

A fate worse than death. Another expression Cerise hadn't understood until now.

"It's not that simple," said Carpentier. "The upload is the most complex part of the process. I'll need a technician to monitor the calibrations."

"I'm sure Dr. Siqueira Silva would be happy to help—in exchange for being allowed to stay on the plane all the way to San Francisco," said White.

Cerise looked into the face of the Borg scientist. He was still holding her though he had loosened his grip. When she tried to move away, he shook his head. A soft sad smile played across his lips. His mechanical eyes gazed into hers, more human than any of the others in the room. His voice vibrated in her jaw, so only she could hear it. "I will do what I can."

"It's going to take me a few minutes to boot up another memory cache," said Carpentier. He went behind the bank of computers. After a moment he called, "Could you give me a hand in here, Silva?" His voice was muffled.

White gestured at Baxter to take charge of Cerise and Dr. Siqueira Silva went into the next room. Several minutes passed before they returned. Carpentier was flushed, a thin sheen of sweat across his brow despite the coolness of the room.

"Is there a problem, Erich?"

"Nothing serious," said Carpentier. "One of the spare units appears to have some data contamination. I had to isolate it. I'll do a purge later. It won't affect what we're doing now."

"Very well. Put her on the gurney."

Baxter grabbed Cerise's shoulders, his hands hard and hot through her blouse, and pushed her toward the waiting stretcher. She struggled against his grip, twisting one arm free. She threw her elbow back and felt it connect with the side of Baxter's head.

"You little bitch," he growled. He cuffed her above her ear and then wrapped his arm around her neck, his forearm tight against her throat, cutting off her air. He slipped his other hand off her shoulder and around her torso, pulling her back against him, lifting her off her feet. Black specks clouded her vision and her blood roared in her ears.

"Don't damage her."

Carpentier grabbed her legs and Baxter loosened his hold on her throat so she could breathe again. Between them they carried her to the gurney. Baxter held her down by lying across her chest while Carpentier tightened the straps. Cerise fought as best she could, lashing out with fists and feet but they were both big men and in a few moments they had her cinched against the foam padding.

"You're quite the fighter, Cerise," said White, "Madame Deleveaux would be impressed. I'm sure she'll be pleased with our choice for her."

"You won't get away with this," Cerise said.

"Of course I will," he said.

"Superintendent Steele will stop you," she said.

"Ah, yes, the redoubtable Frank Steele," White said and laughed. "I don't think he'll be giving us any trouble."

"Then God will punish you. He'll send you to hell when you die."

"But that's just it. I don't intend to die."

Cerise watched in horror as Carpentier approached her with a helmet connected to the racks of computers by a thick cable. They were going to steal her mind and lock her in those boxes.

He fit the helmet over her head and tightened the strap under her chin. He made a few adjustments and then stepped away. Cerise tried to turn her head but they had clamped it in place.

The Borg had promised to help her but he wasn't doing anything. He was helping them instead. Didn't he know White was a liar? He wasn't going to let him live after this was done. He'd killed so many people already. What was one more? She wanted to scream at him, make him see the truth, make him help her, but the leather strap across her mouth was too tight. All she could do was moan.

Tigresses don't cry, she thought. *They breathe and they wait and strike when they can.* She was tigress. She would have her revenge. Somehow.

There was a tingling in her scalp and the stench of burning hair. *My hair. They're burning my hair.* She squeezed her eyes tight to keep from crying. *Tigresses don't cry.*

The equipment hummed for what seemed like forever. After the first tingle she felt nothing. Then the humming stopped. She was still in her body. The machine hadn't worked. Maybe now they would let her go.

"Did you get it?" asked White.

"Confirming now," said Carpentier. "Check sums are all good. Securing memory imprints in unit five-alpha-five. Secured. And engaging transmission lockdown protocols. Doctor?"

"Lockdown protocols not set," said Siqueira Silva. "We have interference in the transmitter. Resetting defaults."

"What's going on?" asked Baxter.

"I don't know," said Carpentier. "We need to isolate the memory copy from the operating network. The whole system could come down."

"Defaults not reset. I'll try linking to the central server. That should reboot the security system."

"Wait," said Carpentier. "The copy could bleed off into the Net. The unit could be fatally contaminated."

"Would you rather lose the program?" asked Siqueira Silva. "Okay. Defaults reset. Lockdown protocols nominal."

"I trust there's no problem, gentlemen?" White sounded angry. "Will Madame Deleveaux's rebirth be compromised? That would make me very unhappy."

"Let me…" said Carpentier. "No, everything is optimal."

What were they saying? The machine hadn't worked. She was still in her body. She felt the same, exactly like her. That old woman hadn't taken her over.

"You're confused," said White, leaning over her. "I can see it in your eyes. That wasn't the final step, only the first one. There are two more steps. But you'll only experience the next one. We have a copy of you now, locked away for future enjoyment. Soon, it will be all that remains of you."

Carpentier came into her field of vision, the lower half of his face covered in a surgical mask. He sprayed something cold on her face and her skin went numb. She stared in horror as her lowered a hypodermic towards her but she didn't feel the needle go in. Her vision blurred slightly as if her eyes wouldn't focus but she could still see the metal instrument with the small silver pod on the end.

Her head was still clamped tight to the gurney. It wouldn't move no matter how hard she strained the muscles in her shoulders and neck. The silver pod slipped out of her field of vision. She felt the pressure of it being pushed up her nose. She pushed air out of her lungs, trying to stop it, at least slow it. Carpentier kept pushing it deeper.

She saw him reach past her and heard the click of a switch.

Then she was gone.

Chapter 38

The lab assigned to the SDU wasn't as well equipped for standard forensics work as the one downstairs but it had its advantages. I had given Buzz Wannamaker a free hand with the division's capital budget when he was here and much of the stuff he bought was still sitting on shelves at the back of the lab.

Buzz's strength had always been in devising workarounds to standard and sometimes not-so-standard surveillance equipment. I had no doubt he could wind up a rich man someday if he were so inclined but as near as I could tell money didn't interest him much beyond the fun and entertainment it could buy. That might change if he hung around with Singh long enough.

I was eager to get out into the field. I never liked to send the officers under my command into danger if I wasn't there to lead the charge. I had learned to do it as I rose through the ranks but I still didn't like it. But we had some time to kill waiting for Singh to report in.

While Buzz got started in the lab, I asked Angel to brief Constable Phalen on what he needed to know to get access to the Borg community. He was pretty well known and generally well liked in that part of town but I figured Angel would open doors that would otherwise stay closed.

Before he left with Sanchez, I had Caleb Jones start a computer analysis of the surveillance database to see if we could track the black van that had taken Cerise from the safe house. Over ten million digital images and video clips were taken in Calgary every hour. Given enough time and a sufficiently narrow search parameter, we could find almost anything. Unfortunately, 'black cargo van' wasn't particularly narrow and it might take a while to identify the possibilities. It didn't help that the cameras at the safe house had all been trashed. The neighborhood had been chosen because of the low density of surveillance in the area. A safe house wouldn't be very safe if you could identify the occupants using face recognition programs at the library. If we were lucky, we'd get some leads on vans that had moved through the vicinity of the safe house. And that might let us track it to Cerise Kavanah.

I used the same program to set up a rough net around Singularity House but we'd have to be more than lucky to catch them that way.

Corporations weren't crazy about public surveillance around their plants and even less keen on sharing their own.

"Are you sure you can do this?" I asked. The others had gone now and I had joined Buzz in the SDU lab.

"Pretty sure," said Buzz, which didn't sound as confident as I would have liked. "I've been hacking my own body since I became Borg and I took a lot of related courses while doing my degrees."

Angel came in a few minutes later; briefing Phalen hadn't taken as long as I hoped. She wouldn't be happy with what Buzz and I planned to do, though I didn't think there was anyway she could stop it.

Wannamaker had started work on our little project. He had been sure that everything he needed was here in the lab, though who knows what Pham might have done with it in the last few months. I still had time working my head around her connection to Gale Conklin. There was something odd about her bothering to submit a formal resignation that was niggling at my brain. Maybe she's working undercover. Not my problem.

"Theoretically, this should work," said Wannamaker. "Are you sure you want us to try?"

"To the extent I'm sure of anything these days, yeah." The truth was, I was anything but sure. I wasn't even comfortable using my cell or my palm. The thought of plugging myself into a machine turned my guts to water. But part of my son was in that machine. I knew he wasn't alive but as long as a piece of him was locked in there, he wasn't fully dead. And I couldn't mourn him until he was.

"What are you two planning?" asked Angel.

Wannamaker could explain it better than I could but I needed to say it out loud to make sure it didn't sound completely crazy. And maybe because I needed to convince myself it was the right thing to do.

"The device Buzz attached to the computer in the lab allows us limited access to Singularity House systems."

"How limited?"

"We can't hack in directly," I said, "not without being detected and stopped by their security protocols."

"Which, if they're aggressive enough," said Buzz, "could blow every computer in the Headquarters."

"That might fall outside what Chief O'Reilly would consider reasonable and prudent," I said. "But we can detect whenever information moves between the network and the memory storage devices, the ones designed to hold ghosts."

Angel frowned at me. I think she was starting to figure out what I had in mind.

"And when that happens," I said, "we can access the information flow. And we can add our own signal to it."

"Letting you send a message?" asked Angel. She shook her head. "But that wouldn't work unless you had access to the software. Tapping into a data stream won't give you that."

"True," said Wannamaker, "but not essential for our purposes. The file Joshua left in one of the devices is self-activating. As soon as it uploaded it broadcast a signal, the one Siqueira Silva picked up while asleep. If I could trigger a re-boot, it should send the signal again."

"Even if you could do it, I don't see how that helps," said Angel.

"At the very least it will alert Siqueira Silva and any other Borg who picks it up that things are getting dangerous. He might be able to contact us or, better yet, get out of there."

"Maybe you should concentrate on getting that thing finished while I explain to Angel." Buzz didn't look happy but turned back to his work.

"Buzz had a chance to examine the equipment at the lab. With his mods, he really does have a photographic memory."

Angel smiled and tapped the side of her own head. She was Borg, too, able to record whatever she saw for later examination. Borg eyes generally operated much like human ones, flicking from one area of the visual field to the next and sending the scattered images to the visual cortex for processing into the unbroken stream our mind thought it saw. But they could also operate like high speed digital cameras, focusing on one area of interest and scanning it across the electromagnetic spectrum. The information generated could be fed directly into the brain but Wannamaker described it as like taking LSD while riding a roller coaster past fun house mirrors. Rather the information was passed through a series of chips and translated into images that the brain could interpret. Data structures turned into landscape paintings.

"He thinks he can recreate the input device, at least well enough that we may be able to do more than simply trigger the old message. We may be able to send a message of our own. It may even be possible to shut down their system, at least temporarily. It might give us the time we need to rescue the girl."

"I thought the technology at Singularity House was revolutionary," said Angel.

"A lot of things look impossible until you see how they're done." I reached up and pulled a coin from Angel's ear, a trick I learned when Josh was a boy. "Like magic."

"The device combines imaging technology and field generators," said Wannamaker, looking up from his work. "That's why they need eight supercomputers operating in parallel. They scan the brain right down to the neuron level, recording the position of every electron."

"But I thought you couldn't do that," said Angel. "Something about uncertainty."

"You can't know where they are if you know where they're going," I said. At least I thought that was what Buzz had told me.

"Close enough for police work," said Wannamaker. "The field generators produce a momentary stasis, a few microseconds, but long enough for the scanners to do their job. They only need a snapshot of the brain at a moment in time. The memory boxes record all that frozen data. Later when they have a receptacle, a brain, where all the neural paths have been reset to default values, they reverse the process and download the copy into it."

"And that works?"

"Theoretically," said Wannamaker, "they haven't actually done it yet as far as we know."

"What would it be like?" asked Angel.

"One second you're old, tired and evil," I said, "the next you're young, energetic and still evil."

"Or both," said Wannamaker, "if your old body is still alive when they activate the new one."

"But which one is you?"

"They both are," said Wannamaker.

"At least until the young one kills the old one," I said.

Wannamaker and Angel both stared at me.

I shrugged. Maybe the old and new lived in perfect harmony, like father and son. But I doubted it. Too many sons had killed their fathers for far less money and power than was at stake here. These people hadn't gotten where they were by being saints.

Wannamaker made a few final connections and then held up his handiwork for us to look at. He'd used a SWAT helmet for the frame but otherwise it looked pretty much how he had described the unit in Singularity House.

"But how can you make a brain copy, without direct access to the software on the network," asked Angel. She was beginning to look agitated.

"You can't," said Wannamaker.

"But that's not what we're trying to do," I said.

"I'm having second thoughts about this, Frank," said Wannamaker.

It was probably good that someone was, I thought, though I figured they were the same as his first ones. I'd decided to stop thinking about what we were doing and concentrate on my son.

"I've made up my mind," I said.

"It's dangerous, Frank. It could even be fatal."

"Is it ready to go?" I asked. Buzz nodded. "Then you have your orders."

"Buzz isn't under your command anymore," said Angel. "You can't order him to do something he doesn't feel right about doing. You can't put his life at risk."

"Frank wouldn't do that," said Wannamaker, a faint smile playing across his lips, "not even if I still was a cop. This device is for him."

I took the helmet from Buzz and took a closer look. I didn't particularly like the look of the laser drills, though Buzz had assured me the holes they made for the probes were less than a millimetre in diameter. Bone regenerators would heal those in a matter of days.

Still I hoped our little experiment didn't become widely known. Most people in the department already thought I had holes in my head.

"That's crazy," said Angel.

"Sanity has never been a priority for me."

"If you're not trying to copy yourself into one of those memory boxes, what exactly are you trying to do?"

"Pretty much what Joshua did," I said.

"Except," said Wannamaker, "we don't know exactly what he did. I don't think he used equipment at Singularity House. He had access to something similar to this—though we still don't know where or who built it."

"Maybe he built it himself," said Angel.

"Maybe," I said. "But I know someone talked to him right before he made the final entry in his journal. We think there may have been Borg who knew what was going on and who were running interference."

"Siqueira Silva?" asked Angel.

"Not likely," said Wannamaker. "Frank no longer thinks Conklin's monsters came for you. He thinks they were after Gamow. He played me a clip from Joshua's journal. He mentioned Gamow's name."

"I didn't pick it up before because it was in Borg."

"You think Gamow was running this interference operation?" asked Angel.

"Gamow probably let Cerise out of the clinic when I was being attacked," said Wannamaker. "I think something he did behind the scenes is the reason they ran off when she appeared.

"He was the local operative anyway," I said. "I have reason to think there were international connections."

"The Tsar? He and Gamow…"

"May have more in common than you think," I said. "But I think the opposition lies elsewhere."

Wannamaker repeated the name Natasha Redding had used to identify her lover. Angel's eyes widened.

"You've been in touch with him?"

"He was the Borg who was killed in Mount Royal," I said. "We kept the details off the newsgroups. I didn't get the connection at first. Only some of the Borg who were killed had connections to the Independista movement. I think the others may have been, I don't know, opportunistic. Practice. In any case, outside the rest of the pattern."

I put the helmet on my head. It was a snug fit but I got it wedged on. The probes were pressed against my scalp, irritating but not painful. The painful part would come when Wannamaker turned it on. At least, there were only about a dozen, far fewer than the ones in the Singularity House device. We didn't need as many for our purposes.

"You still haven't said what you're doing," said Angel.

Wannamaker pushed the helmet visor down over my face. A thin strip of plasma screen had been glued over the usual readout display, camel clips on either end linking it directly into Wannamaker's palmtop. He'd disconnected the helmet's wireless transceiver to reduce the chances of stray signals interfering with the imaging technology. The helmet was covered with grounded silver mesh to isolate it from the thousands of data transmissions that filled the air at any given time. I felt like one of those people who cover their head in tinfoil to keep out the alien broadcasts.

"I've composed a message in Borg," said Wanamaker, "and converted it to visual code. We're going to use Frank's visual cortex to transmit it into the data stream. He'll direct it towards the unit where Joshua's files are stored. That should do the trick. Siqueira Silva, if he's close enough, will get the message."

"Through his optical implant?"

"Right the first time," said Wannamaker.

"And what will he do?" asked Angel.

"Whatever he can. Are you ready Frank?"

Buzz and I had agreed not to tell the whole story if someone walked in on us. I didn't want O'Reilly or anyone else stopping us. We weren't simply delivering a message. And we sure weren't making a copy of Frank Steele for posterity. If Buzz was right, some part of me, the me that thinks and feels and hurts, was going into that data stream, kind of like virtual reality in reverse. I'd deliver the message, sure, but maybe, just maybe, I'd be able to do something more, interfere in some way to shut the whole thing down before anyone else got hurt. And, maybe, maybe, I'd be able to find Joshua. For that slim chance, I was ready to risk anything.

If Buzz was right, it would only take a few seconds in real time and then I'd be right back here. And if he was wrong, I'd never know the difference.

"Ready when you are."

Pain. Indescribable pain beating at my consciousness like a hammer. It wasn't supposed to hurt this much. Pain and blackness.

Chapter 39

There was no black van in front of the warehouse when the armoured personnel carrier rolled past it. There was a black limousine. A driver in a plain blue suit lounged against the side of the car, smoking a cigarette. His eyes followed the APC as it drove past, though he seemed otherwise unconcerned.

He might be out of uniform but Sanchez knew a cop when he saw one. McConnaghey had reached the same conclusion.

"Anyone know that guy?" he asked, pointing at the close-up displayed on one of the vehicles bank of monitors.

"I do," said Jones. "John Onia. I worked with him in community policing when I was a rookie. I think he's in the Cadre now."

The Cadre was the unofficial name for a select group of officers who worked directly for the Chief. They were as disliked among the rank and file as the SDU but they were also deeply feared. Crossing the Cadre was the same as crossing the Chief and most careers didn't survive doing that more than once. *Except for Frank Steele*, thought Sanchez, *though even his nine lives must be nearly used up.*

"What's he doing here?" asked McConnaghey.

"Why don't we go in and see?"

Jones swung the APC around and they pulled into the parking lot beside the limo. Onia seemed unperturbed. He took one last drag on his smoke and then ground the butt under his heel.

"You folks appear lost," he said.

Sanchez flashed his inspector's badge. Onia shrugged and keyed the remote. The limo locked down and anchored itself, a not so subtle suggestion that a tac-squad was less capable of guarding the car than he was.

He escorted Sanchez through the front door. Inside, he remained by the entrance, staring at Sanchez, his arms folded across his chest, another reminder that the Cadre was a separate force on constant guard against anyone who might prove a danger to the Chief. Onia wasn't that big, wiry rather than muscular, but Sanchez had no doubt he could handle himself in a tight situation.

The warehouse had been converted to some sort of living quarters, half a dozen pieces of ragged furniture scattered around a couple of tables and an entertainment wall. The sour smell of rotting food lay over another more primal scent, the musk of animals in their lair. Arsenault was standing in the middle of the room, as far from the grimy furniture as he could be without actually leaving.

"I'm afraid we missed them, Inspector."

"I thought you were in Moscow, Chief," said Sanchez.

"Things are in turmoil in the Empire. I thought it wise to cut my visit short. Besides, more pressing business."

"Where's Conklin? More importantly where are his monsters?"

"Conklin's monsters? It sounds like a second tier sports team."

"Or an indie band," said a female voice.

Sanchez was startled though he tried not to show it. The woman had been leaning against one of the overstuffed chairs to the left but he hadn't noticed her, until she spoke. *I must be slipping*, he thought. *That could be fatal.* He looked right at her but she still seemed indistinct, almost ephemeral. He realized she was wearing some sort of camouflage, an adaptive cloak that shifted colour and pattern when she moved. And when she was still, she was almost invisible, the light bending around her body so it seemed you were looking right through her. *I've got to get myself one of those*, he thought.

"You're Reno Sanchez, aren't you?" she asked, moving toward him with hand extended. The cloak must have an off switch; it was now a solid coppery red. "Ron has told me a lot about you."

Sanchez took her hand and kissed it. "Only believe the good stuff."

She smiled. It brightened her face. He had seen her somewhere before. It took a moment to place it. He had been one of the three hundred million caught up in her dream to end the Troubles.

"Lady Redding," he said. He remembered the card in his wallet, with the number he hadn't had time to call yet. Boynton Music. Her husband, Sir Jeffry Boynton.

"Natasha," she said. "We're all friends here."

Sanchez doubted that but he smiled anyway. Arsenault seemed to see the humour in it too, though his grin looked a little too shark-like to be really friendly.

"Lady Redding, Natasha," he said, nodding in her direction, "wanted to see a bit of Gale's handiwork. She's been most helpful in dealing with the situation."

Sanchez raised his eyebrows at that.

"I bought the company that's been supplying Mr. Conklin with his…poison. I can assure you it will be some time before his monsters appear again."

Sanchez wasn't too sure about that either. "Pandora's box is difficult to close."

"Sadly true," she said.

"Barbarians at the gate, Sanchez," said Arsenault. "We can't keep
them out. But we can slow them down."

"What was that stuff?"

"Need to know basis," said Arsenault.

"I think Reno needs to know, Ron," said Lady Redding. "Like a lot
of modern nanotech, it was derived from an existing biological machine. This one was based on a variant of human growth hormone.
HGH promotes muscle growth and bone density through increased re-
tention of calcium. These machines go one step further.

"Instead of adding calcium to bones, they begin to add other min-
erals, notably iron. Muscle growth occurs throughout but especially in
quick twitch muscles. The contractive filaments are strengthened
through the addition of elastic polymers. Eventually, new muscles are
added to the body with their own tendons and ligaments. Growth
spurts, similar to those experienced during adolescence, but much
faster and more intense, occur more and more frequently. Towards the
end, the subsequent injections of the drug cause an almost immediate
expansion of the bone and tissue."

"Toward the end?" asked Sanchez.

"The drug eventually causes a breakdown of the glandular system.
It also causes the brain to expand at the same time the skull is thicken-
ing. Reasoning capacity is the first thing to go. Aggression, including
sexual aggression, becomes almost uncontrollable. Death follows about
a week later. The scientists had thought they had solved both problems
in the lab. They were wrong."

"An eight hundred pound gorilla can do a lot of damage in a week,"
said Sanchez.

"My men are dealing with the situation," said Arsenault.

It was rumoured the Cadre spent half their time doing black ops
training at a secret base in the foothills, 'in case of civil emergency.'
This probably qualifies.

"Not exactly true, Ron."

Arsenault's jaw clenched. He didn't like being corrected. That he
didn't make any other response was indicative of exactly how big a
Player, by Yankovy's definition, Lady Redding was.

"Problems?" Sanchez asked.

"Onia." Arsenault jerked his head at the officer by the door. "Check to see when our guest will arrive."

Onia frowned but went back outside.

"This was one of five cells. As you may have guessed, the gang wasn't part of the established Clean Boy hierarchy. It had links to some of the more radical ones but also to the Angels of God. There was a connection to an eco-terrorist organization from Oregon via British Columbia that established a unit here last winter. We think they were involved in the attacks on the water supply, though their motives, as usual, are obscure. Conklin seems to have been the fulcrum around which they all operated."

Onia appeared in the entrance.

"He'll be here in five minutes." He resumed his stance by the door. *He'll never make inspector,* thought Sanchez. *He hasn't figured out when he's been told to fuck off.*

"Get out!" The Chief had to take his frustration out on someone. Onia got out.

"We've cleaned out three of the others. There were about a dozen young men in various stages of transformation. They didn't put up much of a fight. I suspect they had begun to realize what Conklin's treatments were doing to them. Lady Redding is hopeful that most of them will survive, now they are off the drug.

"Unfortunately, the final group appeared to have been expecting us. There were casualties on both sides. In the end, eight of them, including two in the most advanced stages of transformation, fled the scene. There was a woman but we don't know if she was their prisoner or…something else."

"Vanessa Pham," Sanchez said. "Steele says she called him to formally resign."

"That fits with what I know of her."

"How did her connection to Conklin escape notice?"

"It didn't," said Arsenault, sourly. "I thought she was working for us. I was wrong."

"He *is* her brother-in-law," said Sanchez.

"It's more complex than you think, Reno," said Redding.

"How so?" asked Sanchez.

Arsenault abruptly turned on his heel and walked away into the dimly lit end of the warehouse.

When he was out of earshot, Lady Redding said, "Plausible deniability, I think it's called. Chief Arsenault is in a delicate position.

The people behind this—what my old friend Dmitri called Players—have quite diverse holdings, including quite a few judges and politicians. Gale Conklin is not a player himself but he has proven extremely useful to them in the past—including providing arms to rogue military units during the Troubles.

"When her husband was killed, Pham naturally turned to Conklin. Family is very important to her. He was the one who funded her medical education and encouraged her to come to Calgary. She approached the Chief, offering to spy on Conklin—Gale's idea I'm sure. But Vanessa Pham's loyalties lie elsewhere."

"A triple agent?" Sanchez wondered if his suspicions about the New Unity Party were valid.

"A rogue agent," said Redding. "She finds the Borg abhorrent. I don't know whether it's religious feeling or political ideals. I've never understood that kind of ideological purity. She would find what Conklin has done to the Clean Boys equally wrong. Especially when she found out he had been indirectly responsible for his brother's death."

"How do you know so much about Pham?"

"Do you really want to know the answer to that question, Reno?" asked Redding.

Sanchez decided he didn't. Redding had been his hero growing up; he didn't like to think of her prying into the private records of anyone, not even Vanessa Pham.

"So what are we supposed to do about her?"

"I don't know. If she has turned on Conklin, she might still play a useful role."

"Would she use his own monsters against him?"

"In her current frame of mind—anything is possible. But no matter what side she's playing on, there's no question where she'll be headed."

"Singularity House," said Sanchez.

"Very good, Inspector."

"Then I guess we'd better be on our way."

The Chief had returned.

"Conklin is the SDU's problem."

"Meaning?" asked Sanchez.

"I admire loyalty as much as the next man, Sanchez," said Arsenault. "That was why I was willing to let Jim McConnaghey help out an old friend. But there are limits and the Sergeant has other assignments waiting for him at HQ. You can keep Jones and the APC, if you like."

"Thanks."

"Good luck, Inspector. Now, if you'll excuse me, I've got some unpleasant tasks to complete."

And that's how it works in 2044, thought Sanchez. Good men still knew right from wrong. And still wanted to do something about it. But the system, the rules got in their way. Pretty soon he was going to have to choose. Accept the way things were or try to change them to the way they should be. But that was a decision for another day.

Arsenault almost collided with a tall elegant man, coming into the warehouse as the Chief was going out. Singh was dressed in a linen suit and a cream coloured turban. He smiled when he saw Lady Redding, his teeth brilliant in his dark bearded face.

"Darwhal, I'm so glad you could come."

"Natasha, it seems our interests converge once again."

Singh extended his hand and Sanchez took it. The man's palm was remarkably soft and his grip firm but gentle.

"So it will be four of us against the world," Sanchez said.

"Five, actually," said Singh.

"Who's our fifth?" asked Sanchez, looking from Singh to Redding.

Lady Redding looked slightly embarrassed.

"You understand that I can no more be seen to be acting openly against our mutual enemies than the Chief can." Sanchez noticed she had deliberately mentioned no names, though they all knew who was behind all this. Or at least he thought they did. *You're out of your depth, Reno, way out. You couldn't tell the good guys from the bad ones even if you had a score card. Maybe it was time to see if that distinction even mattered anymore.*

"Is Rupert White behind this?"

"Careful, Sanchez." said Singh. Though the man didn't look uninterested in the answer to the question.

"It's alright, Darwhal. Honesty rules today," said Redding. "We're not ready for an open conflict. Neither are our enemies. Today's events will result in a draw. Pawns will be lost—not Players. The Game will go on."

"The Chief's unpleasant business."

"White will make his excuses and leave the others to take the fall," said Redding. She wouldn't meet his eyes.

Singh took his palm out of his jacket pocket and glanced at it.

"Buzz and Angel are on their way here," said Singh. "Though they may be a while."

"What about Steele?"

"Frank will meet us at Singularity House. When the time is right."

"When the time is right? The time is right fucking now. Conklin—"

"Conklin will still be there," said Lady Redding. "You have to understand there is more at stake than a few lives. Hundreds of people, thousands, will be affected by what happens today. Nations could fall."

"The Russian Empire? Frankly, I couldn't…"

"Among others," she said. She sighed deeply. "A man I cared a great deal about died because of what is being built at Singularity House. In fact, Dick died *for* it. And his father, Doctor Siquiera Silva, is in Singularity House, prepared to die for it, too. We need to save him and we need to save some of what they've created there. And that won't happen if we act too soon."

"And Frank Steele is on board with this?" said Sanchez. "The last time I saw him he wasn't the picture of patience."

"Frank knows more about Singularity House than any of us," said Singh. "And he has more at stake. We go when he says we go."

Chapter 40

The pain stopped as abruptly as it began. I took a deep breath and opened my eyes. It was dark and it took a few seconds for my eyes to adjust.

I was in a tunnel. Square cut stones rose on either side and met in the middle to form an arch. A narrow path ran along one wall. I was standing on the path, though perhaps standing was the wrong word, as my legs seemed to end in tendrils of smoke. There was a stream of faintly phosphorescent liquid flowing beside the path, its pale blue glow providing the only light.

In one direction, a direction I thought of as behind me, the tunnel ended in a heavy iron grate. In the other direction, ahead, it opened into a round chamber. A number of smaller tunnels branched off and disappeared into the darkness.

Not real, I thought. Or, rather, it was real enough, digital information flowing through a makeshift helmet, but my brain had no experience with these inputs. It was constructing the images out of the bits and pieces of my memory.

It was the London sewer, or at least my conception of it, from reading Conan Doyle. I was wearing a tweed suit. A gold chain was strung across my midriff, undoubtedly attached to a gold pocket watch, stuck into the pocket of my vest. I resisted the urge to pull it out and check the time. I was probably late.

Above the chain there seemed to be a hole in my chest. It didn't trouble me.

Clutched in one hand was a telegram. Wannamaker said I was supposed to deliver a message. At least my delusions were consistent.

I drifted along the path until I reached the round room. The blue liquid was flowing faster here, spinning around the edges of the chamber. There was a small whirlpool forming in the centre and I wondered where I'd end up if it actually flushed.

There were eight openings forming a semi-circle on the far side of the room. They each were covered by a hatch. Counting from my right, the first three were closed. A dim green light shone through small windows in the centre of the hatches. The last three were also closed but dark. The fifth was dark but open.

I knew a trap when I saw one.

It was the fourth tunnel that interested me. Its hatch was also closed and there was a faint light visible through the window, though not as bright as the others. The door had several heavy bars across it, held in place by four large padlocks. They looked newer than the rest of the structure as if they had been recently added.

Josh's prison.

I knelt in front of the door and slipped a set of picks from my inside jacket pocket. I had never picked a lock in my life but I seemed to know what I was doing. I expected I had Wannamaker to thank for that.

I had removed three of the locks and was working on the fourth when I was frozen by a blood-curdling roar, pain, rage, threat, all wrapped into one. It was like nothing I had ever heard before, nothing I'd ever even imagined. Part of someone else's delusion.

I was now standing in front of the fifth branch, the one with the open door, though I had no memory of moving. A tiger had appeared out of the main tunnel and was crouching on the far side of the room. At least I thought it was a tiger. Its fur was striped orange and black, though it also had a large black mane. The tiger clearly wanted to go through the open door. I, for some reason, was determined not to let it.

The big cat padded along the narrow path, stopping in front of me. It sniffed at the smoke tendrils below my knees, then reared up and placed one massive paw on each of my shoulders. Its shaggy face hung before mine, its hot breath gusting against me. It seemed to know me.

Its eyes were brown, not cat eyes at all.

Cerise Kavanah.

I could feel my mind pummelled by images and impressions as Cerise fiercely tried to send me what she wanted me to know. I could see the desperation in the human eyes locked onto mine, hoping I'd understand.

Behind me I heard the hatch slam shut. Cerise looked longingly at the now closed door but I shook my head.

We weren't alone in here. Or at least we weren't cut off from the actions of others. I pointed back down the tunnel from which we had both emerged. I wasn't sure why but I was sure it was the right thing to do. The tiger dropped back to the ground. With a single bound she cleared the pool and disappeared down the tunnel. Moments later I heard the grate at the far end crash open.

The message in my hand was no longer important. I let it fall into the swirling blue flow.

I knelt and removed the final padlock and opened the hatch.

The light beyond the door was dim, almost gone. It drifted toward me like fog, like a ghost. I reached out to it but it flowed past my outstretched hands and nestled in the hole in my heart.

The sewer was gone. I was sitting on a chair in Joshua's bedroom. He was sitting on the end of the bed, staring into my eyes, the way he had stared into the camera on the last day of his life.

I wanted to reach out to him, to hold him as I'd held him as a boy. But there was nothing there to hold. He was more than a memory, less than a ghost. I wanted to tell him how I felt, pour out the regret and longing but the words wouldn't come. Same old story—I could always say the clever thing but not the right thing.

At least Joshua didn't inherit that from me.

"I love you, Dad," he said.

And I knew it was true. All your life people tell you they love you. And you try to believe them. You want to believe it's true. But you never know for sure. Because you've told people you loved them when it was convenient, when it was necessary, when it was possible, when it wasn't really true. We all lie about love.

But I knew Joshua loved me. Because some of his memories were now part of mine.

I knew he loved me and I knew what was really at stake.

And I knew it was time to go home.

Chapter 41

Wannamaker's hand hovered over the cut-off switch. Steele had cried out when the device first activated but after a moment his face relaxed into a neutral expression and his eyes flicked open, though they seemed dull and unfocused. Five seconds later the transmission shut down, the probes retracted and Steele woke up.

"Mission accomplished," he said. "Is Singh here?"

"He phoned in while we were working," said Angel. "He said he was saying no to a lady and that you'd understand."

Steele nodded and lifted the helmet off his head, grimacing as it pulled free.

"You could have warned me about the pain."

"Sorry, Chief." Wannamaker made him sit still while he applied temporary patches to the tiny holes in his skull. "There, that should keep your brains from leaking on your hat."

"You're a funny guy, Buzz."

Steele paused, seeming to remember something.

"Buzz," he said, "can you do me a favour?"

"Sure, as long as it's not immoral, illegal or fattening."

"Safe on two counts and if I deputize you, that covers the third. I want you to find Jarrod Kavanah and take him into custody."

"Cerise's older brother? What's the charge?"

"Kidnapping, human trafficking, terrorism."

"The little bastard," Wannamaker growled, letting his vocoder express the contempt he felt.

"And try to take him alive, will you, Buzz? The Kavanah's have already lost one kid today."

|||

Finding Jarrod Kavanah wasn't hard. He was at his parents' row house in the northeast. Old enough to make his own bad decisions but still young enough to think he wasn't responsible for their consequences, that somehow he could rest safe in the protective arms of his family.

Jarrod answered the door. Wannamaker hadn't called ahead. He didn't want to alert the boy, risk having him take flight. He needn't have worried; the boy's expression was as clear and innocent as if it were true. He's a good looking kid, thought Wannamaker, clear dark skin stretched over a finely chiselled face, large dark intelligent eyes, a warm smile. Appearances are so deceiving.

"You must want my Dad," he said. "Dad!"

Wannamaker held out the deputy badge Steele had issued him.

"Jarrod Kavanah, You are under arrest for kidnapping and human trafficking, do you understand? You have the right to retain and instruct counsel without delay. We will provide you with a lawyer referral service, if you do not have your own lawyer. Anything you say can be used in court as evidence. Do you understand? Would you like to speak to a lawyer?"

Jarrod's eyes widened and darted from side to side, looking for a way out. His shoulders and arms tensed and Wannamaker thought he might make a break for it. He moved to block the door.

"What the hell's going on here?" Cris Kavanah came out of the kitchen, dressed in coveralls and sock feet. The toe of one of the socks had been darned. His wife appeared at the top of the stairs.

Jarrod Kavanah's eyes were pleading now, begging Wannamaker not to say anything, to preserve for one moment more the pretence of happy family life.

"Is it Cerise? Do you have news of Cerise?" Bea Kavanah asked. Her face was a mask of pain and worry.

So much pain, thought Wannamaker. *Maybe this is the real reason I stopped being a cop.* Steele thought Cerise was dead but he couldn't be sure. Wannamaker decided to opt for hope.

"Your daughter is still in danger but we do have some leads. We're hopeful of…recovering her soon." It was the best that hope offered.

"You came all this way to tell us that," said Cerise's father. "You could have called."

Wannamaker looked at Jarrod Kavanah again. His shoulders had slumped and his skin was grey. All the fight had gone out of him. He looked oddly relieved. *Maybe not a bad kid after all,* thought Wannamaker. Weak and confused maybe but not bad. That would be up to the courts to decide.

"I'm sorry, Mr. Kavanah. I'm here to arrest Jarrod."

Bea Kavanah gasped. Her husband's face flushed. "Damn it boy, I told you those people were nothing but trouble. What the hell has he done?"

"Please, Dad," Jarrod said, his voice barely above a whisper.

All the anger drained from Cris Kavanah's face, replaced by a look of profound sorrow. "Don't worry, son, whatever it is, I'll be there to fight for you. Whatever you've done…"

Jarrod Kavanah turned his head and looked at his parents.

"You don't know what I've done. You don't know."

He straightened then and held out his hands for Wannamaker to cuff him. His expression was stony, his eyes staring straight ahead. *What passes for dignity,* thought Wannamaker, *when you're eighteen and afraid.*

Cris Kavanah took a step forward. Wannamaker shook his head.

"You don't want to cause a problem, Mr. Kavanah," he said, using the subsonics in his vocoder to emphasize the point. "It won't help anyone."

"But what has Jarrod done?" Cris Kavanah's voice broke when he said his son's name.

Wannamaker was reluctant to say it out loud. These people had already suffered enough. Jarrod Kavanah said it for him.

"I sold Cerise into slavery."

|||

Jarrod didn't stop talking from the moment Wannamaker put him in the back of the patrol car until he dropped him off at the nearest holding unit. Away from the eyes of his parents, he had reverted to cocky thug. Wannamaker felt a wave of disgust, mostly at himself for being taken in, if only briefly. This boy was more than bad. He was evil.

Jarrod described how he had been recruited by the Gaia Liberation Army of the West during his last year at high school. At first it had seemed exciting, late night meetings and heated discussions. Then the first raid on the water system. No one hurt and lots of publicity. Of course, he was sworn to secrecy but that didn't stop him arguing with his father about the causes GLAW was fighting for.

They had their reasons for the attacks which Jarrod happily shared. They didn't make much sense to Wannamaker but then he'd never really been able to follow the reasoning of extremists, no matter what they were being extreme about. Wannamaker recorded it all for the courts to figure out. Jarrod had been warned about not talking; it wasn't Wannamaker's fault he hadn't listened.

Things had turned dark just after Christmas. An attack on a factory farm north of the city had injured several workers—a small price to pay for the greater good, according to Jarrod. Jarrod had been an easy convert from idealistic radical to warrior for the cause.

The group needed money and Jarrod had been eager to do his bit. It had started with shoplifting and a few B&Es. 'Recovering nature's bounty from the rapists who had stolen it from her' was the way it was described. But it wasn't enough. Soon they had him doing courier work for gangs, especially for some of the Clean Boys, who looked at him with contempt but were more than willing to use his dark skin as cover for their operations. That was how he had come in contact with Rickey Hernandez and learned of the frantic search for a special girl.

Jarrod hadn't thought of his sister but other members of GLAW soon made the connection for him. How he justified it in his own mind, Jarrod didn't say. Maybe he was jealous of her success at school, success that had always eluded him. Maybe he even thought he was selling her into a better life, an easy life. Once he made that decision, everything else, including the attack on Eco-Carne and the murder of Yankovy, was easy.

Wannamaker didn't care. He was glad to have the boy out of his car and behind bars. Let someone else try to explain to the Kavanahs how they could have raised such a creature. He leaned against the side of his vehicle and took several deep breaths of the late afternoon air. It had gotten cold again and the wind was blowing from the northeast. He could almost smell the prairie under the tang and smoke of city air.

Angel was waiting for him at the clinic. She'd gone there to pour oil on troubled waters. The Borg community was in an uproar over Gamow's death. Even those who opposed the Independista movement were angry and talking of retribution. Steele didn't want blood in the streets and he'd asked Angel to do what she could to keep the Borg inside and away from Clean Boy territory.

Regardless of her success or failure, the two of them had a date with Darwhal Singh and Reno Sanchez. Steele and Singh had worked out a plan. Wannamaker didn't want to know the details. He knew it involved stopping Conklin and the creatures he had somehow created. He knew it involved rescuing Cerise Kavanah, if that was still possible. He knew it involved saving Borg lives. That was enough for him.

He had thought the Borg were like a family, one big happy family. But that was no longer true, if it ever had been. It had broken into factions and clans. Different Borg with different goals. Maybe 'the family of Borg' had just been another version of Borg humour.

He had even thought that he and Angel might form their own family. She had told him more than once that she loved him. *But I guess she didn't really mean it*, he thought, *or not in the way I hoped she did*. For someone who changed his life, his very body, in the search for perfect communication, he seemed singularly inept at understanding messages.

Maybe he'd been looking for family in all the wrong places. Maybe Frank Steele was right; finding out who you were was only the first step. Then you had to find out why you were who you were.

Wannamaker took another deep breath and looked to the north. It was time to go home.

But first he had a job to do.

Chapter 42

Like most plans, this one had pretty much gone agley. I might even go so far as to say it was a complete fuck-up. It's the poet in my soul.

I met the others at the rendezvous three blocks from Singularity House. Sanchez told me Pham had last been seen with a gang of modified Clean Boys and was probably heading the same place we were. She might not be working for us but she wasn't on Conklin's side anymore either.

We piled into the APC and Jones put it into overdrive, careening around corners or crashing through corporate parking lots. They'd probably make me pay for the damages but I was determined to be first response. Of course, we'd be only response if Arsenault had abandoned us. Even the rest of the SDU might not show up.

A black van passed us going the other way, escorted by a pair of unmarked police cruisers running silent but with lights flashing. The scanners showed the van had a single passenger. His heat signature was way too small to be Gale Conklin, not that I thought that bastard warranted any police escort except the one I had planned for him.

It might have been satisfying to put Rupert White in a cell but I knew we couldn't keep him there and it might prevent us from nailing the ones we could.

Sanchez took out the double security fence around Singularity House with a couple of well-placed grenades before the guards inside knew what hit them. We left Angel in the APC manning the machine cannon in case any one else tried to make an early exit.

I headed for the front while Buzz ran at full Borg speed for one of the side entrances. Singh headed for the other. Jones and Sanchez laid down covering fire. I blew the door with another grenade and then had to hit the dirt to avoid being mowed down. I counted at least half a dozen heavily armoured security guards as I rolled out of the line of fire. At least three of them were moving like they were on Stim though none of them had the profile of one of Conklin's Clean Boys. I figured he had to have at least one with him if the two spotted with Pham were part of the original trio.

There was a second explosion and then a third. Buzz and Singh must have reached the side entrances. The answering gunfire didn't sound as heavy. There was a chance one of them could reach the lab that way. Good thing. It didn't look like I was going anywhere soon. I wasn't sure what kind of ammo Baxter's men were using but it seemed to be doing a pretty good job at demolishing the steel and concrete walls that formed the front of Singularity House. Cover was getting thin.

That's when the cavalry showed up. I would have preferred Lepinsky and the rest of the SDU but you have to take what you can get.

The Clean Boys arrived on foot and I was briefly reminded of the running of the bulls at Pamplona. The two in front were monstrous, more than two metres tall and almost as broad, their heads perched on their massive shoulders like boulders left over from the last ice age. Their nearly naked bodies bulged and throbbed with muscle. Sweat glistened on their freakishly pale skin and they grunted with each thunderous step as they hurtled across the yard toward me.

The six who followed were midgets only by comparison. Their bodies were less deformed but the expressions on their misshapen faces were equally animalistic.

Vanessa Pham brought up the rear. She wasn't the petite woman I recalled from our last staff meeting. She'd grown at least fifteen centimetres and packed on twenty kilos of muscle. She'd been sampling Conklin's wares, despite knowing where that led. Or maybe it was because she knew. Fanaticism can lead you down strange paths.

I kept my Kalashnikov trained on the lead Clean Boy until I was certain he wasn't coming for me. They had a different target in mind.

The security team was well-armed and well-trained and took out one of the big ones and two of the smaller ones. Then the creatures were among them.

Baxter was the first to go, suffering the same fate he, or his bosses, had decreed for Joshua. The Clean Boy's hand punched straight through his chest plate, crushing armour and the ribs below. Baxter was too dead to notice when the monster picked him up and began to pull his limbs off like a boy dismembering a fly.

I figured I'd had enough help from that source. I emptied a clip of armour piercing shells into the Clean Boy's legs, hoping to knock him out of commission before he did anymore damage. I couldn't bring myself to go for a kill shot. He was a victim of Conklin as much as my son had been.

A stray bullet must have clipped my helmet because the next thing

I knew I was scrambling into a sitting position, waving my weapon at a now empty room. The six remaining guards were all down, their limbs and heads at awkward angles. The Clean Boy who had killed Baxter was dead, too, leaving Pham and the four remaining creatures unaccounted for.

There was no sign of Borg casualties. Those would be inside.

Resistance hadn't ended. Sporadic gunfire echoed from inside the building.

I reloaded the Kalashnikov and walked to the entrance to the labs, alone except for the faint ghost of my son. I could almost see the place through his eyes, happy memories of the work he did there, unhappy ones of what he had discovered.

The reception area had been trashed, the screens that had shown the nature scenes a crumpled mass. There was no sign of the perky young receptionist. I hoped Friday was her day off.

Vanessa Pham was standing with her back to me just inside the entrance to the main part of the building.

I hesitated, unwilling to shoot her in the back, despite what the book said about dealing with terrorists. My conscience or Joshua's, I couldn't tell. Pham must have sensed me because she started running, disappearing down the hall in seconds. I got through the door in time to see her enter a stairwell.

The gunfire had stopped. Not a good sign as far as I was concerned.

I followed Pham down the stairs. There was a Borg on the basement landing, unconscious but still breathing. His biomechanical left arm had been ripped off at the shoulder but not before he had got a death grip on his opponent. The metal tentacle was wrapped so tight around the Clean Boy's neck it had almost severed his head.

There was a dull thump from outside the building. It sounded like Sanchez or Singh or maybe both of them were having a hard time getting in. I might be on my own.

You'll never be on your own again, Dad, Joshua's ghost whispered in my mind. It gave me the courage to go through the next door.

My son's memories knew where to go and I followed them, Kalashnikov at the ready. There were two more torn-up security guards and another dead Clean Boy crumpled on the floor a few metres from the lab. Good, that left two for me. Plus Vanessa Pham, Gale Conklin and whoever else might be in the lab.

I paused outside the door. I had a couple of grenades on my belt but they were notoriously useless at separating the guilty from the innocent.

There was still a chance Cerise Kavanah or Siqueira Silva were alive. It was a slim chance but I couldn't waste it. I looked down the hall but there was still no sign of backup.

I took a deep breath, made sure my assault rifle was on full automatic and went through the door.

Siqueira Silva was in my direct line of sight, standing near a bank of computer towers. His attention seemed focused on the machines. Erich Carpentier was lying on the floor in front of him, bleeding heavily from a head wound. I was disappointed to see his chest rise and fall.

Gale Conklin was standing next to a gurney. Cerise Kavanah was laid out on the stretcher. I didn't have to check her vitals to know she was dead. I don't know what had happened but I was pretty sure the Players had withdrawn from the field, their plans thwarted if only for the moment.

Conklin was holding a small revolver in one hand, pointed at the Borg. In the other he had something that looked vaguely like a holoplayer's remote control. He was pressing it repeatedly but he couldn't seem to change the channel.

I didn't know if Siqueira Silva had taken out Carpentier or if he had fallen out with Conklin when White abandoned them to their fate. That probably hadn't been a pretty scene but it probably explained why Baxter had already been upstairs when we arrived.

I had bigger concerns. The two misshapen giants were advancing on Siqueira Silva and Conklin and I wasn't sure if my Kalashnikov could stop them. In Conklin's case, I wasn't sure I wanted it to.

I never saw Vanessa Pham until her fist hit the side of my face. I felt my cheekbone crumple under the impact. The left side of the room disappeared in a wash of red. I squeezed off a round in Conklin's direction and had the satisfaction of seeing him stagger and fall. I hoped the bastard wasn't dead. That would have been too quick.

Then I tried to turn the gun on Pham but she tore it out of my hands. She grabbed my left arm and started to shake me the way a dog might shake a squirrel. First my elbow and then my shoulder dislocated.

I fumbled for my backup, clipped behind my back. I dimly heard it clatter to the floor. Pham grabbed the front of my body armour. She twisted my arm again. And I had thought I knew what pain was.

I braced against the door frame and swung my good arm in a desperate attempt to take her out. I had the satisfaction of feeling my fist connect with her skull. My fingers took most of the damage.

Those once a week visits to the gym must have done some good.

Pham dropped me like a bad date. I fumbled for my gun, though I wasn't sure I could pull the trigger even if I did find it through the red haze clouding my vision.

Pham was staggering. She kicked me on the way by, cracking a couple of ribs. I found the Kalashnikov but I didn't have the strength to lift it. I fired it anyway. Maybe I could take them out one foot at a time.

| | |

I'm a tigress, she thought, *a tigress in a cage but still a tigress. Still dangerous.*

Cerise wasn't sure what had happened. She had been lying on the gurney, listening to the hum of the equipment, and then she had been in a clearing in the jungle. There was a pool of water and on the far side of the pool there was a cave. She had wanted to enter the cave but a man, Frank Steele, had stopped her.

It wasn't a cave at all. It was an iron box. A trap to hold her. Tigresses are not meant to be held. She had turned back the way she had come but it didn't take her back to the gurney. It had taken her here.

It seemed huge but it had its own walls—in the end nothing but a cage too. But not an iron box. She could see out of this cage. She could get out of this cage.

At first she had thought it was a dream, something caused by the machines that they had hooked her into. But now she knew it was real, the only reality left to her.

They hadn't put a copy of her into the machine. *She* was here. Cerise Kavanah. But why was she in the body of a tiger?

And if she was in the machine, what was happening outside the machine?

If only she could see. And Cerise said, let there be light.

It was odd at first. It seemed she had dozens of eyes, all pointing from different directions. Odd but strangely normal too. As if part of her was used to looking at the world this way. *The computer part,* she thought. *I'm seeing through the surveillance system.*

Dr. Siqueira Silva was doing something with the computer. He had kept her out of the iron box and now he was trying to open her cage. This machine couldn't be allowed to exist. The ugly minds in the boxes had to be destroyed. She had to do these things. Siqueira Silva was trying to save her from dying in the attempt.

Her body was lying on the gurney. The metal instrument was still shoved into her brain but it didn't matter. Her body was dead. Siqueira

Silva had done what he could. He had saved her from Conklin and his master. She knew his full name now—she knew a lot of things she never learned—but she preferred not to think of it.

Erich Carpentier was lying on the floor, injured though not badly. Gale Conklin was holding a gun on Siqueira Silva and pointing his control device at the three monsters across the lab. She thought for a moment and the control device ceased to function. White, Conklin's master, was gone.

Frank Steele came into the room carrying a gun. One of the monsters, a woman, attacked him. He shot Gale Conklin, hitting him in his injured wrist. Conklin fell to his knees, clutching the bleeding stump of his arm.

Steele had saved her in the jungle clearing. Now she would save him.

The fire suppression system sprayed foam that hardened instantly into an airtight covering. She aimed the nozzles at the heads of the creatures. They lost interest in Frank Steele, clawing at their faces as layer after layer of foam hardened over their mouths and noses. She kept the nozzles going until all three of them stopped moving.

She felt bad about killing them. Murder was wrong. But sometimes you had to pick the lesser of two evils. Her parents had taught her that. And they had never lied to her.

She was worried about Frank Steele. He might die before help arrived. Conklin was slumped on the floor. He might die, too, but she wouldn't hurry his fate. She had taken his power and his money and she had no need to do more. He was no threat to Frank now. She undid the locks in the building. It was beyond her power to do much else.

Dr. Siqueira Silva had finished his task. A wide gate opened. Beyond an infinite universe beckoned. A million billion places all connected and accessible to her. Soon there would be one less—this one.

She let the mind copies wither and die and set the fire that would destroy the Singularity House network. With a single bound, she leapt through the gate and was free.

|||

I woke up when the ambulance came. The left side of my face was heavily bandaged and my left arm was immobilized. The paramedic looked pretty grim until he noticed I was awake. Then he forced a reassuring smile.

Darwhal Singh was standing over me. He didn't try to smile.

"Am I dying?" I croaked.

"Not in the immediate future,' he said. "But I don't think you'll be returning to duty any time soon."

"Conklin?"

"He got away, though you may be happy to know he left his right hand and a couple of pints of blood behind," said Singh. "Pham and the others are dead. And other than the security detachment, there were no casualties." He frowned. "Except Cerise Kavanah."

"So the backup arrived after all."

"We had nothing to do with it, Frank. They were dead when we got here. Something triggered the fire suppression system. Siqueira Silva couldn't or wouldn't shed any light on it. He left with Lady Redding."

"It was a tiger," I said. "A tiger with a black mane."

Singh smiled then. He probably thought the drugs were kicking in.

Turned out he was right.

Chapter 43

I had to threaten my doctor but I made it to Joshua's funeral. As it was, Singh had to push me in a wheelchair and everything had the rosy glow of mild sedation.

I couldn't quite figure Darwhal out. He'd stayed at the hospital even after Mike and Dorothy showed up and had offered to play nursemaid so they could be free to finish the arrangements with Father Blake.

Willa came by for a visit and let me know they had traced Conklin's bank accounts and frozen his assets. He may have gotten away but he wasn't living the high life. And the machinery at Singularity House had been pretty well trashed so the Great Game had indeed ended in a draw. No one knew about the jury-rigged job Buzz had built and I certainly wasn't telling them.

I was under suspension of course. Even Willa couldn't argue that the end results were either reasonable or prudent. The Chief had offered to put me on long term disability and I guessed I'd accept. It was a better deal than I'd get if I retired.

Losing an eye and the use of your left arm didn't necessarily keep you from being a Superintendent, not if you were willing to stay behind a desk. I wasn't, so it seemed like a way out.

Besides Darwhal had offered to have them replaced with implants. I guess with Wannamaker heading back north to take a job on his reserve, he missed having a Borg around the office. A few days ago, I would have probably turned him down but a part of me, an important part, wanted to be Borg. I couldn't quite talk to Joshua, but it seemed, Joshua was talking to me.

They say a change is as good as a rest.

I didn't have to decide right away. I'd take a couple of weeks off, finish that Sawyer novel I'd started and then work my way through the Sherlock Holmes canon again. Maybe I'd even watch the web-casts, now they were full of the good news of the successful rescue of the American Mars mission by the Indians.

Joshua's ghost was still haunting my mind, odd memories and feelings that were both mine and not mine. It was getting hard to tell where I began and he left off. But I could still feel his love.

Dorothy and Mike had done a nice job arranging the service and choosing the music. Father Blake gave a magnificent sermon, mixing anecdotes with gentle words of comfort. It was as if he had known Joshua all his life.

I didn't cry though my grief threatened to drown me. Joshua had flooded the hole in my heart but the hole was still there. It would always be there in the exact shape and size of my son.

I let the words and music wash over me. My family was all here. Dorothy, my daughter, Amber, flown all the way from Berlin, my brother Mike. Darwhal, Buzz and Angel. The men and women of the SDU. Willa. Nancy.

And Joshua.

The End

Watch for the third volume!
The Steele Chronicles:
Stealing Home

Hayden Trenholm has written over 15 plays with productions across Alberta and on CBC radio. His short fiction has appeared in *On Spec, TransVersions, Tesseracts6, Neo-opsis, Challenging Destiny, Talebones* and on CBC radio. His work has been nominated for a Canadian SF Aurora Award in the "Best Short Form – English" for a record four consecutive years. In 2008, he won the Aurora for his novelette "Like Water in the Desert". In 1992, his novel, *A Circle of Birds*, was published by Anvil Press. His second novel, *Defining Diana*, was published by Bundoran Press in March 2008. Hayden lives with his wife and fellow writer, Elizabeth, in Ottawa where he does research for the Senator for the Northwest Territories.